DAYS OF GRACE

DAYS OF GRACE

Brenda Jagger

William Morrow and Company, Inc.
New York   1984

Library of Congress Cataloging in Publication Data

Jagger, Brenda, 1936-
  Days of grace.

  I. Title.
PR6060.A425D3   1984   813'.54   83-17334
ISBN 0-688-02728-8

Printed in the United States of America

First U.S. Edition

1 2 3 4 5 6 7 8 9 10

BOOK DESIGN BY LINEY LI

ONE

My mother's marriages had not prospered. Her first had been socially impeccable but emotionally austere, beginning with a fashionable English church, a French bridal gown, a Venetian honeymoon, and ending, five or six years later, when she ran off with a lover; taking possession of her infant daughter—myself—but leaving behind her a son who, as heir to his father's broad acres, was too valuable to be included in any woman's elopement.

There had been no elaborate lace gown to wear on her second wedding-day for, although she had bolted romantically and predictably to Paris, the processes of her English divorce had proved so cumbersome that by the time it was granted she had already given birth to two more daughters, a display of fertility which had done much to cool the ardor of her bridegroom.

I called him "Papa Marriott" for a year or two thereafter, since he treated me in identical fashion to his own children, my sisters Victorine and Madelon. We all three quite decidedly and quite equally irritated him, causing him to wince at the noise we made and the need we created for a large apartment near the Parc Monceau full to its brim with the cumbersome and costly apparatus of a city childhood. He despaired at the constant gossiping of nursemaids around an extravagantly piled-up fire, the eternal mending of fine cambric pinafores and white net stockings which we seemed determined to tear or outgrow regardless of expense. He deplored the nanny who allowed us to run wild in the park while she flirted with soldiers. He lived in dread of our childish, careless hands attacking his piano, our enthusiastic, not always spotless shoes menacing his Aubusson rugs. He was a fastidious English gentleman who could detect nothing of his own background or breeding in these alien children and quite simply, despite the best of intentions, he did not like us.

We needed discipline, he declared, although somehow he could never quite find the time to administer it himself. Of course we did, agreed our mother, handing out to us sweets and caresses and whatever loose change she happened to have in her pockets. We needed standards. The solid virtues of self-restraint, obedience and economy.

"Darling, how right—and how clever," murmured my mother without even listening, wanting simply to please him, yielding in the same warm caressing fashion to his opinion of her children as she did to all his other fads and fancies, his politics and his religion, his physical and moral appetites, his obsession with the impurity of French water, the unreliability of French drains.

"Listen to your father," she told us. "We are to mend our manners and save our money." And to celebrate his wisdom she rushed out at once and bought him—quite possibly on credit—a gold pin for his tie and then a silk tie to match the pin, her own effervescent pleasure in the gift being more than enough to conceal the absence of his own.

Poor man. He had carried off a warm, alluring mistress who had failed to transform herself into an efficient wife and on the day Victorine and I had croup and Madelon, living up to her reputation for frailty, seemed on the brink of something even noisier and nastier, I suppose he found it easy to listen to the Marriott family lawyer, who, from time to time, came bustling across the Channel to pay him his allowance and advise him to go home.

His father, it appeared, was in poor health. There were arrangements to be made, the possibility of a legacy. He would return by the month-end, he told my mother, not even expecting to be believed. And, having given some furtive instructions to a shipping and forwarding company about his piano, away he went, unfortunately for him as it turned out since, by that same month-end, he was dead of a low fever brought on not by the French drains he had so dreaded but by the even more pernicious system in use at his father's Northumbrian estate.

"I am a widow," my mother said. "How odd. It is something I never expected"; meaning of course, "Does it suit me? How does one dress for it?" But black lace and chiffon, black satin roses and a veil of black spotted net on her hat became her pale, willowly fairness so well that consolation was offered from all sides, taking her out a great deal in the evenings and increasing her milliner's bills.

"You are poor little orphans now," she told Victorine and Madelon, throwing perfumed arms around them, her tone implying that this made them important and interesting.

"So am I," I insisted, determined not to forfeit my share since I had entirely forgotten my real father, still sitting on his own land in the County of Yorkshire, just a little farther south, I noticed, when I explored the map of England, than the place where "Papa Marriott" was now lying.

He had left no money. He had been, it appeared, a "younger son," a breed despised by the English ruling classes who, in their anxiety to keep their estates intact, left everything to the first-born male, thus obliging any other sons to make their own way in the world, to be lawyers or soldiers or dignitaries of the church or, best of all, the husbands of rich wives. Papa Marriott had neglected all these things, committing instead the supreme folly of adultery. And the allowance upon which he had supported a faithless woman and her children had been entirely in his family's gift, to continue or to cancel as they chose. That they ardently desired to cancel it, my mother was in no doubt.

"I am penniless," she announced, making this sound interesting and important too. "I fear there is nothing to be done except take in washing or go out to scrub steps. Ah well—it is only money, which comes and goes and it is foolish and even rather common to set too much store by it." And since she was well versed in folly and exceedingly uncommon, she bought, with what must have been the end of her capital, a gift for each of us, perfectly adapted, she declared, to our separate personalites, a pearl on a fine gold chain for Madelon, a dark, square-shouldered ruby for Victorine, a diamond chip set in a gold heart for me.

"We will have chocolate cake tonight," she said, "and flowers on the table, and wear all our finery. A last supper before I apprentice myself to a washerwoman."

But the next morning, leaving cake-crumbs and costly hot-house blooms to decay altogether, she took us off to a rather grand hotel in Nice where she made such an excellent impression on certain

7

distinguished English residents of the Côte d'Azur that wheels were set in motion powerful enough to convince even a stubborn Northumbrian squire that, in all decency, he could not allow his grandchildren to starve.

Instead of withdrawing my mother's income, he halved it; a victory she declared, and which sent her rushing poste-haste back to Paris, to a new apartment in the Place Saint-Sulpice where she decorated the walls with watered silk, re-upholstered the chairs with satin, bought feathered hats and Doucet dresses, cream cakes for Victorine, fluffy toy animals in vibrant colors for Madelon, lace blouses for me. And, since her extravagance extended also to her affections, she was soon rushing unwisely perhaps but blissfully into the arms of a third spouse—or was he indeed a spouse? I have never been quite sure—who arrived just in time to reassure our landlord that the rent would, eventually, be paid.

He did not, however, *quite* mean that he would pay off the arrears himself, for we left Place Saint-Sulpice soon afterwards and rather secretly as I recall, at what seemed the dead of an airless summer night, a closed carriage waiting around a corner into which we were bundled wearing several sets of clothing one on top of the other; a procedure which might have alarmed us had not mother and our new "Papa Junot" clearly found it so amusing. I was eight, I believe, Victorine six, Madelon still a dreamy, round-eyed four. Victorine and myself dark and sturdy like our respective fathers, those sporting English squires, Madelon with our mother's pale hair and light blue eyes, her air of never quite paying attention to what one said to her, the same capacity for sudden, easy tears and laughter. Three little girls who forgot Papa Marriott almost as quickly as our mother did and adapted readily enough to Papa Junot's mercurial swings from feast to famine and back to feast again, from days when we could tear our pinafores as often as we pleased and be cheerfully rewarded with a dozen more, their pockets stuffed with *marrons glacés* and chocolate creams, to days when the cry was "Dear God, there is not a halfpenny in the house. Bolt the door, Lavinia, and say I am dead." On which occasions we accepted, with true philosophy, a diet of whatever he happened to bring home from the café or the casino and understood that if we spoiled our clothes there would be nothing for it but to take the consequences and go in rags.

We went to school, of course, sometimes with all the chaperoned splendor of young Infantas in fur-trimmed coats and muffs and ridiculous, quite wonderful swansdown hats, to be expensively taught the social skills and graces, the art of acquiring a rich husband and spending his money. But at other times—in fact more often than not—we were sent off alone in plain serge frocks with instructions not to speak to strangers but to hurry along to dubious establishments whose purpose was not so much to educate us as to keep us out of our mother's way.

"Look after the others, Olivia," she always said and it seemed natural and right for me for I was the eldest, the biggest, the one less likely to cry when scolded, less likely to take fright. And when no governesses, no nuns, no fiery spinster ladies, no educators even of the most sinister kind were available, we were obliged to make do with the "vast school of life" as Papa Junot called it following the demands of his business—whatever it happened to be that season—to all four corners of France, to Monte Carlo and Biarritz, Rome, Naples, Lisbon and Vienna, to a chalk-white villa, one luminous summer, not far from Athens where my mother gave birth to Papa Junot's son, a black-eyed, vocal little imp who was placed almost immediately in my care, since even the simplest of Athenian nurse-maids knew better than to work without wages; while I—just then—did not.

My mother was happy and indolent with Papa Junot, purring all day long at her mirror, as graceful and insubstantial as a pale gold butterfly. When there was money he showered it upon her, nourishing her vanity for their mutual pleasure and because, in times of supposed affluence, she was his show-piece, living proof of his supposed worth. And although the furs in which he draped her, the jewels he put in her ears, never stayed with her for long, she wore their memory like perfume, retained their excitement in her easily flowing laughter; her mind and her senses replete with this voluble little man, never doubting—in true butterfly fashion—his capacity to go on producing these treats forever.

And then abruptly, he was gone.

"Taken him away and locked him up for fraud—or forgery—or bigamy," chanted the undernourished daughter of our *concierge* who knew no more about it than I did, except that the rent was probably overdue again and we would be moving on. And because Papa Junot had taught me that when one had a hundred francs one behaved like

9

a thousand, when one had no francs at all one acted a million, I ignored her, dismissed her, and walked upstairs, imperious in my distress, to an apartment where the furniture already wore the air of being marked down to the highest bidder, realizing—with neither the words to express it nor the intention to criticize—that my mother, when she composed herself enough to get out her Chinese box of facepowders again, would be equally for auction with the rest.

I was fourteen by then and already knew about such things. Victorine was a snub-nosed, determined twelve, still plagued every hour or so by her keen, persistent appetite for confectionery. Madelon of the dreamy disposition and delicate physique had grown prettier but no stronger, having recently developed a weakness of the lungs that puzzled our doctors and multiplied their bills. My brother Luc was a chattering, agile little monkey just five years old, as mischievous and maddening, as adorable and just as likely to get into trouble as Papa Junot may have been himself at that age. My mother was thirty-six, a woman of spun-glass enchantments who, incredibly, had borne five children if one counted the English brother she appeared to have forgotten. Yet, as I watched her weeping for Junot, no ugly reddening of the eyelids or blotching of the complexion but a grief that flowed from the surface of her as easily and as gracefully as her laughter, I knew that I was truly the eldest, older perhaps than she would ever be. And, once again, I felt not the slightest need to criticize. She was irresponsible perhaps but the word meant nothing to me then and even later, when I understood it more fully, I could only apply its meaning to my mother with a tolerant, affectionate shake of the head, a certain shrug of resignation and amusement. She was irresponsible. She was also beautiful, affectionate, tender-hearted, ready at any moment to give her last penny, without a backward glance or any thought of repayment or gratitude, to me or almost anyone else who appeared to need it. She was unwise, lacking in judgment. Undoubtedly. But her presence attracted me as warmth and light and moisture attract in their seasons. There was no one else I wished to talk to or look at if I could be with her, no one else who colored the world so brightly. She was as she was. To change her would have been to destroy her and, in any case, it had never once occurred to me that she might be different. I loved her not as some accepted ideal of motherhood but as my mother, the imperfect but unique individual upon whom my own individuality had initially depended. For if she had been other than herself how could she have given birth to me?

"I expect we'll manage, mother—in the end we will, at any rate."

She sighed and gave me a misty smile that quivered almost equally on the brim of tears or laughter. "Oh darling I do hope so, for I believe I have rather passed the season of scrubbing steps or being a laundry-maid . . . "

I believed so too and set the matter completely aside, knowing full well that if anything of the kind should ever be necessary, then I would do it myself. I was the eldest and what was surprising or alarming about that? I had always taken care of the others, had always remembered the guard on the nursery fire, the chain on the door, had learned very soon to recognize the dangers of city streets, to detect with unerring flair the step of a creditor on the front stairs and to engage him in artless conversation while Papa Junot escaped by the back. And although I had liked Junot and would miss him, it had never crossed my mind to depend on him. He was gone and what it really meant to me was that now I would have to take care of my mother too.

"There's no money, Olivia," she said bleakly. "My English money was stopped when I became Madame Junot and now I have none." But that, too, could not really alarm me since what money had there ever been other than Junot's golden snow showers, which had soon melted away? And I was used to that.

"We'll manage," I replied, feeling quite sure of it, and she raised her head, tears still beading her lashes but the eyes beneath them already—if only slightly—alert at the hint of some new and possibly delightful opportunity; for she was used to this too.

"Well, if they could not let us starve before," she said, meaning before Junot, "I do not see why they should permit it now." And so we applied ourselves, my mother and I, to the writing of lengthy and explicit, if not entirely truthful letters to the lawyers of Mr. James Heron of Clarrow Fell in the County of Yorkshire—my father—and Squire Marriott in Northumberland, requesting these gentlemen to be apprised of the sorry state into which Madame Lavinia Junot and her Heron and Marriott daughters had fallen.

"Really," she trilled, having borne with remarkable calm the sight of her best furniture being taken away, since these were not the first chairs and tables she had lost and she was probably tired of them anyway. "Really, Olivia, I believe that with letters like these we might melt the heart of a stone."

11

But the heart of Mr. James Heron of Clarrow Fell was beyond melting, my father having died, we learned, six months ago—should I somehow have known that? Should it have mattered more to me?—although Mr. Neville Heron, *his* father—and I had not even known I had a grandfather—was prepared to contribute one hundred pounds per year towards the maintenance of his relative, Miss Olivia Heron, on condition, the curt legal document implied, that he might hear no more of her.

"He was always cold," my mother told me, having been accustomed, in Junot's good years, to spending twice as much on her hats. "Cold and hard and gritty—yes—like the land he lives on. Promise me never to go there."

It seemed unlikely. I was a French child, or very nearly, not by birth like Victorine and Madelon, nor by blood like Luc, but my childhood memories were of the Parc Monceau, the Luxembourg Gardens, the awnings of boulevard cafés unfolding every spring like the buds of the chestnut trees, the ancient, enchanted patchwork of rooftops glimpsed from our attic window the year we had lived high up in Montmartre; not the hard, gritty land of the North my mother remembered. I had left England at eighteen months old, hastily wrapped in a corner of my mother's satin evening cloak, carried off as a sentimental gesture on her part, perhaps even an afterthought. Victorine and Madelon, although they chattered just as well in English or French or our personal mixture of both, had never set foot in England at all. We belonged to no precise geographical location, simply together, and it was, therefore, a severe shock when Squire Marriott replied from Northumberland that, although he was unwilling to put money into my mother's hands, having no more faith in her judgment now than on the day she had enticed his son into so disastrous an attachment, he did, nevertheless, acknowledge limited responsibility for Victorine and Madelon, to the extent of educating them in a select residential establishment for young ladies near Newcastle.

"Don't let them take me," whispered Madelon, distress bringing on that strange malady of the lungs as it always did, tightening her chest and restricting her breathing to painful gasps and coughs.

"I won't go, that's all," declared Victorine, reaching out for the chocolate cake with which she always fortified her determination, her pugnacious little chin marking her as no mean adversary for a dozen Northumbrian grandfathers.

12

"Mother," I warned her, "you must put a stop to it, you know. *Newcastle*—I can't even imagine Newcastle. You'll just have to make it clear that they can't separate us. It's not possible, mother. You must see that."

"Oh, dear," she said, biting her long elegant lip, "I believe I must. But I wonder if *you* see, Olivia dear, that life on your grandfather's hundred pounds a year . . . Well, if you cannot imagine Newcastle, I think you might well imagine *that*."

I imagined it and at once rejected it, convinced—as Junot had taught me—that one could always find a way.

"Well then—tell my grandfather that you can see no alternative but to abandon me on his doorstep. That might embarrass him into paying more."

"Darling," my mother said with her luminous, rather breathless smile, her sudden gasp of delight, "what a wicked, absolutely splendid idea!"

And so, to tide us over until good fortune smiled on us again, until some unknown relative might appear and leave us a rich legacy, until my mother or one of her daughters—probably Madelon she thought—might marry a millionaire, Squire Heron and Squire Marriott were induced to "see reason." Even Papa Junot's old mother, who kept a fish restaurant in Toulouse, agreed, after a sentimental glance at Luc's black eyes, to put something more substantial into the pot than an occasional stew. While, as a final bonus, we had word of Papa Junot himself, no longer in prison, it transpired, but in a place we could imagine rather more easily than Newcastle called Mexico, evading his creditors, of course, but doing it cheerfully and so successfully that he was able to make an arrangement of some kind which rendered our lives not easy, but tenable.

We moved to a plain but adequate apartment in the rue Vavin, furnished with pieces acquired cheaply here and there, since face creams and powders and those discreetly applied touches of rouge from their Chinese lacquer pots were of more importance to mother in the thirty-seventh year of her age than inlaid tables and deep upholstered sofas. She needed a touch of warm apricot near her face these days, she declared, giving me an armful of white bodices and blouses and collars with a wistful, "Here take these and wear them while your skin and teeth can stand the glare. Do you know, Olivia, I would give a fortune—anybody's fortune—to be dark and definite like you and my good red ruby Victorine. Oh yes, I have done very well in my day but it is the tall brunettes with the good strong bones who *last*." But she was being kind, not truthful, for I knew how much the subtle shadings of her own blonde coloring enchanted her, the translucence of the pale skin and the clear blue gaze she shared with Madelon, the fine hair swirling like feathers against a neck as long and delicate as a stem of porcelain. She was only playing with age, flirting with it as she did with everything else, and quite soon there was a new admirer, not a husband this time since it was discreetly understood and never mentioned that for religious or financial or political reasons the gentleman could never be free, although he appeared to have a sufficiency of time and money at his disposal, taking us all to Marienbad one spring where, remembering our British origins, he pointed out to us the portly, elderly Prince of Wales.

"Dear old Henri," she called this new-found benefactor and with him and "Dear old Gustave" who came after, she followed the fashions of every season, concealing only from "Dear old Jean-Paul," who turned out to be a year younger than herself, that she was the mother of three daughters already erupting into boisterous young womanhood. We moved from the rue Vavin, of course, in tribute to these better days, to grander accommodation on the lively, not unfashionable boulevard des Italiens where, at the window of what seemed to us to be a magnificent *salon*, we perched every fine evening, looking down through the tree-tops to watch the cafés receive their dinner guests, silk-hatted, cigar-smoking gentlemen, regrettably similar in appearance, I thought, to Queen Victoria's wayward, fifty-year-old son, and a satin splendor of ladies, bare-shouldered, enticing; our mother—in our informed opinion—the loveliest of them all. It was a time of relative ease and comfort, of bowls of hot chocolate in bed every morning reading our mother's love-letters and invitations, of lazy afternoons in the *salons* of self-important dressmakers, sipping white wine and listening, watching, learning, as my mother made the major decisions of her life, the all important choices between chiffon and silk *mousseline*, Brussels lace or *Valenciennes*. A happy time, as I recall it, with hugs and kisses and new coats and shoes in abundance, lasting until folly overtook us in the shape of a lean, probably fascinating, certainly unreliable officer of Hussars who, by escorting my mother to the Races at Longchamps and neglecting to bring her back for a night or two gave lasting offense to "Dear old Maurice"—or was

14

it "Dear old Abelard"? And, with a graceful shrug of the shoulders, a "Well, it is only money, you know—it comes and now it has gone," we were reduced to a horrid attic flat in the faubourg Saint-Denis.

I was sixteen then and before I was eighteen we had moved seven times more, sometimes up and sometimes down, settling finally in the rue du Bac where, having noticed how each new upheaval brought on an attack of Madelon's "chest," we made up our minds to stay.

We had a cheerful, untidy *salon*, three sparsely furnished bedrooms made cosy by chintz cushions, paper flowers, a great many "artistic prints" and a servant's attic above, which we gave to Luc since we had no maid, relying largely on the good offices of Victorine who, driven by the demands of her own keen appetite, had become an excellent cook. And we were far—very far—from being unhappy.

No one cared enough about us now, it seemed, to try to separate us. Occasionally Grandmère Junot would invite us to Toulouse where the warm air was good for Madelon. Occasionally my mother would go off with a "friend" to some marine destination from which she would return feeling loved or not loved, which in real terms, meant feeling young or feeling "desperate, exhausted, *old*—dear God!" But usually we were to be found in the neighborhood of the rue du Bac, sharp-eyed Victorine interviewing the butcher and the grocer, demanding good measure and a bargain price; Luc hopefully but by no means certainly at school; my mother, with Madelon as her apprentice, devoting herself to the care of her complexion which—after the shock of her fortieth birthday—required the constant nurturing of creams and lotions purchased secretly and at great cost beneath the arcades of the rue de Rivoli.

"Madelon—a touch of aquamarine on the eyelid? What do you think?"

And Madelon, her head on one side, would consider the matter with the gravity of a dedicated *artiste*.

"Yes, *maman*. And rose *cendrée* below the cheekbone—or the Chinese vermilion."

"Darling, how clever. The vermilion. Lord, have I really used it up again? It is becoming like opium to me. I wonder if I have the courage to go out without it this afternoon?"

But she would set off, nevertheless, around two o'clock when the cruel noonday glare had abated, for it was still her policy to be "seen," usually with Madelon, in the appropriate places, the avenues of the Bois de Boulogne, the terraces of certain boulevard cafés, two exquisite alabaster dolls, existing to be admired. Madelon was restful, my mother said, not constantly chopping vegetables and stirring soup like Victorine, or forever rushing around the town with not a moment to spare like Olivia. And indeed, during those two relatively stable years in the rue du Bac I found it expedient—for who knew when a new gown or a doctor's fee might be needed in a hurry—to accept whatever gainful employment came my way.

Work as such, of course, was beyond the limits of my experience for, despite the irregularities of her own life, my mother considered both herself and her daughters to be ladies designed not to fend for themselves but to be maintained, one way or another, by gentlemen. But there remained, nevertheless, one or two unobtrusive little occupations at which, without losing caste, I might earn myself a franc or two and I was soon busy from morning to night writing letters in my best copperplate for socially ambitious ladies who could not quite afford a permanent secretary, answering their invitations, copying out their menu-cards, running discreet little errands on their behalf to chemists and perfumers and—for a slightly higher fee—to lovers.

I was constantly in and out of other people's houses, listening to their gossip, their anxieties, their secrets and letting it all wash over me, murmuring, "How terrible, *madame*. Naturally you cannot stand for it," saying whatever the lady wished to hear—while in the manner of paid sympathizers, I jingled my hard-earned pin-money in my pocket. I was a pupil, once again, in the vast "school of life," as Junot had aptly named it and I learned, quickly enough, how to tell which husbands would be likely to make advances and which would not, how to draw a firm but friendly line between *flirtation*, which could be pleasant and had its uses, and *invitation* which must be avoided at any cost.

And although I was cautious and proud and knew I could afford no blemish on my reputation I *did* hover, from time to time, on the fringes of romance. I even accepted—just now and then—an invitation to dine at a boulevard café, held hands in a cab, exchanged a few uncertain kisses, and was troubled the whole of one dark winter by a young man as stormy and brooding as the weather who harassed me, excited me, pushed me into dark corners at every opportunity

16

and flung himself upon me with a kind of despairing ferocity I found all too enticing.

My mother would have succumbed instantly and joyfully, I knew it. But her supple, shallow nature had taken love lightly a dozen times and relinquished it just as easily without lasting pain. I suspected my own nature could not and I withdrew, retreated, cried a few tears into my pillow, forgot.

The summer that I was twenty I met a young man by arrangement in the Tuileries Gardens, a lieutenant in the British army on his way to South Africa where trouble was expected with the Boers. And I was very nervous hurrying across the Pont Royal to meet him through a misty curtain of August rain, late as always, my basket of correspondence and other women's secrets on my arm. Very late. Would he wait for me? Would he even come at all? And reminding myself how very unlikely it seemed, I slowed my step, drew breath, prepared myself—as seemed wise—for disappointment. Of course he would not be there. His letter, making the appointment, had clearly been written on impulse, a sentimental, even a tipsy moment, no more. He would have regretted it as thoroughly as I was now regretting my reply.

He would not come. And in any case how could we possibly recognize each other?

He was there, standing by the statue I had described; and I knew him immediately. A tall, fair young man—twenty-three years old, I supposed, calculating his age from mine—waiting with the amused, faintly superior, slightly apprehensive expression one often sees in the English abroad. He was my brother, Guy Heron, of that improbable place called Clarrow Fell who, before marching off to war in the Transvaal, had decided to have a look at this mysterious foreign sister of his. Why not? I had wondered about him myself often enough, the more so because my mother's refusal to discuss him had kept my curiosity unsatisfied. And so, when he had written asking to meet us and my mother, turning pale and shaking her head, had given the letter to me, I had suggested this rendezvous.

It had seemed exciting, moving—distant. But now that it was upon me what could I say to him? How could I even introduce myself? There was no need.

"Olivia?" he called out.

"Guy? How did you know?"

"I didn't, I just thought—I suppose you remind me of somebody."

Clearly not of himself and my whisper of disappointment told me I had been hoping we might resemble each other. We did not. Incredibly he was my mother's son, fair and pale with a long elegant upper lip like hers and her light blue, rather absent-minded eyes. I was dark-eyed and amber as a Spaniard with strong teeth and bones and long, enduring limbs, an earth-child, my mother called me sometimes when she was feeling witty with champagne, not a creature of the air like herself and Madelon and this new, undeniably attractive brother. Yet the notion that I resembled some unknown person in Clarrow Fell intrigued me, moved me to a point beyond shyness where I simply wished to know more, both of him and of myself.

"You didn't mind my writing to you, Olivia?"

"Oh no."

"And your mother?"

My mother? His mother too, of course. But it was too soon for that.

"She thought it better not to meet. Not this time, anyway."

"I see. What very perfect English you speak, Olivia."

I had never thought of it before, but so I did. His speech was easy, careless, taken from life, mine from the textbook; my accent quite neutral, containing no distinguishing marks, nothing to identify me as a resident of Clarrow Fell or anywhere else. Too perfect, he meant, since only aliens who needed to try harder spoke so flawlessly. But how fascinating to discover even this much about myself in his company. How eager it made me to discover more. And quite soon, as we walked up and down in the damp air, the pavements all around us shiny and scented with rain, it no longer mattered what we said so quickly did the rapport and the laughter grow between us.

"So why are you going to fight the Boers? What have they ever done to you except refuse to give you their gold?"

"Oh, I expect that's their side of the story. Don't listen to it Our side is bound to be different."

"Bound to be? Don't you know?"

"Oh—one doesn't ask that kind of thing, my dear. One just obeys—for Queen and Country and all that."

"Which means, I suppose, that you have your own reasons Why did you join the army in the first place? You're the young squire, aren't you, up there? Shouldn't you stay at home and look after your land?"

"Yes," he said, half teasing, half sad, so that it might have been a joke; probably not. "So I should. But maybe the girl I wanted had the good sense not to want me. And my grandfather knows all about the land."

"My grandfather too, I suppose, although I expect he wouldn't care to be reminded."

"I expect *my* mother feels just about the same."

"I expect so."

But they were members of a narrower generation, brooding on past wrongs for which we were not to blame. And we were young and clear-sighted and wiser by far than they had ever been.

We found a café with a sheltered terrace were he drank cognac—a great deal of it, I thought—and we held hands openly, carelessly, needing to touch one another as I told him about Victorine and Madelon and Luc—his own mother's children, after all—and he spoke to me, in his casual, undemonstrative, English fashion of the home I had never seen, of cousins I had never suspected.

"Let's see—there's Alys, quite beautiful, of course. And Robin. Yes, I suppose he's beautiful too, in his fashion. I expect Alys will marry him one of these days when she gets around to it. And then there's Amyas. You should come and meet them."

"I never will. What was father like?"

"Unyielding."

"And grandfather?"

"A devilish fine old gentleman."

"Which means—what? Have you quarreled with him?"

"Shall we say that he wanted me to stay and I wanted to go."

"Why?"

"My dear, I've told you already—to defend my Queen and Country."

"But no one is attacking your country. It is the British who are attacking the Boers, since they discovered those goldfields."

"Is that what they are saying in France? They may well be right. But all I want out of it is a change of scene. Or a reprieve perhaps, since I shall certainly go home in the end."

"A reprieve from what?"

"Oh—from knowing that tomorrow will be just like today . . ."

He smiled, took my hand, pressed it against his cheek and then kissed it, his mouth dry and cool, my fingers retaining, for a very long time, the tingling sensation of his touch.

"Guy, is something wrong?"

He shook his head. "Nothing today. Listen, Olivia, later on, when I'm *the* squire, not just the young squire, will you come and see me? I'd be the envy of the country with a girl like you."

He had said "a girl" not "a sister." I understood and did not recoil from it, aware that the emotion, the attraction, building between us was too precious to be denied. We were brother and sister, yes, but we had never met until today and what I saw was a handsome, vulnerable, most lovable man; what he saw was a girl he believed he could love, and it would take time—more than we had available that wet afternoon—to channel such love in its ordained direction.

And so we walked for hours through patches of sunshine and showers of soft needle-fine rain, the pavements empty and shining like glass around us, saying anything that came into our minds, easy together, in harmony, the sweetest experience, it seemed, of my life.

He came with me to the corner of the rue du Bac and stood for a moment leaning an arm against the wall behind my head, shielding me from the rain which had become heavier now, and cold.

"So, it's a promise, then? You'll come to Clarrow Fell when I'm the squire?"

Would I? Of course not. It was a dream, richly textured with hopes and excitement, so ardently desired that it must be impossible.

"I'll come."

He bent his head and brushed his mouth against the corner of mine, smiling at me a shade ruefully.

"I'll send for you, Olivia. Grandfather won't be alive by then and if the others shouldn't like it—well, as I say, when I'm the squire . . ."

I nodded, my throat too tight to speak; he turned to go, finding speech difficult himself, I think, and I called out "Guy—take care."

He came back, grinning boyishly. "I'll do that all right, little sister. Don't fret."

Little sister! I had never been called so before. I had been the eldest and glad of it, more than ready to tackle anything it might bring. But how wonderful, now, to be smaller and frailer; a pleasure so intense that in a moment or two when he had turned the corner, I would certainly surrender to it and cry.

20

"It's a war you're going to," I scolded him, aware of its implications for the first time. "A war, not a picnic."

"Oh, one doesn't make too much of it, you know. The blighters take one look at us and run away—thought *everybody* knew that."

I shook my head, amused, exasperated, wanting to say something tremendous, one word to contain the whole complexity of my feelings, their sudden quite terrifying strength, their bewildered yet total sincerity. No word existed and so I flung my arms around his neck in a fierce hug, my whole body clenched tight to hold back, just a while longer, my tears.

"Oh—just *behave* yourself," I told him as if he had been Luc and, laughing, he slid his arms around my waist and hugged me too.

"How absolutely splendid," he said. "It's what every front-line soldier feels entitled to—a pretty girl in tears to see him off. Promise to worry about me, will you, love, and cry for joy when I come back?"

"Very likely."

"I'll hold you to that, Olivia. And don't worry about me. It's not even certain there'll be a war, in any case. By the time I get to Cape Town the chances are we'll all be the best of friends again."

He was wrong.

I had never thought, before, of how wars were made. They had seemed simply to occur in the pages of history books, as tedious and obscure as the disputes which preceded them and the treaties—signed by contingents of dry-as-dust old men—which marked their end. Yet, since war did break out so frequently, and since it was inconceivable to me that ordinary men could take pleasure in killing each other, somebody must want it.

Not the British Government, of course, who, having expressed total disinterest in the Boer Republics when there had seemed to be nothing there but dry *veldt*, thin cattle, hot winds and hot tempers, could not openly change its mind now that diamonds had been discovered at Kimberley and gold in the Transvaal hills of Witwatersrand. Certainly not the Boers who, being simple, homespun farmers with no mining skills, ought to be glad—the British newspapers alleged—to see the population of their country doubled and trebled overnight by gold-hungry adventurers, mainly British, who had nothing simple or homespun about them at all.

I sent Luc to the boulevard Saint-Michel every morning to fetch me the English and French newspapers which could often be found there abandoned on the café tables, and read them avidly and privately, over and over again. It was unreasonable of the Boers, one editor informed me, to feel that this admittedly very large foreign presence might be threatening to take over their land. It was blatantly obvious, declared another, that British Imperialism was up to its old tricks again, "Perfidious Albion" no less, sending in first her merchants and then her soldiers, just as she had done in India. I absorbed every word, every turn of phrase, searching each one for traces of my brother, yet it was not in cold newsprint but only later, in the published letters of survivors, that I learned the details of a certain October morning—the war only ten days old—when a *commando* of Boer farmers, many of them in their Sunday suits, attacked the British town of Dundee in northern Natal. The weather was drizzly and overcast, more British than African, the garrison unprepared, the Commanding Officer, General Sir Penn Symons, declaring, with some spirit, that in his view it was damned impudence, if not downright bad taste, to start shelling before breakfast. But by the more civilized hour of ten o'clock, when a gentleman might be supposed to have done with his ham and his toast and his kedgeree, General Symons lay dying, having sustained a stomach wound which proved fatal, partly because he concealed it from his men, mounting his horse unaided and riding off alone—can one doubt with a cheerful wave of the hand?—to the dressing-station so as not to alarm them. And in the resulting confusion, the mist, the shock, the inexperience, a moment arose when a battery of British artillery, their view for some reason obscured, opened fire on their own infantrymen who, with fixed bayonets, were attempting to take what they—or at least *someone*—evidently considered to be a strategic hill.

"Stop that firing," shouted a British colonel, jumping to his feet and waving his arms at a British gunner who promptly shot him through the heart. And among the two hundred and fifty British officers and men who fell with him that day was Lieutenant Guy Heron, my brother, slaughtered by mistake while taking a hill in Africa, in support of what cause? What ideal? For what gain? Had he even cared in the moment of his communal, regimental death, about anything but his own body, bleeding into the alien earth, his clean, twenty-four year old limbs, his intricate, multi-faceted brain and heart which had been generations in the molding, reduced, with official apologies from Whitehall, to butcher's meat?

He had taken a hill in Africa and they had called it victory. Who would even remember it next year—tomorrow?

I would remember.

The news of his death was conveyed to my mother by the Heron family solicitor and I experienced, for the first time in my life, an immediate and absolute need to be alone. I went up to the attic where Luc slept, knowing he would not be there, sat on his narrow bed and shook with one violent spasm after another, a hard, dry, angry grief that rattled the teeth in my head and jarred my bones. Yet how was it possible to grieve so painfully for a stranger? I had known him for half a day. I had known him always. It was possible.

And, numbed by this first true grief of my life, I was very slow to understand the document delivered the following day from that same solicitor, informing me that, due to some family settlement of a truly British complexity, my brother's demise had made me the heiress of Clarrow Fell.

TWO

My mother shed a great many tears for several days thereafter and for a great many reasons; the death of her unknown son, death in itself, her own frailties and follies and the sorry conviction that, if restored to her youth, she would be more than likely to commit them all over again. And then, drying her eyes, she warned me "Do not trust the Herons and their lawyers, Olivia, for they will find a way to cheat you if they can."

But, as my grandfather's lawyers were quick to reassure me, my right to the property was in no way disputed. By Act of Settlement, which had been in force for generations, the estate of Clarrow Fell was destined to pass in direct male line from father to eldest son, the squire of every generation holding it in trust for his heir without whose consent he could neither sell nor mortgage any part of it. This system of entail, it was explained to me, had been devised to keep estates whole and entire and safely within the family to which they belonged. Entailed land was protected land and could not be disposed of, acre by acre, to pay off the gambling debts or the unsuitable romantic entanglements to which country squires were apparently prone. The sons of the house of Heron were, therefore, bound hand and foot to their land but it had always been recognized that one could not so bind a woman. No man, particularly in medieval times, would be likely to marry an heiress unless she had the power to transfer her property to him on their wedding-day, and my ancestors had made reluctant but realistic arrangements to that effect in case the direct male line should fail. It had failed now with me.

Following the deaths of my father and brother, my grandfather had no choice—as I understood it—but to leave the estate to me. Had Guy lived to inherit, he too would have had no choice but to keep the property secure for a son or grandson of his own. But in my case, in order to provide me with a dowry, the entail was broken, thus placing the estate of Clarrow Fell freely at my disposal, to keep, to give away, or to sell exactly as I pleased.

And there seemed to be no question in anyone's mind, including my own, that I would sell.

I would not be rich. The Heron lawyers had been at some pains to caution me that the sale of an ancient manor house with no more than four or five small farms and some village property attached to it would not make my fortune. Land values in the North of England, they told me, were never high, rents notoriously low, but at least it was something solid to pave the way into the future, and if my mother saw it rather differently, as a few more years of Worth dresses and Grand Hotels, I never doubted my ability to restrain her.

"He should invite you up there," she declared, speaking of Mr. Neville Heron, my grandfather. "Not that you could possibly want to go and will positively loathe it if you do. But any other man would at least have been curious. Heavens! Such a cold man. I can still shudder when I think of him and really could not wish his acquaintance upon you, except . . . Well I am sorry to say it, but you *ought* to see him, Olivia, or let him see you. He may be forced to leave you the land but I believe he has other things—valuable things–which are free of entail, and he must leave them to *someone*. It seems sensible to go and see. Heavens, how suddenly life changes. I have been so *bored* lately, Olivia—very nearly ready to buy myself a pair of sensible shoes and a blanket shawl and take up knitting. Thank goodness that is over."

She bought instead a white lace evening gown that moved around her like sea-foam and, at a candlelit dinner where her fine, pale skin appeared to great advantage, acquired a new and undeniably attractive lover of a type even she could recognize as unreliable.

"How sad," she told me, her eyes bright with a familiar excitement. "Poor Jean-François. He has no money, of course, and he is quite reckless with cards and horses and all those other costly things— not a hint of sensible shoes about him anywhere."

"He is rather young, too, mother."

"Well—thirty—thirty-five? Old enough, darling. I am being very foolish again, I suppose."

"Yes, mother, I suppose so."

"But you do see, darling," she said earnestly, "that if I am to suffer for it then it will only be *later*. And there is no guarantee that I shall have to suffer at all."

The winter passed, January presenting us with the birth of a brand-new century, February bringing me not precisely an invitation to Clarrow Fell but an intimation from my grandfather's overworked lawyers that I might, if I so desired, present myself before him, possibly in the spring, not to satisfy his grandfatherly curiosity, it seemed, but to settle the matter of the legacy I had received from my brother. What legacy? Small things, the lawyers replied, the result of a "soldier's will" which his commanding officer had no doubt required him to make and which amounted to the contents of his bookshelves and his wardrobe, some old property in a neighboring town which an elderly relative had recently left to him. Small things but immediate, surprising, intensely moving, sending me up to Luc's attic bedroom again until I had shed my tears and regained my calm. Why me? I could cope with money, the impersonal profits of bricks and mortar and land, but not these precious, speaking souvenirs. Why had he willed them to me and not the girl he had almost told me he loved and who had not, it seemed, loved him—perhaps the beautiful and presumably flirtatious Alys. Was there something he wished me to know or to do for him, which could only be discovered at Clarrow Fell? Naturally I would go anywhere for that.

"You are right, dear," my mother said. "Spring—April—can I have you ready in time?"

And, having treated me for twenty years with a brand of warm inattention all her own, she suddenly and most surprisingly began to concern herself with such mundane matters as my gloves and my underwear, issuing strange warnings that the maids of Clarrow Fell would judge me by the quality and condition of my linen and that in no circumstances would it be possible for me to make the proposed journey alone.

Indeed yes, she was fully—even sadly—aware that I had been running unchaperoned around the streets of Europe's major cities since the scandalous age of fourteen.

"Ten, mother—or less."

"Impossible—and I shall swear to that should anyone inquire."

"Ten, mother."

She shrugged, shook her head. Did anyone really understand the problems of a woman alone? Particularly in England where women were so bound by the rules and regulations of conduct devised by their pious, prickly Queen that I, with my Parisienne freedom of manner and my strange delusions about roaming the streets in positive infancy, would need to take the greatest care. In England, or at least in the quieter, more provincial part of it, there was nothing more fragile than the female reputation and—should I not believe her—she had never forgotten the case of a friend of hers, not too many years ago, whose bicycle had been seen one afternoon leaning against a hedge, alongside the bicycle of a young man. The guilty pair had done nothing more serious, my mother could swear to it, than stroll down to a riverbank nearby, the day being hot and the young lady desirous of washing a grease spot from her glove. But the evidence of those stationary bicycles had been enough. The young lady had neglected the rules of the cyclist's moral code. She had not *kept moving*, had made herself the subject of speculation and had been ruined so irrevocably as a result that there had been nothing for it but to pack her off to India, the only place left where—among all those over-heated bachelors—she might still get a husband. And, as for trains, surely it was common knowledge that the corridor train had been introduced into England as a direct result of the public outcry when another young lady, traveling so unwisely alone, had been attacked by an officer, although evidently not a gentleman, at some point on the London to Liphook Line. No, no, my natural independence may have stood me in good stead in the past but "over there" it simply would not do. England expected to see discretion in its young ladies, I had best make up my mind to it, and it would be pointless to suggest that things had changed since my mother's day. Things did not change in England, let alone in Clarrow Fell. Victoria was still there, was she not, sitting on her throne as she had been doing these past sixty years. What greater proof did I need than that?

"You're not serious, mother?"

"Of course not," she said, "I am not serious about anything. Otherwise I would not have had three husbands and four children and not even a home of my own to show for it."

"Five children, mother."

"I don't forget it. I only like to think I do. But I have told you the truth about English manners. You are not obliged to believe in them but you would be well advised to *behave* as if you do. Had I been more deceitful I would have fared better, I daresay, but somehow I could never get the hang of it. When I thought something was tedious or unnecessary I usually said so and there are no prizes for honesty up there—just for propriety. So you will have to tell lies, my darling, like everybody else. My sister, who might think herself the first lady of Clarrow Fell nowadays, will show you how."

"You have a sister! You never told me."

"Which means—surely—that I do not think of her. But yes I have a sister—dear Sibylla—a most admirable person. Everyone has always said so. She will watch you like a hawk, Olivia—admirable people often do that, I notice. So if we are to achieve our purpose, you must pass her inspection, darling, really you must. And since I am the only one who knows what she will be looking for, you had better leave it all to me."

And with a rare surge of maternal energy, she tracked down and effectively mesmerized an English clergyman and his wife into escorting me to London and keeping me with them for a night or two until an acquaintance of theirs should find it convenient to accompany me to Leeds. From which point Mr. Neville Heron might be expected, she felt, not only to make himself responsible for my care but to have me returned to her, in due course, in the same cumbersome, respectable and quite unnecessary fashion.

She came to the Gare du Nord to see me off, her cheeks still flushed from a luncheon in the Bois de Boulogne which had lasted until after four o'clock. She was very evidently elated—"tipsy" was the word I saw hovering on the clergyman's wife's thin lips—Madelon a pale little shadow beside her, Victorine scowling and munching a *brioche*, Luc . . . ? Where was Luc? Had anyone remembered to fetch him from school?

"Victorine . . . ?" I urgently inquired.

The train began to pull away.

"Darling," my mother called out, a marvel of chiffon and satin and that suspicious elation. "Watch out for that terrible grandfather, in case he is luring you up there to poison you . . . !"

"Do shut the window," the clergyman's wife, very much shocked, and before long my mother's voice, Madelon's quietly waving hand, Victorine's determined good cheer, the possibility of issuing those last-minute instructions about Luc had all faded away.

It was an easy journey, a train through the perfectly balanced countryside of France, a Channel crossing dominated by the clergyman's fear of misplacing his luggage, another train taking me to London where I spent two chilly nights, two tedious days in a suburban vicarage assisting the vicar's wife with her positive obsession for serving tea. And it was with a considerable feeling of reprieve that I was at last transferred to the care of another clerical lady who might have been the sister to the first, a little brown mouse of a woman returning to her husband's parish in Leeds who, having agreed to "take a young girl to her grandfather" had clearly understood "young" to mean "little" and was visibly startled, not only by my height, but my ability to tackle such perplexing matters as station porters and the handles of train doors.

And after enduring for a polite ten minutes or so, her warnings about the chloroform pad which would very likely be pressed against my nose should I venture into the corridor alone rendering me an unconscious victim of present lust and future white slavery, I closed my eyes—feeling I had given politeness its due—and thus traveled two or three hours north before noticing how the scene had begun to change, to *darken*, the smooth southern lawns and neat red-brick villages giving way to stone, not only in walls and buildings but somehow in the thinking and feeling of these magnificently sweeping, arrogantly bare uplands.

It was early spring by then—the first of the new century—a cool season, I thought, in this hard land, thin soil broken by outcroppings of rock that were sometimes no more than loose gray scatterings of pebbles, sometimes green slabs overlapping each other, their jagged edges shading from gray to black; even the grass and trees a duller, tougher green. And, increasingly, as my watch told me we must be nearing our destination, I saw towns that did not end in walls or rivers or boundaries of woodland and pasture like other towns I knew, but ran one into the other, a meeting of dark streets, rows of narrow stone houses covering dismal, identical miles, a pall of yellow-gray smoke hanging low in the air, the tangible evidence of manufacture, mass-production, the factory system which may well have made England the first, and at present the greatest industrial power on earth but which now, inserting itself through the ill-fitting windows of the train, seemed intent on soiling my gloves and making me sneeze.

"Are you cold, dear?" inquired the second clergyman's wife, unwrapping still more of the parcels of bread and cheese, fruitcake and cinnamon buns she had been pressing upon me ever since London.

I shook my head but in fact I had shivered, chilled by an awareness that this was a foreign land. In London streets I had heard accents as strange to me as the cries of Venetian gondoliers. Now, whenever we came to a halt, the station porters, small, stocky men with creased-apple faces and wiry curls, called out to each other in a language which obliged me to listen, very hard. Surely my own too-perfect speech would set me instantly apart, marking me as the visitor from abroad I was and should not have been. For what did I know of England beyond the casual knowledge of any Parisienne?

There was a dumpy, intensely domestic queen who had adored her husband so immoderately that when he died forty years ago she had gone into mourning and never come out again. There was a Prince of Wales, already in his late fifties, who had found little to occupy his time while waiting for the throne but eating, drinking and changing his clothes.

There was great wealth in England, I was well aware of that, having seen English milords in their hundreds thronging the boulevards, their fortunes coming not only from ancestral lands but from the merchant adventuring on the high seas; from trade routes forged through far-off continents—with or without the permission of their inhabitants—from mills and mines, coal and iron and steam. Great riches and great traditions, great inventions and exploits which had dazzled the world—industrial machinery, railways, bridges—and great poverty too, it seemed, since four out of every ten of the recruits who had offered to take the Queen's shilling a day for fighting the Boers had been declared unfit for service because of malnutrition. While as for the war itself I had heard, not only in the boulevard cafés but from the reported speeches of a British politician named David Lloyd George, that it was not only unjust but unlikely to succeed, these *backveld* farmers possessing an uncanny ability to blend into their own arid landscape, to disappear, when pursued, through a heat haze or, even more disastrously, to appear when least expected from trenches cunningly concealed by acacia thorn. And in the first month of the conflict the Boers had cut off and besieged a British garrison at Ladysmith, another at Mafeking, and had even shut up Cecil Rhodes himself in his own diamond town of Kimberley from where he made it plain—his personal fortune in Cape diamonds and Rand gold being upwards of five million pounds—that he expected the British generals to come very quickly and set him free.

I understood that young men like my brother—Boer as well as British—would be asked to die for that and, as the train creaked and panted further north, I experienced a vague and curiously heavy sense

30

of foreboding, accompanied, every now and then, by a sensation of unreality. I had dreamed of making this journey but *with* my brother, not instead of him. Now I was coming to take his place and even I— much less those unknown cousins, that unwilling grandfather—could not approve of it.

Leeds—the first industrial city I had encountered—remained in my mind as a station-yard, acrid with smoke and the sudden hiss of steam, dim with yellow swirls of fog glimpsed as we crossed one platform to another, the minister's wife needing my guidance, not I hers, in that purposeful throng. And taking in these new sights and sounds in eager double-helpings, my sense of foreboding lifted and dispersed, powerless against the force of curiosity. I had arrived in the North of England and how strange it was, how very interesting.

"My dear," whispered the clergyman's good lady whose image of me as a "poor orphan lamb" had been fading with every mile since London. "Far be it from me to criticize but one does not, at least in England one does not, stare about one in quite that fashion. One might be thought bold, which would be a great pity. Now *do* please follow me."

And hurrying forward, her own eyes at a correctly demure level, she collided first with a portly gentleman who did not seem to object and then with a lady of rather aloof bearing who, raising fastidious eyebrows, looked beyond her and inquired of me "Miss Olivia Heron?"

"Who wants her?" demanded my officious little companion, wishing it to be known that she was a woman who always did her duty and would not relinquish me now without some proof of identity, some expression, even, of gratitude.

"I am Sibylla Heron," the lady replied, her disdainful eyebrows conveying that this in her view was explanation enough.

"Indeed . . .?"

"Indeed."

And who dared to doubt her? Certainly not the clergyman's timid little lady who, after only a moment's exposure to Mrs. Sibylla Heron's distant yet penetrating gaze could hardly contain herself from dropping curtsies like a parlormaid.

"I am in your debt for bringing my niece, Mrs.—ah—Mrs. . . . ? And was it a pleasant journey?"

But she did not care about the journey; had made no effort to remember the little woman's name and, while gracious enough to acknowledge that there was a debt, her tone implied that, in her view,

31

it had already been paid. The services of a chaperone were no longer required. The still arched and decidedly supercilious line of Mrs. Heron's eyebrows expressed surprise that the clergyman's wife did not see that.

"You may go," the eyebrows said, although the words she actually spoke were "You will be glad to get home, I imagine. We must not detain you."

The command was clear.

"Oh yes—quite so," muttered the clergyman's little lady, apparently unaware that the very superior Mrs. Heron was a clergyman's lady too.

"Goodbye," said my aunt, not merely dismissing her but forgetting her, allowing nothing to disturb her inspection of me.

"Well, Olivia . . . ? Of course, you know who I am."

I did and did not, for with some emotion I found myself looking at a bleached and somehow elongated copy of my mother. She was tall and very thin where my mother was fine-boned and delicate, cool where my mother was vague, the shades of her appearance and her character being white and steel-gray and a subtle lavender while my mother remained so vibrantly, artfully gold. But the pale blue eyes and long, eloquent mouth were the same, the slenderness of the neck, the narrow hands and feet, the same air of good breeding. Not that this newly discovered aunt had ever possessed my mother's charm, or so my mother—growing indiscreet over a bottle of Chablis on my last night at home—had told me.

They had been famous in their locality, the two Blackwood sisters, one enchanting, the other merely pretty. The exquisite Lavinia who had married the young squire of Clarrow Fell and clever, ambitious Sibylla, her father's favorite, who had been obliged, nevertheless, to make do with a Heron cousin who was first the Curate and then the Vicar of Clarrow Church, his living in the Heron family's gift.

"Poor Sibylla," my mother had said with more amusement than sympathy. "Married six months after me and ten years older. And Toby Heron with nothing to put in the pot but his classical education. Poor Sibylla, and lucky me. But that is just the way of it sometimes and it was not fair of them all to say that I deliberately stole the scene at Sibylla's wedding by fainting in church and letting it be known that I was in the family way. Well, now she has Clarrow Vicarage to live in which is not very grand but at least no one is dunning her for the rent. And she has all my mother's furniture, which I simply adored, and all her jewelry too, I imagine, since no one offered any of it to me. You will not like her, Olivia. Indeed, I shall be offended if you do."

Would I like her?

There was a moment of silence which my Aunt Sibylla certainly intended me to find awkward but which, in fact, I did not, having been looked over many a time in this gimlet-eyed fashion by prospective employers who, before trusting me with their correspondence, had considered it necessary to ascertain whether I might be likely to make off with the family silver or unearth the family skeleton from its hiding place. I, therefore, endured her scrutiny without embarrassment, feeling that I had not the slightest need to be ashamed of my gray broadcloth skirt and short military jacket with its rows of black braiding, my black straw hat with its white ribbon, a discreet costume of half-mourning which Clarrow Fell, my mother had declared, would expect of me. Despite the lengthy, dusty journey, my white cambric shirt and high frilled collar looked perfectly fresh—I had taken good care of that—my boots were well polished, my gloves beyond anyone's reproach, my hair carefully, even modestly dressed.

My aunt would have to look hard and long to find anything amiss with me and while she made up her mind to it I studied her too, seeing at once that I did not impress her in any way that might be of use to me. For the second time that day I had not lived up—or down—to expectations. The little lady who had accompanied me from London had wanted a child to mollycoddle and perhaps to bully on the way. What had my aunt been hoping to see? An undernourished, ill-educated, little drab, easily overawed and unlikely to answer back? A flighty, foreign version of my mother, too self-absorbed and pleasure-seeking to threaten anyone? Did I represent a threat to her? Very likely I did, since the owner of Clarrow Fell must control the destiny of Clarrow Vicarage and its incumbent too. Could I dispossess her husband of his living, oblige her to pack up the furniture my mother had coveted and take it elsewhere? Possibly. But instinct warned me that nothing I did would remove that faint smile from her lips nor lessen, by one degree, the supercilious arch of her brow. Other people had money. Some—like my mother—had charm. Aunt Sibylla had self-esteem and, having my own share of it, I knew that I must show her no weakness, must never, in my dealings with her, be humble.

"Well, Olivia," she said at last. "This must be very difficult for you, I know."

"For both of us, perhaps. I am very pleased to meet you Aunt."

"Let me bid you welcome then, although I fear I must also hurry you along. Should we miss our train we would be obliged to wait twenty-four hours for another. This is Mr. Amyas Hird, by the way, the land agent at Clarrow Fell, who is about to be efficient with your luggage—are you not Amyas?"

Amyas? My brother had mentioned an Amyas, including him so casually, so intimately in the landscape of his boyhood that I had assumed him to be another cousin, or at least a relative of some kind, not a land agent, an employee. But, nevertheless, concealing even the murmur of disappointment, I turned swiftly to the man who had been there all the time, seen but not noticed, and smiled, held out my hand, feeling on much surer ground with a male of any age or variety than this shrewd, suspicious, cool-eyed aunt.

He was thirty or thereabouts, dressed as correctly as a lawyer or even a clergyman, his appearance so unremarkable that, an hour after leaving his company, one had to think hard to remember him. And even then, although one managed to recall his medium build and medium height, the brown—neither particularly dark nor particularly light—of his eyes and hair, one could not easily blend them together into a whole, could hazard no more than a guess as to what manner of man lay underneath.

How disappointing. I had expected more than this of Amyas. Yet he was, indeed, most efficient with my luggage, installing it and us in an asthmatic little train which, after wheezing painfully for an hour or two through those long industrial suburbs, more sinister than ever in the gathering twilight, came finally to a halt at what seemed just another station, as gloomy and smoky and *dark* as the rest.

"Bradeswick," announced my aunt, as I might have said "Vienna" or "Rome," and then, with the total self-confidence of royalty who know that doors will be opened for them and that the crowd will respectfully give way, she waited while Amyas Hird organized her careful removal from one train into an empty compartment of another, even more ailing than the first, which took us in slow, shuddering stages through bare fields and unlit windy spaces, to Clarrow Fell.

And having expected to engrave every detail of that journey on my mind, to spend it in a state of high excitement, anxiety, defiance, unease, I remembered little but the effort of talking to my mother's sister as if my mother did not exist, of answering her questions about my early life as if I had resulted from some form of immaculate conception, since she clearly could not bring herself to mention my father, considering, perhaps, that he was no concern of mine.

"Where did you go to school, dear?"

I told her at great length, peppering my narrative with references to Victorine and Madelon, of which she took no notice whatsoever, possessing a most convenient form of deafness, it seemed, to words she did not wish to hear.

"You say that you have spent some time in Athens?"

"Yes. My brother, Luc, was born there."

She smiled, her expression polite but registering no greater interest than if I had been speaking of a pet cat.

"Athens is doubtless very educational," she said, annihilating Luc by the civilized process of ignoring him. "My daughter, Alys, longs for the culture but could not stand the heat, I fear . . ."

"It never troubled me, *madame*. But my sister, Madelon, was often incommoded, her skin being fair like mother's."

But, far from defeating her, I had not even ruffled her calm. "It is a problem we do not have in this part of the world," she told me, her faint smile never wavering. "I imagine we may see rain by the end of the day. We are rarely without it, which can be a great nuisance, although so good for the gardens. And, indeed, the wealth of our County, in the old days, was founded on rain. Why yes, my dear, for without it there would have been less grass for the sheep and consequently less wool for the looms. And they used water power, after all, to drive the engines of our first textile mills before steam came in and turned so many of our common weavers into millionaire industrialists. So I suppose we must be grateful for our rain."

Mr. Amyas Hird took no part in our conversation, although his silence had nothing in the least heavy or uncomfortable or timid about it. He was simply there, unobtrusive to the point of invisibility until the train, with a great shuddering sigh that might have been its dying breath, halted at our destination—not a station, it seemed to me, but a platform abandoned amidst empty fields—whereupon he became efficient once again, conveying us from our compartment and into the waiting gig with the minimum of fuss.

"Everything all right, sir?" inquired the stationmaster, hat in hand, his obsequious manner indicating that a land agent was entitled to be treated like a gentleman. "I walked the horse like you said."

"Quite all right thank you, Grigson!" Mr. Hird replied, his voice

35

speaking the words, no more than that. And a few moments later, when he had mounted the gig and was driving it at a not inconsiderable pace with his back to me, although I could remember distinctly the stationmaster's tip-tilted nose and boxer's chin, and every single detail of my brother Guy, I was no longer *certain* about Amyas.

But I could barely control my excitement now and knew of no real reason why I should, leaning forward to seize with eyes and mind the village Guy had described to me; a single street clambering bravely up a steep hillside, its cobbles clinging with square-jawed determination to the rock below; a line of low, stone cottages on either side blackened by time and the soot-bearing winds of industrial Bradford, Halifax, Wakefield and Leeds, not far away. There were a few women in the cottage doorways, who sketched quick curtsies as we passed although their stares held more curiosity than subservience, a few men on the bench outside the ale-house who raised their flat caps to us, salutations graciously acknowledged by Aunt Sibylla and which Amyas did not appear to see.

A grim place, perhaps, to someone whose expectations had been nurtured so much farther south, no softening of flower gardens or mellowing of vines, just those bare, black rows of dwellings, a farrier's yard, a shop—or so it seemed, although the goods were hidden well away inside—another ale-house, an ancient church, its stonework blacker than the rest, its tower square, uncompromising, thrifty. And beyond it, where the village petered out, a continuing prospect of dull green earth and dull gray sky, an impression of water all around me, in the skirts of every trailing cloud above my head, rushing in fast-flowing underground streams beneath my feet, falling in thin, sharp-scented torrents down every bald hillside.

"An acquired taste," Guy had told me, speaking of the village, the Manor, the land and the grimy fringe of industry around it; yet my eyes had seen it all before and something in me remembered.

"Here we are," said my aunt, making some minor adjustments to her gloves and instantly, having had good training in such matters, I sensed the approach of insult and stiffened angrily, very willing to defend myself.

"Here, *madame* . . . ?" For the gate into which we were turning could not possibly lead to the Manor. But if she noticed my annoyance, she did not condescend to be disturbed by it, merely offering me once again her cool, impersonal, almost perpetual smile.

36

"You will be staying at the vicarage with us, of course."

"Really, *madame?*" I could see no "of course" about it.

"Why yes, dear, since the Squire lives quite alone with no woman in the house of greater standing than a housekeeper to chaperone you, which is hardly enough . . ."

"Not even when the Squire happens to be my grandfather?"

She alighted from the gig, her composure absolute, and continued to smile at me as if I had made some commonplace remark about the weather which hardly merited a reply.

"You are very tired, dear."

It was not a question. It was even true. But as I joined her on the gravel drive, I was not defeated.

"Tell me, *madame*, is my grandfather a feeble man—incapacitated in some way?"

And for the first time I had succeeded in startling her.

"Good Heavens—my dear child, absolutely not. *Whatever* can have given you that idea?"

"Oh—I simply wondered why he did not come to meet me himself."

"Ah!" she said, and we stood on the gravel for a moment taking each other's measure in a way which could have generated open conflict had not her mouth suddenly produced its empty smile again.

"My dear, no doubt our English notions of chaperonage seem very quaint to you . . ."

"No—no. Not quaint—provincial."

"I daresay. But there it is. Each country has its customs and you will bear with us, I feel sure of it."

"Certainly, *madame*."

"Ah yes—Olivia dear, forgive me for mentioning it, but since we *are* on the subject of customs . . . In England we do not use the word "*madame*" in quite that way. One could say "madam," of course, but only if one happened to be a shopkeeper, or a waiter in a hotel, or a parlormaid. A natural mistake, dear. Don't let it trouble you. Do come inside. My daughter, Alys, is longing to meet you."

The vicarage was a square, Georgian box, plain and rather low, its long windows opening onto grass, its hall very cool and quiet and rather dim, my cousin Alys's desire to meet me evidently kept well under control since she was not there to express it. I saw a long, narrow passage with a garden door at the end of it, rooms at either side that looked empty, *felt* empty, although in fact they were furnished with a grandeur somewhat out of keeping with the refined economy often found in clerical households—small appetites, a calculated minimum of hot water and dinner guests—since on a vicar's stipend very little, certainly not these inlaid sideboards and velvet chairs which must have come from my mother's mother, could ever be replaced.

"Alys," called my aunt, her voice echoing down the well-scoured stone passage. No Alys.

"Alys!"

And then, through the garden door—not immediately and not even in a great hurry—came a girl with an open book in her hand, having just and not a moment too soon, remembered the time and the demands of hospitality which must now take precedence over her obvious desire to go on with her reading under the chestnut tree.

"Alys—*there* you are. This is your cousin, Olivia."

And I took a step forward into the early evening shadows to get a better look at her, for this was the Alys my brother had spoken of, the girl who—I had now firmly decided—had rejected him and sent him off to war.

"Quite beautiful, of course," he'd said of her. "I expect she'll marry Robin one of these days when she gets around to it." And so I had been expecting a brilliant, flirtatious butterfly, flitting from one bedazzled suitor to another, my mother's niece who might resemble my mother far more than any of her daughters. But she did not, and having already felt acute disappointment with regard to Amyas, I thought in that first moment of acquaintance that I was to be disappointed in Alys too.

She was about my own age, her coloring perhaps the fairest I had ever seen, pale skin, long straight hair just a shade away from white, eyes of a faint, transparent blue, her features not individually pleasing since her nose was too large, her forehead extremely high, her mouth wide and with scarcely more color than her cheeks but which, when put together, made an interesting face, plain, rather than pretty but original, the only one of its kind I had ever seen.

She wore a trailing dark skirt, a white blouse, a little girl's velvet ribbon holding back her hair, her manner absent-minded rather than cool as if, having journeyed very far away in her book, she needed a little more time than we had allowed her to come back again. And since the only Englishwoman I really knew well at that time was my mother, who lived perpetually on the frothy surface of her emotions, who laughed when she was happy, wept copiously when she was sad, who told everything, gave everything, I did not immediately understand that Alys's reserve was not hostile—as her mother was hostile—but a uniquely English combination of good manners, shyness and the fear of seeming to intrude.

"Olivia—I am so pleased . . ."

"So am I."

But it had been a very long day, during which I had endured an uncomfortable journey, a surfeit of clergymen's wives, and still no sign of my grandfather; and I was rapidly approaching a point where nothing could please me.

"Olivia wishes to go upstairs, Alys," Aunt Sibylla said, the tone of her voice not impatient but, just the same, wondering why Alys had not seen this herself. "Go up with her, dear, and then we will have tea in the drawing room in—shall we say—three-quarters of an hour? Yes, three-quarters, since we are to dine at seven. One would not expect you to dress elaborately tonight, Olivia, unless you particularly wish it. I am sure Alys will not—although one may hope she will find something better to do with her hair than bundle it back with that schoolgirl ribbon. Really, Alys!"

I was taken to a bedroom that had little in it but a great deal of scouring and dusting and polishing; a single, straight-backed chair, a low oak chest too scarred and not quite old enough for value, a wash-stand with a plain white basin and jug, a narrow bed, Aunt Sibylla's legacy of fine furniture evidently not extending to her upper story. The counterpane and the walls were white, the fireplace, in which no fire had burned, I thought, since February, was a dull brown; the grate and fender polished far beyond their humble station. The floorboards gleamed with dark brown varnish, a small rag rug in shades of earth and dead leaves lay by the bedside. The window was wide open, homespun curtains blowing in a breeze that came straight from a Yorkshire moor where April was rarely a gentle season. I would be very clean here, there was no doubt of that, very cold and decidedly uncomfortable. Yet here I meant to stay until I had achieved my purpose, until I had looked just as hard and just as long as I liked at my place of origin and rediscovered something of my brother. And when the maid had unpacked my boxes and Alys and I had exchanged our birthdates, the details of my journey, the preliminaries necessary to our civilization, I sat down on the bed, finding it every bit as hard as I had supposed, and asked her, "When might I expect to see my grandfather?"

"Oh yes—indeed," she said, smiling and frowning at the same time, an expression I would come to know well—for, having no temper of her own, she was always puzzled by anger, truly sorry that she could not instantly assuage it by the sweet, clean-limbed powers of logic and reason in which she so ardently believed.

"Quite soon, Olivia, I think. I am to take you up to the house tomorrow morning, that is quite certain, so that you may explore it undisturbed. And there is a dinner-party arranged there for you tomorrow night. You will be sure to see him then."

"That is hardly soon, when one considers that I have come all the way from Paris."

"Oh dear . . ." she said, biting her lip, trying with great goodwill to put herself in my place and failing utterly for the simple reason that had anyone exposed her to neglect or insult she would have been too engrossed in her reading, her sketching, her *thinking*, to notice.

Could it be that my brother had loved her and that she had failed to notice that too? No flirt, then, playing off one young man against another—Guy against the unknown Robin—but a dreamer, a creature neither of the earth like me nor the air like my mother but of thought, ideas, abstractions, living in some fragrant meadow of the imagination where other people's urgencies could not really touch her.

But, nevertheless, my situation and the likelihood that I would be neither philosophical nor good-tempered about it, *did* become clear to her and at once she was full of concern, eager to put things right and anxious, above all, that my opinion of my grandfather should not suffer.

"You see, he is such a terribly conscientious man," she told me earnestly, frowning again in her desire to be believed. "They call him a pillar of the community, which sounds very pompous, but it is actually quite true, for I can think of several things, hereabouts, that would fall down the very moment he ceased to prop them up. He has the farms and the tenants to see to and practically everybody in the village relies on him for one thing or another. And he is a magistrate, of course. He went all the way to York this morning to hear a case which concerns a local family . . ."

She paused, hoping I would find this admirable and when, by an expressive and rather foreign movement of the shoulders and hands,

I indicated that I did not, she sighed and hurried on. "He was really needed there, I do assure you, for if the man is convicted he leaves a wife and several children in one of the Clarrow cottages."

"Really. How inconvenient."

"Oh no, Squire Heron will not find it so. There are squires, of course, and many of them, who would simply evict and repossess and that would be the end of it."

"So I imagine."

"But not your grandfather. He accepts responsibility, you see, for the people who live here and before thinking of re-letting the cottage, he will find the woman a refuge somewhere or other, *and* apprentice her sons to a trade and place her daughters in service, no matter how many train journeys or how many hours in the saddle it costs him. And he is quite old, you know."

"I imagine he must be. Would my brother have done all that?"

"Guy?" She smiled, her expression full of warmth and sadness, her affection shining out sincere and true but without passion, no more than one might be expected to feel for a cousin, a childhood companion. "Ah well, you see, Guy liked to be different—different that is, from his grandfather. I don't think it was really antagonism. I think Guy cared—respected . . . It was just that he felt he had to be—*different*. He told me in one of his letters about coming to see you in Paris and how close he felt to you. When we were children we used so often to wonder about you—Guy and Robin and I."

Letters! *I* had no letters. I had been on the verge of liking her and now, while the stab of jealousy lasted, I could not.

"Did he write you often?"

"Oh yes, quite often!" she told me, entirely without guile. "Just about every day, I suppose, on the voyage out. But I expect that was because he was bored on the ship and had nothing else to do."

Had they been love letters? Yes, of course, they had, written with all the quizzical, nonchalant charm that had touched me so lightly and penetrated so deeply; affection understated, underplayed, offered with a shrug for her to take only if she chose. She had not taken it, and because my memory of Guy had become the exact image of the man I wanted for myself, her decision amazed me. In her place I would have fought tooth and nail to win him and keep him, not throw him away, and fiercely I hoped that at least she had given him something to take with him into the African *veldt*.

The door opened apologetically and a little maid about twelve years old and fragile as a sparrow, appeared with a can of hot water and the information that "missus" had sent her.

"Oh Lord," said Alys, having clearly forgotten her mother's instructions about drawing-room tea. "I had better leave you, Olivia, for you will want to wash and—yes—did mother say something about my hair? I had better brush it and pin it up which never takes me long, and I will see you downstairs for tea in—well, Betsy, how long before tea is ready? Don't say it is ready now and I am late again?"

"Yes, miss."

"And mother already in the drawing room with her eye on the clock? Oh dear. I am in disgrace again, Olivia, which need be of no concern to anyone, I do assure you. It happens to me so often that one could call it my natural habitat. I will just do *something* with my hair—not a great deal, you may believe me—and then I will run straight downstairs to make our excuses. Mother will know better than to blame you, Olivia, so you may take your time."

I remained quite still for a moment when she had gone, the bare, brown room closing in around me, my spirits as sombre as the patch of cold sky, darkening towards evening, on the other side of the window. And then, jumping to my feet, I slammed the window shut with a bang which claimed it, for the time being, as my window, my room. I washed, brushed *my* hair into a high-piled Pompadour, put on a gown of gray foulard and white lace which my mother and I thought suitable for drawing-room tea no matter what my Aunt Sibylla might think. I bit my lips and slapped my cheeks to give them color, dabbed lavender water on my wrists and on my handkerchief, added, as a final flourish, a black velvet sash and breathed in as I tied it, which was the most effective method I knew of accentuating a small waist.

I was hurt and disappointed but would take good care not to show it. I was angry too and would be quite prepared, at need, to let everyone see that. I had not expected to be welcomed with open arms, being well aware that my claims on the estate must have come as a shock to some of my relations, a threat to others, even a source of grief to those who most regretted Guy. But my grandfather had invited me here and I expected better treatment from him than this. I was not responsible, after all, for my mother's misdemeanors and had no need to feel humble before anyone. Naturally I would have preferred to meet friendship and the possibility of affection. I had even hoped, forlornly but persistently, that it might be here. But I would not ask for it. I would not beg. I would simply toss my head and let them know that, having made their acquaintance, it was no longer surprising to me that my mother had found it so easy to run away.

I walked briskly down the uncarpeted stairs, allowing my heels to slap smartly against the gleaming wood, for if I had sometimes lived in conditions of hardship and squalor far beyond the comprehension of this faintly threadbare vicarage, I had also had my sips of grandeur. And in the spirit of pure loyalty to my mother, I now planned to enliven my aunt's provincial tea-time hour with descriptions of Grand Hotels, villas in Cannes, Alpine chalets and Mediterranean yachts— whether I had stayed in them or not—strewing my conversation with all the names of the rich and famous I could lay tongue to, transforming even Grandmère Junot's very simple, back-street café in Toulouse into a crystal and silver palace of *haute cuisine*.

Aunt Sibylla would know all about my mother's poverty but *that*— I would soon show her—was simply lack of money, not lack of style.

"I am so sorry to have kept you waiting, *madame*," I announced from the doorway, delighted to see that Alys, far from running straight downstairs, had apparently forgotten to come at all. But Aunt Sibylla was not alone with her silver kettle and cake-basket, for there was a young man sitting—or rather lounging—on the window-seat, someone tall and fair and loosely put together, who sprang to his feet when he saw me, crossing the room in long, eager, curious strides.

"Olivia—I never thought I'd see the day. This really is the most absolutely marvelous pleasure . . ."

I smiled a polite inquiry, held out a tentative hand, not giving too much too soon but, already, my spirits lightening, my own curiosity flowing free. This was the kind of welcome I had been hoping for. This— in those same lazy accents of privilege—was the way Guy had spoken to me.

"I'm Robin Esmond," he said, "which makes us second or third or at least some kind of cousins. I've been dreaming of you for years, Olivia. We all have."

And, giving him my other hand, I felt the fatigue and the chill of the day depart, banished by his interest, his admiration, his open-hearted excitement in me. I was excited too, very much moved, although one did not show *that*, of course, to a young gentleman. But the fact remained that this was what I had wanted most from Clarrow Fell; and my hopes, in such dismal ruins a moment ago, were now incredibly fulfilled. I had found my brother again.

THREE

I awoke to a pale gray morning, a tremor of remembered excitement and the warning that I must not expect my grandfather to return from York that day before dinner time.

"The squire is most meticulous in the performance of his official duty," explained Aunt Sibylla, offering me thin toast and an unfamiliar smoked fish, her tone implying that one could hardly expect a daughter of Lavinia Blackwood—Heron—Marriott—Junot to understand much about that. And so it was with Alys that I first crossed the sparse and stony field which lay between the gates of my grandfather's house and its village, the two existing in such close proximity—even sharing the single name of Clarrow Fell—that the house was known and spoken of throughout the entire neighborhood as "The Manor," somewhat to the irritation of other local landowners whose properties far exceeded it both in grandeur and yield per acre.

I already knew that the estate, even by northern standards, was small, just the home farm and four others of which the tenancies—I had learned at dinner last night—were habitually passed down in the same family from father to son or, if they became vacant, were eagerly sought after. Indeed, Squire Heron's reputation as the best of landlords had spread so far and wide that Aunt Sibylla seemed surprised, in her quizzically amused fashion, that it had failed to reach me in France.

He owned the village too, of course, since it had come into existence not merely with the house but because of it, prospering as the estate prospered in the good years and depending upon estate help to weather the years of drought, depression, bad harvests, bad government, Act of Parliament or act of God. A closeknit community, Aunt Sibylla had told me, of mutual dependence and respect where each thrifty, hard-working man was content with the role life had allotted him, and each woman was content to be the deep-scrubbing, hard-polishing wife of her man.

"Hardly, mamma," Alys had said, looking down at her plate.

"Oh the absolute best of all possible worlds," Robin Esmond had murmured, winking at me across the dinner table in a way that I had been thinking about ever since. But my aunt had chosen, with a certain rather pitying graciousness, to ignore their objections. They were young and while she was not precisely old, she was *right*. Life had a pattern here, she insisted, the squire in his manor, the tenant in his cottage, the farmer in his fields. And Clarrow Church was full three times every Sunday with happy men and women thanking God for it. One knew one's place. One kept one's place. What could be wrong with that? It offered security and *she* knew—even if her clever daughter did not—that men liked, above all things, to be secure. And security entailed an acceptance of authority, submission to a natural and rightful master; God in the first place, of course, and then the squire.

"Oh dear . . ." sighed Alys.

But as we took our short, steep walk towards the manor the next morning, Alys's pale hair hanging to her waist not so much in coquettish profusion as because she had forgotten to pin it up, she dutifully told me, in her vague and definitely sweet fashion, everything I wanted to know.

Yes, she had been born here at the vicarage and had never left it except for summer visits to the sea, a few months at a finishing school in Cheltenham, and was now leading the traditional life of a young lady helping her mother at home, except—regrettably—that she was no real help at all, her inclinations being far from domestic, her disasters in the kitchen and the still-room too numerous to relate. Her mother, of course, was always busy, fulfilling her pastoral duties as the vicar's wife with unflagging energy, thinking nothing of walking into any one of the cottages as she passed to inquire, not only into the progress of sickness and injury, but to lift the lids of the cooking pots to see if an adequate, or even a too adequate supper was brewing. For my aunt was strongly of the opinion that the villagers spent far too much of their very limited incomes on food and had no sympathy to spare for tales of rent arrears or unpaid doctor's bills from a housewife who had been caught broiling mutton chops instead of scrag-end.

Did no one object, I wondered, to what might, without too much of a strain on the imagination, be called interference? Well—and here Alys sounded a shade less than certain—the older people who had always lived and worked on the squire's land, were accustomed to follow the lead of the gentry, to live "under" them as they put it, and glad to do so, since the gentry in return for all this doffing of caps and bobbing of curtsies, would look after their people, more often than not, in times of trouble. But the younger men were no longer so dependent on the squire for their employment, now that the railway line had come to Clarrow Fell and given them the choice of remaining on the land or taking the train every morning to Bradeswick, to jobs in workshops and factories where feudal obedience was not required. And, perhaps naturally, the wives of these young men did not always conduct themselves to suit the requirements of the vicarage.

Her mother, of course, considered this drift from the land to be most harmful, nothing more or less than a Liberal Nonconformist plot to weaken the authority of England's Tory high church squires. But Alys, on the whole, thought it a good thing. Not that Bradeswick could be anyone's idea of paradise but at least it was bigger and, therefore, must hold out greater opportunities than Clarrow Fell.

She was not happy there? Oh—she could not say that. It was her home and although she could not share the local obsession with ancestor worship and tradition she could not deny the fascination of the Manor.

It was, quite simply, the most prestigious house in the locality, considerably less grand than Lord Potterton's magnificent Queen Anne residence just on the other side of the hill, which had three thousand fertile acres around it; considerably poorer than the Palladian mansion equipped with a positive bewilderment of modern gadgetry which the Nasebys of Naseby's Brewery had recently constructed five miles away, from the profits of their light ales. But no matter how stubbornly Lord Potterton might refer to his property as "The Park," or the Nasebys offer their address simply as "The Court," the natural seat of authority throughout the area remained "The Manor," smallest perhaps, and with not even a baronetcy attached to it, but the oldest, the first; just

46

a square, three-story tower of guard in its early stages, hurriedly piled up rock upon rock as protection against enemies, neighbors and the marauding Scots.

The village had grown up around the Manor walls, catering for the Manor's needs, a farrier to shoe the Squire's horses, laborers for his fields, a ready supply of housemaids, dairymaids, maids to scrub his linen and mend his hose. While the Herons themselves had proved to be a breed of survivors, producing surplus heirs in plenty who, at a time when every mother could expect to lose at least half her progeny, not only managed to withstand the natural weeding out of accident and disease but grew tall and strong and dark-complexioned, becoming high sheriffs of the County, churchmen, soldiers, minor pillars of the Tory Party, husbands of well-dowered, invariably fertile wives.

There had, of course, been an occasional black sheep or two, young bloods of the last century with nothing on their minds but cards, fast horses and fast women; and rather more recently the estate had withstood the deprivations of the present Squire's younger brother, Vivian Heron, whose sole talent had been his ability to put ten deadly accurate shots through the ace of diamonds at a distance of twenty-five feet.

But in the main the squire of every generation had shown himself to be a sound man who kept a close watch over the affairs of his parish, a moderate sportsman, more often than not, shooting grouse every autumn, hunting foxes every winter, having regard to law and order at all seasons. As a Justice of the Peace, holding Court from a room at the manor set aside for the purpose, he was fully empowered to administer justice or retribution to poachers and the absconding fathers of bastard children, to tradesmen who had cheated on matters of weights and measures, to rioters, burners of hay-ricks, breakers of industrial machinery in nearby Bradeswick, to trespassers, vagrants, and habitual drunkards. He it was who gave licenses to ale-houses or withdrew them, and granted permission for the Annual Horse Fair to be held at Clarrow Green. He it was who administered the Poor Law in his parish, and supervised the running of his local orphanage, workhouse, infirmary, primary school. He it was who gave the vicar his living, and who maintained, at the Manor, an ever-changing miscellany of impecunious, invalid or simply idle relatives, refusing not even the slightest of claims on his hospitality. He it was who reduced his rents in times of agricultural depression or cancelled them altogether; who found or created employment for his tenants' sons and sent his own sons—except the eldest—out into the world to serve their country usually in a military and often fatal capacity—a Heron at Waterloo, various younger Heron sons speared by Zulu assagais at Ulundi or Rorke's Drift, massacred by wild dervishes in the Sudan, dead of the cholera at Sebastopol, a whole batch of them slaughtered by tedium, by drink, by rebellious sepoys, by escapades in the mess and accidents on the polo-field during our long occupation of India.

Yet the eldest son—the heir—had always remained on the land, schooling himself in the disciplines of ownership, the responsibilities of inheritance so that he, in his turn, might become that good Heron landlord, that guardian of justice and the poor. So that, above all, he might take a suitable wife and breed a new generation to come after him. Could Alys tell me why my brother had turned away from that?

But she was a little breathless, just a shade more elusive than I had bargained for, as we reached the gates and began the long approach to the house between hedges so high and thick that each glimpse of the formal garden behind them came as an astonishment and a delight. I saw rhododendrons massed heavily together, not yet in flower, old trees standing huge and hoary and magnificent beside new-born daffodils, narrow stone pathways disappearing through tunnels of interlacing leaf and branch, sudden spaces of grass. And then, quite incredibly, the house was *there*, as naturally as if it had grown, like the trees, from the same wet earth, a long, low building of dark stone which had clearly taken gradual shape between the two medieval towers, rooms and wings and sections added as they had seemed convenient or affordable, to make a haphazard blending of styles which was harder, darker, so very much smaller than I had expected.

Perhaps I had imagined a French *château*, pale, graceful spires and turrets, long windows gleaming in the sun. Yes, I believe I had. But if I felt a whisper of disappointment I cannot remember it for I seemed to know, at once, that no other house would have been possible here; that, in fact, there was no other house even remotely like this one.

The entrance was not imposing, just three shallow steps, a heavy oak door opening into a stone-flagged vestibule, but then immediately beyond it I saw, exactly as Guy had said, the great hall, two storys high, stone-clad, a balcony running along one side of it,

48

an enormous window of stained heraldic glass dominating the other, each pane—through which the sun was slanting in reflected tints of emerald, ruby, sapphire, topaz, ebony and ivory—representing the coat of arms of every family allied by blood or by marriage with the Herons.

And closing my eyes, I imagined it on festive winter nights as my brother had described it, candles burning in the wall sconces, a great log fire crackling in the stone hearth, the vast refectory table drawn up beneath the great window and laid with crystal and silver for two dozen guests.

"How marvelous."

"Yes—I suppose it is," said Alys, who had seen it perhaps too many times before. "I expect Mrs. Long will want to show you round." And I became aware of another presence beside us, a housekeeper if the rustle of authority in her black silk skirts and the keys at her waist were anything to go by. She was a taut little woman, narrow of build, black hair drawn into an uncompromising bun, her eyes and skin a shade or two darker than one expected to find in England, a low voice saying exactly what a housekeeper ought to say on such occasions, before conducting me on a professional housekeeper's tour of her domain.

She had done it many times before and with the same disinterested efficiency, her concern with the family portraits lining every wall having more to do with the dust which gathered so persistently on their frames than with the dark-complexioned faces therein.

"Who is that?" I eagerly inquired realizing with awe and amazement and just a shade of disbelief that these men and women, with their black hair and heavy-lidded eyes, belonged to me: that I belonged to them.

"*Who's that?*" The housekeeper peered at the portrait of a spurred and booted cavalier and could not tell me.

"Alys?"

But Alys, shrugging and shaking her head, her long, pale hair falling around her like a curtain, could only advise me to ask Amyas.

"You will notice the pewter dishes on the mantelshelf," murmured Mrs. Long, on considerably surer ground with dishes. "Tudor, I believe—or earlier." And very smoothly, having exhausted the possibilities of the great hall, she transferred me to the Justice's Room, a low, bay-windowed apartment entirely paneled in dark wood where until as recently as twelve years ago when such matters had been handed over to the newly established County Councils, my grandfather had held his manorial courts, and where Amyas Hird still attended him night and morning to discuss the management of the estate.

There was the eighteenth-century wing to the right, a drawing room, dining room and parlor, cast in a lighter mold, the ceilings high and elegant with the kind of decorative plasterwork I was accustomed to see in France. And apart from the kitchens and other domestic offices which neither Mrs. Long nor I felt to be my concern, there remained on the ground floor just one more room, immensely long and narrow, running parallel with the great hall and lit not by one spectacular window but by a dozen small ones set between stone mullions; part library, part smoking-room, I thought, a place of leather armchairs and after-dinner brandies, of slow, warm afternoons curled up on the window-seat with a book.

There was no imposing staircase upon which the squire's lady might receive her guests, just a flight of stone steps leading to a corridor where the floorboards, at the very lightest tread, creaked out their age. And here, since there were no state bedrooms kept in readiness for public view, I was taken directly up a further tortuous flight of stairs to the top of the medieval tower where my brother had slept.

It was a roughly circular room, the paneled walls retaining an impression of stone in thick slabs beneath the wood, the walls themselves a little uneven, the structure having sagged rather more at one side than the other; decidedly a boy's room, a place of adventure high in an ancient tower where, from those arrow-slit windows a restless, imaginative lad could watch the savage borderers come swarming over the hill, could see the pikes and hear the drums of Yorkists and Lancastrians, Roundheads and Cavaliers, could watch the Charge of the Light Brigade, the Zulus, the Boers.

"You will find everything in order, Miss Heron," said Mrs. Long, indicating the closed cupboard doors, assuming that I wished to go through his things, to sort out his shirts and jackets into practical groupings of "usable," "saleable," "give-away," "throw-away," to peruse his account books and his correspondence, to make some assessment as to what I might get for his shaving brushes or his hunting boots.

Clearly it was what Mrs. Long would have done herself, what she believed *ought* to be done now. I could not. Alys could not either and with a whispered "Thank you, Mrs. Long," she ushered the hard-wearing woman from the room, shut the door and hesitated on the extreme fringes of my mood, knowing it to be vulnerable, sincerely wanting to help me yet unable to risk contact with an emotion which might spark off her own. And if she wondered what reason or even what right I had to grieve for a man who had been far closer to her than to me, she gave no sign.

"I think there is very little here," she said, "just the box on the table over there, and Mrs. Long can surely see to the rest. There were his horses, of course, but they have all been commandeered by the army and sent off to Africa. Amyas will know about the compensation. And then there is the house in Bradeswick—"

"House? I thought it just a warehouse of some sort—a shed."

She shook her head very slowly, her mind, like mine, on far deeper and more complex issues than houses and horses and boxes of shirt studs.

"I am afraid not, for I think a warehouse would have had more value. It is very far from grand. An old Heron lady lived there, with an ancient housemaid who died a week before her, and a positive army of cats. I doubt if anyone would buy it in its present condition, for old Marth-Ellen was years and years beyond cleaning and the cats were—not very particular. Amyas will show it to you and advise you how best to go on."

"What happened to the cats?"

"Oh they took care of themselves, I suppose, as cats do. Amyas will know. Shall I leave you now, Olivia? If I wait for you in the library can you find your own way downstairs?"

I nodded and she went out, gratefully I thought, needing a more tranquil atmosphere than the one I created. And suddenly, quite horribly—left alone between these massive stone walls—I felt crushed and menaced, not by the specter of Guy which, if I had judged him aright, would be too light and easy to haunt this place seriously, but by all those others, in their worthy, self-respecting hundreds who had been blended into that single identity "Squire Heron": those dark-complexioned, tough-grained men who had looked out at me from the canvases in the hall, faces like mine, stubborn wills like mine, keen appetites and urgent desires, marching down the years to a point which ended now with me.

It was an ironic fate, an awesome responsibility; and contem-

51

plating it I felt the weight of that collective identity descend full upon me, the strivings that had gone into it, the hopes, the lifetimes of effort, the rebuilding, more than once, from spiritual or financial ashes; the deep joys. I was not even certain whether or not I liked this house. But what had something so pale as liking to do with it? This was *the* house. I was aware of that with every bone and breath in my body, so deeply and increasingly aware of it that if I remained here much longer—listening to it, sensing it, making no resistance—the house would claim me and blend me too with all the others. I would not possess it. I would be absorbed into its service. And I understood how easily Guy, with his share of my mother's airy nature, could have been repelled by that.

It was indeed a heavy burden. But my own burden, one day, would be the greater, for when my grandfather died I would have to take this beautiful, breathing house and sell it to strangers. And so strongly did I feel that *they* would not allow it that I darted a swift glance over my shoulder, made for the door and then came back again, refusing to be beaten so easily by anything; much less an adversary which I could not even see.

I had come here for Guy, only for Guy, and now I would be well advised to steady myself, perform the sad tasks of bereavement as quickly as possible, and have done. Leaving aside the matter of blood, I had no place here, no real right either to my brother's possessions or to his memory. And, in that case, what else could I honestly do but hand over his trinket box untouched to Alys, ask Amyas to get what he could for the house in Bradeswick and use the money to feed the old lady's cats?

I would take no more from the house of Heron than the price of my journey back to France and by so doing would escape the appalling confusion of belonging here too deeply and, at the same time, not at all. For what good could it do to listen to those voices whispering to me from the past when no living voice at Clarrow Fell, certainly not my grandfather's, could offer me a true welcome?

I put my hands on the lid of the plain, leather box Alys had indicated and, considerably against my better judgment, allowed them to open it. Guy's box. And inside it, a pearl stick-pin to wear on gala evenings, a knife with a jeweled handle and a broken blade, a surprising strand of turquoise and coral beads, a signet ring with an engraved heron which they had sent back from Africa. Small things.

52

Speaking things. Impossible to touch. Yet I picked up each one and held it, separately, differently, recognizing the knife as a boyhood treasure bought in secret, I supposed, from a peddler, and then concealed from the prying, anxious eyes of nursemaid and nanny, just as Luc would have concealed it from mine. I held the pearl tie-pin to the light and saw him in evening dress, laughing, flirting, telling me his secrets. I touched the coral beads with the tips of my fingers, knowing them as a gift he had never made and which had not been intended for me. I took his ring and sat down with it for a moment, remembering it on his hand as he had drunk his cognac that day at a pavement café, believing himself to be immortal. I had believed it too and even now, no matter how often I reminded myself of that drizzly morning in Natal, no matter how cruelly I made myself count those hours and those miles of human destruction, I could not relinquish him.

I had loved Guy. I had wanted to love my grandfather. Just like my mother and Madelon I too could spin my share of dreams and ever since the arrival of my grandfather's invitation, I had been telling myself tales of intense discovery, great and moving revelations. The Squire would be stern and sad, even cold as my mother had described him, but that would be just a shield which surely—surely?—I could penetrate. And throughout my long journey north I had refused to doubt that behind it I would, if only gradually, find the man my brother might have been. The young squire grown old who would learn to be glad of me.

I doubted it now. My fingers closed hard around the ring, my head swimming suddenly with the sounds and images of distress, my nostrils troubled by the dry odor of dust, the sourness of churning mud. Guy was dead. I opened his box again and replaced everything exactly as I had found it, fussily, painfully coiling the beads in their remembered pattern, his knife to their left, his pin to the right. His ring emptied my hand. The room was still.

My life was not here. I had my own loves and realities in plenty elsewhere. I must take Guy's beads and his ring, absolutely here and now, and give them to Alys.

I picked up the box, my resolution firm, and put it down again. Of course I must give it to Alys. The coral and turquoise necklace had assuredly been meant for her. But not just now—not yet. For *something* might happen. There might be some better moment to make the gift. Or *not* to make it. Who knew? Unlikely, perhaps. But I could not be sure.

I found my way easily to the disappointing main staircase and down into the hall and then, looking for the library where Alys would be waiting, missed my way, caught the scent of a kitchen and, anxious to give Mrs. Long no cause to suspect me of prying into her domestic affairs, opened the first outer door I came to and in case anyone should be watching, straightened my shoulders and walked across a cobbled courtyard with the air of one who at least *appears* confident of her direction.

A certain dank odor warned me I was approaching stables or kennels, an environment equally unsuited both to my temperament and my shoes. Horses, in my city-bred eyes, were to be found safely harnessed between the shafts of hired cabs, or to be admired at a discreet distance, galloping along the *allées* of the Bois de Boulogne, not left to their own devices, as they seemed to be in this littered, malodorous yard, tossing nervous heads and shuddering a fretful menace as I passed by. While dogs, most certainly, were fluffy, beribboned creatures residing on velvet chairs and silk counterpanes, as greedy for *marrons glacés* and chocolate creams as my sister, Victorine, not these heavy-jowled, yellow hounds who stiffened at my approach, regarding me with an altogether understandable suspicion. A wiry, bandy-legged man, presumably a groom, appeared suddenly with a tangle of harness in his hands, stared at me for a moment, every bit as scornful as the dogs, grunted what may have been a greeting or a warning, and moved on. What should I reply to him? What prevented me from admitting I had lost my way and asking his assistance? I merely knew that *something* did and venturing a "Good morning," making my voice as nonchalant as I could, I smiled rather graciously and walked on deeper into the mire.

Guy, I well knew, would have been perfectly at ease in this situation. It would not seem strange to Alys. But, biting my lip quite painfully, I was forced to acknowledge that, against all my hopes and intentions, it was very strange to me. Had I spent my childhood here, of course, I would have ridden to hounds—I was in no doubt about that—and, moreover, I would have done it not just with enthusiasm but superbly. For a brief moment I allowed myself to see the notable equestrienne I might have been, leaping hedges and ditches in full sunlight, fearless and tireless in a man's tall hat and a riding-habit cut so tight that my maid would have had to stitch me inside it every hunting morning. Yet, as it was, my one solitary riding-lesson in the Bois de Boulogne had terminated abruptly when my instructor—an acquaintance of my mother's—had tried to kiss me. And I had shown no aptitude in any case. The horse had seemed most alarmingly bony and unstable, the ground beneath its feet extremely hard and far away. I had hung on blindly, feeling inelegant and foolish and, telling myself I could not afford the luxury of breaking a limb, had never tried again. But the dream persisted. Wild gallops across open fields, stirrup-cups drunk in the saddle at dawn, winter mornings of hard frost and brilliant sunshine, my breath—and Guy's?—leaving feathery trails in the air; all this remained in my hopeful imaginings. It could have happened. Surely it had been meant to happen and now, hearing the approach of trotting hooves, I stood back against the wall and, with a surge of excitement strong enough to banish all unease, watched Robin Esmond ride towards me through the thin, gray mist.

I was incompetent to judge his skill as a horseman. I merely assumed it to be magnificent, for he sat easily in his saddle and although he was bare-headed and wearing rough, dark tweeds with leather patches which would have been quite unacceptable in the Bois de Boulogne, it took my imagination no more than a moment to clothe him in the splendor of hunting-pink. And having done so, the result was far more than sufficient to take my breath away.

But naturally—very naturally—one did not allow a young gentleman even to suspect so much and I remained quite still, allowing the most persistent of the dogs to sniff my skirts, allowing the mud to stain the new shoes I could not easily replace, allowing my nostrils to be assailed by these natural odors I found so very offensive; *waiting* until he saw me.

"Olivia!" And recognizing the leap of pleasure in his face, feeling its answer bubbling inside me, I nevertheless replied pleasantly but not *too* eagerly, "Good morning, Robin."

He dismounted without effort, thinking nothing of what to me would have been a major undertaking—possibly a major disaster— and, throwing his reins to the groom, reached me in three long strides, looking—how could I describe it?—exactly as I had imagined a young English country gentleman *ought* to look after a morning in the open air, a little mud-stained and wind-blown and making light of it, taking life's pains and pleasures equally with a shrug. Well-balanced, sound, healthy, *familiar*. So familiar, indeed, that for a moment it was possible just to smile at one another, a silent and very nearly intimate greeting.

But our intimacy was too new and fragile to last and wishing to break it before it grew awkward I said again, my voice unwittingly asking a question, "Good morning?"

"Yes—absolutely. But Olivia—what *are* you doing here? Please don't discount my sheer delight in seeing you. But the stable-yard . . . ?"

And at once his good humor touched me, reducing my predicament, which I had been inclined to take so seriously a moment ago, to a matter for laughter.

"Oh—I just opened a door and there it was."

"You lost your way? Why aren't they taking better care of you?"

I needed no one to take care of me. Should I tell him that? Of course not, for I would willingly get lost every day of my life if I might be rescued in this delightful fashion.

"I was looking for Alys."

"You won't find her here."

"She doesn't ride then?" I was surprised and then rather pleased about that.

"Lord no. That's not her style. She'll be in the library lost in a book."

"Really?"

"Most decidedly. But it's better outdoors, I reckon—don't you?—on a day like this?"

Indeed I did. A moment ago I had thought the weather overcast, uninviting. But now there was a freshness in the air, an April stirring of scent and light which made even that unsavory yard with its wet straw and mud puddles, the potential savagery of its dogs, no longer intolerable. I had been cold and very worried about my shoes and the hem of my dress. Now it no longer mattered. *Now* I would stand ankle-deep in muddy water if necessary talking to Robin Esmond, and be glad.

"Do you ride every morning?"

"Well there's not much else to do, you know."

"Is that your horse?"

He shook his head, both of us speaking words simply to detain the other.

"Oh no—just the Squire's old hunter in need of exercise. Wav past her best, I'm afraid."

I had mistaken the tall gray mare for a fiery stallion, the kind of mount a knight-errant would ride. But no matter.

"We've nothing left now of any quality," he told me. "The army commandeered all the bloodstock and shipped the poor brutes out to Africa for their cavalry officers to ride. There'd be no point, really, in taking out any of these old Dobbins—if you were thinking of it."

I was considerably relieved about that. Old Dobbins, perhaps, to him; mettlesome, dangerous beasts to me. Yet I said quite airly, "I was really just exploring."

"Then let me show you the garden."

There would be nothing to see, surely, at this season, except the anonymous beginnings of plants I could not imagine, and great blasts of that icy moorland wind. Yet, as we turned the corner of the house, it seemed I had seen nothing anywhere more delightful than those formal squares of damp, upturned soil planted with spiky shrubs just in bud, which could have been anything.

"Forsythia," he said. "Broom. And the rhododendrons, of course, about a million years old and quite breathtaking in a week or two. You ought to stay and see them."

"I'd like to."

"Is there a chance of it?"

"Oh no. I shouldn't think so."

"Is there no way to persuade you?"

A dozen ways. A few words of kindness from my grandfather, should he ever decide to show himself. A simple indication that I would be welcome to remain. The pleasure—although I was by no means ready to show it—of *watching*, not really listening to Robin Esmond as he told me the names of my grandfather's plants.

He was amazingly handsome. I had seen that, of course, last night at the vicarage but, with my aunt's suspicious eyes upon me, had not cared to examine him too closely. And earlier this morning I had soon convinced myself that the remarkable good looks I remembered had been no more than a trick of light and shade and my own tired but always hopeful imagination. Yet now, in full daylight, I saw the same long, elegant mouth with a perpetual half-smile just touching its corners, the straight, patrician nose, hair falling like pale gold feathers across a high forehead, a whimsical blue gaze from eyes that were long-lashed and wide apart. I saw the same light, lounging charm which had so moved me in Guy, spiced by a hint of complexity not quite concealed by a deliberately boyish air which made him not only beautiful but vulnerable.

He was taller than Guy, his body even more finely chiseled and delicately balanced, but either one of them, in a boulevard café, would have been instantly recognizable as an English milord. The same culture and customs had molded them. They had absorbed, since their shared infancy, the same Spartan self-discipline of the English public school which had made them good sports and good losers, good comrades at arms, which had given them their good manners and good digestions, their perfect knowledge of how to play life's games. They had the same well-bred, well-polished shell with emotion safely, perhaps even fiercely, repressed beneath it; a reserve which I—accustomed to the superficial passions of my mother's friends—found so intriguing.

They were alike and I had loved Guy immediately as if the possibility of loving him had always lain dormant inside me awaiting its opportunity. Naturally, I could not permit myself to love Robin Esmond in the same headlong fashion. Naturally not. But I could think about it, could imagine it, could feel the possibility, the excitement of it effervescing, foolishly perhaps and dangerously inside me. And having avoided danger all my life I felt suddenly very much inclined to shrug my shoulders at it, to toss my head and fling down my challenge. To risk myself just once—as my mother had done a dozen times—and be ready, like her, to suffer afterwards. Suddenly, without any warning, my well-shod, capable feet had left the ground, my mind soaring from the mediocre level of offended pride to a rare peak of elation from which no one, having once attained it—certainly not my mother's daughter—could possibly wish to descend. A moment ago I had had a great many problems to solve, arrangements to make, dozens of essential things to do. Now, something inside me had called a halt, bidding everything wait until I had considered this startling, glorious thing which had happened to me. Perhaps I had simply discovered my own capacity for love, an impulsive spark of sensuality, an inherited recklessness which now that I could no longer suppress it attracted me like a candle-flame. But it was Robin Esmond who had aroused these sensations and until I had restored myself to order, all I really wished to do was think about him, study him, *look* at him.

"Who are you exactly, Robin? Last night you said a half-cousin—or less?" He swung round to face me, exaggeratedly, mock-

58

ingly debonair and bowed over my hand, "So I am. Robin Saint-Giles Heron Esmond, ma'am, at your service. The fourth, I believe, of that name."

And although I laughed at him as he had clearly intended, in spirit I endowed him with the pedigree of a prince, being unaware just then that a dozen Olivia Herons had gone before me, including my grandfather's late and very much lamented wife.

"Which makes you . . . ?"

"No one of any consequence, I'm afraid. My mother was the Squire's niece and my father is related in some way to the Blackwoods, your mother's family."

"So Alys is your cousin, too, as well as mine?"

He smiled, a sudden radiance of good humor inclining him to be anyone's cousin who should desire it.

"Oh yes. In these country places, you know, one ends up related to everybody. Not that it could matter less, I find the old family tree a crashing bore, don't you?"

As a matter of fact I found it fascinating, being well on the way to developing an obsession about my ancestors because I had not even realized, until recently, that I had any. But I saw no point in telling him so, for at that stage his opinions, his views, the words he actually spoke were of far less importance to me than the sound of his voice, that lazy accent of public school and privilege, speaking them.

"Do you live here at the Manor?"

He smiled again, nonchalant, easy, taking most things, especially himself, none too seriously.

"On and off—mostly on, it seems. I *do* keep meaning to set out and conquer the world, you know—but one wonders just where to make a start."

It was an attitude with which I was not familiar. I raised an enquiring, possibly a critical eyebrow, and then, seeing the twinkle in his eye, the almost impish good-humor of his smile, I surrendered once again and very easily to laughter.

He had been born in India, he told me, the cradle of the British Raj, where his mother had spent her time serving tea and cucumber sandwiches on imitation British lawns, while his father, a professional soldier of great zeal and dedication, had contented himself—when no armed or, in some cases unarmed uprising of subject peoples required his attention—with the massacre of any available lion, buffalo, hippopotamus or anything else unfortunate enough to wander within range of his sporting gun. A very successful and conventional couple, Colonel and Mrs. Esmond who, in conventional fashion, had sent their son back to England at the age of seven, to be educated under the guardianship of his mother's cousin, Squire Heron. He had gone to Hexingham, the school which every Heron and Esmond male had attended for generations, and then to Cambridge where, for the simple reason that nothing else appealed to him, he had taken a law degree. His mother had died in a cholera epidemic ten years ago, his father had continued to serve his Queen and Country overseas, "slaughtering rebellious natives on demand—that kind of caper, you know." While Robin himself was currently "thinking about life," as he put it. And, until he had reached some satisfactory conclusion, it seemed likely that he would remain at Clarrow Fell.

"And then?" For I required much more positive information than that.

He shrugged and offered me once again that lightly mocking smile.

"Then I'll launch myself in some brilliant career or other. Can anyone doubt it—except the Squire, that is, and the Colonel?"

"The Colonel? Your father? You don't get on with him?"

"Don't I? I hardly know him. But as a matter of fact—well—one feels bound to admire him, you know. One can't resemble him, that's all. Poor old chap—there he is, the Great White Hunter incarnate, going after tiger with his bare hands, in a manner of speaking. It cut him to the quick, I can tell you, when he realized an English fox is plenty big enough for me."

"So he doesn't approve of you?"

"Not desperately. I disappoint him, I suppose—just like the Ashanti."

"Ashanti?"

I had not the least idea what an Ashanti might be, nor did I care. Once again what mattered was his voice speaking words to me, any words would do, so that I could watch that half-smile flickering at the corners of his mouth, catch the exact moment when the light or the tilt of his head changed his eyes to a smokier blue.

"Don't you know about the Ashanti? Good Heavens, what *do* they teach you in France? An African nation, no less, who couldn't seem to understand why Victoria should be their Queen when they

60

already had a perfectly agreeable king of their own. So we had to teach them, didn't we?"

"Did we?"

"My dear, of course we did. That's what they call the White Man's Burden, don't you know."

"I didn't know."

"I'm delighted to hear it. Not so the gallant Colonel. He came all the way from India to fight the Ashanti war, put himself to no end of trouble to get there in time for the kick-off, and what do you think the cringing beggars did? Took one look at our maxim guns, shook their spears and slunk home again. *Can* you credit it? The Colonel still hasn't got over it. Luckily the Boers have given him a better run for his money."

The remembrance of Guy fell instantly across my mind and I realized, with shock, that for the past half-hour I had quite forgotten him unless it was that the process by which I came to blend his identity with Robin Esmond's had already begun, and I was losing the need to consider them apart. Yet the wasteful brutality of his death in Africa could not be obliterated and now, remembering it acutely, I turned to Robin Esmond with a dozen questions chasing each other to the surface of my mind, reasons, explanations, motives, pictures of his childhood—and his manhood—with Guy and Alys.

"Robin, tell me . . ." But before I could ask him "Robin, why haven't you gone out to Africa?" he said quickly, far too casually:

"Yes, the Colonel has a kind of sneaking regard for the Boers. They had him surrounded at Ladysmith all winter, shut in like a rat in a trap with the typhoid and the dysentery and the enteric fever, living on a pound of horsemeat a day and getting shelled night and morning for good measure. He'll have been splendid about it all, of course."

"And where is he now?"

For the first time, and very briefly, he hesitated, his smile tightening a little, no longer quite so skillfully boyish and debonair, a tremor of unease just below the surface which suddenly and very badly I wanted him to share with me.

"Ah well, just as soon as he got out of Ladysmith the irrepressible old sport went dashing off to Mafeking. You've heard of Mafeking?"

Vaguely. But I merely nodded and smiled.

"The garrison commander there is an old crony of his—General Baden-Powell—and the Boers have got him penned in pretty tight."

"How terrible . . ."

"Yes, I think it is—quite terrible. As a matter of fact he wrote asking me to join him."

"Will you go?" And I was in no doubt whatsoever that I would do my utmost to dissuade him.

"I believe I should," he said, speaking rather slowly, his smile fading without quite disappearing, "which is not to say I will. They're short of cavalry, you see—among other things like food and water, not to mention horses for the cavalry to ride. And they *have* been appealing for volunteers who can ride and shoot—foxhunting men, in fact. The idea being that if a fellow knows how to go after foxes and bring down flying game he might just as well go off to the Transvaal and pot himself a Boer or two. They've even got up a Committee of Masters of Foxhounds to organize it and called themselves the Imperial Yeomanry. They'll be quite splendid too, just like father."

I waited, knowing there was no necessity to press him to speak, making my whole body an inquiry which offered, in advance, all the sympathy and encouragement he could possibly need.

"We've lost a lot of men already, killed and wounded," he said abruptly, needing to say it while he could, "not counting the thousands who've been sticking it out under siege at Kimberley and Ladysmith and Mafeking all winter. They won't all be as eager to get back into action as my father. So a volunteer brigade of young foxhunting squires is just what's needed to fit the bill. The gold-mining interest must certainly think so, since they've paid fifty thousand pounds cash down to help equip it."

"And you ride to hounds. And shoot—what—grouse and pheasant?"

"I do. In season and in moderation. Unfortunately, I'm not entirely certain that I could shoot a man. Is that very feeble of me?"

"Absolutely not."

Did I mean it? Did Alys expect him to go to war? I did not know her well enough to judge, but of one thing I was quite certain. I would go to war myself and endure all its agonies and humiliations rather than send my loved ones, my dependents, my young.

"*Will* you go, Robin?"

We had reached the limits of the formal garden and stood for a moment, looking out across a paddock where two spindly, unsteady foals and their handsome chestnut mothers were calmly grazing, the hillside strewn with sheep as thick as daisies, a fragile blue sky above. And we might have walked a hundred miles, so far had we traveled from the chance acquaintance of half an hour ago.

"I believe they can manage without me," he said slowly and then, in a great rush, "It's very sporting of you, Olivia, to understand—I mean not to hand me a white feather and all that . . ."

"A white feather? Heavens—what nonsense."

"Just the same, I may get one by the next post."

"From your father?"

"Indeed."

Hotly, I positioned myself to defend him, from critics and colonels and diamond millionaires and all those other old men in the world who believed themselves entitled to create young, dead heroes.

"War is stupid," I said flatly. "Everybody knows that." And when I made pronouncements in that particular tone of voice I intended to be believed.

"My father doesn't—nor the Squire. And the girls one knows do tend to go overboard for a gold-braided uniform—my word, they do."

"Then, perhaps, *one* knows the wrong kind of girls."

I had startled him but I had intrigued him too, for I felt quite certain that no young lady of Bradeswick or Halifax or Leeds, no gentleman's daughter from the neighborhood of Clarrow Fell would have spoken to him in quite that way. No doubt many of them were very pretty, one or two even ready to fall in love with him, but, cast in the mold of these provincial cities, their values, their aims, their conversation, would all be the same. They might please him but they would not surprise him, could not arouse in him the tempting excitement of discovery, as I—a girl from another country, another climate—had been able to do. And how could I continue to regret my strangeness when it gave me this glorious advantage?

"Olivia . . ." But whatever he wished to say had become too complex far too soon and, sensing a threshold of intimacy which I was uncertain, as yet, how to cross, I took advantage of the cold and suggested we should return indoors. And at once he was full of apology and concern, his attitude wrapping me in imaginary furs, shielding me with his own long, lounging body from the wind and rain, as Guy had done.

"I should have thought of it, Olivia—this beastly weather. If you catch a chill I may never forgive myself."

I was very, very far from being so fragile as that. I knew it and, with a great almost feline pleasure, allowed myself to forget it, allowed him to worry, to see me as a delicate and therefore precious creature who might melt or break but who would be very brave and exceedingly endearing about it.

"I'm quite all right, Robin—really."

"I do hope so."

"In fact, I'm very well."

"Yes . . ." he said, his eyes puzzled and narrowing with concentration, wholly intent, as I was, on this new experience, the richness, the danger, the wonder of this new possibility. He did not touch me and would not have dreamed of doing so, for he was a gentleman who had been taught how to control his desires, I was a young lady for whom sensuality was too perilous to contemplate. Yet, although the correct physical distance was maintained, contact nevertheless was made, a transference from his eyes and his mind to the surface of my skin, an invisible but undoubted caress which I accepted neither fearfully nor bashfully but in triumph. I had been desired by men before and turned it swiftly aside, defending myself with humor or scorn or brute force as had seemed appropriate. Now I stood slightly on tiptoe and basked in it as one luxuriates in sunshine, my whole body glowing with a proud delight.

And then, because it must be the woman who controls these things, the woman who must exercise her power, I said very softly "Shall we go?"

We walked back to the house with a hush around us, not a leaf stirring or a bird singing, a stillness so profound that the appearance of Alys seemed jarring, unbearably loud.

I had quite forgotten her and now, remembering everything I knew and suspected, I stood back and observed every detail of her, minutely, shrewdly, her long pale hair in all its charming disarray, her narrow figure with that vulnerable innocence of the child-woman about it which I knew better than to underestimate.

"There's Alys," he said, smiling a frank, affectionate welcome.

There she was, elusive, dreamy, wistful Alys who would probably marry him one day, I had been told, when she got around to it. On the whole, I could see the sense to that, could even acknowledge their marriage to be a practical, reasonable arrangement.

But I was twenty years old and that month of April was simply not my season to be cautious, rational, or wise.

64

FOUR

I returned to the vicarage, ate a frugal luncheon and spent the rest of the day preparing myself for evening, an occupation completely beyond the comprehension of Alys who, when her mother had found her and reminded her of dinner-time took all of ten minutes to put on whatever came first to hand; a pastel blue gown, on this occasion, with a deep lace frill, a spray of white roses at the waist, billowing sleeves with fashionable beaded cuffs but with a bead or two missing and a few more coming loose, I noticed, on one side.

"That dress is very light-colored, Alys," her mother told her, "considering that Guy is so recently dead."

"I do not believe in the wearing of mourning, mamma."

"Of course you do."

"No I do not. It is the sincerity of grief that matters, not the amount of black crêpe on one's gown."

"That is just what I said, dear, since the two go inextricably together. Run along quickly now and change. Your dark green will do."

But in the end, when it was realized that my aunt's husband, the Reverend Mr. Toby Heron, was missing from the study where he appeared to spend most of his time, attention was at once diverted from my cousin's gown.

"Where is he?" demanded Aunt Sibylla, her tone implying "What have you done with him?"

"He's not here," said Alys, quite unaware, I thought, that she had given so exasperating an answer. And clearly feeling that her father's whereabouts were none of her concern, she climbed into the carriage and waited with the patience of long habit, until he should choose to appear.

He came, his wife an irate step behind him, a tall, rather willowy man, handsome in a muted, wispy fashion, and apparently quite accustomed to being called to order by my aunt.

"I was just cataloging my butterflies, my dear."

"Indeed," she told him, her lack of surprise neither lessening her irritation nor quite concealing her contempt. "And are we ready now?"

"Yes, dear," he sighed, evidently resigned to it.

"Yes, mamma," said Alys, her eyes cloudy, her thoughts so obviously elsewhere that I felt my aunt's fingers itching to slap her, heard my aunt's voice rise to a pitch one could only call shrill.

"Then let's be off, shall we, since I have told you both many a time that when one is invited for seven o'clock, even two minutes past the hour is *simply not good enough.*"

I believed myself to be very well dressed, perhaps even more than the occasion required, too much being preferable at all times, in my opinion, to too little. And I had chosen to wear a gown from the fashion house of Poiret, an indication to anyone who really knew my circumstances that it could only be secondhand; just a stem of grape purple silk, high in the neck, long in the sleeves yet, by some subtle miracle of the couturier's art, revealing far more than the boldest negligee, so that now, with my mother's pearl drops swinging in my ears, my hair swept up into a great cloud of a Pompadour, I felt elegant enough to be defiant or gracious or even forgiving, as the evening should require.

"My word, how tall you are tonight," was Aunt Sibylla's opinion, tartly expressed, as we were shown into the library at Clarrow, the dark, slender dress and high-piled hair giving me a height which slightly outmatched her own. "Alys—do stand up straight, dear."

But Alys, without the slightest hint of rudeness or rebellion, had already blended calmly yet quite irretrievably into the atmosphere of this long, mellow, quiet room, to be followed almost as swiftly by her father.

They were, quite simply, "not there," leaving me with the cool surface of my aunt and the unobtrusive courtesy of Amyas Hird who inquired my opinion of the weather, the landscape, the respective

66

literature of England and France, and offered me a sherry I found far too sweet.

Time passed, far too much of it, every moment increasing the tumult of my nerves and my determination that my discomfort must not show. When my grandfather finally appeared he would see no supplicant, no prodigal, but a composed and critical young lady in need of nothing he could give. And in my effort to retain that composure, I had only a brief smile for Robin Esmond when he came up to me, wonderfully blond in his evening clothes, and with every reason to expect a warm welcome.

"Olivia, you look absolutely stunning."

I sincerely hoped so, for I had worked hard all afternoon to make sure of it. But no matter how glad I might be to see him, no matter how wildly my pulses had started to beat, I could not afford to be distracted even by him from the coming encounter.

For, at that moment, it was not the presence of Robin Esmond but the continued absence of Squire Heron which required my full and absolute concentration.

I had expected him to be at the door to greet me. Climbing down from the carriage I had felt certain that his eyes were upon me, and had taken great care with the management of my narrow, trailing skirt, had kept my head high, my manner pleasant but by no means effusive, a performance I at once abandoned when I realized that the dark, narrow-shouldered old gentleman glimpsed from my eye-corners was not after all my grandfather but his butler. On entering this room I had steeled myself afresh only to encounter, once again, the insult of his absence, the hostile void occupied by the crushing anticlimax of Amyas. And on my way through the hall I had seen no signs of the lavish hospitality Guy had spoken of, no long, baronial table beneath the great window, brilliant with crystal and silver branches of candles, no firelight turning the windowpanes to jewels, illuminating the cool spring evening as was always done—Guy had told me—for an honored guest.

"We are to dine in the Regency wing," murmured Amyas, in answer to my aunt's question.

"Ah yes," she said, her mouth well satisfied. "You saw our Regency wing this morning did you not, Olivia? You will agree that it is very fine."

"Indeed yes. Very French, *madame*."

"Really!"

"Oh yes. One is accustomed to meet that style quite often in Paris."

And it was to Paris that I would return, I suddenly decided, just as soon as I could and have nothing more to do with this house again until the time came to dispose of it—family portraits, baronial table and all—to the highest bidder. How dare this arrogant old man, my grandfather, keep me waiting here like a parlormaid begging for employment? How dare he, above all, allow our first meeting to take place like a spectacle, an entertainment before an audience of his own choosing? It was intolerable and since nothing obliged me to tolerate it I would pack my bags and go.

The door opened quietly and a man who had once been physically powerful and very strong came into the room, nothing left now of that strength but the long, hard bones which had supported it and the air of authority of one who cannot so much as imagine disobedience. He was older than I had expected, a weathered open-air look about him, age having bleached his hair but not the sallow skin, the dark eyes, the high-bridged, autocratic nose I had only to look in my mirror to recognize. He was a dark-complexioned Heron like the portraits in the hall—like me. Yet, although his features were well formed and even now at this advanced age he should have been handsome, the cast of his countenance was far too sombre for that, his mouth a hard, thin line drawn so disdainfully that his smile, when it finally came, had no meaning beyond the merest concession to the requirements of etiquette. My mother had described him as hard and gritty like his land and, as I turned with everyone else to watch his progress down the long room, I thought him arrogant too, a weary old aristocrat embalmed in the sense of his own superiority, taking entirely for granted the deference with which he was greeted, Aunt Sibylla's unnecessary "*Here* is the Squire," as if he had suddenly descended upon us from heaven; the way Robin's lounging posture straightened like a rakish, young captain in the presence of his general; the almost feline alertness of Amyas, ready to anticipate orders before they were spoken; the sudden and most surprising glow of welcome from Alys.

"Good evening, sir."

"Good evening, Squire."

"*Hello*," said Alys. "How was York? All sorted out now, I

imagine." And it was to her alone that he responded, not in words but with a moment of his attention, a brief nod, a true communication for which I believed Aunt Sibylla or Amyas Hird would have given a great deal, and which should, by right, have been mine.

I watched him come, and waited, holding myself erect, my whole body taut with nervous anger.

"Olivia," whispered my aunt, urging me to make a move towards him, to show an eager or a contrite face, to stir myself and at least attempt a good impression. I ignored her. I would never have forgiven myself had I done otherwise.

"Olivia—it is your grandfather."

Nonsense. It was a cruel and selfish stranger who had taken it into his head to humiliate me if he could. It was essential to show him *now*, right from the start, that he could not and so I continued to stand my ground until he had accepted the obeisance of his dependents and came to a halt before me, his alien granddaughter who depended—as he would soon discover—on no one.

There was a moment of silence, of assessing and measuring, his weathered face and dull, deep eyes so expressionless that I had not the faintest notion as to what he might be thinking or feeling, no clue at all as to what he had expected to see. But what, after all, could he say to me? What, in all honesty, could I reply? Even my aunt's vague, wispy husband had laid down his book, sharing the general eagerness to discover, while my aunt herself was craning forward with the avidity of a Roman matron at the Circus, awaiting a Christian massacre by lions. Even Alys, I noticed, had turned her head, catching a distant scent of *something* in the wind. While Robin Esmond's face, glimpsed just behind her, seemed to be conveying to me a message I interpreted as "Well done," as if he too, on occasion, had wished to be defiant and his courage had failed him.

But my courage would not fail me for what else had I to rely on? Who would defend me or do battle on my account if I did not? I could not afford to be weak, it was as simple as that. I would not even consider the possibility of surrender nor, I suspected, would the Squire. And this territory, after all, was his.

"You must be Olivia."

"Yes." There was no more I cared to say about that. "You had a good journey, I trust?"

"Unfortunately not. It was most tedious."

"I am sorry to hear it."

"However, it was most kind of you to invite me."

I had challenged him to say "You are most welcome," but the beginning of his reply was swept away heedlessly and artlessly by Alys who, having heard only part of our conversation, and none of its undertones and being apparently unaware of the awe my grandfather inspired in others, suddenly cried out "Oh, Olivia, how can you say that? I should think any journey quite fascinating. And to travel alone, as you do—simply to get on a train and go . . . ! How I should adore that."

"No dear," Aunt Sibylla said flatly, "you would not."

"On the contrary, mamma, I would never tire of it."

"My daughter," her mother declared, looking very much amused, "has such fanciful notions. Traveling, indeed. We all know that even if she managed to get started she would lose herself somewhere between Bradeswick and Leeds. Come Alys—do you not see that the Squire is ready for his dinner?"

I went into the dining room on my grandfather's arm, gingerly touching his sleeve, as he led me with a cool courtesy to his table and drew out for me the chair to the right of his own, Alys seating herself without the least ceremony at his left where she proceeded to ask him in a flurry of quick but evidently pertinent questions about his business at York with all the ease and certainty of a favorite child. To Aunt Sibylla was allotted the place at the opposite head of the table, an arrangement to which I could have no objection since she was the senior lady present, the natural hostess. But as she took her seat with an undoubted flourish, her eagle eye checking the arrangement of the silver, the starched perfection of the table linen, the correct angle of the parlormaid's lace cap and ribbons, I found, most strangely, that I *did* object. A moment ago I would have been glad to see this house in ashes. Suddenly and quite unreasonably I could bear no hand to touch it but mine. I had been born here, after all, not Sibylla Heron who despite her great air of consequence was only the vicar's wife. And it followed, therefore, that I should have been sitting at the head of the table, being generally gracious as my aunt was now doing, playing Queen Bee in what ought to have been *my* hive. I did not like it. I detested it, in fact, so fiercely that I was surprised at myself.

70

We had a brown, peppery soup, a huge joint of beef, Aunt Sibylla insisting that I try the mustard, the horseradish, the carrots because they were good for me, the cabbage because the vegetable garden at Clarrow was famous for its spring greens, the potatoes so that I might be made aware that not even the produce of Jersey could be finer.

"You will find," she told me, "that English food at its best will compare very favorably with anything to be had in France."

"I believe so, *madame*. My mother often says the same." I leaned back a little in my chair and on an impulse of pure wickedness proceeded to regale them with a gastronomic tour of the Continent of Europe, from the *haute cuisine* of France with its fine wines and cheeses to the robust flavors of Italy, the stuffed vine leaves and honey and almond pastries my sister, Victorine, had so enjoyed in Athens, the rice and fish and omelettes of Portugal and Spain, the excellent *bouillabaisse* served by my brother's grandmother in Toulouse. And, despite all Aunt Sibylla's attempts to silence me, I went on talking—and talking—until I had mentioned every member of my family at least twice by name, every place we had ever visited and a few we had not, and had thrown in, for good measure, the titles of every bogus count, every impecunious baron, every imposter we had met along the way.

"Indeed—indeed," murmured my uncle, the Reverend Toby Heron, laying down his fork, entirely forgetting to eat his own dinner, so frankly, and with a somewhat un-Christian touch of malice, did he enjoy his wife's discomfiture.

"Athens . . . ," breathed Alys. "Rome . . . ! How marvelous!" her interest in these cities far outweighing any curiosity she might have felt for my variously conceived sisters and brother.

"Bravo," said Robin Esmond, the whisper just reaching me across the watchful silence of Amyas who might not comment but would—I felt—remember.

But the person to whom my performance was really directed, my grandfather, paid no attention to it at all.

"Do try the syllabub," he said when I finally paused for breath. "We are very fond of it, are we not, Alys?"

"Fond?" she said, making a wide gesture of enthusiasm, her pale blue sleeve already stained from an encounter with the sauce-boat. "I adore it. You know I do."

"Yes. You always have."

And once again, adroitly, cruelly, he had excluded me.

My mother had warned me of the English custom by which the ladies departed after dinner to take their coffee elsewhere, leaving the gentlemen still at table with their port and brandy and *risqué* stories, although I doubted if there would be much of *that* while my grandfather was about. And so, when my aunt arose and gave the signal to withdraw, it was Alys not I who was caught unawares, remaining in her seat, her elbows on the table pouring out a rapid flow of argument addressed to the Squire and Amyas, totally engrossed in her subject which seemed to be the voting rights of agricultural laborers—I had never even heard of such a thing!—and her indignation that a certain Lord Potterton had recently served eviction notices on several tenants who had failed to elect his nominee.

Voting rights? What a very peculiar concern for a young lady. Evidently Aunt Sibylla thought so too.

"Alys!" she gave warning once and then, producing no results, once again, her color but not her voice visibly rising.

"Oh Heavens above," said Alys. "Is it time to beat our retreat? *Must* we, mamma, since we are just family, after all?"

"Alys," the matron replied, superb in her understated indignation. "The gentlemen have things to discuss which *have nothing to do with you.*"

"Ah yes, I know. They are going to talk politics and religion and finance—*real* issues with the fancy wrapping paper taken off, instead of the fairy tales they tell to us. I know."

"You know nothing of the kind. Come, Alys." Aunt Sibylla, already, had had a difficult evening and this—the sight of her own daughter lounging among the men, putting forward this preposterous argument while Lavinia Junot's daughter had risen so obediently— was becoming more than even she, with her long practice, could bear.

"Alys!"

"Oh well . . . ," Alys got to her feet, good-humored, resigned, her sleeve gathering the crumbs from her plate as she did so, her napkin and her gloves slipping off her lap, falling somewhere under the table where she was perfectly content to leave them. "Oh well." And I did not miss the glance of amused complicity she directed at Robin, asking him to make haste to join her, not for the purpose of flirtation but in order that she might be rescued from the aimless coffee-table chatter of women.

We made our brief curtsies to the gentlemen and took our leave, settling ourselves in the Regency drawing room in chairs that were too fragile and too valuable for comfort, Alys and I sipping our coffee in a reflective silence, both of us having things to ponder, while Aunt Sibylla proceeded at once to lecture her daughter on her posture, her vagueness and her scathing remarks about their neighbor, Lord Potterton.

"It is simply not your place, Alys, to question his Lordship's decisions regarding his tenants, any more than it would be seemly of you to interfere with the management of his laundry or his kitchen."

"His laundry does not interest me in the least, mamma—nor his kitchen."

"I am relieved to hear it, although not surprised, since I doubt you would recognize a laundry if you stumbled upon one." And when Alys merely sketched an inattentive shrug, my aunt, her temper dangerously near its limits, shot me a vicious look, as if I were to blame for it, and said tartly, "Such things as the washing and ironing of linen are miracles to my daughter, Alys. She has not the faintest notion how all these clean garments are constantly appearing in her cupboards, nor how the larder shelves are filled with pies and jams and preserves unless they *grow* there. You will have to marry a rich man, Alys."

I heard Alys sigh, the mild exasperation of someone going over old ground again—and again—no longer hoping for a reprieve.

"*Must* we go on talking of marriage, mamma?" But evidently she knew they must and, sighing again, seemed as resigned to it, and as distant, as her father.

"My dear, what else do young girls talk about, or think about? What else have young girls to do but get themselves a husband?"

"I think of a great many other things than that, mamma."

I wondered, with Robin Esmond so constantly beside her, just what these things could be. But I had suspected, indeed I had been counting on the fact that familiarity did not generate excitement in the way I believed Robin wished to be excited. And now, listening only vaguely to snatches of their conversation, I was nevertheless pleased to discover that Alys, too, did not appear to be in love, or not in the way I understood it.

"I think of friendship, mamma," I heard her say, "which to me is the very best of emotions."

And I was not in the least surprised by the disdainful quality of my aunt's reply.

"Friendship? My dear child, *friendship*—I regret to inform you—is the refuge of old maids. No more and no less."

"Mamma—really."

"And if you know of any condition more pitiful than spinsterhood then I do not care to be informed of it. You are already nineteen, Alys . . ."

"I am twenty," I ventured, coming to my cousin's defense because I was pleased with her for not being in love with Robin.

But my case was clearly beyond redemption and having allowed Aunt Sibylla's pained expression to wonder exactly what kind of a man would be likely to marry a daughter of her wayward sister, Lavinia, I retreated into my own preoccupations, hearing nothing of their argument beyond its suppressed yet deeply rooted bitterness.

Aunt Sibylla wished her daughter to be married. Alys, who could have married Guy, would prefer a journey to Rome or Athens, I rather imagined, before embarking on a honeymoon. Their conflict was not uncommon and compared to the coming interview with my grandfather, it did not interest me.

When he had finally consumed his port and finished his cigar then—I was in no doubt of it—he would request a few words alone with me. We would go to his study, I supposed, and would either reach an understanding or a compromise, or would fail to do so, in which case I would at least know where I stood. I was prepared, I thought, for any eventuality since what had I to lose, after all, but daydreams, possibilities, pleasures and affections which I had never had. But when the door finally opened, my grandfather was not among the gentlemen who were coming so tardily to join their ladies; just the Reverend Toby, Robin and Amyas who closed the door behind him, excluding the possibility of a late arrival.

"The Squire sends his apologies," he said in his neutral tones, addressing no one in particular. "He has gone to the Justice's Room to glance at his correspondence and then—well, he has had a long day."

"Cream and sugar?" inquired my aunt, pouring out his coffee, her smile of entirely malicious satisfaction telling me plainly that she had suspected all along and entirely approved the Squire's policy of ignoring me.

Very well. I had not liked him but it had not occurred to me that he would refuse me an opportunity to explain myself. But the solution, as always, was in my own hands.

"Would you excuse me a moment," I said, daring Aunt Sibylla to question me, and walking briskly, as if I knew exactly where I was going—which I certainly did not—I found my way to the Justice's Room, rapped smartly on the door and entered without permission, being totally disinclined to wait like a housemaid or a tenant until it should suit him to ask me in.

The room was very dark, very enclosed, four paneled walls black with twilight, a shuttered window, a single lamp dimly illuminating the desk where my grandfather sat alone, his face, in the gloom, entirely without animation, a mask painted in the same deep browns and yellow ochres as the portraits around him. And it seemed to me, not then perhaps but later when I thought it over, that he was neither working nor brooding but simply *waiting*, with the weariness and resignation of old men disillusioned by the past and with no great interest in the future.

I could not call him grandfather, would not call him Squire, and so I addressed him in the French manner with which I, at least, felt comfortable.

"I am sorry, *monsieur*, for this intrusion."

"Are you really?"

No, of course, I was not. But for the moment I wished to be correct, to demonstrate that my frivolous, much-despised mother had succeeded, nevertheless, in teaching me better manners than Alys.

"Yes, indeed. The more so since Amyas said you were very tired."

"I am tired, yes. I am also not in the least surprised to see you here. You strike me as a young lady who will intrude whenever she thinks it to be necessary, or to her advantage."

It was the longest speech I had so far heard him make, his voice completely toneless, neither rising nor falling, nor conveying anything but the sense of the words themselves. And although I could read no compliments into their meaning, at least—*at last*—he had, by making even this unflattering assessment of my character, acknowledged me. He had disliked the idea of me. Now his weary voice and hard mouth told me he disliked the reality. But I would allow him that dislike for, in order to feel it, he had first been obliged to *look*. And even then, right from the start, it was his notice that mattered.

"There are some questions I would like to ask you—*monsieur*."

"Ask them—*mademoiselle*."

I could have smiled at that. But there was no humor in him. Nothing at all, it seemed, but a certain snap of impatience, an evident wish to get through this tedious business which was the tag-end of living and be done. I was a nuisance to him. He was not interested in my hopes and fears, my injured pride, my capacity to feel love and loyalty and sorrow. All that concerned him was that I should state my business quickly and leave him in peace.

"Ask."

It was a command which would not be repeated. If I disobeyed it, the next one would be "Go".

"I wish to know—yes, indeed I do—why is it that you seem to blame me for the circumstances of my childhood—for things which happened before I can even remember?"

"I do not blame you."

"Nor for the way my mother has conducted her life since then?"

"No."

"And do you know of anything in my own conduct which could be called irregular?"

"I know nothing about you, Olivia. But, if asked to make a wager, I would incline to the view that your life has been beyond reproach. Light women are usually light-headed and I see no sign of that in you."

"Then you have not been just to me, have you."

"No. But life is not famous for its justice, child, or very rarely. I am sure you know that."

"Yes I do. But in this case, I think you should tell me your reasons. I feel entitled to that much."

"Entitled?" He leaned back a little in his chair, a magistrate trying a case and just faintly amused by the defendant's insolence. "And, of course, when you feel *entitled* to something, you will not easily let go, will you, Olivia. I know this, you see, because I am much the same. Tenacious, acquisitive, possessive, intent on having my way . . ."

76

I believed him. I believed too that he would have rapped on the study door, as I had just done, to voice his indignation and state his case. I recognized that aspect of myself in him very clearly, the Heron character, a hard, gritty breed that hung on, raked through the ashes and built them up again; survived. No doubt, he recognized it too but, whereas I was still young enough to feel immortal and would have rushed headlong towards a truce, a reconciliation, a glorious new beginning, he had passed the season for such things, having lost not merely his faith in the future but any desire to have it renewed. I would have thrown my arms around his neck, given half a chance, and adored him, for there was no doubt that in other circumstances we would have dearly loved each other. He knew that too and even his capacity to regret it had withered. Quite simply it was too late for him.

"Very well," he said briskly, for already he had approached me more closely than had been intended and wished to give me no further encouragement. "What reason can I provide? I am an old man and you must allow me my prejudices."

"That is an excuse, not a reason."

"Yes, Olivia, so it is. Then let me put it this way, as briefly as I can, since it has been, indeed, a very long day. Your visit here was necessary because of the property you inherited from Guy. But, since it must be a reminder of what you will one day inherit from me, I cannot take pleasure in it. Therefore, I think it best, my dear, if you finalize your business with all possible speed and return to your home in France. The proceeds from the sale of the house in Bradeswick will be transferred to you there, along with an allowance I propose to make you. The allowance, in fact, that I made to Guy. It is not princely since cash is never freely available on an estate such as this, but it will enable you to live in moderate comfort and security until the time comes for you to see Clarrow. Even then, of course, you will not be rich. Amyas will do his best for you but unless he can find some city merchant with a fancy for a sporting estate you may have to divide the property into several lots. In that case the tenants should be given the opportunity to buy their farms and cottages themselves, while the house alone without the land should be easily disposed of. Anyas will see to it. Is there anything else?"

A hundred things, but first and foremost my blank amazement that he could talk like this as if the house were no longer worth a fig to him.

"Don't you *care?*"

"About what?"

"About what happens here—afterwards."

Once again he almost smiled.

"That shocks you? Yes, I can see it does. Once it would have shocked me. Indeed, I would not have thought it possible. But things change, not only men and events but the world itself. And I am no longer adaptable. Your knowledge of our life here is very limited. You have been here only a day and cannot be expected to see beneath the surface as I do. Clarrow is vastly altered since my youth, not because I am old and look from a different angle, but because the world has moved on to another stage of its development, better or worse I can't tell, but one in which I am ill at ease. I believe that this new order of things, once it is established, will be ill at ease with me. The surface appears little changed as yet. Life *appears* to go on very much as ever. But it is not so. It is not so much the change itself which disturbs me but the *pace* of it, which I freely confess has left me far behind. I am becoming a relic of the past, my dear, a far, far slower past. My mind was cast in the same mold as my father's mind, you see, and even my grandfather's. Our values and aspirations, our methods, were the same. But the young men of your generation are of another breed. Neither better nor worse, perhaps, as I have said already, but *uneasy.* And uneasy men tend to knock things down, I find, before they have considered how to build them up again. It may well be that they will sweep my kind away and I rather imagine that what happens to me will happen to Clarrow Fell. The building may remain, of course, but its essence will be irrevocably altered. In which case why should it matter to me who lives here when I do not? Naturally you do not believe any of this."

No. Old men had always talked of impending doom, I thought, sitting on benches in the sun and muttering how the old ways were best. No I did not believe it.

"Will you tell me one thing more?"

"Possibly."

"If I had been brought up here with Guy, would you still be advising me to sell up and go?"

There was a long pause, an old man's pause with closed eyes, laborious breath. And then he said, "I wonder what purpose would be served by answering that question?"

"It might ease my mind."

"Oh, I doubt that. But, very well, Olivia, since I know you are persistent and will not let the matter rest. Yes, if your mother had left you here then I can see quite well that you would have been closer to me than Guy, for he was a difficult boy in many ways and we rarely saw eye to eye. But I am too old now and far too tired to play games of what might have been. I concern myself only with what *is*. Guy remained. You did not. And I expected neither one of you to succeed me. I had a son of my own, your father, to take my place. I am an orderly man. It grieved me immensely when that natural order was broken."

"No one has even told me how my father died."

"He fell from a horse, my dear, when he was drunk, and broke his neck. I see that shocks you . . ."

Dreadfully. But far more by the weary, matter-of-fact way he had spoken than by the accident itself.

"Will you tell me no more about him than that?"

He eased his position just a little, the fingers of one long, gnarled hand beginning to tap out a message of impatience on the desk top.

"I will tell you what I can. To suffer for a woman like your mother is a humiliation. Your father suffered and was humiliated. He knew her to be utterly worthless but still could not rid himself of a most destructive jealousy on her account. It destroyed him. I wonder how often she has thought of him these twenty years? Rarely, if at all. He knew that. Yet he thought of her every day. She dominated his life. She could not be banished from this house because he would not let her go. He was tenacious too, you see, persistent and possessive, as you are, as I am myself. It cannot have escaped your notice that you resemble me." He sighed and then, straightened his almost flesh-less shoulders, shook his head, denying far more in me than the cast of my countenance, the color of my eyes and skin.

"And what conclusion shall we draw from it? That your mother would have done better had she taken Guy and left you behind? A pointless supposition, my dear. You did not choose your environment but, nevertheless, you are the product of it. Some years ago, when your mother approached me for money I considered removing you from her charge and seeing what could be done with you. I concluded, even then, that it was too late. It is most certainly too late now."

"And so you are writing me off and sending me on my way."

"If that is what you wish to call it. Your allowance will be paid to you monthly from my bank to yours, or through Amyas, should you prefer. It will help you to get married or whatever it is that you are hoping to do and should make you less impatient to bury me. I trust you will not annoy me by any talk of refusing it."

My throat had become very tight, my jaw most painfully clenched in the effort to hold back my tears, a whole flood of them, I suspected, that were touched at their roots by both grief and anger. Yet I must not cry, for if I did I would simply be giving him an extra reason to despise me.

I *would* not cry and so, instead, I would have to make some other noise, would have to laugh if I could, or talk and keep on talking until the vulnerable moment passed. He had offered me money and denied me affection which was the treatment one meted out to a courtesan. Very well. I had nothing more to lose. And feeling the need not only to defend myself but to strike out, to hurt him if I could, I got up and tossed my head, a flippant and polished young lady again. My mother's daughter.

"Heavens—I would not dream of refusing the allowance, Squire Heron. I cannot afford to make grand gestures of that sort."

"So I had supposed."

"Yes. For as one of my mother's husbands—a dear man called Emil Junot—used to say, one should never refuse a penny unless by doing so one saw a way to attract two. I have never forgotten it, although poor Junot did not take his own advice and ended sadly."

"You will spare me the details, I trust," he said very wearily.

"You would not understand them. Junot was a scoundrel, I suppose, and you are certainly not that. But he was kinder to me than you have been."

"Yes, Olivia. I will readily believe it."

"Then perhaps you will also believe that I am not ashamed of him, or of my mother. And I am certainly not ashamed of myself. Where is the credit in keeping one's good name if no one threatens it? Well—I have been tempted and pursued and threatened in ways a girl like Alys could not even imagine. And I have kept myself decent not because a governess or a grandfather or an Aunt Sibylla told me I had to but because I believed it to be right. No doubt this will surprise you but I grew up believing that we—my mother and brother and sisters and I—were the best people in the world. I still believe it.

You call this the Justice's Room, I know. But you have not given me justice."

He stood up too, much taller now even in his hollow, stooping age than I was, much stronger, his face shuttered so that I could only guess his anger, could only hope that I had touched something in him; as he, to my rage and sorrow, had touched me.

But he was not angry. He was . . . What name could I put to it? Sorry. Was that it? Embittered, certainly, bone-weary, wanting rid of me and wanting it badly. Yes. But, beneath it all, *sorry*. And I could not bear it.

"Do not deceive yourself, Olivia. You do not belong here. I cannot change that and neither can you. We do not suit each other, child. Your loyalties are already bestowed elsewhere and so are mine. There is nothing left. Should you care to inspect the house in Bradeswick, Amyas will accompany you, although it hardly seems worthwhile. You may trust him to handle the sale most efficiently. Yes, Olivia, in your own words, that is the best advice I can offer you. Take your money and go."

I turned and walked out of the room, out of the house; not running away, since where could I run to on a dark night in my evening shoes, but needing a little time to breathe before facing Aunt Sibylla again. I was shaking from head to foot. I felt sick. I felt bruised. I felt—I didn't know what I felt except that it was terrible and there was too much of it. And I was dreadfully alone.

The garden was dark and heavy, full of green fragrances and damp air, a chill little breeze showing me how to explain my trembling, should anyone inquire. But who would ask? And there was no one here I wanted to see. No one, until I caught the drift of tobacco smoke in the dark, saw the glow of a cigarette and, as if by assignation, came face to face with Robin.

"Olivia, I was looking for you."

"Yes."

It seemed quite right, quite natural, and suddenly my mood taking a tremendous swing from one extreme to the other, I was alert, excited, still fiercely miserable yet, somehow or other, just as fiercely glad.

"You went to beard the Squire in his den, didn't you?"

I laughed, amazing myself, since a moment ago I had expected never to laugh again.

"Yes, I did."

"Incredible. I would never have had the courage."

"Of course you would."

"No—no, I assure you, when it comes to facing the Squire I know my limitations."

"He is not so terrible."

"Olivia—he is *terrifying*. Just one of those withering glances and I crumble clean away."

He was teasing me—naturally—and I entered into the game with him, happy to say anything that would keep us here standing close together in the dark.

"And I suppose your father is terrifying too."

"Oh no—the Colonel is a different proposition altogether. What he has is bluster, not strength, and one can always handle bluster by making fun of it. I'm rather good at that. No it's real strength, and courage, that one finds so disturbing—so attractive."

Yes Robin, I thought, be disturbed, for he was talking about me now, surely, looking at me once again with that puzzled, tremulous gaze of desire. And I had never before realized the power it gave me. I had only to reach forward, it seemed, and he would fall into the hollow of my hand and I could keep him there, this charming, vulnerable, slightly elusive man, so like my brother but not my brother, a wonderful recompense life had suddenly offered me.

"Olivia," he said, speaking with difficulty, "what an absolutely splendid girl you are. But of course you know that."

Yes, at that moment of course I did. Splendid and strong, brave as a lion and as I savored my exultation, tasting it drop by drop since I knew it could not last, I was overtaken once again by that impulse to possess, an intense urge to claim and to keep not only my inheritance, the house and the land, the way of life, the authority, but the man who seemed born to accompany it, as Guy had been. And when, after a moment or two, the desire for bricks and mortar and acreage had eased to a bearable, sensible degree, I knew with a total and therefore dangerous certainty, that I still most urgently desired this man.

FIVE

I returned to France ten days later, without giving any precise instructions to Amyas about the house in Bradeswick, making no firm promises to anyone about anything, taking no positive action at all except to give serious offense to Aunt Sibylla by inviting Alys to visit me in the rue du Bac.

I spent the journey indulging myself with alternate daydreams of Robin Esmond falling at my feet to vow he loved me and my grandfather, browbeaten into a position where he was obliged to confess not his love for me precisely, since even daydreams can only go so far, but his respect.

I reached Paris in excellent spirits, full of energy, information, plans, but although I was very warmly welcomed and everyone had missed me just as they should, it was clear from the moment of my arrival that my mother had lost all interest in Clarrow Fell, listening with a suspicious lack of attention to my account of what, after all, had once been her home and family.

"Thank God you are here, Olivia." But it was my experience as a letter-writer she wanted, my practiced turn of phrase, acquired from so many professional beauties and flirtatious wives.

Her *affaire* with Jean-François was not going well. He had grown cold at the precise moment when her emotions had reached a white and evidently desperate heat. She had accused him of infidelity and dismissed him as she had done a dozen others before him, fully confident that he would return. She had not seen him since. So, if I could just compose a line . . . ?

"Yes, mother, what do you want to tell him?"

"That I believe he is killing me, only say it in such a way he will know, should he come to see me, that I will not weep and rave and make one of those distressing scenes which he might be expecting, and which could well be keeping him away. Men do so hate a fuss and Jean-François—well, he is young, I make no secret about that, and young men hate fuss even more than the others. They cannot cope with it, you see, and so they run off and hide and get up to mischief like little boys, to show they don't care. Bravado. That must be it, Olivia. He wants to come back but can't find the way, so if we could just point it out to him! He is killing me but I can still smile, that is the tone. Let him know that I care and I am wounded but I will forgive."

I composed the first letter before my bags were unpacked, two the next day, a long and beautiful epic followed by a curt note breaking everything off.

"So, that is the end of Jean-François."

No doubt, in a week or two, there would be a Jean-Paul. But she woke me at five o'clock the next morning, pale and distraught, shaking me from a warm dream of Robin Esmond to the reality of her overstrung nerves, her sleepless night, during which she had been tormented by the thought of her lover with her last, cool letter in his hand.

"Olivia, I can't bear it. What might it do to him?" What had it done to her?

"We must write again at once, please Olivia, and ease his mind. He has too little experience to know that one says these hard things sometimes without meaning them, just *because* one cares deeply. It is almost a part of caring. You will know how to make that clear, darling. Just scribble it out for me and I will make a fair copy. Victorine will deliver it."

There was no reply.

"But Victorine dear, I told you to wait for an answer. Well, of course he would have written a line if you had only waited a little longer—just to say that he was coming. Now he will have to get his valet to bring it here, poor man."

And for the rest of the day she hovered about the hall, listening to every step on the stair.

"Olivia, is that the bell?"

"No, mother."

"I swear it is. Victorine, quick, open the door."

No one was there.

I had seen her in love before. I had seen her tire of men and had seen men tire of her. It had been part of the same glorious game of chance in which one hazarded oneself joyfully and lightly without taking either the pains or the pleasures too much to heart. Whatever happened one recovered from it, and one had the constant comfort of knowing that the best cure for love was simply to take another lover. But now Jean-François was gone, or so it seemed, and she could neither forget him nor replace him. The time of suffering, the "later" in which she had never really believed had overtaken her and, within the apartment, the familiar signs of tension began to grow, Victorine eating, Madelon coughing, Luc disappearing.

"Where has Luc got to, Victorine?"

"Upstairs? No? Well, he was here under my feet a moment ago."

And I would find him in odd and dangerous places, fairgrounds, railway stations, the Place Pigalle, very late at night collecting pennies for a blind man who, when it came to evading the police or ogling a pretty girl, turned out not to be blind at all: once, curled up asleep on a barge on the river.

"You'd have woken up in Belgium, you little pest."

"What fun!"

"If you do it again I'll murder you."

"You'll have to catch me first."

And when I had demonstrated that although he could run faster I could still hit very hard, and had convinced him of the wisdom of keeping to the neighborhood of the rue du Bac, then came the complaints from the parents of the boy he had punched in the eye, the parents of the boy he was leading into temptation, the boy whose pearl-handled penknife, once admired by Luc, had never been seen again.

"He gave it to me, Olivia," he said, arranging those fluid Junot features into the injured innocence of an angel.

I went up to the attic and there, to my horror, uncovered a magpie hoard of small, shiny things, spoons from the neighboring cafés, shirt studs and dress buttons, a cigarette holder, the ebony top of a walking cane, chess pieces, a string of amber beads.

85

"And who gave you these?"

"Oh *those*," he smiled at me engagingly. "I just found them. You'd be surprised, Olivia, at the things one can find, under the tables and in the toilets at the *Deux Magots*, for instance, or the *Brasserie Malakoff*."

I went to my mother and warned her. "He'll end up in a house of correction, that one."

But her life, from the deepest shades of tragedy, had entered into full sunshine that morning for she had received, at last, a note from her lover and was radiant, ecstatic, opening her arms to a cloudless future.

"He is just a child, darling, and children get up to these monkey tricks. Everyone understands it, scolds maybe just a little and then hugs them better when they cry."

"Which, I suppose, is what you are planning to do with Jean-François."

"Darling, what a lovely idea. He is coming to dinner tonight and Victorine has promised to cook. I have just sent her out to buy *foie gras*."

"Can you afford *foie gras*."

"My dear, when could I ever afford anything? If one lived one's life by what one could *afford*, what a meager existence that would be."

"She is using the rent money," Victorine told me as we sat together in the kitchen that night, my mother and Jean-François having dined sumptuously *en tête-a-tête*. "She has sold her pearl ring too, so you had better keep a tight hold on your inheritance."

"Sold it, to entertain *him*?"

"Yes, either to entertain him or to pay his debts. He has not been near her since you went away. And if you want my opinion he has only come tonight to borrow money or to flirt with Madelon."

It was possible. Sickening but possible, even very likely when one thought how very pretty Madelon was, how much like mother had been in the days when handsome men had tempted *her* to folly, not the other way around.

"Does mother know about this?"

Victorine shrugged, her shoulders by no means fluid like Luc's but solid with hearty nourishment, her appetite larger than ever in times of uncertainty, annoyance, or stress.

"She doesn't want to see it. Madelon is still a pretty child to her, young enough to be asked to give a gentleman a kiss. And what he whispers in her ear—well, mother is not to know."

Poor Madelon. I had gone through it all myself at her age, the "uncles" with straying fingers, all the sly stroking and squeezing which accompanied the gift of a few chocolates, the elderly, overheated leg pressed against mine beneath the dinner-table. I remembered. I had been embarrassed, scared, and then, understanding the relatively small degree of peril, learned to cope with it. It *was* disgusting but unlikely to be fatal, unless one happened to be timid yet, at the same time, desperately eager to please, like Madelon.

"We shall have to put a stop to it, Victorine."

"How?" my sister said, as earthy and shrewd and heavy as any peasant. "When Jean-François goes there will be another. And at the moment if he tried to make love to Madelon under mother's nose she still would not see. Madelon must learn to handle it, as you had to do. Fortunately I am too solid to suit the tastes of mother's gentlemen and they do not bother me."

Had that been Victorine's solution? But Madelon had no toughness, no resource, no ability to fend for herself. Madelon, unless something was done about it, would be badly hurt.

"She can't do it," I said flatly. "Not Madelon."

"Then she'll end up in a nunnery. Or worse."

"How cheerful, Victorine. And what about us since you're telling fortunes tonight?"

"Oh, we'll be all right. I'll marry the fishmonger from the rue de Bellechasse and you'll meet an old man rich enough to do as he pleases, no matter what his family have to say about it, who'll take you as his second wife."

"I don't think I'd like that."

"You'd be lucky to get the chance."

"And what of the fishmonger?"

I did not even realize, at that point, that he existed.

"Marcel Lefevre? He's forty-six, big as an ox and almost as simple. He'd be good to me."

"*Victorine.* You can't be serious!"

"Why ever not?"

"You haven't promised anything have you—haven't *done* anything . . . ?"

"He hasn't asked me yet, Olivia."

Victorine, a fishwife, married to a middle-aged ox! It was unthinkable. And then, suddenly, it seemed quite likely, just as Luc—unless I did something swift and drastic to prevent it—might go to prison one day like his father before him. And what of my mother, approaching the end of her looks, the final pretense of youth? She did not believe, as yet, that she was growing old, but I believed it, just as I believed Victorine deserved more than a fish shop in the rue de Bellechasse, Madelon far more than the "protection" of elderly men who would discard her when her fragile bloom was gone. Once again my loved ones were being threatened by a greedy, grasping world, were being exploited by young men who should have been kinder and old ones who should have had more sense. And I—who else?—would have to do something very sure and very positive in order to protect them.

Jean-François, who was soon to merge in my memory with Jean-Paul, Jean-Louis, Jean-Pierre, who had preceded him, left early, my mother remaining a long time alone at the dinner-table, contemplating the remains of the *foie gras*, the *canard aux cerises*, the champagne which had failed, after all, to restore to her the tender, tantalizing bloom of Madelon.

He did not come back. No one came. She sat in our little *salon* at the table by the window, thin, nervous hands laying out cards for fortunes or for solitaire, quick, nervous eyes flickering constantly to the street, waiting, listening, a burden to herself, a gnawing anxiety to us. She wanted neither money nor power nor any kind of material benefit from men and had never wanted such things. When mink was freely available she would wear it but would sell it happily next morning to help a friend. Nor was she moved by any great physical urges, taking the old-fashioned view, perhaps not far removed from her sister Sibylla's, that sex was for the gentlemen, God bless them, and who was to deny their little pleasures?

She understood flirtation, dalliance, her nature—and this was her tragedy—having remained a restless, questing adolescent within a body unable to stand its pace. And what she craved, as ardently as any craving for opium or cocaine, was not the deep fulfillment of love's maturity but the sunbursts and summer lightning of a perpetual seventeen. She needed to be outrageous, had nourished herself all these years on the scandals she had created. She was now faced with normality, the condition of an ordinary middle-aged woman, and it appalled her. My grandfather had judged her incapable of real suffering. Remembering her previous heartbreaks and miraculous recoveries I had been inclined to agree. We had both been wrong.

She lost sleep and appetite and weight, swallowed laudanum and alcohol in quantities which left her gray-faced, heavy, lethargic, unequal to the effort of powdering her face or brushing her hair or even getting dressed when there was no one to see. Why go through the tedious routines of beauty, why even be clean, when her world was in ashes, when every time she put her head outside the door someone, some kind friend, and dear God, with such friends she had no need of enemies, would come rushing to tell her such tales, to pour out such jealousy and spite. Why not simply sit here and decay, *molder*, since who cared, who would come running to inquire, who would shed more than a casual tear in her memory? What a cruel world! What a cruel city! If she could get away from this flat, this street, these false friends. *That* would be her salvation.

"There is the house in Bradeswick, mother," I suggested carefully. "It might be fun to go and look it over. Sell it, or knock it down, or something. . . ."

But at this stage she wanted neither consolation nor solutions. She wanted to agonize, to burn, and even then at the height of it, she might never be desperate enough to consider Bradeswick.

"Dear God," she said, "does Bradeswick still stand? I thought they must have leveled it to the ground years ago as a service to humanity. You cannot seriously imagine that I would set foot in Bradeswick or anywhere near it in my present sorry condition?"

"He is not worth this agony, you know, mother. No man could possibly be worth it."

"Oh darling," she said, shaking her head and opening her arms wide in a rueful, graceful gesture. "Are you really so sure of that?"

And because, with the memory of Robin Esmond still engraved on my mind, I was not in the least sure of it, I found myself swallowing hard and blinking away the tears which, since my return, had kept on taking me, most annoyingly, by surprise.

"There you are," she said, triumphant yet a little tearful herself. "You did not mean it. No daughter of mine ever could. It has nothing to do with worth or good sense or reason. Heavens—I do still have a little of all that. It makes no difference. It is what one feels. And I cannot feel old, Olivia, I almost wish I could."

"You are not old, mother." And I did my utmost to sound absolutely certain of *that*.

"Of course not. It is just that sometimes I am a little tired . . ."

"Then come away, mother—a change—a rest . . ."

"In Bradeswick?"

Her nostrils wrinkled with distaste, her long fine mouth expressing its utter abhorrence of these provincial manners and morals which inexplicably had so attracted me. And then, blue eyes suddenly wide open, she leaned forward and peered at me, an odd mixture of perplexity, satisfaction and regret in her face.

"Darling—I am so very sorry."

"Mother! Whatever for?"

"Because I have not been listening, have I? All these days since you came home, I have been bombarding you with my own misery and I just didn't see . . . There is a young man in Bradeswick. *Now* I understand. Darling, I am so glad."

She threw out her arms again in a gesture expansive enough to embrace a whole world of young girls in love, so very ready, in the midst of all her sorrows, to rejoice for me that my voice, in reply, sounded gruff with a familiar mixture of affection and exasperation.

"Heavens—I may never see him again."

"But you do want to see him?"

"Oh yes." My answer came swift and fierce with eagerness to be followed instantly by a denial. "It doesn't matter."

For I had no intention of letting her know that it was she, who so believed in love, who was keeping me away from him.

She hesitated a moment and then sat down at the table where she had laid out yet another solitaire, her head bent for a moment, considering the cards, her long, thin hands clasped tight together.

"Oh dear . . ." she said. "Oh dear. . . ."

And she raised her head, rather slowly, to look at me, all her elegance and sophistication faded, briefly but most alarmingly, to reveal the timid, infinitely breakable spirit of my sister, Madelon.

"You must see him, Olivia."

"Oh well—perhaps I will. There's no great hurry . . ."

"Nonsense. We know better than that, darling. You must see him soon. And if he turns out to be less than you remembered then never mind. What matters is that you know you can *feel*. Not everyone can—not really, not in the way that counts. And you may believe me, my darling, when I tell you that nothing can compare with it. It is worth anything. There is nothing one should hesitate to give up, or lose, just to experience it. I am so pleased for you. And you must not think of wasting it, as one does sometimes, for reasons which may seem sound but which turn out not to be—which *could*n't be. So if your heart is in Bradeswick or Clarrow Fell then, however ironic, I suppose . . ."

"Mother!" Had I sounded too eager? "Couldn't we go to Bradeswick for just a week or two? It might be fun . . ."

"Fun?" Her total, blank amazement told me that, in her view, fun was a commodity which had never been available in Bradeswick, and then, remembering my reasons for thinking differently, she bit her lip and sighed, "Oh, darling, I'll try. But not now. Really not now. There are reasons—my fault, of course, and I must take the consequences—all my fault. I can't tell you—except that I *am* to blame."

What had she done? She went to her room, closed the door and left us wondering.

"She's pawned her jewelry," said Luc, appearing for once when we would have preferred him to go away. "Her earrings are in the window of that little shop in Saint-Germain-des-Prés—you know the one."

We knew. But there must be more than that.

"She seemed so frightened," whispered Madelon, looking terrified.

"Her man has taken up with a dancer from the Deux Moulins," announced Luc, a conjurer producing a verbal rabbit from his hat and expecting my applause for it. "Everybody knows."

"No they don't, little beast. How do *you* know?"

"Because I saw them together, weeks ago, and he gave me ten francs not to tell."

"Why should that have stopped you?" He shrugged, examining my question from all its angles to see if I had spotted some way in which he could have further exploited the situation and earned himself another ten francs from somebody else.

"Poor mother," breathed Madelon sadly, knowing exactly how she would have felt herself in that situation.

"She owes money in all the shops too," said Victorine, slapping out pastry dough on the kitchen table, having acquired great quantities of over-ripe berries somewhere or other which, all day, she had been putting into pies.

"What money? Did one of the shopkeepers ask you for any?"

"No. Marcel Lefevre told me."

Her fishman. And if he knew about it then did it mean that my mother owed money as far afield as the rue de Bellechasse?

"Victorine—mother has never bought a pound of fish in her life, not even on credit."

"No. She sends me, which is how I met Marcel. But there is the hat-shop on the corner, and the place that sells embroidered stockings and doeskin gloves, and the antique dealer with the carved ivory in his window."

I had seen no new hats or gloves, no carved ivories. Had they too gone to pay for Jean-François' champagne or to calm the nerves of *his* creditors?

"How long have you known about it, Victorine?"

"Not long," she said, continuing to slap her dough about the table, dogged in her determination that any void, no matter how painful, could be filled with food. "Marcel mentioned it last night. He thought we should know."

"And just where did you see your fishmonger last night?"

"He came here, to the kitchen door, if you must know."

"*Victorine*—like calling on a housemaid."

"Yes," she snapped, her chin clenched at its most pugnacious angle, her hands still deftly shaping the pastry and trimming its edges. "Yes, Olivia, just like that."

"*Please*," whispered Madelon. "Please don't quarrel."

I had a great deal to occupy my mind that night and lay awake until the approach of a cold dawn sorting out the list of my anxieties, arranging them first in the order of their gravity and then on a varying scale of what I could realistically hope to do about them. I could not control Luc, and, therefore, I would have to find some way of removing him from the source of his temptation. Madelon too was badly in need of a refuge for I had long been of the opinion that a little stability, a little peace of mind would cure her cough far more effectively than medicines. And how long would it be—unless positive action were taken against it—before Victorine's Marcel made sure of his bride in the traditional kitchen-door manner of making her pregnant? *He* must be only too eager. What middle-aged fishmonger could be otherwise? While she, I suspected, was becoming every day more resigned to a marriage *she* might call convenient but which I considered to be a waste. Ten years from now she would have grown fat on fried fish and potatoes, loud from the racket of the fish market, rough-skinned from gutting and filleting and scouring. And since I could not forbid her to see him, the solution, in her case too, would be to move away.

Everything—my personal desires not least of all—pointed to Bradeswick. There was a house there, a reason to make the journey, a task to perform on arriving. My sisters and Luc presented no problem for they had been brought up to follow me. But how—with all the persistence of which I knew myself capable—could I possibly get my mother there?

I had no longer the slightest doubt that she had been buying on credit and re-selling or pawning the goods. Could one go to prison for that? It sounded quite possible. And why—*why?*—had so many of these close-mouthed, over-cautious shopkeepers given her credit in the first place? She was plausible and inventive, I well knew, but what tale could have loosened their purse-strings better than the good fortune of her daughter, Olivia, who was about to inherit—any day now—a great estate, a noble house, to become "milady" in her own right like the English "milords" who spent their money so freely along the boulevards.

I could imagine her telling the story, breathless and scatter-brained and innocent, giving her orders for kid boots and gloves and wickedly expensive little fur collars almost as an afterthought. How had she hoped to repay? The answer was that she had not given it a thought, repayment like suffering belonging to the list of things which might happen later and possibly not at all.

What could I do? What could Emil Junot have done in this not unfamiliar situation? Taken a cab to the station, I thought, one dark night and disappeared. Bradeswick again. Although Junot, of course, would have taken her to Rome or Lisbon or London. But no matter how humiliating it would be for her to return to Bradeswick in a condition it would be difficult to pass off as triumphant, I remained convinced that it might be the making of us all.

I had spent one day in Bradeswick and had found it ugly, dark, extremely dull, a factory town bordering my grandfather's land which had nothing to recommend it but its solidity, its lack—surely—of fascinating young men like Jean-François, its distance from the fish shop in the rue de Bellechasse, its close proximity to Clarrow Fell and Robin. My mother might be bored in Bradeswick but she would be safe. Madelon would prefer boredom to her present uncertainties. Victorine, as the sister of Miss Heron of Clarrow Fell would be above the importunities of the local fishing trade. Luc would be well away from the temptations of the *Deux Magots* and the *Brasserie Malakoff*. I could be with Robin.

I went no further than that. Bradeswick, not Clarrow Fell. The tall, shabby town house Amyas had shown me, not the Manor. I was too harassed tonight, too busy, too scared, to think about falling in love. But the possibility of love existed. If I never saw him again, then eventually I would forget. But if I did see him! It was as I sank into this most enchanting contemplation that I heard a sound, tried hard to ignore it, heard it again, stiffened, told myself no, it was nothing, and then dry-mouthed, my senses certain of disaster while my mind still tried to reject it, I flung myself out of bed and ran to my mother.

I had not, in any way, expected it. Yet, when I reached her room and saw what she had done, it seemed incredible that I had been so near-sighted, so insensitive. I had judged the degree of her passion to be no greater than usual and in that I think I had been right. But I had underestimated her fear of debt, a laughing matter once when Emil Junot had been here to spirit her away; appalling now when it was for her, and her alone, that the officers of the law would come looking. I had also misjudged the strength of her attachment to life for its own sake, basing it on my own fierce desire to stay alive forever. And there was more than that. Far more. For I was the one who had pressed her to go to Bradeswick, had made her aware that, even for Robin Esmond, I would not leave her behind. And if she had done this, in any way for me, how could I ever bear it? How could I ever be at peace again?

She had taken laudanum and brandy—I could see and smell that—and a great many other things I could not give a name to, her bedside-table cluttered with pills and powders, a whole lethal array of dark brown and dark blue chemists' bottles. And for an unbelievable moment I stood there in the half-dark looking down at this woman on the bed, this stranger, just female bones and skin, no longer very

94

young, damp hair pulled cruelly back from a face one could see any day of the week in its hundreds and thousands, drawn and plain and weary, plodding home with the laundry, the shopping, a truculent grandchild. My mother? Yes indeed, or the husk of her with the essence drawn out and blown away, the charm and grace and style which had been her true identity gone now so that she could have been anyone, just a poor, sick, worn-out woman, the kind they fish out of the river often enough in any big city. A woman who, despite her shallow, irregular breathing, looked dead, felt dead, had wished to be dead. Mother! And suddenly I was grinding my teeth with what proved a sustaining fury. How could she? How dare she? I loved her. I needed to love her. Mother—please mother—don't leave me.

I made no conscious decisions. I simply followed the lead of my hands as they grabbed her shoulders and started to shake her hard, my fingers encountering bones as brittle as a bird, but refusing to pity her yet, since I would have to hurt her first—and badly—if I hoped to keep her above the level of that final sleep.

I dragged her out of bed and into the corridor, the dead weight of her more than I had bargained for, and screamed out for Victorine, Madelon, anybody, anything. And for a while I could see nothing but flapping white nightgowns, chalk-white circles that were their faces, open mouths stupid and noisy with panic, my mother staggering like a rag doll from one to the other.

It could not continue. I had to think. Pick up the pieces. Clear up the mess. *Think!*

"That's enough—now listen, Victorine, help me hold her up. Madelon, get Luc and quickly. And then the two of you must go and fetch a doctor. *Do it*, Madelon. And Madelon, you may have to knock on his door and refuse to go away unless he comes. You'll do that, won't you, Madelon. *Now run.*"

"Yes," she said, very pale, just a thin, unformed child in her cotton nightgown, fine hair hanging down her back, a cough beginning in her chest and then quickly suppressed, her small chin quivering in its heartrending attempt to be resolute.

She went. There were footsteps up and down the stairs, doors banging, Luc—who would know the whereabouts of every doctor in the *quartier*—dashing past me and then away again. But all this occurred only on the fringes of my vision, my mind entirely filled by the need to keep my mother awake, *moving*, up and down the hall, up and down, a weight of seaweed hanging limply against me, mindlessly entangling me so that twice I stumbled, taking her down with me as if we were drowning, pulling her to her feet again, using my own rage as my best weapon since it would have enabled me to drag her about by the hair had it become necessary.

"Make her drink this," said Victorine, appearing with some peppery-smelling concoction in a jug. And so we sat her down, held her head, and spooned the mixture into her while she moaned and spat it feebly back at us.

"She has to be sick," said Victorine, dogged even in panic, "and if she won't swallow . . ."

"She'll swallow—one way or another. Come on, mother—come on!" But she merely slumped lower down in the chair, her body boneless, fluid, looking as if it might evaporate, like water and become just a puff of steam, hanging in the air for a moment or two: then nothing. How dare you, mother? Mother—please, mother—don't go. And in desperation I caught hold of her nose, pinched her nostrils viciously together and, when her mouth opened in automatic need for air, poured the whole content of Victorine's jug inside it.

For a moment of blind terror I thought I had choked her. So did Victorine.

"Dear God, Olivia!"

Bending her forward we thumped her back while she gagged and spluttered and heaved, her breath eventually wheezing up to us like old machinery creaking through layers of rust and injury. And it was a sign of triumph when she fell on to her knees and vomited with the abandon of a child—or a dog—on the carpet.

"I'll fetch the mop and bucket," said Victorine.

"Mother," I heard myself whisper stupidly, "are you there?"

The doctor was small and precise and irritable, far too accustomed to dealing with hysterical women in unusual situations to be even mildly curious as to why this woman in particular had chosen to poison herself in the middle of a wet Friday night.

"Her bedroom?"

I showed him. He and I together got her to bed, he closed the door, leaving the others outside, Madelon very white, Luc's eyes looking twice their normal size, Victorine still at her mopping, and having raised sardonic eyebrows at the bottles on her table he asked me to undress her which I reluctantly did. And then, having stripped her, I suddenly could not stop myself from darting forward and covering her with a blanket.

"I beg your pardon, *monsieur*," I said feebly in reply to his evident irritation.

"If you would prefer to wait outside, *mademoiselle?*"

I shook my head and removed the blanket, disturbed not that he should see her naked but that he should see her ugly.

"Very well."

And deftly, without too much interest, he inserted a tube down her throat and pumped out the contents of her stomach, a brutal process from which I averted my head, although my nostrils could not escape the stink nor my ears the gurgling.

"Hardly necessary, in this case, *mademoiselle*," he said, "other than to discourage her from doing the same again. And now if your maid would bring me the wherewithal to wash my hands. . . ?"

My maid? Victorine, of course, with her mop and pail, her sturdy fishwife's build. Victorine, slowly withdrawing from the family circle, abdicating her position as a daughter of the house who must marry a gentleman or stay single. Turning herself into a housemaid for whom the fishmonger of the rue de Bellechasse would be an excellent catch.

"Yes—of course. I'll ask."

But when I opened the door she had anticipated the need and was there with a steaming basin, a new bar of soap, clean towels.

"Thank you," he said, to me not to her, washed his hands, buttoned his shirt cuffs, mentioned his fee, having learned by experience, one supposed, the folly of sending in one's account at the month-end to a house such as this.

"Certainly, *monsieur*."

I paid him, accompanied him to the street door, finding myself obliged to lean suddenly against the cold wall, my legs shaky, my body feeling hot and hollow, lamentably unsteady.

But experience had also taught him never to involve himself with young ladies in distress.

"Good night, *mademoiselle*."

"Good night, *monsieur*."

Upstairs my mother lay as I had left her, flat on her face, whimpering through her daze and shock, her hair still damp, her skin clammy, her shoulder bones protruding at an awkward, somehow childish angle which reminded me of Madelon.

There was nothing, yet, to say to her. Much to be done. The house was quiet, the floor in the passage clean. I picked up the debris the doctor had left behind and disposed of it in the courtyard, startled by the unexpectedly full light of day. Saturday, I supposed it was, and as I let myself back into the hall I caught the aroma of fresh coffee coming from the kitchen where Victorine, fully dressed, had already started her placid beheading of carrots and sprouts for the day's *pot au feu*.

"Are you all right, Victorine?"

"Yes. I've just warmed this blackcurrant syrup for Madelon."

"I'll take it."

In another room my younger sister had crept into bed like a little mouse and lay there, her breathing an agony to the ear, her face gray.

"There's nothing to worry about now, Madelon."

But her hands were shaking, her teeth chattering on the rim of the cup, black smudges in the hollows of her eyes; a sick and very frightened child.

"You did well, Madelon."

Very well, in fact, for although she could not have found her way through the dark streets without Luc to guide her, she had known, far better than Luc, how to convince the doctor of the urgency of the call. And she had not broken down until her work was done.

Yet where was Luc? Instantly my mind filled with railway stations, night trains to God knew where, boats drifting upstream to destinations beyond my imagining. Not that! But I found him upstairs in his attic sorting through his glittering, stolen treasures, small objects, which were easily portable if one had to run, objects which would not break, could not be damaged by poison in the night or by the infidelities of dashing young men, objects which, when they grew old, tended not to lose but to increase their value, and were, therefore, *dependable*.

"Luc—are you all right?"

He was holding a crystal button up to the light, the hardest, brightest thing he possessed, turning it this way and that, assessing its worth and its market value, by no means the same, of course, but, even then, very well within his grasp.

98

"Yes, I'm all right. Are you?"

"Yes. So is mamma."

"Oh good. I thought she might like this." He squeezed the crystal tight in his hand, his shrewd little face puckering suddenly with tears. He was giving away his most treasured possession, part of his security, and would probably regret it tomorrow when she was laying out her games of solitaire again and telling him to be quiet. But, nevertheless, he was performing a generous, loving act. He was, and I was quite surprised by it, just a little boy crying for his mother. Hugging him hard, ruffling his hair, I pretended I had not noticed his tears and took him down to Madelon, asking her to look after him, asking him to look after her: leaving them curled up together like a pair of stray kittens sheltering under a blanket.

And then I returned to my mother's room, sat down in her bedside chair, and kept watch.

Remorse came first, a terrible flood of tears and sobs which moved me to cry a little too, then embarrassed me, then unnerved me. She slept a little after that and then, waking to strong sunlight, wanted to die again, hating herself for the condition she was in and me for witnessing it. But this I took to be a better sign and suggested that now she might like me to wash her hair. But I was somewhat too premature. No. She would lie in her own vomit forever. It seemed appropriate. She began to shiver and to cry again. Her throat was sore and swollen. Her stomach ached, she was bruised from head to foot, and as these physical preoccupations began to cancel out her thoughts of death—for if her body hurt then it must surely be alive—there came the hoarsely whispered confession, "I am ashamed, Olivia. I can never hold up my head again."

But she and Junot had scattered debts all over Europe and she could hardly feel humiliated by that when so many counts and dukes and princes did the same. She had been scared, certainly, and heart-broken, of course, but the thing that had broken her, the thing she still could not bear was that all those milliners and glove-makers and ivory-sellers should know that she, to whom so much adoration had been given in her summertime, had attempted and failed to buy the affections of a younger man.

"What a sordid little tale," she said, wrinkling her nose with distaste, her eyes still hunted. "I have heard it a hundred times. How commonplace it all is. I can't stay here, Olivia. You do see that?"

I saw it. When the news leaked out our doorbell would know no rest, not merely from the demands of anxious creditors, but the constant parade of my mother's "friends," men whose advances she had rejected in her heyday, young women who wished to see for themselves that she was no longer a rival, a woman of her own age who had been less beautiful but had had more sense. They would bring flowers, chocolates, tears and kisses, and then as a final gift, some little tale about Jean-François which *everybody* had known all along and nobody had quite liked to tell. It would be altogether unbearable, I quite agreed with her.

"I can't stand it, Olivia."

"Then we'll just have to get you away—somewhere or other."

"If only I could—if I could just turn a page, start again . . . "

"Yes. But it wouldn't do just to run off, helter-skelter, would it?"

"Dear God—I don't know. Why not?"

"Because people would say you'd let that girl from the *Deux Moulins* drive you out."

"I don't care what people say."

"Yes you do. So we'd have to go somewhere that would seem to be to our advantage. We'd have to make it look as if we were going up in the world, or might be."

"Never," she said. "You go to Bradeswick. Just let me go to hell."

But her voice lacked conviction, the seed had been sown and, in the manner of Emil Junot before me, I proceeded to make it grow. She would be returning to her own country which might seem a defeat in her eyes but would look natural enough to everybody else. And who in Bradeswick would ever guess that she had left debt and disgrace behind her? They would simply see the mysterious Madame Junot who, between thrilling engagements elsewhere, had come not to ask favors or borrow money but to inspect her daughter's property. She would, inevitably, be the talk of the town, queen of a small country— very small, in fact—but nonetheless royal for that, since what other woman in Bradeswick could hold a candle to her? Certainly not her sister, Sibylla, the vicar's wife, nor any other of the stout, high-complexioned matrons I had seen, with their tight-laced corsets and strait-laced manners. While her friends here in Paris could have no notion of the exact size and nature of my inheritance and might easily be encouraged—as easily as our local shopkeepers—to think of her as living in circumstances of considerable affluence.

It would be the perfect answer.

"No," she said, but very wearily, her voice lifting slightly in interrogation. "No?" And then "Oh no," rather more firmly. "Don't plague me so, Olivia."

But, somewhat opportunely from my point of view, the milliner from the rue de Bellechasse chose that very afternoon to send round an account for a gray satin hat my mother did not appear to remember.

"How many more of these to come, Mother?"

The doorbell rang again. Only Victorine's fishman as it turned out, bringing her a present of hake, but enough to convince my mother that she was living under siege, as Emil Junot had so often done.

She lay back on her pillows and closed her eyes, looking as frail and almost as small as Madelon. When she spoke again they were the words I had often heard her speak to Junot.

"I'll go anywhere. Just arrange it."

"Are you sure?"

"Yes—yes," she said, too frightened now for questions or reasons, wanting simply to be off, to be safe, to snatch once again at that mythical clean page, that fresh start. And, as Junot had always done, I began to make my preparations quickly, knowing that for as long as her panic lasted she was mine.

Madelon would go anywhere I led her. Luc was still small enough to tuck under my arm. Half an hour of my persistent logic assisted by ten minutes of my sharp tongue convinced Victorine that she could not possibly desert her family for a hard-working marriage in the rue de Bellechasse. And having settled that quite satisfactorily I left my sisters busily sorting through our linen and set off, not to pay my mother's debts, but to get them paid.

Money, I knew, would be a constant problem, for Guy's allowance, which had been ample for one, must now make do for five. And, the expenses of the journey apart, there would be a hotel in Bradeswick to pay for, since my mother, in her role of Madame Junot, could not take up residence in my house until it was fit to live in. What such repairs and decorations might cost I did not know, except that it would leave me nothing to spare for those shopkeepers who ought not to be left to pay the bill for my mother's folly and her lover's *foie gras*.

I spent the morning among my mother's friends, just happening to meet them by chance in the places I expected them to be; a tightly knit circle where everybody knew the secrets of everybody else and secrets, like promises, were not meant to be kept. That afternoon I called on Jean-François and informed him pleasantly that his aunt in Normandy, upon whom his future prosperity depended, would not be pleased to know how ruthlessly he had preyed on a woman and her innocent children, particularly if I went myself to tell her about it, taking frail, gentle Madelon and Luc, who could look very soulful when necessary, with me. Were a few tradesmen's bills really worth the loss of his aunt's good opinion or his share of her fortune? For I had heard that she had other nephews who would be only too willing to replace him in her favor. I told him the exact total of my mother's debts and that I would return for the money the following morning. He paid. I have never cared to inquire how. But by noon my mother's reputation was entirely restored in the rue du Bac although it was no part of my plan to tell her so.

She had eaten a little luncheon, her hair washed and curled, her face pale but painted very discreetly, blue shadows on a porcelain-tinted skin, cleverly creating a lovely, suffering face, in case anyone should call.

"Don't let anyone in to see her, Victorine. I think she knows by now that she can live without Jean-François and if she finds out her debts are paid, we're done for."

She smiled, gave a heavy shrug.

"You're not troubled by scruples, are you Olivia?"

"Victorine—it's for her own *good*."

I went out again, sent telegrams to my grandfather's lawyers and Amyas Hird, wrote a short statement of intent to my grandfather and a long, friendly letter to Alys. I bought train tickets and boat tickets, booked sleeping compartments and cabins, calculated the cost of a night or two in a London hotel and checked it against the dwindling contents of my purse, hoping I had allowed sufficient margin for the emergencies and unforeseen eventualities which would very likely become all too clear. I paid calls on every lady who had ever employed me as a secretary, collecting a great deal of good advice, a few cast-off pairs of gloves, a silk scarf, a parasol and, from the better-hearted, a franc or two. And then on my way home, I stopped at the milliner's shop in the rue de Bellechasse where my mother had accumulated the largest single debt and, with my secondhand gleanings strewn on the floor around me, bought my mother, cash down, a brand new hat, a gorgeous extravaganza of peach and lilac chiffon, swirl upon swirl of it crowned with a yard of white plumage, a rose-garden of white tulle blossoms on the brim.

There had never been such a hat. I had never felt so sure and so strong. Our boxes were packed, our tickets in my hand, my intentions crystal clear. I was going back to Clarrow Fell on no mission of discovery this time, but to take it by storm.

SIX

We arrived at the start of a wet July, a novelty in itself since we were none of us accustomed to gray skies and this particular kind of cold, stinging rain at high summer.

"The West Riding of Yorkshire," my mother explained to Victorine and Madelon, in much the same manner as, three months ago, Aunt Sibylla had explained to me, "is famous for its rain. It has something to do with the hills. The clouds bump against them and, *voilà*, down it comes. They say it makes things grow, weeds and mill chimneys, for instance, and the wool on the sheep's backs."

And although I had deliberately exaggerated the ugliness of Bradeswick, it seemed even worse than I remembered it that day, its gutters overflowing with muddy water, its stone houses low of stature and thick with grime, its narrow, uphill streets either cobbled and dangerous to the ankles or criss-crossed with tramlines, the surrounding hills looking bald and empty as if all this colliding with wet clouds had rinsed them of their vegetation.

"The promised land," said Victorine, turning up her coat collar.

"Where is everybody?" said Luc, glancing about him in bewilderment at the half-empty, sullen little square which announced itself as Corporation Place, finding the few carts drawn by heavy horses and the occasional tram discharging its load of purposeful, hurrying people, no substitute at all for the high-stepping thoroughbreds and the fashionable strollers of the boulevards.

"It is an acquired taste," my mother told him with a shrug, "and since Olivia has decided that we must acquire it . . . !"

Bradeswick. I had spent a morning here with Amyas Hird who had explained to me in his dry fashion how the town had grown up from a scattering of cottages at a shallow stretch of the River Brade used by the local keepers of sheep and weavers of wool to get their carts safely across the stream every market day when they took their finished cloth to the Piece Hall in Halifax.

A quiet town in an obscure setting of moorland and rainwater surrounded by other towns cut to the same quiet pattern until the invention of steam engines, spinning machines and mechanical looms had transformed the cottage craft of weaving into *industry* and supplied a new breed of men, "industrialists," to control it. Some of these towns—Bradford for instance—had doubled their size annually in the ten or fifteen years it had taken to build those awesome, black-browed factories and to rush in a motley population of starving Irish, unemployed English fieldworkers. Anyone from anywhere who was desperate enough to take these small industrial wages in exchange for their labor.

But Bradeswick had somehow remained aloof from these grand explosions of progress, nothing of any magnitude having occurred here at all, it seemed, except the discovery of iron ore, a couple of generations ago, on nearby land belonging to the Herons of Clarrow Fell. The squire of his day, having no interest in mineral rights or, just possibly, no true conception of their worth, had sold them to a Mr. Greenlaw and a Mr. Clough, founders of the Bradeswick Ironworks Company, whose enterprises and the labor-force imported to man them had quickly spread out towards Bradeswick itself, the town and its new colony soon meeting and becoming one. And their fusion quite naturally had stimulated growth in other areas of commerce, a great multiplication of butchers and bakers and grocers to meet the ironworkers' needs and the establishment, since foundries are notoriously hot and thirsty places, of Naseby's Brewery, now famous throughout the North for the excellence of its light ales.

In Bradeswick, therefore, one worked for the ironmasters, Messrs. Greenlaw and Clough, or for Mr. Naseby, the Brewer; or else one's trade depended upon the favor of one or all of those gentlemen and their descendants. One lived in houses of varying condition and value which belonged, for the most part, to the Ironworks or the Brewery who fixed their rents and, in some cases, made sweeping decrees as to their tenants' personal behavior, forbidding them to hang washing lines across the street or to scour their doorsteps on Sundays. One attended schools which, although now becoming subject to the policies of government ministers, had originally been founded, staffed, maintained and had undoubtedly pandered to the educational whims and fancies of a member of one or the other of these ruling families. One followed the doctrines of the High Church of England as laid down by the vicar of Bradeswick parish church if one wished to rise in the service of the Nasebys, or, on the other hand, one presented oneself twice every Sunday at the Congregationalist Chapel which had secured the eagle-eyed patronage of the Cloughs.

Bradeswick Infirmary and Technical School had both been built on Greenlaw and Clough generosity. The public gardens and recreation grounds with the ornamental lake and somewhat regimented flower-beds were the inspiration of a Naseby. The Bradeswick Ironworks Brass Band was famous for its exuberance, a great favorite with the Sunday strollers in the park; its distinction matched, assuredly in their own opinion, by the tug-of-war team from the brewery which, throughout the summer, attended and occasionally won the contests that were held in every mill town and mining town during the week of its annual holiday.

And if one did not happen to be in the employ of Greenlaw or Clough or Naseby and did not do business with them or serve them in some official or professional capacity, one had really no reason for being in Bradeswick at all.

Amyas Hird met us at the station, betraying no hint of curiosity as to my intentions or motives, no sign of anything which could be called curiosity when my mother, surrounded by hat boxes and vanity bags and holding a large bouquet of roses and carnations she had insisted on buying in Leeds to give herself the air of a visiting prima donna, fixed him with her wide, blue stare and murmured "Good Heavens, is it really Amyas? You were just a child when I saw you last."

"Not really, Lavinia." Lavinia! I had not even expected him to know her name, much less use it so freely, having forgotten that her knowledge of this place and of these people must be very much greater than mine. But when I questioned her later, just as she was scattering her hats and her feathers and her flowers all over the best front bedroom at the Station Hotel, she shrugged and pouted a little, unwilling as yet to venture too deeply into her past.

"Oh, Amyas. Good Lord, he has been here forever—at the Manor I mean."

"But he is not a relation. Or is he?"

"Oh well, I daresay he is not, although there again who could ever be sure of it. These large families are always in such a tangle. You must know something already of the Squire's feudal inclinations, his positive position, in fact, for taking in waifs and strays. Until he got his fingers burned, that is, which is quite another story. There were always two or three boys being brought up at Clarrow in my day. All of them in love with me, of course . . ."

"Of course. Even Amyas?" It sounded excessively unlikely.

"Every one of them without exception and without fail. I was the bride of the young Squire, you see, and what waif or stray could possibly resist that. Poor Amyas. He was always so silent and intense, the kind who bleeds easily. Although now, I must say, he looks quite bloodless. Perhaps that was only to be expected."

"I would hardly be in a position to know. But he *is* waiting downstairs in the foyer to take us to see the house. Are you coming, mother?" She shook her head.

"But mother, are you not even curious?"

"My dear, why should I be? It is the house of Jemima Copthorne Heron; a spinster from the hour of her birth. The nearest she came to marriage was with the manager of the Bradeswick Commercial Bank, until she caught him one Christmas Eve kissing me under the mistletoe, when I was fifteen and he must have been over forty. My word, what a fuss. And if she was fool enough to send him away, then it was hardly my fault that he did not come back. She forgave me, of course, because she was a Christian, although that never prevented her from hating me too. The house is tall and cold and narrow, just like her. And I do not imagine that Aireville Terrace can still be considered the best part of town."

It was not far away, of course, since nothing in Bradeswick was far from anything else and by no stretch even of my hopeful imagination, could Miss Jemima's house be called attractive. It was narrow in the extreme, as my mother had said, with a long garden both front and back choked with weeds and thorns and waist-high grasses, the ground waterlogged in places and covered in others by haphazard paving stones that were slimy and dangerous with moss. The front door was dark green and uninviting, opening into a dingy hall that had nothing in it but a threadbare carpet and the distinctive odor of cats.

Two sitting rooms were placed one behind the other, both

stuffy and overfurnished in shades of dull red, sepia and unpolished mahogany. There was a dining room of minute dimensions entirely dominated by a carved wood fireplace, a gigantic banqueting table and chairs. While behind it, through a second passage, we discovered a whole complexity of kitchens, pantries, a still-room complete with an ancient still, keeping cellars and coal cellars where the recent presence of Miss Jemima's cats stung my eyelids and caused Madelon, hastily, to withdraw.

The main staircase was a steep tunnel coated with dark brown varnish. The upper floor consisted of four small square bedrooms and a considerably superior one at the front, its large bay-window giving us a view of Aireville Terrace in all its prim splendor, houses like our own sheltering behind hedges and firmly shut iron gates, their own windows close-curtained against neighborly curiosity, their gardens achingly neat.

The furniture throughout was of Gothic design and Herculean proportions, the cumbersome pieces of Queen Victoria's young womanhood, now fifty years out of date. Towering sideboards complete with fancy shelving and elaborately carved cupboard doors sprouted a super-abundance of mahogany flowers and fruit, heavily upholstered chairs with wide seats designed to accommodate a crinoline seemed planted immovably on their carved hardwood frames and massive claw and ball feet. The downstairs windows were uniformly curtained in dark red plush and yellowing lace intended, one supposed, to keep out the soot, the air, and the sun. Bathing, very clearly, would consist of nothing more elaborate than a tub or a hip-bath drawn up to the kitchen fire. The water closet was at the far end of the backyard.

"It's a home," I said flatly to Victorine. "We own it. Nobody is waiting at the month-end for the rent."

It was even more than that. It was a future.

"Very well," she said, giving her heavy shrug. "Then there's work to be done."

Work indeed. I had come to Bradeswick to build a nest but first I must test the security of the tree, must ascertain what dangers, if any, might be threatening my roots or casting malevolent glances at my branch. I took the train to Clarrow Fell and presented myself before my grandfather, standing once again in the Justice's Room in my best gray coat and skirt, my heart still foolishly brimming with hope until the very moment he said "Please do not trouble to explain why you have returned to Bradeswick. Whatever your reasons I cannot approve them."

"I'm sorry. I came because it was necessary."

"You came because you wanted to, Olivia. Otherwise no amount of necessity would have brought you back. I cannot force you to leave. I do not encourage you to stay. You will, of course, do exactly as you please. You must allow me to do the same. And now, if you will excuse me—Mrs. Long will give you tea."

No miracle had taken place. There was to be no reconciliation. No truce. But no retribution either. Being a man who believed in the strict performance of his duty he would allow me—strictly and to the letter—every one of my rights. The allowance he had promised me would not be withdrawn. But should I incur debts, or should my mother incur debts, I must not assume his assistance to be guaranteed. I might visit the Manor as I pleased and should he decide to hold a reception, which seemed unlikely now at his age, he would not arouse local gossip by excluding me from his list of guests. But I must come to Clarrow Fell alone. He would not receive my mother and could not feel her other children to be any concern of his. He would fulfill his obligations but, at the same time, must warn me never to overstep the mark. I was not to be punished, but, as far as possible, I was to be ignored.

I drank the tea Mrs. Long gave me and then, walking down to the vicarage, took a second cup with my aunt who informed me at once that, with the best will in the world, she could do nothing, either for or against my mother, until my grandfather had made his wishes on the matter crystal clear. After all, her husband's living depended on the Squire. The vicarage—her home—belonged to him and she could not use it, without his express permission, to entertain the woman, albeit her own sister, who had so blighted the life of his only son. Nor could she visit us in Bradeswick since to do so would be to set upon us a seal of approval of which she was by no means certain. Where Sibylla Heron led, others would follow and she did not care to expose her acquaintances to influences which might well . . . !
I would, no doubt, take her meaning. While as for Alys, she was away just now, spending the summer in Bridlington with her father and, on her return, her anxious mother would have to consider most carefully how best to proceed. Alys, she supposed, would want to see me, for we were cousins after all and it seemed natural and right. But Alys was at a vulnerable, impressionable age, when it was essential to

maintain a flawless reputation, to associate—and to be seen to associate—only with those who were likewise beyond reproach. Her daughter, my aunt informed me, was a popular young lady greatly in demand who, this coming season, was expected to make her final choice among the suitors who would cluster around her at the hunt ball to be held by the Pottertons at Dawney Park, at the Christmas Eve dance offered by Mrs. Naseby of Naseby's Brewery, at Bradeswick's civic banquet and the dozens of dinner-parties and theater-parties which always enlivened the autumn and winter. Whether I attended all or any of these functions would depend on the Squire, since none of the local gentry would wish to offend him and would invite me or leave me out to suit *his* pleasure, not their own. But even if I did find myself invited to a dance or two I must realize that no such courtesy could be extended to my half-sisters. What was it she had heard me call them? Ah yes. Naturally the Squire could not be expected to vouch for them. Pretty girls, were they?

"Beautiful."

"Indeed." She raised pained eyebrows, imagining them as youthful copies of my mother made even more enchanting by their Parisienne airs and graces, and hastened to inform me that in Bradeswick it was not prettiness that mattered. To find a husband in Bradeswick one required the far more solid attributes of a good name and a good family. One required, above all, a dowry. A narrow view of life, perhaps, but she could not complain since her daughter was amply provided with all these things.

"A dowry!" my mother declared later that day when I had described the interview to her. "If my niece Alys has a dowry then I wonder how Sibylla has obtained it. For Toby Heron had nothing to recommend him when they married but his classical education and what can a country vicar be expected to earn? Very likely she has sold my mother's jewelry. It must all have gone to Sibylla, I suppose, since no one offered any of it to me. But what do we care, my darling? We may be poor and disreputable but she is still jealous of us. It is because you are so much better looking than Alys."

"You have not seen Alys, mother."

"No, and there is not the least need for it. I have seen you often enough and therefore I *know*. I have not seen this wonderful young man of yours either, by the way."

I had learned, from Mrs. Long, that he was in Cambridge

visiting friends and would not return, she supposed, until the grouse-shooting began in mid-August. I went upstairs early that night to my impersonal hotel bedroom and lay on hard pillows, listening to the street noises and thinking, with exquisite leisure, of Robin Esmond. I knew almost nothing about him and although, with every other new acquaintance, I was invariably curious, very much inclined to examine and assess every facet of disposition and character, in Robin's case none of these appeared to matter. I had seen him. Therefore I knew him. It seemed as simple as that. I had always tended to admire dark-complexioned men, a lean, slightly sinister cast of countenance, black Spanish eyes. But now, with Robin's blue gaze acquiring the radiance of sapphires in my eager memory, his fine, feathery hair the pale sheen of silver, I could not for the life of me imagine why. I had always been considerably attracted by ambition, too, by success itself and the single-minded ruthlessness, the tough, predatory male instincts which achieved it. Yet now, Robin's declaration that he was just "thinking about life," which would have dismayed me in anyone else, seemed altogether charming, his nonchalance, which could so easily have irritated me, was an intriguing delight. What, after all, I asked myself, had he to strive for when he had been born in the very circumstances which suited him best? He was, by nature—I felt quite sure of it—as well as by education, a country gentleman and since he had all the sporting facilities of the countryside already at his disposal why should he think any further than that? Admittedly, I had heard of no ancestral estate waiting for him to inherit. But there was Clarrow Fell. It was, of course, very foolish and far too soon to think of that but, closing my eyes tight, I thought of it hard and long. Robin and Clarrow Fell. Could life or fate or destiny—or should I call it chance?—which had never seemed to be entirely on my side, suddenly offer me these riches? When my grandfather died could I possibly keep the Manor and live there with Robin? Lying motionless and breathless in the dark I knew with the absolute but not always reliable certainty of youth, that it was all I wanted. Was it too much? To me it was everything but, in other eyes, the Manor was in need of repair, the land of no great value, while Robin himself had no particular fortune that I knew of, no brilliant prospects to make him a matrimonial prize. Surely Chance could spare me this? And I would be more than ready to go out and give her a helping hand. I would not sit idly by waiting for life to happen to me and turning sour when it did not. I would not merely

111

dream of myself in white, spangled tulle dancing with Robin at Lady Potterton's hunt ball but would take whatever steps seemed necessary to get myself an invitation. Nor would I bow my head meekly to Aunt Sibylla's gloomy predictions concerning Madelon and Victorine. I had had no need of her to remind me that, unlike myself, they had no property, no expectations, and even less claim to respectability than I.

But Madelon was sweet-natured, affectionate and beautiful, Victorine strong-minded, capable, shrewd, and my opinion of the opposite sex was high enough to feel sure of finding at least two—which was all one required—who would appreciate these things.

But, in the meantime, we had come here to build our nest, to provide ourselves with a secure base from which to direct our campaign. There was work to be done. And work, moreover, which ought not to be seen to be done by us, since work was for housemaids and women of the lower classes, not for young *marriageable* ladies who, if they indulged in it, might be thought odd or, even worse, to have committed the unforgivable sin of poverty. Unless, of course, they could call their labors by another name, presenting them to the world as a summer whim, a joke, one of the unlikely novelties which bored and pampered females are forever seizing upon to while away their time.

"My girls have taken it into their heads to play house," my mother languidly announced in the deep crimson foyer of the Station Hotel where she sat in state every afternoon wearing her French hat and sipping China tea. "One feels bound to permit it, for it seems harmless enough."

Harmless perhaps. Backbreaking, beyond all question, helped not at all by a sudden return to fine weather which made the shabbiness shabbier, the pungent memory of the cats even more offensive. And it became essential to make a start, for the Station Hotel was expensive, my money was running out and I had a long way to go before the month-end.

"Would you care to borrow a half-dozen girls from Clarrow Fell?" offered Amyas, his nostrils wrinkling fastidiously at the feline odor. I would have liked nothing better, especially since everyone would be bound to assume that such generous assistance had come directly from my grandfather. But who learns the secrets and uncertainties of a household more thoroughly and more rapidly than its

112

maids? And knowing that these girls would be more than likely to report back to Mrs. Long, I declined, hiring for the time being, a daily woman of sturdy appearance and dull understanding, whose main function was to show that we *had* a servant should anyone call. And for the rest of that exhausting summer I led a double life, officially residing at the Station Hotel until the house should be considered ready, maintaining, for all I was worth, the image of myself as a young socialite playing at dolls' houses in Aireville Terrace. Concealing the reality.

And what I remember of those hectic days is not the fatigue but the exhilaration, the joy and the fun of working altogether towards the same goal. There were grazed knees and chapped hands and frayed tempers, of course, in plenty, but nothing which could not be quickly absorbed by our shared excitement, our sometimes quite giddy laughter.

At Victorine's direction, I sorted through acres of household linen, soaked it, boiled it, scrubbed it, wrung it out until my back ached and then, doing up my hair, putting on a lacy blouse, a satin sash, a dainty summer skirt, went tripping down Commercial Street and Corporation Place to Station Square, acknowledging with an appropriate smile every tall silk hat that was raised to me, every matron who condescended to nod in my direction from her carriage. I cut up old petticoats and stockings for dusters, dipped the household brooms in boiling suds—an awkward procedure—to toughen them and make them last and then, with the air of a girl who has nothing to think of but pleasure, I would spend an hour browsing in what passed in Bradeswick for fashionable shops, invariably purchasing some folly, some extravagance, usually as a gift for my mother who needed gifts every now and then, in order that I might be recognized by these milliners and haberdashers and grocers as Miss Heron of Paris and Rome and Clarrow Fell.

On Sunday mornings we took part in Bradeswick's church parade, attending a service with which we were not familiar, accompanied by a display of social climbing and clawing, of jockeying for position which we recognized only too well. On Sunday afternoons we walked for an hour in the park and listened to the ironworks band, my mother causing as great a sensation as she intended in her glorious hat, sweeping back into the hotel rather as if it were an amusing little *pied-à-terre* she was thinking of buying, the waiters hurrying to bring

113

her tea and sugary little cakes which, with an air of complete inattention and no conception of the size of our bill, she would eat by the basketful.

Bradeswick had never seen her like and to my immense relief, found no reason to hide its fascination.

"Here's Madame Junot," was the daily chorus of the Hotel's commercial guests, competing like schoolboys for her attention.

"Goodness me, it's Lavinia Blackwood," said a dapper little man, coming to a halt before her with the air of an aging fox-terrier.

"Alas, no more, dear Septimus Cross," she replied, scrutinizing him through a languorously raised lorgnette.

It was the former manager of Bradeswick Commercial Bank, now also a director of the Bradeswick Tramways and Omnibus Company and a town councilor, he hastened to inform her, the very same gentleman who had once kissed her with such enthusiasm under the mistletoe that he had broken Miss Jemima Copthorne Heron's heart.

"Dear Septimus," she enthused later, "he was so desperately in love with me. Quite ancient, of course, even then, and one could hardly think of becoming a banker's wife. Not at fifteen—since they are obliged to be so fearfully proper. But he has never married, you know. How sweet."

The following afternoon, at her tea-time, the foyer quite suddenly was filled by the bulk of a single man, sixteen or seventeen stones of prosperous living encased in the very best quality gentleman's suiting, a fancy brocade waistcoat, a ponderous watch-chain.

"Good God," he declared, evidently thunderstruck, "it's Lavinia Blackwood."

"No, dear Samuel Greenlaw, it most decidedly is not. Lavinia *Blackwood* was a hundred years ago."

He was *the* Mr. Greenlaw, or one of them, of Greenlaw and Clough, the Ironworks, semi-retired now, of course, and a widower with sons in the business and nothing to do all day but eat his four square meals, drink his hock and his claret and walk down to the Station Hotel for a game of whist.

"Dear Sam," she said that night, her mouth amused but her eyes shining, admiration proving itself once again the only balm her soul required.

"And he was in love with you too, I suppose."

"Do you know, I rather think he was, for he followed me around the whole of one summer like a great faithful sheepdog, except that he was not faithful, of course, because he was engaged to Evelina Clough. He had been engaged to her *forever* and could somehow never bring himself to name the day. Naturally he had to marry her, one knew that, because she was his father's partner's daughter and he could hardly let her shares in the company go to another man. But he was a most reluctant bridegroom just the same and even when I had married your father he was attentive to me, very much on hand when I needed someone to chat to as one so often does.''

"You are not bored then, mother?"

"No, dear. Not yet."

But I was aware, nevertheless, of the need for haste. If suddenly she should tire of her card-parties and her tea-parties with Mr. Cross and Mr. Greenlaw who, to my relief, seemed quite happy to pay for the cakes, I could not be certain of preventing her from flitting off, not to Paris, perhaps, since she still believed her debts unpaid, but to London at the very least, where types like Jean-François must surely abound.

To work, then. Victorine and I together took up the carpets one by one, carried them outdoors, shook them, beat them, washed them in vinegar to refresh their colors and then in rosewater to kill the vinegary smell. We swept and washed the bare floors, sprinkled the clean boards with a concoction of black pepper and tobacco that was guaranteed, according to Victorine, to drive the moths away and laid each carpet carefully down again. We forced Luc—no easy task— to whitewash the cellars while Madelon, who needed no forcing at all, sat patiently mending curtains, sewing tiny muslin bags to hold lavender and sweet herbs for our linen cupboards and drawers, or leaves of pennyroyal to press between our sheets and mattresses, a sure remedy, we hoped, for keeping bed bugs away.

I peeled the dark brown paper from the walls or allowed it to fall off, exhausted by age, while Victorine mixed gallons of flour and water paste. And then, having argued mildly over colors and designs, considering at length the nosegays of primroses and forget-me-nots on a white background which were Madelon's choice, the bold, full-blown roses which appealed to Victorine, the gold damask which took my eye, we consulted a price-list and realized our alternatives had narrowed to an insipid paisley pattern or plain bottle green.

"Hideous," exclaimed my mother when consulted. "But no

matter. Mr. Samuel Greenlaw has lately been doing up his boardroom, most elegantly he tells me, with a new kind of wallpaper which can hardly be distinguished from watered silk. I feel quite certain that he has simply rolls and rolls of it left and would be positively grateful to have it taken off his hands."

It arrived a day or so later on an ironworks delivery van, expensive, elegant, equal quantities of apple-green and the pale gold I had so coveted.

"And you shall have your roses and your forget-me-nots too, girls," my mother said with a wink, "just as soon as I have explained to Mr. Septimus Cross how badly *his* parlor is in need of refurbishing."

She brought Mr. Samuel Greenlaw to Aireville Terrace the following afternoon to inspect his generosity and, having duly praised the excellence of his taste and his disposition she took him outside and, with an air of limpid innocence, spoke words I had never expected to hear on her tongue.

"My goodness, those drainpipes have a most peculiar look about them! What can it be?"

"Rust," declared Mr. Greenlaw.

"Heavens! How very unhealthy. Whatever can one *do*."

One could leave it to Mr. Greenlaw, as she had always intended, and quite soon the ironworks van stood once again outside our door, attending to our drainage and our guttering and installing a pair of wrought-iron gates for good measure.

We stood around Mr. Greenlaw and thanked him in chorus.

"If a job's worth doing," he said, not in the least embarrassed by our praises, "then it's worth doing well. And preferably by a Greenlaw of Greenlaw & Clough."

"I am going to Leeds tomorrow with Mr. Septimus Cross," murmured my mother, "to help him choose a new carpet for his drawing room."

His old one was delivered to us soon afterwards, in excellent condition; a design of pale rosebuds on a cream ground which seemed most surprisingly youthful when one considered the withered appearance of Mr. Cross.

My mother brought Mr. Greenlaw to have a look at it and having agreed, somewhat peevishly, that it was a generous gift, he cast a swift glance around him and announced abruptly, "That fire-grate could do with changing. And I'm bound to point out to you, Lavinia, that the gas in this house has never been reliable."

"Heavens! You mean dangerous? That settles it. We cannot stay here to be poisoned in our beds. Come girls, we must pack and return at once to France."

"I do believe," said Mr. Greenlaw stoutly, "that I can find a simpler solution than that." And returning at once to the premises of Greenlaw & Clough he sent us a cheerful, talkative little man who replaced our fire-grates and our fenders, adjusted our gas brackets and, as a final flourish, brought us a quite hideous but doubtless well-intentioned hat and umbrella stand in massive black iron which entirely dominated our hall.

"Thank you, Mr. Greenlaw," we dutifully said.

We spent a long, tedious day removing the stains and ring marks from Miss Jemima Copthorne Heron's mahogany sideboards by rubbing them with the corks of champagne bottles—my mother and Mr. Greenlaw having drunk the champagne—and then polishing each piece thoroughly, if not lovingly, with linseed oil and turpentine. Victorine and I, our sleeves turned up beyond the elbow, our hair bundled into mop-caps, washed five years of Bradeswick grime from the windows and then polished them to a diamond sparkle with the juice of a lemon, while Madelon, whose body was not adapted to perching on ladders, busied herself with the more delicate cleaning of Miss Jemima's silver, using the tops of cotton stockings which the ever-resourceful Victorine had boiled in milk and hartshorn, a witch's brew which had converted them to polishing cloths.

We found unexpected treasures, lace tablecloths as fine as cobwebs stuffed at the back of a dresser which Madelon, with the aid of some skillful needlework and a few ribbons transformed into evening shawls: a box full of exquisite embroideries under a bed which she carefully framed and hung on the drawing-room walls: a hoard of china figurines, rustic but colorful, quite valuable we thought, which helped provide the personal touch, even if not personal to us, which made a home.

"I do believe we have finished now, Victorine," I said, having arranged these ornaments several times over until they were *almost* to my satisfaction.

Surely, if not absolutely, we must be near the end? Surely now I could settle our account at the Station Hotel before it grew any larger, and move my mother in? Victorine, who had been born, it seemed, with an awareness of these things, would be the one to know.

"Yes," she said, casting a critical eye about her, "I'd say the house is just about done. So now there's the garden."

I found myself perfectly happy to accept Amyas's offer of help for that, pretending to anyone who cared to inquire and just a little to myself that the two taciturn countrymen soon uprooting our weeds and pruning a wilderness of shrubs and hoary, querulous old trees had been sent at the express wish of my grandfather, the Squire. And in the somewhat forlorn hope that he might experience a change of heart and come to call, I hired, in addition to my bovine scrub-woman, a little twelve-year-old housemaid straight from a charity school, chosen neither for her willingness to please nor her domestic skills, of which she had none, but because her fresh complexion and trim shape would give her the air of a luxury servant when she answered our door and served our tea.

The first stage of my campaign was nearly won.

There was a morning in mid-August when I truly believed that Chance had finally tired of the game of throwing obstacles in my path and made up her mind, instead, to smile. The day began with a present of grouse from the Manor, the first of the season, delivered by Amyas but, he hastened to assure me, the Squire's gift just the same, shot by his own gun over his own moor at Clarrow Fell. I decided to believe him.

"What a beautiful day, Amyas."

"Yes. Is there anything I can do for you?"

"If you would please give my best wishes to my grandfather."

The sun came out, parting the clouds, offering me a glorious preview of a future in which I would sweep away old prejudices, the shadows of old wrongs, as surely as these beams of sunlight. How could I fail? Failure, particularly on this lovely morning, was an attitude I simply did not possess. And an hour later, in confirmation of my optimism, a smart town landau stopped at my new iron gate, the coachman descended, my maid opened the door looking as pert and pretty as anyone could desire, and received from him, the visiting cards of Mr. Samuel Greenlaw's two daughters-in-law, Mrs. Albert and Mrs. Benjamin.

I walked out into the sunshine again, considering the significance of these cards and the best use I could make of them. I had

118

seen the Greenlaw ladies in church several times, stout, serviceable matrons in their middle thirties, whose only motive in wishing to be acquainted with us must be alarm about my mother's association with their father-in-law, who still firmly held the family purse-strings. Naturally they, and no doubt their husbands, would be concerned with matters of inheritance, shares in the Ironworks Company, seats on the board, and would know all too well what havoc a woman of my mother's reputation could play with such things. And in these cases there were two recognized methods of attack. One could snub the woman and encourage one's friends to snub her in the hope that, starved of society, she would give up and go away. Or one could get to know one's enemy, assess the extent of the threat she represented and, hopefully, uncover her weaknesses, the better, at need, to dismay her. Clearly the Greenlaws had decided it would be safer to confront Madame Junot than to ignore her, but their motives did not greatly worry me. The important thing was that they had made the first move, which could only have come from them. As newcomers to the neighborhood it would have been incorrect for us to leave cards or to visit anyone to whom we had less than a specific letter of introduction. But now, with those two squares of glossy, deckle-edged paper prominently displayed in a silver dish on our hall table, I was in a position to persuade my mother, who did not care whether the Greenlaw ladies snubbed her or not, to send cards of her own. The way would then be open for Mrs. Albert and Mrs. Benjamin to visit us, just a polite quarter of an hour, perhaps, between the conventional calling hours of eleven and four o'clock, nothing more than a cup of weak tea and a few stilted remarks about the weather which would, nonetheless, give us the right, at a discreet interval, to pay a similar call on them.

It was the *entrée* I needed, not just to the Greenlaws but to Mrs. Esmeralda Naseby of the Brewery who was known to keep a sharp eye on any social innovations of the Ironworks ladies, and through Mrs. Naseby to Lady Potterton, mistress of Dawney Park and the hunt ball. And if Mr. Samuel Greenlaw should prove to be as susceptible as his relatives feared, then I saw no reason why my mother should not marry him. What better solution could possibly be devised for her than this safe anchorage? Why, when it was so very right for her, had I not thought of it before? Mrs. Samuel Greenlaw, my mother, her butterfly wings clipped by respectability but no longer in danger of the bruising and scorching so casually inflicted by men like Jean-

François. Mrs. Greenlaw! Yes. For I might not always be on hand to protect her, and it had a reassuring sound.

Papa Greenlaw. Had she ever dissolved her union with Papa Junot? Had there been anything of a legal nature to dissolve? I must remember to ask her this evening while it was fresh in my mind. But then, my head suddenly empty of everything but equal measures of joy and fright, I heard a horseman at the gate, turned and saw Robin Esmond already on the path, his arms full of roses.

And having waited for him, longed for him, having uprooted my family and brought them to Bradeswick in order to see him again, I suddenly could not bear to look. Had I longed and dreamed too much? Had I imagined him, invented him even, to suit the needs of a particular moment which may now have passed? He was little more than a stranger, after all, and of a type, a background, a culture so unfamiliar to me that I had no real competence to judge. Why had I waited until now to remind myself of this cold reality?

"Olivia," he said, and I was standing in blue air and sunshine, giddy with relief and excitement, holding out my hands to a lover.

He was exactly, not so much as I *remembered* but as I *knew* him, his hair falling in those fine, pale feathers across a tanned forehead, his long mouth whimsical, smiling at his own eagerness and haste, his unkempt burden of roses. He had returned from Cambridge late last night and had joined the Pottertons' shooting party this morning on their moor just beyond Bradeswick Green. A run-of-the-mill sort of day, he had thought, until somebody had casually mentioned my name. Luckily he had ridden out to the shoot and, abandoning everything, had come absolutely hell for leather to Aireville Terrace, acquiring the roses on the way.

He had no idea now what to do with them. Neither had I. They were transferred from his arms to mine, stray thorns catching in his shabby, comfortable tweed jacket, their perfume, so close to my nostrils, threatening, with no consideration whatsoever for romance, to make me sneeze. And we stood smiling at each other, just smiling, absorbed by gladness, dazzled by the sheer splendor of standing close together in an untidy garden on an ordinary August afternoon.

Chance was still proving herself not merely generous but bountiful, heaping upon me the richness of his reality. I was so immeasurably happy that had it been only a degree or so less I might also have been terrified.

"Is that your horse?" demanded Luc, materializing from the branches of the chestnut tree above us. "That one, I mean—the skinny brown one?"

But Robin had been a boy himself, not too long ago, in the monastic, mischievous world of the "good public school" and Luc's appearance did not dismay him.

"Yes, that's my horse."

"Well, it's loose."

"And you had nothing to do with it, I suppose?"

"Never."

"All right. But I expect you'll be able to catch him."

"How much?"

"*Luc!*" I said, my voice giving warning that unless he mended his manners retribution would certainly follow.

"Sixpence," said Robin, man to man, taking no notice.

"Eightpence."

"Sixpence. Or, of course, I could whistle and he might just come back on his own."

The black Junot eyebrows flew upwards at a wide angle, the cherubic mouth starting to form the word "sevenpence" until the Junot mind, which was not too sure as yet of the purchasing power of the English penny, thought better of it and he ran off to catch the brown mare which had not, in fact, strayed very far.

"You won't pay him, of course, Robin."

"Oh yes I will. One should never underestimate the nuisance value of a little brother. It's well worth the odd sixpence or two to have him on my side."

I smiled again, blissfully self-satisfied. Every one of my instincts about him had been right. He was not only handsome. He was humorous and amiable. He was kind.

Victorine was around the back hoeing a border, a red scarf tied gipsy-fashion around her head, her sleeves turned up and her collar down.

"Hello," he said, recognizing a lady, "I'm so glad to meet you. I say what a marvelous idea. You're making a herb-garden, aren't you? What are you putting in?"

"I'm not certain," she said, leaning on her hoe, ready to talk sense to him if he turned out to be sensible; not in the least shy, "Parsley and chives, which seem straightforward enough. Coriander

121

and dill, lemon verbena. And something big to fill in that windy corner."

"Try lovage. It grows six feet tall and the flowers are pretty. Or marshmallow. It grows to about four feet if you can nurse it through the winter. You'd have to plant it very deep."

How wonderful that he knew such things, that he could speak with such quiet assurance on these eternal issues of soil and seed, flowering and ripening, which would be so alien to the breed of Jean-François.

"You must be Robin," murmured Madelon, hovering on the edge of the pathway, uncertain with young men since her encounter with Jean-François but making the effort for my sake.

"Yes I am. And you're Madelon." There was no need for him to say more, the innate *pleasantness* of his tone, of his nature, convincing her at once that this man was no threat but almost certainly a friend, a brother.

The miracle had occurred. The people I loved were showing every sign of being ready to love each other. Chance was not merely a great lady. She was a queen.

"The thing is," he said, smiling down at me, leaning towards me with that easy lounging charm "from tomorrow morning, I've got the loan of a motor car."

"Robin! What kind of people have motor cars to *lend?*"

"Oh—just a chap I was at school with who always seems to have two of everything. He's asked me to feed it and water it while he's in Biarritz."

"Like a horse?"

"That's right. And if I can manage to get it down here in one piece tomorrow morning I was wondering . . . ?"

"Yes, Robin—I will."

No sunshine, ever, anywhere in the world, had ever been so warm and bright. I could feel it still dancing on my skin as I returned to the Station Hotel that night, my eyes still dazzled, my exultation reflecting, perhaps, in the smile I gave to my mother's commercial gentlemen, my mind according only a minimum of notice to the newcomer who—and I remembered this—appeared to be keeping his distance, not physically but, nevertheless, quite positively from the rest.

He bowed to me very slightly as I entered the foyer and went to fetch my key, watching me, I knew, as I walked away. A little later I passed him on the stairs and he bowed again and wished me a good evening, his shrewd eyes calculating whether or not I was here alone and what advantage he could best take of it, his accent, which was quite neutral like mine and Victorine's, identifying him as yet another man who came from everywhere and nowhere, a rootless and, by the cut of his coat, expensive wanderer. He was there again when I went in to dine, his table close enough for me to hear him ordering his oysters and his wine, his presence strong enough to intrude, just a little, into my blissful haze. I had, in this short afternoon, arranged my life, my mother's life, everybody's lives, entirely to my satisfaction, and what I wanted now was the leisure in which to work out the details of my various schemes, not the casual, self-interested admiration of strangers.

I saw him again, much later, returning from whatever pleasures Bradeswick had to offer a gentleman of his type, a tall silk hat on his head, a black silk-lined cape swinging about his shoulders, the discreet glimmer of gold shirt studs, the sudden and decidedly indiscreet sparkle of a diamond on the hand that removed his hat.

"We meet again," he said.

"Again? I beg your pardon. I was not aware that we had met at all."

"Have we not? Then I think we should—don't you?"

But my cool, sharp words of discouragement were never spoken for at that moment my mother swept out of the cardroom, slightly tipsy and disheveled, immeasurably entrancing, ponderous Mr. Greenlaw and dapper little Mr. Cross at her side. And my lovely, miraculous day was ended.

"It's Lavinia Blackwood," the stranger said, just as those other two gentlemen had done a month ago.

"Yes?" But this time there was no recognition in her face, no witty response about Lavinia Blackwood being a hundred years ago, just the question in her voice, the leap of curiosity and pleasure in her eyes at the sight—after this long abstinence—of a handsome, sophisticated man.

He looked at least thirty, I calculated, of no more than medium height but with an impression of great physical alertness, a kind of whipcord toughness that made him a shade less civilized, perhaps, than his white brocade waistcoat and jeweled cuff-links implied. He was extremely dark in a bronzed, sun-dried fashion that was not wholly

European, with something about him, despite those truly immaculate evening clothes and beautifully manicured hands, of the caution that comes from hot and dangerous places where the climate itself is an enemy. A man whose practiced drawing-room manner, I thought, did not quite conceal his air of calculating the distance to the next oasis or the next crock of gold; his air of not only keeping a sharp lookout for a knife in his back but of being ready, at any given moment, to retaliate.

"Yes, I was Lavinia Blackwood." And it was clear that, although she still did not remember him, she would dearly like to.

"Max de Haan," he said, giving her his slight bow, his long hard mouth looking amused and, most oddly familiar to me, although I could not place it."

"Max!"

"Yes, Lavinia. Max."

For a moment she looked quite stunned and then, with the effervescence of champagne escaping its cork, delight came bubbling out of her.

"Max! Is it possible? My dear boy, I thought you were dead, or simply expected that you would be—romantically, of course, with a jealous husband's dagger in your back at the very least."

"I would find nothing romantic in that, Lavinia."

"Well no, dear, I daresay, although you cannot deny it would seem appropriate. But Max! And looking so very prosperous too, which should surprise no one. Now then—you will find it hard to credit, I know, but this beautiful woman standing beside me is my daughter. I hope you are going to be very astonished about that."

"Amazed."

Amused, I thought, and abominably sure of himself, standing there looking us over, making up his mind which of us would suit him best, never doubting his ability to persuade or to purchase either or both.

And it was unfair. It was cruel. And, even worse than that, it was entirely predictable for I should have known it all along. I had relaxed my guard, disobeyed my own rules, permitted myself to believe that I could have what I wanted simply by wanting it. I should have known better. I would have known better, had not that raddled old hag called Chance blinded my eyes. Oh yes, she had had her sport with me today, there was no denying it, had led me on and lulled me, and then, just as I was feeling so ridiculously safe and certain, had tittered behind her faithless hand and beckoned Jean-François back into my life again.

SEVEN

His real name, I learned the next morning, was Maxim Heron, his parents having been a Miss Rosella de Haan, half Spanish, half Dutch, more than half mad according to my own still highly excited mother, and Vivian Heron, the Squire's unsatisfactory younger brother who had possessed the art of piercing the ace of diamonds with ten consecutive pistol shots, and not much else.

"So he is the Squire's nephew—my father's cousin?"

"I daresay he is. But you will never see him at Clarrow. The Squire forbade him to set foot on Heron land—oh—years ago, just before I ran away. And I believe it was the Squire who took his name away too. Either he called himself de Haan or nothing would be done to clear up the scandal and the debts."

Of course. He was a gambler and a spendthrift. I had known it all along. He had borrowed money he could not pay or had never intended to pay, in true Jean-François fashion. What else?

"But no," my mother said, blissfully unaware of my desire to think ill of him, "Max had no debts. Max never lost at cards, and that was the trouble, or part of it, for I never knew the whole. Money was owing to him, not the other way round, and what the Squire objected to was the way he set about collecting it. Debts of honor must be paid, we all know that. But there are ways and means, after all—*honorable* ways— of twisting a man's arm and Max never took any notice of that. He just wanted his money. But to say that the whole upper school at Hexingham was in terror of him and to expel him for it was a little hysterical, in my opinion. Heavens—how the

Squire thrashed him the night they sent him home. It was quite terrible. Even your father thought it on the harsh side, and I seem to remember Amyas being sick. Poor Max—not that he cared, of course. Max never cared about anything but money and now he seems to have plenty of that."

He had been yet another of the unwanted or inconvenient children—like Amyas and Robin—growing up at Clarrow under the guardianship of the Squire and, during her brief first marriage my mother had known him, not well, perhaps, but as well—she thought— as anyone. His father, the feckless Vivian, had caused the Squire untold sorrow and expense, yet when he died in squalid Italian lodgings of a gunshot wound, self-inflicted, they said, to avoid his creditors— although my mother wondered about that—no one could have moved more rapidly than Squire Heron to the assistance of the widow and her difficult, half-foreign son. The lady had taken no persuading, it appeared, either to return to her de Haan kin in Madrid or perhaps in Amsterdam, my mother was not quite certain, or to send to Clarrow Fell a handsome seven-year-old who had been a thorn in the Squire's side ever since.

But the Squire, nevertheless, had done his duty, had taught the boy to ride and shoot and pay lip service, if nothing else, to the code of the English country gentleman. He had engaged tutors to teach him and Amyas Latin and Greek and then, keeping Amyas at home, had sent Max to Hexingham, the school all the young Herons attended, where he had not only relieved his classmates of their pocket-money but had committed other misdemeanors of a sexual nature, my mother supposed, since no one had been too explicit about it. But it had been very serious, very bad. The Squire had been thoroughly disgusted, Max unrepentant. And she vividly remembered their final encounter, the cynical young man and the disillusioned old one standing in the hall at Clarrow beneath the great window, the jeweled glass shedding its emerald and azure rays on their hard faces, huge logs crackling in the hearth, exploding every now and then into lethal showers of sparks, anger reflecting anger. A clash of wills which had ended with the dismissal of Maxim Heron from the family; Max de Haan being sent off that same night to Amsterdam or Madrid or wherever it was that one might locate his mother's kin.

And after that, who knows? My mother shrugged fluid shoulders. They had discovered gold in the Transvaal had they not, fifteen

126

years ago, reefs of it running thirty precious miles long across the Rand which, until then, everybody had been content to leave to the Boers. She knew all about it because it had been one of the great regrets of Emil Junot's life that he had taken part in neither the gold-rush to Witwatersrand nor the diamond-rush to Kimberley which had preceded it.

But Max de Haan, although too young, she thought, to have done anything spectacular with diamonds, had certainly been involved in the rough and often murderous scramble for gold. He had explained it all to her last night over a bottle of the hotel's best champagne, so clearly that she felt she had actually seen it for herself. Fifteen years ago he had owned a pickaxe and a tent pitched alongside the diggings of the mining camp they had called Johannesburg, a perilous place beyond the reach of any law but the most basic rules of survival, where men settled their own disputes with fists and knives and either learned to watch their backs—like Max—or died. A couple of years ago, or thereabouts, he had left behind a stone and gas-lit city—still named Johannesburg—where fifty thousand Europeans conducted themselves with style. And he had considerably fired her imagination by his account of the quality and richness of life any man of initiative might now enjoy in Colonial Africa; the excellent French champagne to be had, of all places, at the Grand Hotel, Pretoria, which for years he had regarded as a second home; the warm evenings of old brandy and good conversation on the verandah of a house he had owned at Bloemfontein—Flowers-in-the-Springs, what a lovely name; the receptions held by the great "gold-bug" himself, Mr. Cecil Rhodes, at what sounded more like an imperial palace than his home, high in the hills above Cape Town. And in these conditions, taking into account that Max de Haan had never shown himself to be either scrupulous or tender-hearted, how could I ever doubt that he actually possessed the fortune which, last night, he had certainly implied.

Of course he was rich.

Nonsense, I cautioned her, hoping I was right. Fool's gold. Emil Junot's gold. The kind that evaporated at the turn of a card; unreliable, unsound like the man himself. I could even prove it. If his goldfields had been reaping so rich a harvest, why had he left them all behind?

"Ah well, dear," she said, "discretion, you know, has always been better than valor. *Of course* you know. Emil Junot would not have stayed there either, not now when all those shells have started to fly."

And, apart from shells and Mauser bullets and siege-fever, had I never heard of Jameson's Raid? That gallant attempt by a force of Rhodesian policemen and English public schoolboys out for a lark, to take over the Transvaal for themselves? Or rather for Cecil Rhodes who, having failed to persuade the British Government to send in its troops, had decided to hire his own. Had the raid succeeded, Johannesburg would have fallen, the Boers would have been driven into the sea or at least into a position from which they could no longer interfere with foreign—predominantly British—administration of Transvaal gold. Unfortunately, for reasons Max did not specify, it had failed. And for a while, Johannesburg's Europeans had felt themselves to be somewhat at risk, a great many of them—anyone, in fact, who was suspected of even the slightest involvement in the Raid—being liable to short but decidedly uncomfortable terms of imprisonment. My mother did not *quite* know whether Max had actually gone to prison or whether, seeing his friends rounded up one by one, had again put discretion before valor and made his escape, to Madeira she thought, where it rather sounded to her as if he had a financial interest of some kind in wine.

"Well then, mother, if he ran away, he must have left his gold behind him."

"Oh no, dear," and now she was tremendously amused. "This is one instance in which you must admit that I have more knowledge of the world than you, Olivia. Men like Max de Haan do not leave their money behind. He could spend it, or even give it away—although that is unlikely—but leave it behind—my dear!—*never!*"

I had more need than ever now of haste. The following morning my mother declined, albeit most charmingly, the offer of a ride in Robin's dark blue Lanchester, declaring that motor cars, like telephones, were of neither her style nor her era, and drove off instead in a high-perch sporting phaeton with Max de Haan at the reins. The day after she went with him to the fashionable spa town of Harrogate from which she returned very late and highly elated, to face the combined reprimands of her eldest daughter and Mr. Samuel Greenlaw to whom she had promised an evening of bridge. The day after that I settled our bill at the Station Hotel while she was still upstairs lingering over her breakfast, packed her bags myself and had them

128

carried around to Aireville Terrace, arranged fresh flowers in the best front bedroom, installed her gowns, her hats, her feather boas, her trailing chiffons, in their new cupboards, and served dinner that evening in our own home.

"I am sure this is all quite delightful," she said, "if a little sudden . . . ?"

"Essential, mother. Our money is running out."

"Oh darling—*that!*"

She had made an agreeable niche for herself at the Station Hotel. She could not stay there forever, she fully accepted that. But nothing prevented her from importing to Aireville Terrace the aspects of life which had pleased her best, her five o'clock teas, the sugary cakes and biscuits baked now by Victorine, the unending river not of conversation but of small-talk, gossip, clever remarks made for the sake of cleverness, *chat*; the almost continuous game of cards she carried virtually unbroken from one evening to the next, at which Mr. Greenlaw and Mr. Cross—but not Mr. de Haan—would usually let her win.

For the moment she was comfortable, carefree, she was *amused*, and would do herself no harm so long as I remained on hand to divert her attention from Mr. de Haan to Mr. Greenlaw once in a while. The first part of my plan was not merely complete, it was a resounding success. We had a home. We had an income which, however slender, was paid regularly at the end of every month into a reputable bank. We had the framework of a life and now it was up to me—since no one else would stir themselves—to create the fabric, weaving into it, after all, only the things to which most girls felt themselves entitled.

And no matter how often Aunt Sibylla might suggest that my sisters could not hope for marriage while even I would have my work cut out to get myself off the shelf, I refused, categorically, to believe it. Watching the Sunday afternoon strollers in Bradeswick Park, I had seen a number of solid young businessmen who would have sense enough, I thought, once it had been pointed out to them, to realize that capable, tireless, resourceful Victorine would make a far better wife, in the long run, than some insipid little chit with nothing to recommend her but a virtuous mother and a few hundred pounds a year. I had seen other young men gazing at Madelon in a thunderstruck fashion I found most encouraging, being well aware how easily men in that condition are apt to lose their heads. I *wanted* the handsomest man I could find after Robin to lose his head over Madelon, who, I rather imagined, would be only too pleased to lose her own head in return. I wanted to see Victorine happy and settled, perhaps in one of the smart new villas I had noticed in suburban Bradeswick Green, keeping her own carriage and visiting me at the Manor. I wanted to see her children and my children and pretty, eternally childlike Madelon gathered around a log fire at Christmas time, her husband and my husband and Madelon's husband drinking spiced punch beneath the great window in the hall. I wanted Luc to attend a good school, Eton or Hexingham, where he could be turned into an English gentleman like Guy and Robin. I wanted Sam Greenlaw for my mother.

It was not impossible. Aunt Sibylla might continue to raise her eyebrows whenever I happened to meet her and mention the invitations which were already *pouring in* for Alys from Pottertons and Nasebys and others who remained apparently unaware of me. I would not be despondent. And in the meantime, while I considered how best to tackle the problem, we prepared ourselves—at my insistence—like careful athletes for the fray, soaking our hands and our elbows nightly in oil of almonds and honey to soften them, lemon juice to whiten them, washing our faces in an infusion of elderflowers and violets to procure a fashionably pale complexion, rinsing Madelon's hair with water of chamomile flowers to make it lighter, my hair and Victorine's in rosemary and sage to enhance the dark sheen.

"What an absolute bore," said Victorine, "and an even more absolute waste of time."

"But one simply *must*," said Madelon, who believed, like my mother, that to be beautiful was the first essential of life.

"Yes, one must," I replied, for I was determined that no one in Bradeswick would ever mistake my sister, Victorine, for a housemaid as a Parisian doctor had once done. I wanted her to become dignified if she refused to be pretty. I wanted her and Madelon to be happy. Now that my own relationship with Robin had begun to blossom and seemed to flourish, I was suddenly in a great hurry to meet the men who would make my sisters blossom in the same glorious way.

And I knew of three people who might, either by accident or design, stand in the way of it, my grandfather, Max de Haan and Alys.

The Squire continued to hold himself aloof, inquiring as to my welfare occasionally through Amyas. Alys remained with her father

130

in Bridlington. But Max de Haan, although never to be seen in the mornings, would put in an appearance most afternoons around two o'clock, driving his sporting carriage or riding a sleek, pitch-black mare which my brother Luc—far from turning loose to collect a six-pence—would walk for hours up and down Aireville Terrace, entirely free of charge.

Luc was, from the very first, enormously impressed by Max, not only by his air of fashion and consequence but by his *possessions*; the diamond on his finger, the pearl stick-pin in his tie, his black snakeskin cigar case with the letter M displayed in precious stones, the mother-of-pearl case he used in the evenings set with a large ruby, the dazzling display of cuff-links which drew one's attention, whether one cared to admit it or not, to the thin, puckered line of an old scar running along the back of his left hand and disappearing inside his sleeve.

But it was the sleeve not the scar which interested my brother who, with an inbred knowledge of such things, went into raptures over the quality of the de Haan wardrobe, the fine textures and subtle shadings of his country tweeds and flannels, the superb cut of his morning suits, his narrow trousers, and elegant pointed shoes; the multiplicity of his hats, the Homburgs and straw-boaters, the silk toppers and curly-brimmed beavers, the tweed caps and deerstalkers, the bush hat which Luc declared he must have taken—or won in a card game—from a Boer.

There was no doubt that for each and every activity appropriate to a gentleman, for riding, driving, hunting, shooting, for strolling through city streets or tramping across a plowed field, for dining, theater-going, or simply lounging, and flirting in a lady's drawing room, Max de Haan could present himself correctly, fashionably, even daringly dressed. His embroidered Chinese dressing gowns were the cause of great flutterings—according to Luc—among the chamber-maids at the Station Hotel, his blazers and silk scarves having much the same effect in Bradeswick Park on Sunday afternoons, the scarlet silk sash he sometimes wore with a dinner-jacket arousing the con-tempt of Mr. Greenlaw who, even for the most informal of evening entertainments, wore his old-fashioned dress-coat, its tails far too long nowadays—said Luc—for anybody but a butler or a head waiter.

But the portly and rather pompous Mr. Greenlaw continued to stand his ground.

"Dinner-jackets," he snorted. "Monkey jackets, more like. And what's that fellow doing here in Bradeswick in the first place? That's what I'd like to know."

I would have liked to know it too. But, whatever it was, too much of it was being done in Aireville Terrace, Mr. de Haan taking up far too much of our space and my mother's time during the very hours of the day when *new* acquaintances, *useful* acquaintances might be expected to call, continuously smoking his thin black cigars in leisurely progression, one after the other, leaning against the mantelpiece or reclining in the best armchair in arrogant repose. He left his hat on the hallstand too, a familiarity I detested, its blatant presence there proclaiming him as one who had special privileges, rather than an ordinary guest who would enter a lady's drawing room with his hat in his hand.

One left umbrellas in hallstands with galoshes or document cases. Guests invited for the evening handed over cloaks and wraps and toppers to a servant who quickly put them away somewhere out of sight. But if any lady of consequence saw a gentleman's hat in our hall between the hours of luncheon and dinner-time she would think the worst. And even if the worst had not yet occurred, and I had made it my business to be very sure of that, we were not sufficiently well-established to be given the benefit of the doubt. Only those women whose reputations were beyond reproach could afford to take chances with etiquette. And, therefore, in our delicate circumstances, we could only hope to redeem my mother's past by the impeccable tone of our present lives. Not permanently, of course, but just long enough to get us married, after which I believed, cheerfully and wholeheartedly, that we would be able to do as we liked.

I had already returned the courtesy of the Mrs. Greenlaws' calling cards by sending cards of our own, my name printed in small letters beneath my mother's in the approved fashion. There seemed every likelihood that they would now proceed a stage further by paying us a visit quite soon and, therefore, knowing how sharply they would be on the lookout for any irregularity, I mentioned to my mother, without much hope, that it might be wise to restrict the visits of Max de Haan.

"Darling," she protested, giving me her startled blue gaze and her sweetest smile, "it is Bessie and Hattie Greenlaw we are expecting, not Queen Victoria. Poor Max—I had no idea you disliked him but since you do you will be pleased to know that he is going to Madeira for the winter. He describes himself as a wine-merchant, after all—Madeira wine—or at least he *sometimes* does, and I believe the climate in Funchal is permanently July. You need not worry that he will invite me to go with him either, for there will be fascinating acquaintances to be made in plenty on Madeira and he will see no sense in importing his own."

But "winter" lay several months away and although she did promise to see rather less of him, I noticed no sign of it.

"Damn fellow," continued to mutter Mr. Greenlaw. "Nothing but a professional card-player, if you ask me. Walked away with twenty-five of my guineas last night, cool as a cucumber."

"Well, we all knew his father," murmured little Mr. Cross, who as Bradeswick's principal banker for so many years, could be presumed to know a great deal about everybody.

"I've heard of him, of course," said Robin, his lack of interest causing me to hope that his mind was full of something else—or *me*. "But whatever he did—or didn't—it was twenty years ago and since I'm only twenty-five that makes him a shade before my time. Amyas must know all about him since they were brought up together, like Guy and me."

Amyas knew a great deal, as I was to discover the following afternoon when he and Max de Haan came face to face, one entering, the other leaving our garden gate. And before a word had been spoken I felt the enmity rise up between them, a quick rapier dart of it from Max, something heavier and deeper, something that could have been a long time festering, from Amyas.

"You must know each other," I said, most unusually flustered.

"We do. How are you, Max?"

"How am I?" Max de Haan tipped his hat to a jauntier angle, his diamond taking fire in the sunlight, a gesture openly designed to display the fortune he carried on his person, a gentleman whose affluence could be ascertained at a glance, without need for inquiry.

"I'm very well, Amyas. And you? Still running errands for the Squire?"

"I have been his land agent now for over fifteen years—as you know."

"And he pays you good wages?"

"He pays what a land agent is worth."

"I doubt that."

"Of course you do."

"Will you give him my regards, Amyas?"

"I'll tell him I've seen you."

"That's hardly the same. But it will suffice. Tell him I was looking prosperous, of course. Don't forget to mention that."

"I'll tell him. Is there anything else?"

"Yes, Amyas. You can remind him of the offer I made him. The way things are going he might soon be glad of it."

He tipped his hat again and strolled away, and after a long moment Amyas said quietly, "He is not a person with whom you should associate, Olivia."

"Good Heavens, Amyas, I know that very well. Just tell me about this offer—what and why?"

"He is trying to buy Clarrow Fell."

The house? Instinctively, fiercely, I meant my house.

"But no one can do that—surely? There's the entail—well isn't there?—which can't be broken."

And even in this dire extremity, when the foundation of all my hopes seemed threatened, Amyas retained his perfect calm.

"Only if you and the Squire both agree to it, in which case the entail would be declared void and the house could be offered for sale like any other."

"How dreadful."

"Do you really think so, Olivia? Shortly after Guy's death a letter came from Max suggesting exactly that, and offering a realistic enough figure. Naturally the Squire refused."

"And he has come here to try to persuade him?"

"Oh no. The Squire will not even see him. He knows that."

"Then what purpose . . . ?"

He smiled, a very small, very rare occurrence which had little to do with humor, nothing with pleasure.

"With Max there is always a purpose, you can be sure of it. The Squire will not sell to him. But you might. Why should you not, since there is no axe to grind between you and. presumably when the time comes, you will have to sell to somebody. He will have known all about you and your exact circumstances for years, you may be quite sure of it. For he is very thorough and when he wants something he will take endless pains. And he has connections or associates or people who owe him favors—and money—just about everywhere. He knew of Guy's death almost as soon as we did. He will have known of your visit here in the spring, and your decision to return. And now I believe he has come to negotiate with you."

He would negotiate in vain, I was in no doubt of it, for, in that golden month of August, I had discovered a great soaring cathedral of faith not in any particular creed but in life for its own sake and in myself, in the strength of my own good intentions, in my own ability to stand my ground and see things through. I awoke every bright, blue morning not only to the certainty of sunshine but of a bubbling, effervescent joy which never left me. My happiness was enormous, exuberant, irritating, no doubt, at times to those around me who were slightly less inclined to view the world through my rosy, breathless haze. Nothing, throughout those long, drowsy days of high summer, had any real power to disturb me. Nothing was too complex for me to unravel, no obstacle so solid that I could not laughingly blow it away and watch it scatter like the down of a spent dandelion. I knew exactly where I was going and, while this blaze of jubilation possessed me I carried everyone else along, my eyes far too dazzled to notice whether or not they really wished to come. And if any of the cooler, shrewder, or more sophisticated of my acquaintances—Max de Haan, perhaps, or even my grandfather—had told me that such exaltation was vulnerable and dangerous, since anyone who rides so high must expect a fall, I would have paid no heed.

I was invincible. I was irresistible that August. For who could resist me? Not Victorine, who might grumble but who, nevertheless, continued to anoint herself with my herbal preparations and to do her hair in the new way I had taught her. Not Madelon, who dutifully attended the piano lessons which bored her and the tennis lessons she feared would roughen her hands, because I believed they would be useful and would do her good. Not even my mother who, although fond of smoking one of Max de Haan's cigars after dinner at Aireville Terrace, had so far remembered my request not to do so in public.

Not Robin.

I saw him almost every day, drove with him in the borrowed motor car he found so exciting and which I detested; walked with him through deep summer woodland to the very peaks of those bold northern hills, excursions from which I returned wind-swept, a little footsore, easily inclined to fury when someone—was it Max de Haan?—

suggested it might have suited me better to take a civilized stroll in Bradeswick Park.

I saw him, in fact, so often that I, who so anxiously protected my mother's reputation, was fast compromising my own, our relationship causing sufficient comment for Aunt Sibylla to feel compelled to inform me that, despite anything I may have heard to the contrary, Robin would never be rich. Comfortably off, one day, perhaps, for his father had private means and future expectations as well as what must be supposed an adequate salary. But it should be borne in mind that the Colonel had recently married a new wife young enough to present him with a dozen sons for whom due financial provision would have to be made. Robin's share might, therefore, be less—far, far less—than I may have heard.

"She is warning you off," my mother said knowingly, looking rather pleased about it, "so that she can keep him in reserve for Alys. Not as a first choice, perhaps, because my sister's ambitions, at the moment, are running higher than that. I have it from Mr. Septimus Cross, who hears and sees everything in Bradeswick, that Sibylla is angling for a Potterton, no less. And why not? There is Clive, as I recall, the Potterton son and heir who was packed off to India to be a soldier for the very good reason that nothing else could be done with him. He must be nearly forty now, which is about the right age for an 'heir' to come home and marry. And then there is his cousin Felix who wants to be Member of Parliament for Bradeswick and Clarrow Fell and can't seem to manage it. Well, perhaps not Felix. I doubt if even my sister Sibylla could convince a politician that he can buy votes with Alys's good character. But considering the tales one hears of Clive, the Pottertons might be glad to settle for virginity. Because that dowry my sister speaks of *cannot* be extensive. Mr. Septimus Cross entirely agrees with me and, moreover, he has only an uncertain opinion of Alys. Sibylla may go on as much as she pleases about an engagement between Alys and my son Guy, but according to Mr. Cross, it was never official. And Mr. Cross finds that strange since he knows beyond question that, not only were Sibylla and the Squire very much in favor, but Guy himself was very keen to marry her. You will scarcely credit this but it was Alys who backed off, declaring that she was not yet ready for marriage. Not to Guy, in particular, you will notice, but to anyone! I actually felt sorry for Sibylla when Mr. Cross told me that. It is friendship, apparently, which Miss Alys values and, that being the case, one can perfectly understand why Sibylla feels the need to keep her options open. She will have to employ every scrap of her ingenuity to bring Clive Potterton up to scratch and, what then, if the young lady is still not ready? How very provoking for Sibylla who was ready for marriage herself, I can tell you, before she had turned fifteen and failed to bring it off until she was nearly thirty. But don't worry about them, darling. Sibylla may want a son-in-law and Alys may want a friend. It is what Robin wants, surely, which conerns us?"

Did I know what he wanted? What, at the end of every crowded day did I really remember of our conversation? He told me, with the sun in my eyes and a warm breeze in my hair, how much at ease he felt in the scholarly, somewhat unreal atmosphere of Cambridge. And I was simply glad that he had no taste for the café society of London. He told me of journalist friends, artist friends, whose views on life he found stimulating. But I never really heard the nature of those views, so relieved was I that none of these friends were women. He explained, at length, his reasons for taking a stand against the war in Africa, his dislike of imperialism, his rejection of the very things his father stood for. The Transvaal belonged to the Boers, India to the Indians. His father would have an apoplectic fit if he ever heard him say that, and the Squire would be none too pleased about it either. But there it was. It had never so much as crossed his father's mind to wonder what right one had to march into India or Africa or anywhere else one fancied and just take over. Men like Cecil Rhodes—or Max de Haan— would probably come straight out and say they were there for the money. Not so Colonel Esmond who considered it bad taste even to talk about money, much less make it. Colonel Esmond, and the Squire, simply knew themselves to be on the right side. Men like Max did not care. Robin possessed neither these comforting certainties nor so convenient a lack of scruples. Clearly he was one of the uneasy young men my grandfather had spoken of, seeing all the faults of the old order but undecided, as yet, how to build the new. I listened, hearing the anxiety in his voice, watching the trouble in his face, and what it really meant to me was that I had been spared the danger of seeing him obeying his father's summons to join the Imperial Yeomanry and hurry out to Africa. He would not throw his life away, like Guy and a dozen other of his schoolmates, so that men like Cecil Rhodes— and Max—might grow richer. He would stay here with me.

He asked me about my travels abroad and I brushed them aside, for those days were over, and asked him instead a quick flurry of questions about local matters, the Clarrow Hunt, the annual steeplechase from Clarrow Fell to the neighboring village of Appleburton, the famous public school of Hexingham.

He smiled, apparently more than willing to answer. He hunted three or four times a week throughout the winter, which was moderate enough when one considered the Pottertons who hunted every day of the season and talked of nothing else all the year round. He also took part in the steeplechase, but only for the fun of it, being disinclined to risk breaking his neck for a wager, like Clive Potterton. He had loathed Hexingham. It was all very well, he supposed, for the intrepid types and the regimental types, the "thin red line" and "stiff upper lip" men, the kind who rode to Johannesburg with Colonel Jameson or queued up to join the Imperial Yeomanry. Or the card-sharps, of course, like Max who would see themselves all right wherever they happened to be. But Robin had never quite seen the point of Hexingham. He had no team-spirit, he confessed. A game was a game and he had never been able to whip up the required degree of enthusiasm about which side won. Hexingham had been a bore.

I did not believe him. Not that I suspected him of telling lies. Rather, I read into his attitude the understatement, the deliberate playing down of reality to which I knew the English were prone. In my eyes he remained the perfect product of Hexingham and, therefore, could not really have disliked it. He had simply outgrown it, passed on to other things, and having suffered from time to time in the past the company of overgrown schoolboys, I was glad.

There remained the question of Alys. Naturally I had no right to question him about her but, even more naturally, one afternoon when he had stepped into the garden to check the progress of the lemon verbena and the marshmallow, I did question him, very casually of course, as if it could not have mattered less when, in fact, it mattered more just then than anything else.

He made no bones about it. There had always been Alys. Her company was so natural to him that she was just *there*, that was the only word really to explain it. And they wrote to each other, of course, at least once a week, whenever either of them happened to be away. Always had, always would, he supposed. What about? Lord—whatever came into his head—or hers. Sheer nonsense, most of it. But, just the same, Hexingham and Cambridge and his various trips to India had all been considerably brightened up by Alys's letters.

They were good friends. The best.

My heart turned cold.

"She's restless," he said, "in her way—like me. She feels confined here in the village. And being a girl, of course, it's difficult for her to get out."

"Where would she go?"

He grinned suddenly, fondly, his tolerant, affectionate knowledge of Alys's elusive character lacerating me.

"Samarkand. Or Babylon. Or Xanadu. Not somewhere easy or likely, that's for certain."

Where would *he* go? But restlessness, in a man, did not necessarily imply a change of location. And if Alys meant so much to him then why was he here with me? Perhaps he now found it necessary to ask that question himself, for he did not call the next day, or the day after; the only information I could glean coming from Max who had met him out shooting with the Pottertons and afterwards at a moorland inn, of ill-repute Max made a point of telling me, where a great deal of ale had been drunk.

I suffered behind a façade of gaiety, laughed louder than ever, exhibited a marked tendency to burst into song, even spent an evening at my mother's card-table where, with great hilarity, I won five shillings from Mr. Greenlaw and then lost it, ten minutes later, to Max.

He came back the third morning, not on horseback as I so liked to see him, but in that abominable motor.

"Olivia, will you come for a drive—if it's convenient?"

It could never be inconvenient. It was, however, more than a little improper to set off alone with him in a vehicle which had no place for even the unreliable chaperonage of a coachman or a groom. Last week, even three days ago, he had not thought of that. He was aware of it now with all its implications which must surely mean that he had decided to carry our intimacy through to a deeper level, or to end it.

"Yes, Robin." And I was accepting far more than a drive to Clarrow Moor, the excitement of junketing along at a heady fifteen miles an hour, although it did *not* excite me, on roads which had been intended—and very properly, I thought—for farm carts, slow-wheeled carriages, briskly trotting feet. Like my mother, I would have preferred to ride in a park landau wearing an extravagant French hat or to sit aloft in a high-perch phaeton with a gentleman's silk topper at a dashing angle on my head. But if this noisy, dusty, bone-jarring motoring was Robin's pleasure then, at least, until I could persuade him otherwise, I would make it mine, particularly as Aunt Sibylla had told me that she had expressly forbidden it to Alys.

We reached the edge of Clarrow Moor and leaving the unflattering encumbrance of dust-coats, scarves and goggles on the seat, walking perhaps half a mile without speaking a word, moving easily but very slowly across the rough ground as if we were wading into a tufted, spiky, deep purple sea, swimming through clean, fern-spiced air. A few charcoal sketches of birds wheeled high above us. There was the sound of a gunshot, made harmless by distance. No one else was about.

And suddenly, catching my breath, I felt a deep, perhaps primitive love for this high, gray-green landscape, this hard, enduring earth interwoven with rock and water. I did not understand it. My understanding was of city pavements, hothouse flowers, animals in cages. I was not entirely comfortable here. But, quite simply, I loved it. And, therefore, I would learn.

"The thing is," Robin said, "well—I thought I'd better tell you . . ."

"Yes?" Whatever it was I would take it calmly. Even if he were about to break everything off I would not roll on the ground in agony until he was safely out of sight. Pride would hold me to that and the inbred knowledge that if I allowed him to go easily and sweetly he would find it easier to return.

"Olivia, I'm the most desperately unsettled sort of chap. I mean, I'm not at all sure how I see life, or what I believe in. You seem to know so exactly where you're going . . ."

Of course I did. Where else could I possibly wish to be than here, on this shelf of moorland, with Clarrow Fell below me in the gray distance and Robin at my side?

"Yes, I know."

I was ready physically and emotionally for marriage. Perhaps Robin's emotions, at that precise moment of his life, would have preferred a mistress. But his body wanted me, desire suddenly tightening the air around us with such force, such terrifying power, that I think we were both afraid of it.

"I'm just not *settled* . . ."

But what a pale little word, what an insignificant notion, no more than a moth's wing to be consumed, all in a moment, by this glorious blaze of desire. I had nothing to say. I stood quite still and looked at him, felt his eyes on me, not offering him my body as a deliberate temptation, for I was not then so worldly wise as that, but knowing, just the same, that one did not turn away from a flame like this. One allowed it, instead, to burn away the part of oneself which might have resisted, the part which remembered such mundane matters as what to believe in, and "being settled." One allowed oneself to be mesmerized and then, like the drugged initiate of some oriental cult, one fell joyfully into the fire.

"Olivia . . . ?" I did not speak.

"Olivia . . . " I said not a word. I was *there*, the woman he desired, ready to be taken.

"We'd better go back to the motor."

I nodded, obedient and submissive as an odalisque, my body controlled no longer by quick-tempered Olivia Heron but by an amorous, yielding female dedicated to his pleasure.

"Darling . . ." he said, and kissed me, the huge, crushing embrace of a young man who can no longer contain himself, the fierceness of his need making it unnecessary for me either to respond or to struggle since both would have gone unnoticed.

He kissed me and hurt me. I gloried in the kiss and the pain. He took me by the shoulders, positioned me against the one remaining wall of a derelict barn and kissed me again, savoring with more calm yet greater sensuality, my mouth and my skin, my body enclosed now between the length of his and the stone wall, the trembling of his limbs blending into mine so that I could no longer tell which one of us was trembling.

He stood away from me for a moment, his eyes glazed and helpless, and swayed back again. I felt a hand on my breast and instead of fear or indignation I leaned forward into the caress, welcoming the stroking inquiry of his fingertips and his mouth, when it followed them, burning me through the thin, summery fabric of my dress.

"Olivia," he whispered hoarsely. "*Please*. Don't let me offend you."

I saw that, with part of his mind, he was appalled by his behavior and was asking me to put a stop to it. I understood. Yet I

141

could not. We had been born, it seemed to me in that moment of exaltation, to do these wonderful, dangerous, natural things to each other. *This*—this holding and caressing, this contact—was life at its finest and purest intensity, its true reality and we were not wanton but privileged to experience it.

A dangerous philosophy, which my mother would have applauded. But she would also have known, as I did not, the full extent of my peril, and how very badly I might have fared with a man less chivalrous than Robin.

"Good God," he said suddenly, straining hard, I could see, to break the force which held us, shaking his head as if to clear it. "Oh Christ—Olivia. I do beg your pardon. What a damnable thing to have done . . ."

Unflattering, perhaps, if one took the remark at face value. But I understood.

"No, Robin. Don't worry. It's all right."

"I haven't—haven't *hurt* you, have I?"

I shook my head, smiled, realizing now, when the frenzy had cooled, that in fact he had hurt me in places, and that I was perfectly ready to console him for it.

"I'd better take you home."

I shook my skirt free of bracken, smiled again, and walked back to the motor as silently as we had come, his face puzzled and anxious, his manner tense yet touchingly eager to please.

"Olivia, you're not angry, are you?"

"No, I'm not."

"What an angel you are."

"I'm not that, either."

It was the truth, and even though he was not disposed to believe me, at least I had not lied to him.

"You are so beautiful," he said and taking my hand turned it palm upwards and kissed it, not raising my hand to his lips but bending his head very low in the tender, submissive gesture of a knight-errant, a perfect English gentleman who, although prone to the lusts of the flesh every now and then, was pure at heart.

I was dizzy and bemused with love for him. I adored him. There was nothing I would not give him or do for him. Nothing. And he was mine now—or very nearly—for I knew with a great inner shout of triumph that Alys could have no conception of the

142

experience he and I had just shared. She may have given him a great deal in terms of friendship and understanding. But I could give him those things too. And how could she, with her narrow upbringing and cool, intellectual disposition, possibly match the immense power of desire?

EIGHT

Alys returned home and paid her first visit to Aireville Terrace within the week, her hair in its silvery, unkempt profusion hanging loose down her back, her face—despite the good weather—extremely pale since she had spent the whole summer on the beach at Bridlington reading beneath the brim of her hat. And now, having rushed down from Clarrow at once to see me, she had left her gloves in the train and entirely forgotten to bring the housewarming present it had taken her a whole Bridlington morning to buy. But she was *here* and delighted about it.

"Dearest Olivia—how marvelous to see you."

Had Judas Iscariot a female counterpart, I wondered? But once I had recovered from the shock of liking her again, I decided it would be pointless to feel more than slightly guilty on her account.

I had known from the start that some kind of an "understanding" existed between her and Robin and it must be his task—not mine—when the time came, to tell her that it was over. I had made no promises to anyone else and so had none to break. Alys had declared herself unready. Now, however difficult or painful or downright cruel it seemed, she was too late. And when conscience stabbed me hard and treacherously in the back I consoled myself with the belief that she would not really mind.

Our house, as such, was of no interest to Alys. Tables, chairs, wallpapers, topics in any way domestic could only hold her attention for a polite moment. But her delight in meeting new people from the world beyond Bradeswick knew no bounds. The slight French accent,

144

which Madelon seemed unable to lose, enchanted her. The phrases of Italian and Spanish and regional French with which Luc deliberately peppered his conversation both amused and—to his great satisfaction—rather impressed her. Victorine she found most interesting, my mother every bit as fascinating as she had expected. And was it really true that wicked Vivian's son, the apparently just as wicked Max, had turned up again, a Johannesburg millionaire, with the Koh-i-Noor diamond or something like it on his hand and a ruby the size of a pigeon's egg set into his cigar case? Ten minutes later she was able to see for herself when the gentleman in question strolled inside to pass the time of day and seemed very well disposed towards this pastel-tinted young lady whose mother he remembered as Sibylla Blackwood.

"You are not in the least like her."

"I know. She is terribly disappointed about it."

"Why—in particular?"

"Oh—because if I resembled her I would want the things she wants, I suppose, and would therefore be—Heavens, I don't know."

"I think you do. Easier to handle? You are a philosopher, Alys."

"I try to be."

"Oh dear," she said, some time later when he had gone away. "How am I to bear it? He talks of Pretoria and Durban and *Madagascar* as casually as you talk of Paris and Rome and Biarritz. Do you realize that I have been to Bridlington and Scarborough and once all the way to Eastbourne. Think of that."

"One Grand Hotel is very much like another, you know, even in Pretoria."

She heaved a deep sigh and shook her head. "That is very cynical of you, Olivia. I should think any hotel the most exciting place on earth—provided I could be there alone, to stay or to pack my things and go just as it suited me."

"I have been doing that all my life, Alys."

"Yes. And you are heartily sick of it? Shall we change places then, you and I? How would that be?"

Robin suddenly came into the room, visibly startled by his first sight of us both together.

"Oh, hello," said Alys, pleased to see him but far more interested in finding out all she could about Athens from Madelon, who must have been rather young, I thought, during the summer we spent there, to remember much about it now.

He sat down, lit a nervous cigarette without permission, threw it into the fire and quickly made an excuse to leave, Alys sending him a vague smile, her mind still wandering about the Parthenon, while I walked with him to the door, friendly, undemanding, making no fuss, leaving everything—for the moment—to him.

As yet we had exchanged no vows. We had simply fallen into each other's arms on Clarrow Moor and at some part of every day since then he had found some way of touching me, a sudden handclasp, some part of his body, an arm, an elbow, an instep, making contact with some part of mine. There seemed nothing to say. If other people were present we looked at each other. Whenever we happened to be alone we drew together in a silence that had the texture of warm velvet and simply touched, his hand on the nape of my neck, his mouth on my cheek or my ear or the whole length of my forehead, kisses that were light and delicate, each one a unique and separate treasure to store in my mind.

But until Alys returned, my own peculiar brand of chivalry decreed that I should push the matter no further. When the final choice was made I wanted her to be here in Bradeswick. Not from motives of fairness alone—since who can really be fair when they are in love—but because I would give no one, her mother perhaps, cause to say that I could have got him in no other fashion than behind her back.

But she was here now and when he returned to Aireville Terrace rather late that same evening, having spent several hours walking about the town in evident agony of mind, we went, as if by arrangement, into the dark herb-garden and stood close together without speaking a word, far enough apart to be able to see each other, near enough to be aware of the other's pulse beat and heart beat, skin odors and skin textures, rendering ourselves weak and giddy by the potence of our mutual desire.

"I love you?" he said and if we heard the question in his voice neither of us listened to it.

The next day, when it was no longer uppermost in my mind, brought the long-expected visit of the Greenlaw ladies who, looking rather surprised that they were here at all, stayed exactly the quarter of an hour politeness demanded, declining to take tea and making their stilted little remarks mostly to Max de Haan whom they had met several times, it seemed, to my intense annoyance, both at Mrs. Naseby's and at the Pottertons.

146

How very pleasant! And what I badly wanted to know was why a man like Max de Haan should be wined and dined and made much of by the very people who were still ignoring me? Mrs. Naseby had driven past me several times in Bradeswick without so much as a sidelong glance. Lady Potterton, who spent the early part of every year in London, had been back in residence at Dawney Park long enough to organize her shooting-parties and her dinner-parties and no doubt to draw up the guest list for her hunt ball, but had not even sent her calling-card to me. The Greenlaw ladies were here today, I was well aware of it, only because their father-in-law, who was still the chairman and major shareholder of the Ironworks Company, had commanded them.

What an unjust world this was in which I, against whom no personal blemish was known, was obliged to prove myself over and over as a woman of spotless reputation if I hoped to be acknowledged at all, whereas Max, whose reputation was wholly bad, had merely to show his face, stretch out his hard brown hand with its diamond, tip his hat, and was immediately invited everywhere. I bit my lip in a sudden spurt of rage. I understood the rules of the game, the double standard which made heroes of wicked men and outcasts of women. I understood but I did not like it.

The Greenlaw ladies took their leave and as I stood at the window to watch them go Max de Haan came up behind me and said in those low, neutral tones of the traveler—the card-player—who does not wish to be identified, "It has always been easier to be a man, you know."

And by no means pleased that he had read my mind, I answered him airily, archly, borrowing my mother's tricks.

"What *can* you mean?"

"I am sure you know."

"Oh good—are we playing guessing games?"

"If you like. There are ladders to climb in life, are there not?"

I nodded like the good, obedient child I had never been and his long mouth which was not at all like Robin's but hard and subtle and sensual like his father's portrait—like the Squire—smiled at me very slightly, acknowledging a clever performance but warning me not to carry it too far.

"Well then, which kind of ladder am I better equipped to climb than you?"

I made large, angelic eyes at him, the Junot face of innocence, "Oh—ladders into bedroom windows, I should think. Do I get a prize?"

"That depends on what you want, Olivia dear. But you are quite wrong. In that particular case the game is to persuade the lady to open her door. Those kinds of ladders are for losers."

"Well then?"

"Social ladders, my pet."

"Do you know, Max, that I am not your pet?"

"I know. Things change!"

"Not everything."

"Wrong again, Olivia. Everything changes, whether we like it or not. I saw our mutual relative yesterday, by the way—my uncle and your grandfather."

"Did he acknowledge you?"

"Oh yes. I was a guest of the Pottertons and so was he. And Squire Heron does not abuse his neighbors' hospitality by laundering his dirty linen on their premises. He expressed surprise at finding me still alive, as your mother did. Odd, really, since I have every intention of living at least forever. Your name was mentioned too."

"By him?"

"By me. The Pottertons inquired and I told them about your gipsy eyes and your amber skin and that long, lovely arch of your back and those arrogant, Amazon shoulders; and the way you bite your lip and scowl—as you are doing now—when you are angry."

I knew I had blushed and was very far from pleased about it, since to embarrass me had clearly been his intention.

"You said no such thing."

"No, as it happens I did not. They are all in a quandary, you see, about whether or not to invite you, since the Squire will say nothing to the point about it one way or the other. *Someone*, I felt, ought to speak up for you, and so I talked about your skills and accomplishments and how perfectly well-behaved you are—or *would* be, if it were not for that unfortunate little habit of kissing young men in the garden."

"You didn't say that either."

"Of course not."

"And I don't need you to speak up for me, Max."

He shrugged, smiled and gave his slight, by no means respectful bow.

148

"Every little bit helps, my pet. You need them to accept you, we both understand that. They're a dull lot, duller than most, I give you fair warning. But without their seal of approval it's checkmate, isn't it? You'll have your work cut out with Lavinia in tow but I reckon you'll make it. At any rate I shall enjoy watching you make the attempt."

"Max—I really don't know what you are talking about."

"You most certainly do. And I know exactly what you want from this place. I know what I want. A situation may arise in which we could help each other. In which case two kindred spirits such as ours—oh yes, Olivia, I fear so—should really cooperate!"

Kindred spirits? Very likely. But only because I had had to be. Not because I had *chosen* to be hard and devious and tricky, as he had. When I could afford it—as he could now afford it—I would be as tender and yielding as Madelon, as full of integrity as Alys, as generous as my mother.

"Cooperate? You mean you want me to sell you the Manor?"

Again the smile, the slightest inclination of the head. "Possibly. Your grandfather was looking frail yesterday and winter is coming on. When he dies I'll be your next of kin in the male line. At the risk of causing a certain amount of hilarity, I'd like to invite you—when the time comes—to rely on my judgment. To trust me, that is, rather than Amyas."

"Which means—what? That the Squire has told Amyas to sell to anyone but you."

"Very likely. In the Squire's place, it is what I would probably do myself."

"And he will naturally assume that, being a woman, I have no head for business and will do as I am bid."

"Yes, I rather think he would assume that."

"Why should I sell at all, Max?"

"Now I *did* wonder if that was on your mind. Because, my pet, the old man has no money to leave you, or not enough for you to live on in anything approaching comfort. He has some small investments here and there, and a few shares in Sam Greenlaw's Ironworks. But not much. Nowhere near enough to put the house to rights and subsidize the tenants through another bad year. And they're all bad years for farmers nowadays. I'm forbidden to set foot on the estate, as you know, but from Clarrow Moor, with a good pair of field-glasses it's not hard to count the roof-tiles that are missing already and estimate the amount of damage next winter's snow is bound to do. There's no money in land any more, Olivia. Somebody invented fast ships and cold storage, you see, so now the corn comes in from America, the meat from New Zealand, the wool from Australia. And there are no coal deposits on Clarrow land to make the Squire rich, no quarries. Nobody has ever been ready to pay out a fortune to run a railway line through. The only good thing they ever found under Clarrow soil was iron ore and they gave that away. So there's only one future for our birthplace, sweet cousin. It has to be converted from an agricultural to a sporting estate. Get rid of the farms for what they'll fetch at auction. Keep the grouse moor, the woodland, the paddocks, the house and parkland, and sell them to a sporting gentleman with money in his bank."

He bowed again as if in introduction.

"Max de Haan, ma'am—entirely at your service."

We would see about that. I brooded about it for the rest of the morning and then, an hour after luncheon, received a further shock as I saw no less a personage than Aunt Sibylla walking up our path with the air of a great lady bringing charity and good advice to the poor.

"Mother, for Heaven's sake put those cards away."

"Dearest, my sister Sibylla knows how wicked I am."

"There is no need to remind her."

Blessedly none of her usual entourage were present, permitting the first interview in twenty years between these two unlikely sisters to take place in strict privacy behind a closed drawing-room door, an event lasting a full hour before my mother rang for tea and Victorine, Luc and Madelon were allowed to become acquainted with their aunt.

"Charming," she said, "quite charming," looking them up and down with a faint air of disbelief.

"And how are you, Olivia? Very busy, one is given to understand. I do believe Esmeralda Naseby was making some inquiry about you from Alys at dinner the other evening—or was it Dorothea Potterton? Now then, Lavinia, I must be off and I am not sure as yet that I can invite you to visit me. The vicar would not mind, of course— the vicar never does. But the vicarage, after all, does not belong to the vicar. I will let you know."

"Sibylla does not change," my mother said, watching her sister's stately progress along Aireville Terrace. "Poor Toby. He was rather beautiful once and very clever—*too* clever by far for a country vicarage. And he may have been ever so slightly in love with me—a hundred years ago. I believe Sibylla thought so, and so did my mother which is one of the reasons she left Sibylla all her furniture and all her jewelry. Olivia, I would like a word with you. Come up to my room, dearest, so we can be private."

I sat down in the chair by her bed while she perched on the window-seat glowing with the elation of an encounter which had probably exhausted Sibylla.

"What is it, mother?"

"Oh it is all rather amusing. I hope you will find it so. My sister tells me that your behavior has been causing comment, in much the same way as my own used to do—which I accepted, rather graciously, as a compliment. She tells me, in fact, that you have stolen from a certain young man the affections which she considers to be the property of her daughter. Have you really done that, Olivia?"

Nausea gripped the pit of my stomach, squeezing hard, shocking me badly since I was not given to spasms and palpitations of this sort.

"I may have done. What do you think, mother?"

"I think, dear, that the young man is altogether mesmerized by *my* daughter. And I am not in the least surprised at it, since Alys cannot hold a candle to you, my love. Oh yes, she has her fascinations as an original and a *jolie laide*, one can see that. As Max says, she is something of a connoisseur's item, an acquired taste—one of those maidens who live in ivory towers always half-asleep. And according to Max, it is a very piquant enterprise to wake such maidens up. But Robin has not succeeded in waking her and from the tales people tell me neither did my son, Guy. I do not think you have any reason to feel guilty on her account—if that is what you do feel."

"Yes. I believe I do."

"Why? Because he seems so marvelous to you that you think no one could ever recover from his loss? You would recover from it yourself, darling, if you had to. That is the real sorrow, as I should know."

"Do you like him, mother?"

"Of course I do. These English schoolboy-gentlemen have a charm all their own. I felt unable to meet your brother Guy when he came to France but I picture him as another Robin Esmond. But my opinion of him can hardly matter. The great thing is—are you in love with him?"

"Yes."

"Then there is absolutely nothing more to be said. What else could possibly matter but that?"

"Mother—a hundred things."

"Nonsense. True love melts all obstacles clean away."

"*Mother!* It does no such thing. It blinds you, perhaps, but you bump into them just the same."

And leaning forward, still feeling sick and shaken, I began to speak rapidly and urgently, knowing how easily her concentration was apt to wander.

"Mother, supposing I marry him . . ."

"Olivia, I do not suppose it, I expect it. Love and marriage are bound to go together at your age."

"Supposing I marry him—we could not live here."

"No. I rather think you should ask your grandfather for the Gatehouse at Clarrow. It is empty just now. I very cleverly found that out from Sibylla."

"Could you manage here, with Victorine and Madelon?"

"Why ever not?"

"I mean would you run this house along proper lines until we can get them married?"

"I imagine you will make sure of it, Olivia. You will be able to supervise me very adequately from Clarrow. And if you are still worrying about Max there is really no need. On his way back from Madeira he has a call to pay on Corfu where he has a woman and, I rather suspect, a child. So we may not see him again for months, possibly until your grandfather dies. By which time I may be a grandmother myself with all three of my daughters married and my son— I do hope and trust—safely incarcerated in a good school. The fees at Hexingham are high but Sibylla would not have been so keen to get Robin for Alys unless there was the prospect of money. So Hexingham should not be beyond our means."

"You are quite settled here, then, mother?"

"Yes dear, I do believe I am. And when the Squire passes on and you move into the Manor, I shall take delight in helping you outshine that insufferable Esmeralda Naseby who was nothing but a

152

poor schoolmaster's daughter. And Dottie Potterton too who once slapped my face because her Georgie and I were accidentally locked into a store-cupboard together, for rather a long time, I must admit, during a game of sardines. Yes, I shall enjoy seeing you mistress of Clarrow, although Max, of course, will be very much mortified. He has a great fancy to set himself up as squire of the estate from which he was cast out and banished—a romantic notion, really, for such a hard man. But never mind that. Fond of him as I am, you are my daughter and he will just have to stable his thoroughbreds and kennel his hounds elsewhere. Darling—have I eased your mind?"

Robin came an hour or so after dinner when I had almost given up hope of seeing him that day, his face strained and tired yet at the same time eager, excited, his spirits, like mine, balancing between laughter and tears.

"Olivia, can I speak to you?"

We went into the back parlor and sat for rather a long time by the fire, neither speaking nor touching, the warm silence carrying us gradually towards the final point where it would be impossible for either of us to withdraw and then, almost imperceptibly, passing it so that—in the same rich silence—we entered into the long act of belonging. He had spent a painful day with Alys, securing his release from old pledges which may have meant more to him than to her. But I had no right to ask, he had no inclination to tell me and, far from offending me, his reticence seemed merely to confirm his kindness of heart, the distress it caused him to hurt anyone.

But his choice had been made. That was all that mattered. And I would devote every scrap of energy and ingenuity to making certain he would never regret it.

"Olivia, I don't know why you should want to marry me. But you will—won't you?"

"Yes, I will."

The words sang through my mind like a great anthem of joy.

"I love you, Robin."

"You are so beautiful, Olivia—so very beautiful. It overwhelms me."

And then, as if compelled to make some further explanation, some justification, perhaps, for actions he did not fully understand himself, he took both my hands and said rapidly, "I'm not used to this, Olivia. I've always been a pretty unemotional sort of chap. To

153

tell you the truth I never expected to feel so strongly about anything in my life. I didn't think I had it in me. And now it bowls me over. You bowl me over. You're so beautiful."

"So are you."

He looked so very taken aback, so embarrassed that I laughed and shook my head, feeling stronger now and steady enough to lighten the moment.

"You must know that, Robin."

"Well—one doesn't think about it. But I *have* known a girl or two—you know—as one does. I think I'm supposed to tell you that, aren't I—and apologize?"

He was warning me, as Hexingham and the Squire had taught him, that although an Englishman of his class valued chastity in a bride, no one expected a fellow to carry the thing to extremes and remain pure himself. And so, in the interests of fair play, one confessed, apologized, wore a slight air of wickedness for a day or two, and never mentioned the matter again.

"I expect I'll forgive you," I told him, trying hard to sound severe and dimpling instead into laughter.

"Oh good. That's settled then. The next thing is to ask your mother . . ."

"What for?"

"Permission to marry you, my darling."

I had not thought of that. But when we went hand in hand into the drawing room she was waiting for us, intending to play this new role of mother-of-the-bride for all it was worth.

"There is much to consider," she said gravely and proceeded, in the most serious manner, to question him about his prospects and his expectations, his law degree which carried with it the possibility of a partnership in the firm of Lawker & Lane, the Heron family solicitors; the terms of his mother's will by which he was to receive a comfortable amount of capital on his father's death; the size of the allowance his father now made him and whether the Colonel would be willing to increase it, and by how much, when he took a wife.

He answered frankly and fully, having nothing whatsoever to hide.

"Good," she said, and then, breaking into a sunburst of smiles, she told him, "my dear boy, all that sounds most satisfactory but I do not care a fig for it. If you can make my daughter happy I should not

154

mind if you were a Mississippi riverboat gambler or a peddler from the Appleburton Fair. I was merely doing my duty and now we can turn to far more pleasant things—like champagne and what kind of hat to wear for the wedding. See how my daughter's eyes are shining. I would like that to continue."

He kissed her hand and then her cheek, perfectly at ease with her. He kissed Victorine and Madelon, shook hands with Luc. We drank champagne. But I was already intoxicated with happiness, its pure essence rising to my head far more swiftly than wine.

I was in love with a man who loved me. Therefore, I had everything. What more could I desire? But my lover, who knew the turn of my mind and its desires, had found a gift to give me.

"I still have the motor just for tonight. Shall we take a last drive together," he said, the warm twinkle in his eye telling me he had known all along how little I cared for it.

"Where to?"

And with the gesture of a *chevalier* who lays his cloak on the ground before his lady, he told me, "You are a Heron of Clarrow Fell and so, in a manner of speaking, am I. I am going to take you to the Manor, my darling, to collect your blessing from the Squire."

NINE

We were married a few days before Christmas in the parish church at Bradeswick, the inconvenience of the season giving us the excuse we needed for a quiet ceremony since several of our guests were ill-at-ease in the presence of several others, while several more would have preferred not to be there at all. I wore white lace and a cloud of embroidered chiffon for I was, after all—if only barely by then—a virgin bride; attended by my sisters in ice blue taffeta cut to show off the good points of Victorine's figure, since Madelon would always look enchanting in anything.

I walked down the aisle to Robin on my grandfather's arm in a state of bliss far beyond all powers of reason or caution, entranced so totally by joy that I could have floated through a furnace and felt no pain. I *knew*—with a certainty which seemed to render me immortal—that for the rest of my life I was going to be gloriously happy. It was as simple as that. And having achieved the ultimate aim so soon, what else remained beyond my reach?

My interview with my grandfather on the night of my engagement had not been easy. No doubt he had been waiting to see me make a false move, to set my cap at an adventurer like Max or, quite simply, with the lack of true purpose only to be expected in my mother's daughter, to give up and go away. Instead I had chosen a man who had claims of his own on Clarrow Fell, a cousin of the house who had a perfect right to bring his wife there and whose income—in the course of time—would be sufficient to keep the estate intact. My grandfather did not care for this and, summoning me alone to the Justice's Room did not scruple to tell me so.

"What are your motives, Olivia?"

And although my motive was love, his presence was so awesome, so cynical, that my mouth dried on the words and I said primly, seeking to defend rather than to explain myself, "Natural ones, I think."

"Emotion?"

He too could not bring himself to use the word "love," not to me at any rate, perhaps no longer to anyone. And standing before him, enduring a scrutiny that seemed to peel away a layer of skin, I felt the snap of his impatience with all these unruly, inconvenient emotions. What a nuisance you are, Olivia, he was really saying. Could I not see that he wanted nothing more from life but to be left alone with it, to withdraw into the shrinking world of his personal values where this horde of chatterers and posturers and self-seekers which had suddenly descended upon him had no place? Go away, Olivia. Go back to your own high-colored, high-pitched world and take my brother's unscrupulous son and that light woman, your mother, with you. There is no room for your shrill, foreign voices, your greedy eyes fixed on the future, in this house which is all that remains to me of the past.

He neither hated us nor felt threatened by us. We were not sufficiently important to him for that. Yet, nevertheless, our persistent hoverings on the fringes of his attention irritated him, my marriage to Robin was a complication he found distasteful, foolish, unnecessary. Olivia—Olivia—what a *nuisance* you are.

"The marriage is unlikely to succeed," he told me curtly. "You have nothing in common. On his part it is entirely an affair of the senses. On your part I am less certain. You are a schemer, Olivia, I am well aware of it. Perhaps you have had to be. But an understanding of the cause does not necessarily incline one to tolerate the results. And schemes can go awry. Of course you know that. You have seen it happen to other people and are probably still young enough to believe it can never happen to you. It can. Anything can happen to anyone, particularly to someone who *participates* so much in life, as you do."

His own days of participation were definitely over. He did not care to involve himself in mine. But having issued his warning and ascertained—as he had expected—that I would not heed it, he shrugged his spare shoulders and made his concessions coldly and quickly, grudging each and every one.

We were both of full age and good family and no real objection—except his firm conviction that it would fail—could be made to our union. Colonel Esmond, far away in the Transvaal, would be more than happy to welcome a daughter-in-law who happened also to be the heiress of Clarrow Fell, while the local gentry, the Pottertons and the Nasebys and the rest, would follow the Squire's own lead in the matter. Therefore, in real terms, he could make me or break me in local society and while he felt fully entitled to please himself as to his treatment of Olivia Heron he would be bound, by the laws of kinship and hospitality, to show a certain degree of consideration for an Esmond bride. My schemes, he supposed, had taken account of that.

"No, grandfather." But it was not entirely true and raising one scathing eyebrow he went on to inform me of my right to be married in the village church at Clarrow and hold my wedding breakfast in the great hall afterwards, privileges which he would grant—since the tenants and the neighbors and Colonel Esmond would all expect it— on the single condition that no invitation to Clarrow Fell, even on her daughter's wedding-day, could be extended to my mother.

"Darling," she had said, "I don't mind—really I don't. Just go ahead and have your wedding with all the church bells ringing and the log fire blazing in the hall afterwards—and all the candles. I'll just stay here, dearest, good as gold, and wish you well."

But I knew she had already chosen her hat and told all her friends, had already immersed herself in sketches of wedding veils. bridal posies, cake frills.

To have left her behind would have been unthinkable. I knew, at once, that I could not do it and quickly accepted the compromise of Bradeswick parish church, the ceremony—by arrangement with Bradeswick's vicar—to be conducted by my uncle, the Reverend Toby Heron, with my grandfather to give me away.

"The seal of approval you require," he said brusquely, "will thus be quite plain enough." And should anyone doubt its authenticity my future residence was to be the Gatehouse at Clarrow.

And so we were married before a small and in some cases hostile congregation, my mother, with every conceivable shade of blue feather in her hat and a spray of Mr. Greenlaw's prize orchids at her bosom, sharing a front pew with Aunt Sibylla who had been glacial and sharp and with Alys who had continued to be her vague, sweet self, her

158

enchanted, ivory tower sleep evidently still unbroken. Amyas was there, of course, and the housekeeper, Mrs. Long, a fine distinction here arising since, although they had traveled from Clarrow together and appeared sufficiently well acquainted to have given rise to a small but persistent amount of gossip, he—as an estate agent which was almost a profession—joined the family at the front of the church while she—an upper servant—sat at the back.

Mr. Greenlaw was present with both his daughters-in-law and the least enterprising—therefore the most dependent—of his sons, and Mr. Septimus Cross, the banker, sitting among the sprinkling of Bradeswick ladies and gentlemen who, interpreting my engagement as a declaration of respectability, had started to call on us in Aireville Terrace. But the Pottertons had returned to their house in London for the Christmas season, and Mrs. Naseby—that other social lioness—who wintered badly had gone to Rome to avoid the inclement weather and to spend Christmas with her son who was "finishing" his education there. While to my great relief Max de Haan had left, presumably for Madeira, at the beginning of September; having reacted sourly, I thought, beneath all his languid well-polished scorn to a marriage which would be more than likely to complicate his purchase of Clarrow Fell.

"So you are to join the stampede to the altar, I hear."

"Have you such a poor opinion of marriage, Max?"

"I have no opinion of it. If one really cannot avoid it—and I find one nearly always can—then it would seem advisable for like to marry like. And you do not resemble Robin Esmond, my pet, not in the very least."

"You hardly know him."

"My dear girl, I have known him in hundreds. Eton and Harrow and Hexingham are full of him. He is the English country gentleman at his best, that is to say that he hunts and he shoots and he fishes with the rest but he also *thinks*—which admittedly is better than most. But just the same he will bore you, Olivia, when you really get to know him. And if you ever allow him to know you then you will very likely scare him to death."

"Thank you, Max."

"My dear, don't mention it. At least you are saving him from the Yeomanry since not even his father could expect him to go Boer-hunting on his honeymoon."

"I shall ignore that, Max, since I am feeling so very well today and can afford to be generous."

"You'll be lucky to afford a new petticoat should you decide to keep on that ancestral home of ours," he had snapped, for just one moment quite visibly angry. And the day before his departure he had tossed into my lap a wedding present of embarrassing value, a gold bracelet with my initials in diamonds on the clasp and long gold earrings containing a single diamond like a tear drop.

"Wear them or sell them," he'd said. "They'll go a long way to repairing the roof at Clarrow."

"Wear them," my mother urged me on my wedding morning. "People will assume they came from Robin or from the Squire, and Max is not here to say differently. Somebody may even suppose they came from me, since there *was* some good jewelry in my family and I *would* have given it to you, darling, if Sibylla had not made off with it."

And so Max de Haan was present in the touch of his diamonds swinging against my cheeks, their glitter around my wrist as I held out my hand to Robin and became his wife, completing my personal destiny once and for all—I was very sure of it—by that exchange of vows. I would be happy now forever. So would Robin. I stood at the very center of the world on a fabulous, enchanted carpet of silken textures and jeweled colors, walking on patterns of my own devising. The December day was cold and probably dull but I did not see it. I floated through deep blue air and breathed pure sunshine. I believed, as the organ chimed and the bells pealed and the choir sang only slightly out of tune, that I had nothing more to wish for.

We had no honeymoon, midwinter being no time for journeys, the threat of snow hovering about us as we drove in an open landau to the Station Hotel to drink champagne and eat a luncheon of cold pheasant provided by my grandfather and a monumental wedding-cake baked by Victorine.

"Let us drink to the health and happiness of the bride and groom," said my grandfather, strictly doing his duty.

"Darling . . ." breathed my mother, emptying her glass and bursting into tears, remembering how many times she had heard this toast before, to no avail.

"Not all days are wedding-days," declared my Aunt Sibylla, sipping her wine with an air of one who detects the taste of vinegar.

160

"Marriage, like most things, is hard work and perseverance—no laughing matter."

"Olivia will persevere," said Victorine.

"How beautiful you look, Olivia," said Alys.

We remained in Bradeswick when our guests had gone, spending our first night together at the Station Hotel in the large front room which had been my mother's not so long ago, no reticence in me anywhere as I flung myself into his arms, my body sparkling with pleasure wherever he touched it, my breasts straining forward to meet his hands, arching myself this way and that so that no part of me would be deprived of his caress, wanting him to overpower me with love, to possess me in so complete and final a manner that we would never, thereafter, be able to think of ourselves as separate.

I was not only in love with Robin but with the act of love itself. I adored him and I adored everything we had just done together. I adored his nudity and my own, the freedom of unfettered limbs, the sensation of bare skin in contact with mine, and the varying textures and odors of that skin, the quite silken width of his shoulders, the coarser feel of the chest with its scattering of blond hairs, the multiplicity of bone and muscle and sinew, the hollows and angles, everything that he had in him: everything that I had in me. I adored the emotion my body visibly caused him, even the slight pain of penetration and the sudden flood of his desire which so wildly and wonderfully overwhelmed him, leaving me with none of the feelings of subjection, of being used and invaded that women so often experienced—I'd been told—on these occasions. He had entered my body. Yes indeed. But my body had closed itself around him, holding him fast, fusing us together with love and need and self-abandonment, so that—while the need lasted—he was wholly mine.

I did not even realize that my own body had not attained its full orgasm. And had anyone explained it to me it would not, just then, have mattered. I had not groaned and trembled as Robin had done, but I had been the cause of his ecstasy. I had aroused it, held him within me and received its fulfillment, had seen his helpless abandonment to the very senses my grandfather had implied could not endure. But my grandfather was an old man who had forgotten or did not care to remember the intoxication of young bodies clasped together in sensuality and tenderness, and I had no fear.

"Darling Olivia—I do love you." Was there still a question?

161

I had never acknowledged it in the first place and could not hear it now.

The next morning we took the train to Clarrow Fell and walked hand in hand through the steep, black-browed village to the Gatehouse, laughing at the frosty wind, jumping the puddles, giddy and happy as holiday children, my hope for the future so bright and tremendous and golden that I could see it dancing ahead of me on the thin, gray air. Snow began to fall, soft as feathers, and whooping with delight, we ran helter-skelter the last few yards up the hill to our new home.

"Shall I carry you across the threshold?" And swinging me up into his arms, bending his head to negotiate the low doorway, he carried me into the tiny parlor and straight upstairs.

"At least let me take off my hat."

"I'm not at all certain I can wait that long, Olivia."

"Oh yes you can. And you'll take off your own wet things too, Robin Esmond, before you catch cold."

"Do it for me, darling. When a chap has lived out east as long as I have, he never quite loses the fancy for a slave."

I undressed him carefully, caressingly, dried his hair with a new wedding-present towel, turned back the covers of the deep, feather bed which had been scented with herbs and dried rose petals, and when he was installed therein, undressed myself slowly, in languorous display like a harem dancer for his pleasure, shaking loose my hair, offering him the point of a shoulder, the curve of a thigh, the length of a brown and—I believed—shapely leg, until he reached out and pulled me on top of him.

"What a pagan you are, Olivia."

"Is that wrong?"

"Oh, very likely. Brides are supposed to be bashful and coy and not at all sure they like it—or so we're told."

"So I disappoint you, master—or do I?"

"You dazzle me—completely dazzle me. I don't think I've seen anyone else clearly since April when you first walked into Clarrow as if it belonged to you."

"It does belong to me."

"We'll cross that bridge when we come to it, shall we darling?"

Of course we would, for my grandfather could live another ten or fifteen years yet, whether he liked it or not, by which time there would be our children, a new generation of Herons entirely unblemished by any shadows from the past, who could not fail to win his heart.

And, for the time being, I was content to be exactly where I was, here in this deep, soft bed, a bleak afternoon outside the window, rich firelight within, the body's luxurious repose after lovemaking drifting to the edge of sleep.

"I love you, Olivia."

I no longer felt that uneasily whispering need to question it.

The Gatehouse, my first home as a wife, was small but entirely—if only temporarily—perfect, a dining parlor and drawing room with low oak-beams and thick stone walls, two slope-ceilinged bedrooms above, furnished with the unremarkable items left behind by other Heron dependents, all the family widows and spinsters, the pensioned-off colonels and eccentric bachelors, who had occupied the house before me. But I had never chosen furniture of my own, had always made the best of whatever one's landlord thought suitable for one's situation, and I was more than content. I had a solid roof above my head and not just any roof, at that. In nine months I had moved from my precarious perch in the rue du Bac through Bradeswick to the gates of Clarrow Fell, their wrought-iron magnificence filling my front windows, my rear windows giving me a view of a walled garden, anonymous with winter, largely covered over with last year's leaves, but arousing great enthusiasm from Robin. No one had touched it for years, not since a very ancient Miss Matilda Heron had passed away, but Robin would remedy that. There would be purple clematis flowering around my door in summer, he told me, honeysuckle draping itself around my windows, apple blossom and cherry blossom in season and a carpet of bluebells, if he remembered rightly, down by the willow-tree once he had cleared away the scrub. There was a herb-garden too, or what remained of one—for Miss Matilda had been a great one for herbs, quite a witch, he and Alys had once liked to think—and plenty of room to extend it, to plant evergreen rosemary to darken my hair, wild red flowers of bergamot to attract the bees—did I really not care for that drowsy, humming bee chant of midsummer?—lemon balm for its scent, long pink spikes of hyssop and gray-leaved lavender; slow-growing, raven-skinned juniper berries; green flowering sweet marjoram and white-flowering sweet basil.

And now that he put his mind to it he could easily recall, in

163

Matilda's day, a profusion of old-fashioned cottage-garden flowers, clove-scented pinks and their delicate silver-green foliage, marigolds, primroses, hollyhocks, columbines, and over there, just before the hawthorn hedge, trellis upon trellis of sweet peas in every dainty shade of mauve and pink. He could hardly wait for winter to be over so that he could re-discover them, restore them, with his patient gardening skills, to life.

"I should have been a horticulturist, you know—not a lawyer."

"Do you really think so?"

"Yes, I really do. I might even have gone in for it, too, if they hadn't pointed out to me that I couldn't do a thing like that to my father. I mean—'What's your boy doing now, Esmond old chap?' 'Oh, he's a jobbing gardener, don't you know.' *What* a sensation in the officers' mess. The Squire was none too keen on the idea either. So I settled for the law."

I smiled at him lovingly, indulgently, not seeing him as a lawyer or a gardener or as anything else except my lover, the man whose body could not sleep until it had been caressed by mine, who woke early to love me, whose need for me brought him home in the middle of those honeymoon afternoons, laughing and telling me that I had bewitched him.

I had never lived anywhere long enough to see anything grow and so had never planted, had regarded flowers as belonging to public parks and florists' windows and could not really believe horticulture to be a serious occupation. But if Robin wanted a herb-garden or a rose-garden, or even an orchid house like Mr. Greenlaw's, then I would move heaven and earth to make sure he had them. And when, in the fullness of time, we moved the remaining quarter of a mile from the Gatehouse to the Manor, he would have all the broad acres of Clarrow Fell to nourish and beautify.

My anxieties, that first winter, were so few, so insignificant, that they were hard to find, being mainly the small, eternal matters of curbing my mother's extravagance and settling her bills, convincing Luc that he should not only go to Hexingham but stay there, keeping a sharp eye on any young man who paid, or whom I thought ought to pay, attention to Victorine. While my joys were many and various, set within my memory like jewels in pure gold.

We explored the countryside, walking out on crystal mornings of hard frost and brilliant winter sunshine to farmhouses that were

164

long, dark smudges on the horizon, where the farmers' wives, tenants of Clarrow Fell, gave us crusty bread hot from the oven, curd tarts and treacle puddings and spicy gingerbread—the specialties of the region—perfectly at ease with "Master Robin," less so with me since the fate of their tenancies lay in my hands.

When the weather was gray, or snow obscured the moorland pathways, we confined ourselves to the village, each squat stone cottage containing its degree of curiosity about the Heron-granddaughter: old women to whom I was "gentry" and entitled to deference, young women who were less sure of it and rather more interested in my French hats; children who were not interested in me at all unless I had something edible to give them.

"Do you think they like me, Robin?" I asked quite nervously.

"Does it matter?"

Yes. Far more than I was prepared to say.

"Do you like *them*, Olivia?"

Of course I liked them. Enormously. I had neither looked at them closely nor seen them clearly. It was enough for me that they were part of Clarrow Fell.

We kept no carriage but whenever I wished to drive out the acknowledged distance for carriage horses—five miles there and five miles back—I had only to mention the matter to Amyas who would provide me with a park landau and a team of bay geldings from the Clarrow stables. I had one servant only, an unobtrusive little girl, to make beds and light fires and serve five o'clock tea, all the heavy work and the skilled work of my household being done by a relay of maids from Clarrow, sent over several times a day by Mrs. Long. My bread came to me hot and fresh every morning from Clarrow kitchens, my eggs, butter and meat from Clarrow home farm, while my share of the season's pheasant, partridge and grouse was delivered to my back door not by a poacher—the method to which, as a city-dweller, I was accustomed—but legally, if just as silently, by Amyas.

I had become almost, in fact very nearly, a daughter of the house, walking that significant quarter of a mile of driveway to my grandfather's door on the slightest pretext, still marveling inwardly that Robin needed no pretext at all. The Manor was home to him in an easy, casual fashion I envied. When he wanted a book he made free use of the library. When he wanted a gun he helped himself, whistled to the yellow retriever one could always find basking and

165

drowsing near the fire and shouldering a gamebag, walked away. When he wanted a slice of plum cake or apple tart or a handful of raisins he slipped into the kitchen, as he'd done as a boy, smiled at the cook and held out his hand. I followed him one day, feeling an intruder, to be greeted warmly by the diminutive, inquisitive Mrs. Timmins who had been cooking the Squire's dinner for so long that she stood on ceremony with no one. She gave me tea and currant buns and unquestioning acceptance. I was Olivia Heron. She had always expected the Squire to send for me. It was only right. And she proceeded, through many firelit winter afternoons thereafter, to tell me anything I cared to ask about my father and his family, not even lowering her voice when Mrs. Long, in her immaculate housekeeper's black silk, paused in the doorway and raised pained eyebrows at the kitchen clock.

The kitchen itself was an arched vault of stone with bunches of dried herbs, smoked meats and smoked fish hanging from its rafters and a huge brick oven permanently filled with the scents of ginger and cinnamon and vanilla. While Mrs. Timmins herself had little to do in the afternoons the Squire was away from home but gossip, since the maids could eat yesterday's leftovers for their supper and Amyas would take his cold pheasant or his cold beef and his bottle of claret in the housekeeper's room, with Mrs. Long.

"They're very close, those two," said Mrs. Timmins, shrewd and obliging and certainly malicious. "Close in more ways than one."

I had noticed it, regretted it even, since I had come to depend on Amyas just as everyone else at Clarrow seemed to do, and there was something tense and sarcastic, something tight-lipped and rigid about Mrs. Long which would be unlikely to make her an accommodating lover. I believed that Amyas could do better and was sorry.

Every Sunday morning I rose early, put on my best blue velvet with its spotted net veil, my blue wool coat with the squirrel cuffs and collar and three rows of fur around the hem and walked on my husband's arm not merely to Clarrow church but to the Heron family pew, luxuriating in the feel of its ancient, elaborately carved wooden gate, its scarred seat covered with dusty crimson plush. And there I would stand tall and straight and proud as a peacock between Robin— busily sketching caricatures of Aunt Sibylla in the margin of his hymn book—and my stern grandfather.

Ours was the only private pew in Clarrow, a circumstance

which forced Mrs. Naseby to worship in a neighboring and rather inconvenient village; the Pottertons having their own chapel at Dawney Park. We were *the* family. The people crowding the pews behind us, finely graded in accordance with their social status—tenant farmers, shopkeepers, publicans, the schoolmistress and the doctor and Amyas in front, upper servants, smaller tradesmen and Mrs. Long at the back—were *our* people. The farm laborers and housemaids sitting on the wooden benches which came last of all were our people too, all of them singing, with apparent enjoyment, Aunt Sibylla's favorite hymns.

"The rich man in his castle," they cheerfully chorused, "the poor man at his gate. God made them, high or lowly. And ordered their estate."

I did not even hear the words, so ablaze was I with happiness, and therefore did not question them.

On our first Christmas morning we exchanged gold earrings and gold cuff-links, drank hot spiced wine in bed and then walked up the drive to Clarrow to eat our traditional roast turkey and plum pudding beneath the great window in the hall, the candles burning in their wall sconces, a log fire blazing, the Squire doing his duty and no more, even when a crowd of tenants came jostling in to wish him the compliments of the season.

"Long life to you, sir."

"Quite so," he said, his tight, sardonic tone implying that it had already been long enough. But when they made it plain that they wished to drink my health too he merely nodded, refilled their glasses, and stood apart from us in front of his stone hearth, grimly watching me.

"Long life to you, Mrs. Esmond."

And smiling, including them each and every one in my impossible, immeasurable bliss, I was quite certain—like Max de Haan—that I would live at least forever.

But my gift of immortality was clearly not meant for everyone. For on the 22nd January that year Queen Victoria died in the arms of her grandson, Kaiser Wilhelm of Germany, the eldest son of her eldest daughter, a difficult man with a withered arm and a somewhat hysterical disposition who—in common with the rest of Europe's royal highnesses—had all his life been intimidated by the diminutive and, one had heard, equally hysterical Victoria.

She was eighty-one years old, had had nine children and sixty-four grandchildren and great-grandchildren, an elite band including not only the German Kaiser but the Empress Alexandra of Russia, the Queens or queens-to-be of Greece, Rumania and Denmark. She had reigned as Queen Empress of the British Empire for sixty-four years, the last forty of which she had spent in full, deep black mourning for her husband, the German Prince Albert, and had thoroughly mistrusted all men—including her eldest son—who did not resemble him. She had been morbid, self-indulgent, passionate and prim both together, narrow in her views and autocratic in her manners, and had suffered, during her long reign, several bouts of serious unpopularity. But extreme old age had redeemed the worst flaws in her character, since old ladies are allowed to be reclusive and temperamental, and on the day she died she was the nation's mother, for whom the entire nation was ready to mourn.

I visited Bradeswick on the morning of the 23rd to find every shop window and every door knocker draped in black, every man I passed wearing a black armband, even the road-menders who were completing repairs to Aireville Terrace wearing dark-colored sweat-rags and keeping their voices most respectfully low. The haberdashers' shops in Station Square had sold out their entire stock of black ties by noon and three days later ready-made mourning dresses of all qualities—from silk and crêpe-de-chine to paramatta, whipcord and common hopsack—had not only trebled in price but were virtually unobtainable.

By the end of the week a yard of black dress material was harder to find than gold not merely in Bradeswick but from Land's End to John o' Groats, several ladies of our acquaintance having feverishly scoured the warehouses of Bradford and Leeds to no avail; a situation—like all others—which brought grief to some and profit to many. Florists, gentlemen with substantial quantities of black dye in stock, owners of houses along the funeral route who were letting their front windows for amounts as high as £170, did well enough. Jewelers and caterers fared badly as parties and balls and the finery that went with them were canceled. The flower shop at the corner of Aireville Terrace took on extra hands to complete the rush of orders, to be sent with tens of thousands of other floral tributes to Windsor. The tea-shop, recently opened in Market Street—the only establishment in Bradeswick where ladies could obtain refreshment and, as the coy phrase

168

had it "powder their noses"—went out of business, tea-parties no longer being the order of the day. London's theaters closed as a mark of respect, with the result that three thousand theatrical employees lost their wages.

"How sad," my mother said, her deep sigh expressing a passing thought for the Queen and a real anxiety that so much unrelieved black did not suit her. "It is to go on until April, I hear. Do you know, Olivia, I feel quite tempted to take a little trip, somewhere warm and *colorful*, until this sorry business is done."

But by that same afternoon her volatile spirits had been much revived by the unexpected return of Max de Haan, coming himself from a climate warm enough to have added a deeper layer of bronze to his skin and colorful enough to have kept him very adequately amused for the five months he had been away. He looked hard and brown and polished as a nut, wearing, the first time I saw him, a full-length motoring-coat of black fur and his usual air of audacious, questionable prosperity.

"Max—what a *pleasant* surprise. Are you well?"

"Never better."

I believed him. For, hearing of the Queen's death while on his way through France—from exactly where he did not say—he had made a rapid assessment of the situation, hurried at once to Roubaix where he had purchased ninety precious tons of black dress material and shipped it to England; thus making himself yet another audacious, questionable, probably quite sizeable fortune.

"How very clever," my mother said. "He has even brought enough jet beads and black veils for us to look positively *bereaved* for the funeral."

Yet the funeral procession itself took the whole nation, let alone my mother, by surprise for although the number of Highnesses in attendance—Royal, Serene and Imperial—was perfectly satisfactory, Queen Victoria herself had repudiated the black mourning gowns she had worn for forty years and lay in her coffin, at her own express command, in a white dress and her white lace wedding veil, a bride again returning to her Albert.

And so the Queen was dead. Long live King Edward, the name an act of defiance in itself—or of liberation—against his mother's last and dearest wish that he should style himself King Albert in memory of the father he had failed so utterly to resemble. He was sixty years old and because his mother, believing him unfit for responsibility, had never allowed him to have any, his talents had been stretched no further than the selection of race-horses and attractively mature married women. While Prince of Wales he had launched the dinner-jacket so much despised by Mr. Greenlaw, pleated dress shirts and Homburg hats and was entirely responsible for the fashion of leaving the bottom button of the waistcoat undone. He was a man of varied and considerable appetite, eating enormous, complex dinners of a dozen courses followed by suppers of grilled oysters and champagne, smoking an impressive total of twelve huge cigars and twenty cigarettes a day. He was sophisticated, cosmopolitan, vain.

"Good old Teddy," they were calling him a day or two after that startling white funeral. For the Victorian age was now over. We had a new century, a new King. An entirely new set of aims, means, values. What could be better? Good old Teddy.

"I'll drink to that," said Max de Haan, strolling into my mother's drawing room late one afternoon, bringing with him a case of champagne and accompanied, to everyone's surprise, by Alys, dressed in a light brown coat and skirt with not even a black-bordered handkerchief or a black ribbon in her unseasonal straw hat.

"I found this young lady darting across Market Square," Max told us, "in flight from her mamma, I rather imagine."

"Oh dear," she said, laughing and frowning both together, not knowing quite how to sit down or whether it would be better to go on standing; ungainly, vulnerable, impossibly, dangerously charming. "Oh dear—yes I was. Aunt Lavinia will think me very remiss . . ."

"Why no dear—by no means. But what I *do* think is that you are the first female I have seen in ten days who is not in black."

"I do not believe in the wearing of mourning, Aunt Lavinia, not even for those with whom I have been personally acquainted."

"Well, yes dear," my mother said, not taking it too seriously. "I daresay. Many of us would not entirely disagree. But belief, you know, has very little to do with it. One simply *does* these things. It is far easier in the long run and saves a great deal of annoyance."

"My mother says so too."

"And you are able to stand up to her and defy her?" Clearly my mother was now impressed. "Heavens—I never could."

But Alys, smiling, shook her head, tendrils of fine blond hair escaping from their pins.

"Oh no, I never defy her. I am just deceitful."

"*Alys!* I cannot believe it.'

"But it is quite true, Aunt Lavinia. I have been deceitful every day of my life, these past twelve years—at least."

"My goodness . . ." said my mother.

"How intriguing," said Max.

"What she means," said Robin, drawing out a chair for her, "is that she is forever saying 'Yes, mamma' and then going off to do exactly as she pleases. Poor Aunt Sibylla—how many pairs of black gloves have you conveniently left on the train, Alys, or how many yards of black crêpe have somehow just fallen off your hat, since the Queen died?"

"You don't believe in mourning either, Robin."

I bit my lip, conscious of my own beautifully cut black silk which I had browbeaten an overworked seamstress into making for me, my collar of jet beads and the long jet earrings I had purchased, via my mother, from Max. If Robin did not believe in mourning why had he allowed me to go to all this trouble and expense? I had no particular views on the subject and would have seized the opportunity of pleasing him with both hands had I realized it existed, defying the established custom because "Robin and I" not "Robin and Alys" did not believe in it.

Should I have known his opinion? Perhaps. Should he have told me? I rather believed he should. It hurt me and made me angry to think that he had not. It hurt me rather more when I began to wonder why.

"Well, now," said Max, a respectful black tie around his neck, a celebratory glass of champagne in his hand, "having declared Alys a revolutionary *and* having seen Victoria safely—and once and for all—into her grave, shall we drink to our new King? Here's to good old Teddy. Long may he reign. For I have a feeling his reign will be good to me."

He raised his glass, his diamond taking fire in the winter lamp-light, his smile satisfied and a little mocking as if he had just flung down a challenge to this new era, a declaration that the time of men like Prince Albert the Good, the traditionalists, the moralists, the Squire Heron, was over, the time of the *entrepreneur*, the men of openly declared wealth and unashamed appetite, just beginning.

Queen Victoria had only cared for serious men. King Edward liked his friends to be amusing, adventurous and rich.

"Good old Teddy. And here's to your courage, Alys."

"Oh," she said, looking startled, "I have no courage, Max."

"On the contrary—enough, at any rate, to open that cage door one of these days and fly away."

And leaning forward, too intent on his meaning and too serious in her exploration of its possibilities to be embarrassed, she sighed, her face suddenly and touchingly naked. "If I could . . ."

"What stops you? The cage is not real, you know. Nothing holds it together but convention. Nothing holds *you* inside it but your own conscience."

"Max," she said, "it is not so simple. One can open a cage door but even then the bird does not always fly away—*cannot*."

And it was as if he had asked her to fly away with him, today, this very minute, to some impossible, exotic land of freedom, leaving nothing behind but a note for Aunt Sibylla.

"Dear boy . . ." said my mother, evidently sharing my impression.

"Steady on . . ." said Robin, who should have said nothing, noticed nothing, who should not have cared that other men could be intrigued by Alys.

"Don't worry," she said, glancing quickly at Robin, replying to the silent communication still operating between them, her mind picking up the anxiety in his, her voice answering it, reassuring him and at the same time injecting that first cold trickle of fear into my blood; a seed, a germ which, as it bred and multiplied within me, would become the terrible, self-crippling disease of jealousy.

TEN

By the first anniversary of my marriage the Boer War should have been over. The Commander-in-Chief of the British forces in Africa, Lord Roberts, not only thought so but considered he had won it, since—leaving his second-in-command, Lord Kitchener, to conduct mopping-up operations against a mere two or three thousand obstinate guerillas—he came home in April, to be cheered by a grateful House of Commons who promptly granted him an earldom with an endowment of £100,000.

"A splendid fellow, Lord Roberts," said several of my acquaintances, Lady Potterton, for instance, who had once gone to dinner with his sister-in-law; Aunt Sibylla, who often found it expedient to echo the opinions of Lady Potterton; and the Squire, who valued good breeding in military men.

"Wasteful," said Mr. Greenlaw, a Liberal and a firm believer in free trade who had heard what the Tory Government, bolstered up by the military successes of Lord Roberts, planned to impose in the way of import tariffs.

"I do not believe in this war," said Robin.

"I do not believe in any war," said Alys.

"Nonsense, dear, of course you do," said her mother.

And it was generally considered that Lord Kitchener would make short work of those few thousand Boer guerillas.

"Bandits," said Lady Potterton and Aunt Sibylla.

"Farmers defending their homes and families," said Robin quickly because he knew Alys was about to say it and wanted to spare her her mother's anger.

"A splendid fellow, Lord Kitchener," said Lady Potterton who, although this particular lordship did not much care for the society of women, would be sure to know *someone* with whom he was closely acquainted.

"Can't stomach these orientalists," said Mr. Greenlaw who had heard how during his command in the Sudan, Lord Kitchener had permitted the continuance of Oriental punishments such as the cutting off of hands for theft and had held in his own hands for a rather long moment the skull of his arch-enemy, the Mahdi, considering whether he might use it as an ink-stand or a drinking cup.

But at least—whether one could stomach easternized British Officers and newly belted earls or not—the war was over. It had taken 500,000 of our professionally trained soldiers to subdue 40,000 psalm-singing farmers, many of whom had ridden into battle in their Sunday suits. But now, after the humiliation of those initial defeats, after the tragedy of so many young men killed by bullets, by disease and the mistakes of our generals, we had won.

"I wonder," said Max, who knew the country. "Kitchener will have more trouble than he imagines with those burghers. You can't fight an enemy unless you can find it, after all."

And so it proved, the supposedly victorious army of occupation being harassed when least expected in its most vulnerable places, by these small bands of men who, appearing from behind a cloud of hot African dust, would inflict their grievous damage and melt away.

"Cowardly," said Lady Potterton.

"Effective," said Max.

"Tragic," said Alys who had heard the first rumors of Kitchener's new strategy of burning down the farms on which these Boer guerillas—who were farmers first of all—depended not only for their livelihood in peacetime but for the food they now required to keep them in action.

"Regrettable—but necessary, don't you see," said Lady Potterton, in the tone of a parent who, before administering a good thrashing, will often warn "This will not hurt you half so much as it hurts me."

"Appalling," said Alys, for letters from Africa had started to pour home—the Education Acts of the eighteen-seventies having produced the first generation of private soldiers who could read and write—containing graphic descriptions of Boer families, mothers,

174

grandmothers, little children, huddled together in mute horror while men like Private Edgar Birkinshaw of Pasture Cottages, Clarrow Fell, who could identify far more easily with a Boer farmer than with Lord Kitchener, set their homes on fire, drove off their cattle, scorched their land.

"Dreadful," said Victorine, who rarely expressed an opinion in public.

"Murderous. But *effective*," said Max. Yes, indeed. For these homeless Boer women and children could not, after all, be left to starve on the open *veldt* and so they were taken, partly for safekeeping, partly for their value as hostages, and *concentrated* into military-style camps where, as a result of the blunderings of that military machine—which still kept on losing its supply wagons and could never manage to have on hand anything approaching sufficient quantities of bandages and fresh water, medical supplies or medical officers to administer them—a shocking total of twenty thousand captive women and children died of those eternal military hazards, disease and neglect.

"How very distressing," said Aunt Sibylla, meaning that she suspected, without being able to prove anything, that Alys had been attending meetings of some kind in Bradeswick and airing views which would not improve her mother's relationship with the Pottertons.

"It might bring the government down," said Mr. Greenlaw hopefully, his dislike of the Tory attacks on free trade far exceeding any compassion he might have felt for the Boers.

"I suppose—being accustomed to deal with fighting men—Lord Kitchener did not realize that women and children die so easily," said Lady Potterton.

No one answered her.

But in May of 1902 the war *was* over, few men being hard enough to stand back and watch their women die, the final annexation of the Boer Republics with all their gold and diamonds being viewed by Lady Potterton as a fitting Coronation present for King Edward, whose anointing took place in August, a day I remembered largely because it presented me, yet again, with the evidence that I was not expecting a child.

It was a repeated failure I could neither understand nor tolerate since I was healthy, strong, just twenty-two years old, and wanted a baby so badly that there were days—bleak, bitter days indeed—when I could no longer bear the sight of other people's children.

"How strange," my mother said, "when I have spent my life trying not to and somehow or other, have had five—and one or two little mishaps we will not speak of. Never mind, darling, for it is not the be-all and end-all of life, you know—far from it. And Robin's inclinations do not seem to be dynastic."

Indeed they were not.

"In fact, Olivia—and one should take this into account, darling—does he even *want* a child?"

I doubted it. But then, what did Robin want? Or, at least what did he want so passionately that he could not bear to be without it? Sometimes, with an uncomfortable sensation of loose sand shifting beneath my feet, I was not entirely sure.

He wanted me, of course. I still had the evidence of that every night, could still catch the gleam of it in his eyes and his mind as he looked at me across the dinner-table or, leaning towards me suddenly in a public place, would simply whisper, "Olivia. Come home." We were both still mesmerized by the physical sensations we could arouse in one another, caring for each other's bodies as if they had been musical instruments to be tuned and polished and nurtured to perfection.

But what else moved him? What else, besides the harmony of his beauty and the beauty he saw in me, could arouse more in him than a shrug, a smile, a casual "Ah well—never mind"?

Yet it was this very attitude of nonchalance which had first attracted me and which continued, despite an occasional spurt of irritation, to charm me still.

I had got out of bed in the cold dawn many times now to watch him ride off to the meet at Dawney Park in the full glory of his hunting-pink. I had tied his hunting stock and polished his hat myself, my heart bursting with pride, knowing that no other horseman could ever look half so handsome. Certainly not Clive Potterton, home on leave that season from India and apparently intent on riding his mother's tall, wild-eyed hunters into the ground. Not Felix Potterton either, the smooth young politician of the family, whose long drooping moustache always seemed to me as well-oiled as his nature. Not even Max de Haan, superbly mounted and impeccably turned out though he may be, his lean, dark face and whipcord figure by no means ill-suited to the traditional flamboyance of pink jacket, white stock, tall black hat.

But Clive Potterton, unless he should happen to break his neck or his horse's legs in the process, would always be in at the finish. So too would Felix although he may well have taken a circuitous route. Max would speak sharp words to Lord Potterton, Master of the Hunt, if no fox had been found, declaring himself unwilling to waste his time chasing about the countryside after nothing but a pack of bewildered dogs, advising his lordship that unless he could provide sport he should not expect the hunt to be maintained by subscriptions from sporting gentlemen.

But Robin went out for the fresh air and the exercise and, when he had had enough of both, came home or if the fancy took him, called in at an ale-house, letting the hunt go by while he chatted with the locals on surprisingly philosophical matters or flirted cheerfully and harmlessly with the barmaids.

It did not disturb him in the least whether they found a fox or not. Why should it, when he doubted he had been in at the kill more than twice in a dozen years, and then only by accident. He had been "blooded," of course, as a child. So had Guy, and Alys. The Squire himself had daubed their faces with fox's blood, as was customary, just as he had done, in their day, for my father and Amyas and Max. Guy had not minded but Robin had not liked it much and Alys had never hunted again. If one went out into the woods early enough in the morning one could often see families of fox cubs dancing and playing their mischievous, graceful games. The most enchanting creatures in the world, he thought. So enchanting that as a boy he had had to restrain himself from bringing one home in his pocket, since it would only have ended up being massacred by the dogs. How complicated life was.

I wrinkled my nose in a grimace of distaste and sympathy. I did not think I would have cared for that smear of fox-blood on my cheek either. Nor, as a matter of fact—although I would never have admitted it to my grandfather—did I care for the sight of the game-cart trundling past my window at the end of every shoot, heavy-laden with those piles of tiny, feathered bodies on their way to the game-larder at the Manor. But since Robin *did* shoot and professed to enjoy it, there were times when I would have liked him to have taken it just a little more seriously, times when I grew frankly irritated by the praises heaped on Max de Haan who, like his father before him, could bring down a hundred grouse with a hundred consecutive shots any autumn morning.

I believed Robin could do the same if he put his mind to it.

He shook his head. Shrugged. Smiled. Possibly. Possibly not. But sport was sport. He was there to enjoy himself, not turn it into a competition like Clive Potterton and Max who would stand out on the moor all day bringing down anything that flew until one of them—usually Max—had decisively beaten the other. And at least Robin had never lost his temper like Clive Potterton, started firing wild and hit his cousin Felix, not fatally, of course, which—Robin said—could be called a pity. Oh yes, hadn't I heard? If Felix did manage to get himself a seat in Westminster at the coming by-election he would hardly be doing much actual sitting on it for a while.

But at the annual steeplechase starting from Clarrow church steeple and finishing at the steeple of nearby Appleburton, Felix Potterton appeared to be sitting comfortably enough on his neat roan mare, putting in an appearance for the sake of the "sporting vote," Robin assured me since everyone knew that Felix would take no undue risks over those stony, treacherous miles, those high hedges and concealed ditches which separated the two church spires. Felix would not win. But he would arrive unscathed to congratulate the winner.

Clive Potterton intended to win, I could see that, and so did Max de Haan, each one eyeing and measuring the other, both of them on tall, nervous thoroughbreds which looked equally ferocious to me. They were, I thought, about the same height, Max a little younger, Clive a little heavier, but there could not be much in it either way. No real advantage to either, except that I knew Clive had been drinking heavily until late the night before, whereas Max, I rather imagined, would first have placed substantial bets on his own performance with anyone who cared to gamble with him and then retired early, and alone, to bed.

I watched him tip his hat to a group of young ladies which included Alys and, remembering that the Squire had forbidden him to set foot on Clarrow land, wondered how he dared. But he had come here today with the Pottertons whose house-guest he was and on whose property the race ended. And therefore, personal enmity being one thing, courtesy to one's neighbors quite another, my grandfather, with the assistance of Amyas, simply continued to supervise the distribution of ale and mulled wine which, as Squire of Clarrow, it was his obligation to provide, exactly as if no such affliction as Max de Haan had ever existed. Max, I thought, could hardly count that a victory, although I supposed he would very likely win the race.

Robin rode up to the churchyard on the big chestnut gelding he had recently purchased at Appleburton Horse Fair, looking relaxed, slightly amused, competing very plainly, just for the fun of it. I saw the young ladies who were standing with Alys become instantly aware of him, not appearing to look his way but making a great fuss, suddenly, with parasols and gloves, a great swirling of skirts and adjusting of flowery hats, in the hope that he would notice them. I saw a pair of village girls stare at him openly and avidly; while even the handful of farmers who were sullenly consuming as much of the Squire's ale as they could get—since it was *their* fields and fences, after all, that the gentry were about to ride down—brightened up sufficiently to growl out a "mornin', young squire," to Robin.

Urgently, I wanted him to win.

Fiercely I knew that in his place I would do anything and everything to be the first at Appleburton church steeple.

Tolerantly, affectionately and with just a whisper of exasperation, I understood that Robin did not care.

It would be Max, he supposed, or Clive. Clive, he rather hoped, since, if half the things one heard about him were true, he must need the money. Whereas Max, simply liked to win. But either one of them would be quite ready to murder the other, once they got out there and their blood was up, just to prove—what? Guy had evidently understood since he had once set about a Blackwood cousin with his riding crop for getting in his way—Guy had said—and bringing him down. Robin who, year after year, managed, without violence, to come in an effortless third, was accustomed to these scenes at the winning-post. A pity, he thought, on the whole, although one could often see the funny side to it.

At least, *he* could, although Alys, for instance, found the whole thing extremely distasteful. It was the damage to the fields and the animals, of course, that she did not like, everything which lay in that direct line between one village steeple and the other forming part of the race-track. And since the riders would be bound to stray off course what it really amounted to was an invading horde of savages, screaming and yelling, some of them half-drunk before they started, riding into chicken yards and duck ponds, through vegetable patches and washing lines, generally playing havoc with everything. And neither the villagers nor the farmers could complain since these same sporting gentlemen were also their landlords.

It was a state of affairs which Alys deplored. Robin, even though he took part in the race, felt bound to agree with her. Had I been a cottager or a farmer I might well have gone out with a pitch-fork to defend my ducks and chickens. But the fact remained that I too could see no point in entering a race unless one meant, most decidedly, to win.

Clive Potterton was declared the victor on that particular occasion, his arrival at the winning-post being so neck and neck with Max that it had taken the judges—the men of Appleburton—a moment or two to decide.

"Congratulations," said Max, knowing that the residents of Appleburton, who paid rent to the Pottertons, could not possibly have chosen otherwise. It was a fair win, he graciously admitted and then proceeded, that evening at the Pottertons' card table, to relieve Clive not only of his winnings but of a hundred guineas more.

I would not have lost my winnings to anyone.

Yet, what did a steeplechase really matter? It was all a game, as Robin said. Nations would neither rise nor fall as a result of it. Like most things in life, like the broken fences, the startled ducks, like the young men killed in Africa, who would remember tomorrow? Robin was right. But the ease with which he allowed the awkward things of life to wash over him alarmed me and grieved me when it applied to my childlessness.

I wanted a child for its own sake. I wanted a child because I could not accept the failure of my body to bear one. I wanted a child because, without putting the need into words, I suspected that sensuality might not last forever and, in case it should fail, I must have something equally precious and powerful with which to replace it.

I had no real knowledge of the process of conception. One made love. One had children. So far as other people were concerned it seemed as simple as that. I lay in his arms, night after night, my body rich and slumberous with its deep yearning for fertility, governed by a sensual appetite which was hungry not only for pleasure but for the seed he planted in me. And, for three weeks of every month, I nurtured that seed, identified it, adored it, and then sometimes took to my bed on the fourth week when it left me in a painful draining of blood.

I suffered atrocious stomach cramps, sick headaches, intolerable frustration, an occasional flicker of fear. To have a child was the ultimate intimacy. Nothing could be closer than that. I wanted that intimacy. To have a child was also the ultimate safety, or so I imagined, and I wanted to be safe. What threatened me? The suspicion that I had nothing to offer my husband but the satisfaction of his physical desires? And the terrifying knowledge, learned from my mother, that desire was fickle? Did I truly think so ill of myself? Of course not. Did my love for Robin seem so miraculous to me that I felt compelled to spoil it, just a little, by jealousy so that the forces which controlled our lives would not think it *too* perfect for me? How foolish. But why, when I longed for a child so desperately, did it matter so little to Robin?

And if he shunned the irrevocable bond of parenthood then surely it followed—or did it?—that his love had less substance than mine, less finality, that his commitment to me was less certain, less *settled* than the commitment I had made to him. Did I really believe that? Lying in bed alone at the end of every month, bleeding, aching, defeated, I was capable of believing anything.

But, of course, I would never expose my fears, would never take the risk of asking him why he was so wary of fatherhood, in case I could not bear the answer. Eventually I would conceive. *Yes*, I would. And until that day, when I would be immortal again and completely secure, there would be no confrontation. I would never ask.

"Why," I said suddenly, a bolt from the blue, "why don't you want a baby?"

"Darling—have I said so?"

I could have left it there. Much better. Yes I *would* leave it there. No sharp words spoken, no harm done. I would just turn my head into my pillow and pretend to go to sleep.

"But you don't, do you? All I want is the truth. Well—do you?"

"No," he said, "not particularly . . ."

How dare he? Yes, I may have asked him for the truth but how dare it be that?

"Olivia—does it matter all that much? If it happens then I'll be glad. If it doesn't then—well, it doesn't, that's all. If it's so important to you I hope we can manage it, what more can I say? And I certainly do everything in my power, don't I?"

How could he be so calm, so uncaring? Unless it was, after all, that he didn't care, that my mother was right and all men were Jean-François, in disguise.

I glared at him, determined that nothing he might say could ever console me.

"Darling, I'm not a belted earl, you know. I don't need an heir. I'm not even sure I understand what fatherhood is all about. What would I have to turn into? A combination of the Colonel, the Squire and my housemaster at Hexingham? I don't think I'm up to it, that's all. And if it should be difficult for you, or dangerous—and it does rather look that way—then I'd much rather not."

Was he saying he didn't want to risk me in childbirth? Or was he just making excuses? Was he showing consideration and kindness? But what use to me was kindness when I wanted adoration, total joy or failing that, total agony which would be better by far than the bland, half-feelings of liking and disliking.

I sat up, burst into tears and threw one of my pillows at him, following swiftly with the other which he knocked harmlessly aside, laughing, making a comic performance of dodging and parrying blows as he came to hold me in what I forced myself to recognize as loving arms.

But these crises lasted no longer than a day or two and I would soon be up and about, hurrying to the Manor in the hope of a word from my grandfather, gossiping with Mrs. Timmins by the kitchen fire and annoying Mrs. Long, running here and there as I took up my busy, happy life again.

Shortly after our marriage Robin had accepted the situation which had long been awaiting him with Messrs. Lawker & Lane, solicitors to the Squire, his duties being so very far from arduous that he appeared able to discharge them in only two or three days a week, particularly in the hunting season. He found the work tedious, Mr. Lawker a dull fellow, Mr. Lane a pompous bore. But at least those few hours a week spent conveyancing property from one owner to another and drawing up wills, relieved him of the title "gentleman of leisure" which had started to embarrass him. It was high time he had something to do, he told me. One could think about life too long, until it had passed him by. But what, I wondered, did he still need to consider. There would be no time for Lawker & Lane when my grandfather died and Robin, to all intents and purposes became the new squire. We would have plenty to occupy us then with the land and the Manor, and perhaps my brother Luc could take Robin's place with our family solicitor? Unless, of course, my mother should become

182

the second Mrs. Samuel Greenlaw, in which case a surer outlet for Luc's talents might well be found in industry.

Yes, that would do very well for Luc. But, at the moment, he was still only just thirteen, a pupil at Hexingham where he was learning Latin and Greek and good manners which, Robin declared, was as much as Hexingham taught. But at least he was *there*—his fees paid with the economics I made in my housekeeping—and would eventually acquire the status of an old school tie, the correct accent, the air of patrician *hauteur* only rarely glimpsed in Robin, ever present in Max, the Pottertons and the Squire.

Luc was for the future. An English gentleman in the making, perfectly adapted to the Manor. My conquest of local society and the carving of a place for my sisters within it occupied the present.

The first winter of my marriage, Lady Potterton—Dottie to her friends—paid a duty call on the Squire and, as she passed the Gatehouse, her curiosity overcame her. She sent her coachman to knock on my door, alighted and spent ten minutes looking me over in a way with which I was quite familiar and very well-equipped to deal. She had known my mother, but she had known Robin's mother too. My father had been a horseman of considerable prowess and, therefore, since she judged all men by their ability to ride and shoot, one of her closest friends. The Squire was visibly ageing, everyone had noticed it, and if by some miracle I succeeded in keeping the Manor and restoring the former high standard of its hospitality then my acquaintance would be of use to her. One never knew, after all, when one might need to borrow a spare horse to accommodate a houseguest. There were the hunt subscriptions to be kept up and the little matter of getting Felix elected to Parliament, for which she would be obliged to enlist the support of all her neighbors. And could one be certain, in this increasingly uncertain world, that I might not somewhere encounter and invite to Clarrow Fell a woman wealthy and courageous enough to marry her wayward Clive? I had heard rumors that the Potterton fortunes were no longer quite what they once had been. I had heard rather awesome whispers about the size of Clive Potterton's debts. Therefore, without actually promising anything, I led the noble but simple-minded lady to believe that my supply of horses and heiresses *could*, in certain circumstances, be plentiful, assessing what she wanted to hear and saying it. A trick of the poor-relation's trade which I had learned along the boulevards, and which I repeated a few days later with Mrs. Esmeralda Naseby of the Brewery.

I did not greatly care for either one of them. Dottie Potterton was large and bland and dull, a creature of migratory habits who spent every year from May to July at her house in Mayfair, moving north to Dawney Park in August for the grouse, where she would remain for most of the winter, throwing herself with a whole heart and an occasional fractured limb into the hunting season. February would be spent in Monte Carlo, followed by a short fishing trip to Scotland, then back to Dawney Park until May when the start of the London Season called her south again.

Esmeralda Naseby, on the other hand, rarely left her home at Willow Court, a graceful, vaguely Grecian villa set in a large, intensely landscaped garden half-way between Bradeswick and Clarrow Fell. She was a thin, whispering woman, the frail and sensitive widow— in her own view—of a rough-spoken brewer who had left her a great deal of money but had, to her great satisfaction, broken her health. Life with Jack Naseby, she implied, had been harsh and degrading. The spending of his vast fortune had won her enormous local popularity, the chef she had engaged to cook her own invalid diet also providing the most sumptuous and imaginative luncheons and teas, her garden-parties and the masked ball she gave every Halloween in the classically proportioned music pavilion built at the edge of her smoothly manicured lawn, being the highlights of the Bradeswick social season.

Dottie Potterton, so far as I could tell, had two grand passions in her life; horses and what she saw as the natural superiority of the Potterton clan.

Esmeralda Naseby also had two passions, her own personal comfort, no matter what inconvenience it might cause to anyone else, and her son, the heir to the Naseby millions, a beautiful boy—according to his ailing, doting mamma—at present completing his studies in Italy.

"They must be the two most boring women in the world," moaned Robin when he realized I expected him to spend time in their company. "Ever since I first came to Clarrow, when I was seven years old, I've always walked the other way if I saw either of them coming."

So, I rather imagined—although he remembered not to tell me so—had Alys. But neither of them had ever heard the sound of

184

a door slamming in their faces. They had always been respectable, certain of their parentage and from which direction their next meal might be likely to appear. They had always been guests at the party, taking for granted a welcome for which I still had to fight. No longer for myself, perhaps, but for Madelon and Victorine.

"I'm sorry," he said, swiftly understanding. "I'll do what I can." But despite the excellence of his intentions his idea of courting *Mesdames* Naseby and Potterton was simply to refrain from leaving by the back door when he spotted either of them coming to call; just to *be* there, vaguely courteous, not really listening to a word. And I knew it would take far more than that to convert these two capricious women into my most intimate—and therefore useful—friends.

With Dottie Potterton I was a "good sport," with Esmeralda Naseby I was a "good listener," not only sympathizing with the delicacy of her health but appearing to believe in it, showing great interest in the artistic aspirations of her son. I spent tedious spring and summer afternoons in the garden at Willow Court, sipping China tea and eating cucumber sandwiches, enduring Mrs. Naseby's maternal outpourings while bolder spirits played croquet on the lawn. I admired the indifferent water-colors her son had sent her from Italy and went into ecstasies at the many miniature portraits of the young marvel himself, painted from infancy upwards, which she carried in lockets and brooches about her person. I waited until my company had become useful and pleasant to her and then, taking the gamble that her self-centered nature would not relinquish anything it enjoyed, I invited her to tea at the Gatehouse when Victorine was there. Her choice was clear. If she refused my sister's acquaintance she could hardly expect to keep mine. And Victorine seemed such a sensible, *respectable* girl, just the kind who might be very good at arranging sofa cushions behind an aching back and who was not quite pretty enough to be a temptation to her delicate, darling son. She took Victorine's hand and, therefore, was obliged to do the same, very publicly, when Victorine and I happened to meet her in Bradeswick Park. The next time I paid an informal call at Willow Court I took Victorine with me. An invitation to a croquet party soon followed. And where Mrs. Naseby led, Bradeswick at least would follow.

I knew my limitations with the Pottertons and kept strictly within them. Their huge, shabby, chaotic household, which existed solely to accommodate the dogs, the boots and spurs and the appetites

of hunting men, both amused and attracted me. But I was still uncomfortable with horses, had no authority with dogs and, since I could
not conceal it, turned it instead into a laughing matter.

"Olivia is *hopeless*," said Dottie, affectionately.

"But charming," said Felix, his mind on the Clarrow electorate
which the Squire—male or female—should be able to control.

"I could teach you to ride in no time," offered Clive, who was
leaving for India the day after tomorrow. And even had I not seen
the gleam of Jean-François in his eyes, I would have declined.

What I could do, however, was follow the hunt in a carriage
and, at some convenient moment, dispense cold roast chicken and
champagne from a picnic hamper to sporting gentlemen who, being
easily bored and constantly in need of distraction, came clustering
around me in pleasing numbers. I waited until they had started to
look for me, to ride up with an eager, "I say, Mrs. Esmond, we thought
you'd deserted us today." And then, one crisp morning, I brought
Madelon with me in a blue velvet cape with a swansdown muff and
a dashing velvet cap with a tall white feather. No gentleman, of course,
would object to making the acquaintance of this enchanting creature.
In the camaraderie of the hunting-field neither did the ladies. And
having chatted to her so easily in country lanes and woodland clear-
ings, having accepted glasses of wine from her dainty fingers, one
could hardly ignore her elsewhere.

"The girl is perfectly well-behaved," declared Dottie Potterton.
"Better, in fact, than some I could mention." And where Dottie led
I knew that the local gentry, whose sons would be far more likely to
lose their heads over a pretty girl than the shrewd young businessmen
of Bradeswick, would not be far behind.

"Well done, *mademoiselle*," my grandfather told me, his dark
face shrewd and sarcastic. "I see the drift of your mind."

"I do my best, grandfather."

"Indeed. And your best is quite formidable. One may even
regret that you seem unable to channel your energies in a worthier
direction."

But he too—like Robin and Alys—had never been a hungry
fighter and was, therefore, unable, I believed, to judge.

I was popular. I was happy. My mother had so far done nothing
for which I could not supply an explanation. Madelon remained in
better health and Luc remained at school. And as the second winter

of my marriage approached I had even fixed my mind on the ideal husband for Victorine, a Clough of Bradeswick, no less, a cousin of Hattie Greenlaw's, unconnected with the Ironworks but in a good way of business as a master builder. They had met at a tennis party, where Victorine's gypsy coloring had appeared to great advantage in a white muslin dress while her strong right arm and powerful shoulders had proved decisive in a game of mixed doubles which she and Rodney Clough had been delighted to win. They had sat together afterwards at a little table on the edge of a smooth English lawn consuming between them an impressive quantity of sandwiches and sponge-cakes, an occupation the gentleman found so congenial that he soon became a regular caller at Aireville Terrace where Victorine's cakes were rich enough to incline any man of hearty appetite to matrimony.

"He seems to like you, Victorine. Do you like him?"

"There is nothing in him to dislike," she answered calmly. But one would expect calmness in Victorine, and a subtle change in her baking, a heavier, darker fruitcake with far more cinnamon than usual, convinced me that she had Rodney Clough's palate—if nothing else— on her mind.

"Should you meddle?" asked Robin, tolerant, amused, affectionate, yet suggesting, nevertheless, that in his view I should not. But his criticism, if such it was, did not hurt me for what he—like the squire and Alys—may have seen as meddling, I understood as the art of knowing how to survive. And so I smiled back at him and gave, with the utmost sincerity my lifelong answer, "But Robin, it is for her own *good*."

The Cloughs and Greenlaws, of course, did not approve, Hattie Greenlaw giving my mother so positive a hint that her cousin would not be thinking of marriage for years yet, that we were quite convinced he had already decided to marry Victorine.

"Does she like him, mother? I like him."

"I believe she does. In fact she must, otherwise she would say so. For Victorine is blunt and getting blunter."

"Then you had better start leaving them alone together when he calls. Ten minutes here, ten minutes there—you know."

"Yes, darling, I know."

"And she is looking so well lately that she could easily be in love. I do hope so."

"Don't count on it, dear—not Victorine. Madelon, of course,

will spend her life in raptures or in agonies like me, when she is older. But Victorine . . . ? She is not romantic."

"Well—she will be a lovely bride and a marvelous wife. Rodney Clough can consider himself a lucky man."

"My dear," my mother said, her long mouth vaguely smiling, "I believe not even my sister Sibylla goes husband-hunting with such vigor as you. Although I must say you have a less awkward bride-to-be on offer in Victorine than poor Sibylla has in Alys."

It was true. And as always the mention of Alys aroused in me a conflict of desires, the impulse to join in the general gossip about her, to say yes indeed she had turned out oddly, poor Sibylla, and an equally rapid impulse to defend her—as Robin always did—to insist she was not odd at all but unique, special, possibly quite marvelous.

I saw a great deal of her, my house and my status as a married woman which enabled me to chaperone her to and from Bradeswick, providing her with the escape she so often needed from her mother.

"These girls are always running here and running there," said Aunt Sibylla, acid and sugar sweet both together. "Always with their heads together gossiping of this and that. Such busy little bees that one wonders how much time *you* have to spare for your husband, Olivia—or how *you* will ever manage to find one, Alys."

But, indeed, Alys did not understand gossip and had no small-talk, sitting in studious silence for long periods that would have been uncomfortable with anyone else and then suddenly asking me some question to which she certainly did not expect a flippant answer.

"Do you think it right, Olivia, that although women are allowed to complete a course of study at Oxford or Cambridge they cannot take a degree?"

"Do you want a degree, Alys?"

"That is not the point, Olivia. There will certainly be many who do. How would you feel, for instance, if you had passed with great success every examination necessary for the practice of law, and then to be debarred from practice not because of incompetence but because you are a woman?"

"I should take no notice. I should go on practicing just the same."

"No you would not. Men of authority would combine against you and you would be crushed."

"Would I?" I rather doubted it. But Alys was equally certain.

"Yes, Olivia—quite crushed. Our legal system was not designed to suit the needs of women. It was written by men to suit themselves. And you can do absolutely nothing to change the law because, as a woman, you have no vote. *Think* about it, Olivia."

Very well. I did not want to be a lawyer. I had never, for a moment, considered the possibility of a university degree. I rather thought that I could manage to get my way with any man I might be likely to meet in Bradeswick—except my grandfather and possibly Max—without needing to vote for it. But if the vote turned out to be a useful instrument, a handy lever, a weapon, then I would sooner have it than not. That was the extent of my thought.

"Do you feel inferior to men, Olivia?"

Good Lord, no. I felt inferior to no one, or at least not on the issues of sex or age or even status. Sex, after all, was a mere accident of birth, both age and status could be acquired with time, and there had been no heavy-handed father in my life to yoke me to the virtues of obedience and self-denial, no favored elder brothers whose interests had always taken precedence over mine. No one, in fact, had ever explained to me that women were second-rate and should expect nothing more than second-best. I had always been graciously permitted to shoulder my own burdens, fight my own battles, earn my own bread, and I was approaching the mature age of twenty-three before Alys—nearly the same age herself and *still* unmarried—asked me to consider my right to vote.

"Look at it this way, Olivia. When you inherit Clarrow Fell and all the land, will it seem sensible to you that your tenant-farmers will have the parliamentary vote when you do not?"

Sensible? Perhaps not. But when election time came around what difference would it *really* make? They would be faced with the choice of one vain, ambitious young man or another—Lord Potterton's nephew Felix or Mr. Greenlaw's works-manager's brother—who would make all the promises anyone wanted to hear and then, if elected, would do only those things which might be likely to secure their own promotion.

Alys sighed and, straightening her shoulders, tried again. Would I at least consider our electoral system as a whole? *And*, having done so could I possibly pretend it to be just, when it denied the vote not only to women but to five million adult British men who did not possess sufficient property to qualify for it. Whereas Lord Potterton, who owned houses in Mayfair and Leicestershire and Heaven knew where else, could vote eight or nine times in eight or nine different constituencies if he could find the energy to get there on polling day. If I required further information then her friend, Miss Frances Grey, would be delighted to supply it.

"Really, Alys—so *that* is where you have been going—telling your mother you were calling on Victorine, I suppose, and then running across Aireville Terrace to Frances Grey, instead."

"Yes, Olivia. I told you I am deceitful."

Miss Grey, indeed, was a close neighbor of my mother's, a tall, cool spinster of indeterminate years—thirty or forty of them, perhaps— who had probably never looked much younger and would never look much older all her life. She was clever, haughty, fastidious, fond of the company of men in the sense that she enjoyed their admiration and liked them to confide in her, but would have retreated with an air of offended surprise, thought my sisters and I, at the first hint of anything so untidy as romance. She was, it seemed, quite rich and very well-connected, having a multitude of uncles and cousins and "dear friends" in high places at the Foreign Office, the Admiralty, the cloisters of our cathedrals, our universities and our courts of law. An unusual woman by any standards, the only one of her kind in Bradeswick who, despite her well-known preference for dubious company, had held herself rather aloof from my mother to begin with, disliking, we supposed, this challenge to her own notoriety. But, having realized how effective the presence of my mother's daughters could be in attracting young and personable gentlemen to her "*salon*" and keeping them there until they succumbed to the more subtle charm of Miss Grey herself, the hand of friendship was soon extended. And we took our places, sometimes several times a week, among the strange miscellany of her guests, Radicals and Socialists and Suffragists, progressive artists and thinkers, members of strange religions and extreme political groups who wanted to abolish the House of Lords and the workhouse, pay old-age pensions and health insurance, and even give votes to women.

"The Women's Suffrage Movement," my mother trilled. "Good Heavens, does it still live and breathe? Two old aunts of mine were very keen on that sort of thing—my word, it seems a century ago. Two dear spinster ladies, I remember them well. Gentle as doves, but such a rattling of the tea-cups there used to be whenever election time came round. My goodness. They used to draw up petitions to Parliament, as I recall, hundreds and hundreds of signatures in beautiful copperplate, politely requesting votes for women. Dozens of petitions. I wonder what happened to them."

"They will have been filed away somewhere in Westminster," Miss Grey said tartly, "gathering dust."

"How sad," beamed my mother. "Rather like my two old aunts."

"Exactly." Miss Grey smiled too, murderously sweet. "But tell me, Lavinia, are you not irritated or distressed by the inescapable fact that there is one law for men, one rate of pay, one set of moral values, and an entirely different one for women?"

"Oh *that*," said my mother, whose notions of law and morality were somewhat fluid and who understood nothing whatsoever about rates of pay.

"It is the natural order of things," decreed Aunt Sibylla when Alys rather unwisely repeated Miss Grey's opinion as her own one quiet evening at the vicarage.

"Are you aware," inquired Miss Grey on another occasion, "that although a man may divorce his wife on the single ground of her adultery alone, *she* would be obliged to prove adultery coupled with some other charge as serious as bigamy or extreme physical cruelty in order to divorce him?"

"I am most painfully aware of it," murmured my mother.

"It is of absolutely no importance," decreed Aunt Sibylla to Alys, "since no decent woman could even contemplate divorce."

"It has been one of the greatest sorrows of my life," Miss Grey informed us, "that women are debarred from all the major professions. Except medicine, of course, for the simple reason that to be a doctor has only recently become a respectable calling. And even there, the few women who do manage to qualify are subject to the most atrocious prejudice."

"I should not care to be examined by a woman doctor," snapped Aunt Sibylla, when Alys allowed her indignation at this state of affairs to show. While my mother looked startled and astonished, and then, deciding that Miss Grey must at one time have been in love with a series of professional men, nodded her sympathy and smiled.

"And in the trades where women can find employment," Miss Grey went on, "the factory floor, for instance, the shop counter, domestic service, their rate of pay is much lower than a man's, their conditions often far more severe."

Neither my mother nor Aunt Sibylla had anything they wished to say about that.

"It seems harsh to me," Miss Grey remarked, almost playfully, "that a woman who allows herself to be seduced is invariably condemned as an outcast—an untouchable. Whereas her seducer might fare no worse than a mild reproach. The prodigal son, to be welcomed, often quite joyfully, back into the fold. One could wish, perhaps, that Society might find room in its heart for its prodigal daughters."

"Indeed, yes," sighed my mother, seeing no chance of it.

Even Alys knew better than to make any comment on this occasion, to Aunt Sibylla.

"Men exploit us because we do not fight hard enough," Miss Grey said serenely, pouring out her excellent Lapsang Suchong tea. "I expect we would exploit them too if we were able. But they have put themselves in a position of power and strength where they are unassailable. We must do the same. We must have the vote, my dears. And handwritten petitions will not get it. We must fight."

I had been fighting men—and women—all my life and none of this was new to me. To Alys it was a revelation, a whole world of ideas and possibilities she could not wait to discuss with Robin. She had heard of the Women's Suffrage Movement, of course, but had thought it just a collection of genteel old spinsters like my mother's aunts, or young ones who wore bowler hats and ties and smoked cigarettes. Did Robin, with his Cambridge connections, know anything more? A great deal, it seemed, and he was entirely in favor. There was even a book, he thought, in Clarrow library, giving details of the movement from its beginnings in the 1860's. Should he try and find it for her? The achievements, as yet, were uninspiring and trivial, but the aims were positively exciting. There had been a lot of talk about it at Cambridge. Some pretty heated debates. Great fun.

"Why haven't I met Miss Grey?" he asked me.

I had thought she would bore him.

"What a delightful, *charming* man—your husband," she cooed to me after their first meeting and quite soon he—and Alys—were numbered among her most frequent visitors.

"What enlightened views your husband has, Olivia."

"Oh—yes. Yes indeed." What views? What side of his nature had I missed? What stimulation did he find here in this elegant but slightly fussy drawing room, listening so raptly as Miss Frances Grey, surrounded by her antique silver and her porcelain, served revolution every afternoon on Royal Worcester plates with her scones and muffins, her exotic honeys and unusual jams? What had I failed to understand? Alys would know.

"Dear Alys," smiled Miss Grey. "She is like a young tree positively thirsting for knowledge and growing quite visibly with every drop."

Yet when Aunt Sibylla, who had imposed a total ban on Miss Grey's society, discovered how regularly her daughter had disobeyed her, I and I alone was held to blame.

"How could you take her to that house, Olivia," she bitterly complained. "To what influences have you exposed her?"

"Oh, come now, Aunt Sibylla. Frances Grey *is* a lady."

"Really, my dear, so was Lady Macbeth—so was Lady Hamilton. And I must ask you to remember that Alys has not been accustomed to—well—to such varied society as you have, dear, but has been *very carefully brought up.*"

"Yes, aunt. But Miss Grey is very—well *virginal,* you know."

"Indeed, I know nothing about it. My sole concern is my daughter and the acquaintances she makes in that woman's drawing room."

"Yes, aunt?"

"There is a Dr. Rexford who goes there, is there not?" Indeed yes, a lanky and in my view seedy Scot who had recently limped home from the Boer War and having prescribed, quite effectively it seemed, for Madelon's cough, had been drawn into the social life of Aireville Terrace. A man of high ideals and bad manners, I thought him, eating our cakes and drinking our tea, yet despising us all—even Miss Grey—for our social pretensions, our readiness to give away all our worldly goods and march unfettered into an improbable future.

Could Alys be attracted to him? Very likely. For I knew of no greater contrast to the atmosphere of Clarrow vicarage than the one created by Dr. Rexford. Unless, of course, it should be Max.

Madelon was with me that day and, as we walked back to the vicarage with my aunt, we met a young man on the field path who raised his hat to us and would have moved on had not Aunt Sibylla called him to a most decided halt.

"Ivor Naseby," she said, rather as if he might deny it.

"Yes, ma'am," he agreed, having clearly forgotten her name and making no effort to remember it.

"Come now, Ivor, you know me very well. And I imagine you

will wish to pause a moment and make the acquaintance of my nieces, Mrs. Esmond and Miss Madelon . . ."

"Yes, ma'am. How do you do."

So this was the heir to the Naseby millions, by no means the angelic vision of his mother's imaginings, but handsome enough in a boyish, rather sulky fashion, his hair not quite the gold his mother had painted it but a pleasing auburn, his eyes not really amethyst but a perfectly agreeable light blue.

"Ivor Naseby," said Aunt Sibylla, as he left us and walked on. "So our doting Esmeralda has called him home again. One assumed she could not bear to be parted from him for long. My word—I believed him to be much improved, for he was always a sullen, difficult child. He howled a great deal, as I recall, and bit people—rather hard. Quite dreadful. But even then—now I happen to think of it—he was extremely fond of Alys."

"Yes, aunt," I said, my eyes following him with the same degree of speculation. Ivor Naseby indeed, vicious in childhood, clearly discontented now, handsome and rich at all times, the best catch in the neighborhood since his money was not mere dash and dazzle like Max de Haan's but was *there*, within the solid walls of Naseby's Brewery for all to see. Yes, I perfectly followed the drift of Aunt Sibylla's mind as, swiftly abandoning her ideas of Clive Potterton, she began to consider the ways and means of getting Ivor Naseby for Alys. He would, undoubtedly, be the catch of the season, much younger than Clive, no noble name, of course, but no debts or encumbrances either; well worth waiting for. I entirely agreed with her, the more so since I had seen—as she had not—the flash of eagerness in his face, the excited curiosity, when he had looked at Madelon.

194

ELEVEN

I remember very clearly the day on which disaster struck me its first blow, choosing of course, a moment when it was least expected, when I had really started to believe that everything was destined to work out as I wanted it. That is to say for the best.

It was a slow, golden September about a month after our meeting with Ivor Naseby since which time my obliging sister Madelon had been, perhaps only romantically and rather childishly, but most encouragingly in love. She was nineteen now, delicate as spun glass, shy, easily startled, still touchingly eager to please. She was affectionate, with a lovely face and beautiful manners. *I* believed that the King of England himself would have been lucky to win her. And although Mrs. Esmeralda Naseby had risen from her invalid couch at the first hint of mutual attraction and banished her son forthwith to France, "for his art's sake," we knew that he would be twenty-one next June, sufficiently master of his fortune to dispense with his mother's consent should he choose to take a wife.

"Mother," said Victorine, a little sternly, "they have done nothing, as yet, but exchange a few looks and smiles . . ."

"Nonsense, dear. He sat and stared at her the whole evening at Hattie Greenlaw's. A dozen people remarked on it. And when he called on Frances Grey last Wednesday it was certainly not to discuss votes for women. Evidently his mother thought so too, or why else has she sent him off so suddenly? But he will be back, believe me . . ."

"Riding a white horse, I suppose."

"Well, Victorine, now that you come to mention it, why not?

Madelon is exactly the kind of girl to be galloped off with into the sunset. I should have enjoyed it exceedingly myself—in season."

"Good," declared Victorine, without much charity. "I am glad to hear you say 'in season.' For one cannot help thinking that Mr. Greenlaw would look ungainly in the saddle." But Victorine, of course, was blunt and getting blunter, a quality which would not go amiss in the future wife of Rodney Clough, who was somewhat outspoken himself. Whereas Alys, for all Aunt Sibylla's careful upbringing, had developed a preference for distinctly unmarriageable men, sharing my mother's drawingroom sofa that fateful afternoon with the shabby, disreputable Dr. Rexford on one side of her, the elegant, even more disreputable Max de Haan on the other, his diamond still flashing on his hand, the Daimler outside my mother's gate undoubtedly his.

"Max, how very nice to see you—*again.*"

"Olivia, my pet, how sweet of you to say so."

"May one ask where you have been these—well —three months, is it? Or more?"

"One may. Here and there. You know."

I knew. A profit in one direction, a loss in another, a lucky turn of a card, a quick brush with disaster, a man like Emil Junot who still listened for footsteps in the night and never ceased to guard his back. I knew.

"And are you here again on business?"

"Possibly."

He had come to count how many steps my grandfather had advanced towards his grave, to ascertain whether the time was yet ripe to offer me money, probably a great deal of it, for my birthright. And even had I been inclined to sell, I would have required full payment in cash alone and counted it safely into my bank before trusting him.

"Good afternoon, Mrs. Esmond," said Dr. Rexford formally, knowing I did not like him, although, indeed, it was not so much dislike as the caution bred into any female who has had to fend for herself—as Alys had not—and who knows that these idealists, these saints, these champions of the oppressed, are in reality luxury items to be afforded only by the very strongest and most self-reliant of women.

I knew, with every cautious bone in my body, the dangers he represented. So did Victorine, smiling at the impracticality of some remark of his as she, most practical of women, passed him a plate of buttered muffins and what would very likely be his sixth or seventh cup of hot, sweet tea.

So too did Madelon, although she listened to him quietly and rather respectfully, remembering that even if he had not yet managed to heal the sickness of our—according to him—very sick society, he had done wonders for her cough.

Alys, I supposed, would only hear the sentiments he expressed, with which not even I could really quarrel and would not see—as I saw, as Victorine and even Madelon saw—the sheer discomfort of putting them into practice.

He was twenty-nine, perhaps, or only a little more than thirty, tall and thin and hollow about the chest, raw-boned, pale-complexioned, untidy, his shabby tweeds patched with leather at the elbows and liberally dusted with ash from the pipe not even the fastidious Miss Grey had ever asked him to remove from between his teeth.

He had spent a year or two practicing medicine in India, a year in Africa, broadening his horizons, the start of the Boer War catching him in the hornet's nest of the Rand where, when the Europeans had all fled and the gold mines they operated had been shut down, he had assisted in the gathering together of the thousands of African mine boys they had left behind to starve. And, there being no transport available, he had walked with them, giving such medical help as he could, to the comparative safety of British Natal, two hundred miles away.

I had not forgotten Alys's shining eyes, nor the tightness in my own throat, nor even the gruff note of admiration in Victorine's voice, the extra helping of fruitcake she had put on his plate, the night he had told us about that. But my sister and I could also remember the feel, not of dry, hot earth on bare feet perhaps, but of hard pavements through the thin soles of old shoes, a contact quite hard enough, and knew that a man who would sacrifice himself in this heroic way would also sacrifice his woman.

And then there had been the military hospitals, the gangrenes which need never have occurred had that cumbersome military machine functioned a shade more efficiently. There had been the limbs amputated in muddy tents with not even the rudimentary anaesthetic of a swig of brandy, when a surgeon's best hope of saving a patient's life had been his speed—to minimize shock—with the meat cleaver.

There had been the typhoid epidemic at Bloemfontein, three doctors to every three hundred patients who lay without mattresses on the hard ground, the dying and those who might or could recover packed tight together under leaking canvas. And there had been those other, shameful camps where the Boer women and children had died because Lord Kitchener had treated them like British soldiers.

Andrew Rexford had seen service there too, had seen the burned farms, the herding of the dispossessed women, many with babies in their arms, into those terrible enclosures. He had seen the despair, the hatred, the tiny bodies sewn up in sacking and laid out in neat rows every morning. And did Alys imagine that a man, whose soul had been tempered by such atrocious steel as that, would have sympathy to spare for the small ills of her own well-nourished body, the small cares of her unbroken heart? I admired him, or would have done, had he been less inclined to sneer at me, to fire off his quick remarks about social posturing and hypocrisy and the worship of wealth.

"As a religion," said Max, who knew how to sneer himself, "it's more reliable than most. And should you be wondering why I haven't gone back to Africa now the coast is clear . . ."

But no, Dr. Rexford had not been wondering that. Africa was behind him now and his present concerns were here in Bradeswick with the mis-management of our workhouse hospital where, for lack of a proper maternity ward, women in childbirth were put in the same, overcrowded shed as patients with fevers and disorders of the bowels, raving lunatics and those suffering from what—at a sharp glance from Miss Frances Grey—he agreed to call "social diseases." New mothers and new babies were dying there like flies, he asserted—here in Bradeswick right under our delicate noses—at a rate comparable to the Boer women in the Transvaal and he had set himself the task of campaigning not only for a decent maternity unit but for registered midwives to run it. He had seen too much unnecessary dying, from typhoid in the Transvaal to abdominal infections in Bradeswick, caused by the unclean fingernails and unsteady hands of the aged crones employed to deliver babies in our workhouse infirmary, their sole qualification for midwifery being that they had had fourteen or fifteen pregnancies themselves.

Dr. Rexford had denounced this evil on his very first visit to my mother's drawing room, to the great embarrassment of Mr. Samuel Greenlaw who had left early looking considerably offended, and to

198

the visible discomfort of Mr. Septimus Cross, my mother's other love-sick swain, who had succumbed to a bout of nervous giggles, and then left too, clearly considering that such a dubious matter as midwifery should never have been raised in his—possibly?—virgin presence.

"What sort of a damn fellow is Lavinia encouraging now?" had grumbled Mr. Greenlaw, as he put on his hat.

"How very interesting," Miss Frances Grey had murmured, looking for just a moment like an extremely refined child who had been given a new toy. "I must raise the issue at once with certain friends of mine—and, of course, I must know *someone* who is serving at present as a Poor Law guardian."

Such was the world of Dr. Andrew Rexford. I acknowledged it, could even look it in the face, hate it, grieve over it, cope with it in my fashion. But Alys could not even begin to imagine it and Aunt Sibylla would have my deepest sympathies should my suspicions about him and Alys turn out to be true.

Would he even marry her? Or would he be more likely to propose some form of free union of the kind now prevalent, one heard, among the suffrage circles of London and Manchester where, in protest at the inequality of the law with regard to marriage, divorce and custody of children, women were either living openly with their lovers or, if married already, were taking off their wedding rings; to the consternation of the nation's hoteliers who did not permit ringless women the use of a double bed. Would Alys listen to such a proposal? I believed she would, remembering how, only a week or so ago Dr. Rexford had offered us his views on matrimony and how she had responded.

"Marriage," he had said, with just possibly a twinkle in his eye, since he was not a humorless man and knew we would not all agree with him, "diminishes a woman from the status of an individual to a possession—like a man's ox and ass. So until the law changes and allows women equal rights in marriage, I'll steer clear of it. It's a pointless and pernicious institution in its present form. I want no part of it."

"What *do* you want, then?" I had snapped, sounding, to my horror, exactly like Aunt Sibylla.

"Ah well—I'm not sure I can put it discreetly . . ."

"Don't trouble about that."

"A relationship—not just a contract."

"You mean you'd rather have a mistress."

He laughed, a deep chuckle without the least hint of embarrassment, his pipe scattering ash and smoke and masculine self-assurance in a way I detested.

"Now that's a good old-fashioned word, Mrs. Esmond, although not the one I'd use. A friend, I reckon—a partner."

"Well—I expect it works out cheaper, whatever you call it."

"Oh no," Alys had said, raising her head, as if she had been sitting too long in a stuffy room and had just detected a breath of air, "not at all, Olivia—I understand . . ."

"So do I," Victorine had declared flatly, coming, I had thought, to my defense. "What he means is that he's scared of the commitment. Oh yes, you are, Dr. Rexford, so there's no need to shake your head and drop ash on my clean carpet. What you have said sounds very fine, but it's not practical. And when the time comes—since you believe so strongly in equality, you'll have to give the lady of your choice what she wants, not what you think she ought to have."

Well done, Victorine. Spoken like the true mate of shrewd, down-to-earth Rodney Clough. Remembering that conversation of, when had it been, three weeks ago, I felt highly delighted, even a little smug, to think that I had a sister with her feet so firmly on the ground, so reliable and loyal and full of sound common-sense. And so I was totally unprepared for the shock, and therefore totally vulnerable, when I discovered that Dr. Rexford, later that afternoon, had taken the train to Leeds and there, in a civil ceremony witnessed by strangers—although my mother certainly knew of it and had given her consent—became the husband, not of dreamy, idealistic Alys but of my doomed, unfortunate, *treacherous* sister, Victorine.

How could she? For several dazed, incredulous minutes I did not really believe she had. It was a joke and a very bad one. I was not at all amused. And when belief finally struck me it brought the kind of sensation that comes with the release of cramped muscles and restricted breath. Not Victorine. Please—not Victorine. My mother, yes, or Luc—either one of them could take a false or foolish step and I would be ready for it. Even Madelon. But not Victorine. How could she have done this disastrous thing at all? But *how*—how *could* she have done it like this?

"I suppose she knew you'd object," said Robin very carefully, walking on eggshells. "And since her mind was made up it seemed best just to go ahead and do it."

200

And because he was *there* and it was necessary to release at least a portion of my anger and hurt before it choked me, I rounded fiercely upon him.

"Oh yes—it would seem best, I don't doubt it. With my stupid mother at the station to wave her off, I suppose, all sentimental tears and neither one of them with the guts or wit to come and tell me. Good God. She must be crazier than I thought—my mother."

"I wouldn't dare to agree with you," he said, still careful, but taking it all too lightly just the same, far too ready to be amused. "Because if I did—when your temper cools—you would never forgive me."

"*Robin*, don't you see what a mess it is—what a disaster?" And if he didn't see that, then why? I needed his sympathy now, and his support, needed him at least to stand beside me—*with* me—instead of this nonchalant shrugging and smiling, this playing down of what I saw as a conspiracy in which everyone who was supposed to love me had taken part.

"Robin—don't you *see*?"

"Not really. She has not run off with a gypsy, you know, Olivia. She has married a gentleman of the medical profession with her mother's consent . . ."

"Yes, and I shall wring her neck and my mother's, when I see them, which is why they sent you to break the news . . ."

"They didn't precisely send me, Olivia. Victorine is still in Leeds and will have other things on her mind, I imagine. Your mother—well yes, she did send a note round to the office asking me to call and she admitted she didn't feel up to telling you herself. Possibly she wanted my professional advice, which makes a refreshing change since few people seem to take me seriously as a lawyer—including myself. Well, here it is, Olivia. In my view you have no justification at all for making a fuss."

Incredulity once again gave me a sharp slap. No justification? What, then, had kept us afloat all those years if not our unity, the simple fact that we had supported and trusted one another. And since I had fought the hardest to maintain that unity, I was fully entitled, surely, to my anger and my distress now that it had been so treacherously broken. For if my mother had known what was going on, then so too had Madelon. How had they faced me, all these weeks, allowing me to believe in Victorine's attachment to Rodney Clough and Andrew Rexford's to Alys? They had lied to me. What else could one call it? They had taken all the effort I had ever made on their behalf and thrown it in my face. Their perfidy devastated me. My own blindness appalled me. I was in that terrible state of nervous confusion where I required most urgently to bang my head against a wall, smash something large and valuable, knock over some solid object that would make a mighty clatter, and was restrained from doing so only because I rather suspected that Robin would laugh at me. And so I rounded on him once again, turning scornful and hard-hearted.

"Not make a fuss? What do you know about it, Robin Esmond? What do you know about anything, with the soft life you've had— you and Alys?"

"I hardly think Alys can have anything to do with this."

"Oh absolutely not since we all know Alys can do no wrong."

"I know she does no wrong, Olivia."

Stop it. Stop it at once, I thought. Dear God, what a fool I am. This is about Victorine. *Victorine*, not Alys. But the accumulated weight of anxiety, jealousy, fear, was simply too great, toppling me over the edge of good sense into a shout of "Rubbish. Alys had gone behind my back with all the rest. Why else has she been making eyes at that odious man—sitting at his feet like those women in the Bible as if she wanted to dry them with her hair—when she must have known he was carrying on with Victorine. Why? I'll tell you why. To put me off the track, of course. Unless she really is as simple as she pretends, in which case, God help her!"

For a moment he said nothing. We simply stood there, looking at each other across a widening distance which, although it appalled me, I could do nothing to bridge, my limbs and my tongue frozen as they sometimes are in dreams when one sees danger approaching all too clearly, yet cannot move. And then he sighed, very quietly.

"I think we should forget you said that, Olivia."

But words once spoken cannot be forgotten. One can only pretend not to remember them and my temper was still high, my feelings still offended and hurt and hard.

"On the contrary, I shall say it all over again to her face when she shows it. *I* am not deceitful."

No. But you are an idiot, the one cautious area of my brain warned me. A rash fool, running your head into a noose of your own making. Stop it—*now*. There may still be time.

"I must ask you to do no such thing, Olivia."

202

"Ask away. But I shall do exactly as I please, when I please. Can you stop me?"

He shook his head and walked past me, out of the house and into the garden; out and away into space and solitude.

I watched him from the window, moving with slow competence along the neat borders, pausing now and then to inhale the fragrance of a leaf or a blossom, listening—I could tell—to the bee song among the lavender, the bird song high in the chestnut tree, his spirit eased by the pace and texture of these green and growing things, the deep brown patience of earth, the lightness and remoteness of air. I watched him. I loved him and, knowing I had hurt him, I hoped the barb had gone deep for I could not yet begin to tell him how dreadfully he had wounded me. If I opened the window and called I knew he would come to me. I did not call: *could* not, dare not, perhaps, for like some injured jungle animal I was wicked with my pain and I knew I must keep my distance until it had eased.

"I've brought you this," he said at last, handing me a single, long-stemmed rose. "I thought you might like to throw it at me or stab it through my heart—or something."

And the agony—or the first part of it—was over.

Victorine came herself the next morning on her way back from Leeds, unlikeliest of honeymoon cities, although I did not want to dwell in any great detail on that. She was wearing the beige tailor-made coat and skirt with the black velvet collar we had chosen together, a sensible straw hat with a black velvet ribbon, spotless kid gloves. Her boots, as always, were beautifully polished, her hair glossy with good health and good grooming; strong teeth, fine bones, a fresh complexion, the Victorine of everyday, my sister, entirely unchanged except that nothing could ever be the same again. Andrew Rexford— and I—would see to that. I had been so proud of her. I had wanted so much for her. And although I must have known quite well that I would not really abandon her now to face the rigors of the life she had chosen, the time for forgiveness was not quite yet. She would have to feel the rough side of my tongue, and very likely I would have to feel hers, before we could be friends.

"Congratulations. So I saved you from being a fishwife in the rue de Bellechasse for this did I?"

She sighed rather as Robin had done, and then gave her heavy and deliberate shrug.

"All right, Olivia. There's no need to tell me what you think about all this. I know. Mother knows. We knew how it would be right from the start."

"Which is why you ran off like a pregnant housemaid, before I could stop you. Victorine—you are not . . . ?"

"No, as it happens. But I could be."

"Victorine!"

"Don't play the prude, Olivia. You know what's what. And as for stopping me, there'd have been no chance of it. I made up my mind I was going to marry Andrew a long time ago. Quite a while before he made up his, as a matter of fact. And you could have done nothing to make me change it. You know what I'm like, Olivia. You should, since I'm as stubborn as you. And if I'd told you, there'd have been such endless arguments all to no avail. Everybody's nerves—mother's in particular and Madelon's—would have been torn to shreds quite needlessly, because I'd still have married him. And since there was never the remotest possibility of a church and a white dress and all the trimmings, it seemed better this way. At any rate, it's done now. I can't make you accept it. It's up to you."

"So it is."

And for a moment I hovered on the brink of what might have been a final separation, very nearly walked away from her, turned my back, shut her out as she had excluded me, so shaken was I by a most chilling and destructive sense of loss. She no longer wanted me, that was plain. Very well. Then she could do without me. She had made her sordid, narrow, probably unpaid-for bed and she could just get on with the business of lying on it. What did I care? The answer was that I cared deeply, would always care, could not possibly stop caring. She was a part of myself that I could not bear to lose. We both understood that. And after glaring at each other a while longer she shrugged, a little resignedly this time, and said,

"Shall I tell you about it, Olivia?"

I gave a shrug of my own, light, flippant, copying my mother as I often did in moments of stress.

"You might as well. Then I'll know what everybody else seems to have known all along—won't I?"

She dismissed that as irrelevant, just hurt pride which would soon be mended, and assuming I had now invited her to stay, took off her hat and gloves revealing a self-conscious, brand new wedding ring.

"Good heavens, Victorine—a *ring*. I thought all the progressives like Dr. Rexford and Miss Grey were busy persuading people to take them off. Not that *she'll* ever get the chance of one of course."

But my sarcasm was obviously irrelevant too.

"It's all straightforward enough, Olivia. I liked him at once, quite a lot. I liked Rodney Clough too, I never lied to you about that. And nobody lied about Alys and Andrew either. She does like him. Lots of people do. And, to begin with he was very taken with her. But with your experience you ought to have known that he's too—well, too basic—too physical, if you like, for Alys."

"I don't like anything about it, Victorine."

"You'll get used to it. Anyway—if I'd never met Andrew, I'd have done very well as Mrs. Clough, the builder's wife. You were quite right about that. But I did meet Andrew. And really that's all there is to it. At first I just saw him at home or at Frances Grey's, but then he gave me a hand in the garden one day and invited me to go and see him."

"He has a house?"

"Lord yes, a dilapidated old terrace off Corporation Square. I've seen worse. So have you. It needed cleaning, that's all and I soon took care of that. Then he made love to me."

"As a reward for doing the cleaning, I suppose."

Suddenly she smiled, her face glowing with general good humor and one very special memory.

"That's not the way Andrew saw it. It was supposed to set me free—an act of liberation and all that. You know how they talk—Andrew and Frances and Alys. But to be strictly honest, all I really wanted was for it to happen again—which of course it did."

"Yes. It would."

"There's not much more to tell. He wanted me to go and live with him. After all, he'd talked so much hot air about marriage being pernicious and unnecessary that he could hardly propose to me—could he? But I said no. I couldn't have done that to you, Olivia."

"How kind."

"Well, I think it probably was. Madelon would never have got a husband, would she, if I'd been living in sin just up the road off Corporation Square, and the Pottertons and Nasebys and Greenlaws would have had a field-day, I imagine, turning up their noses at you and mother. So I'm not entirely self-centered. I had a terrible row with Andrew about it. In fact, I could have lost him."

"It's a pity you didn't."

"I suppose you had to say that."

"Yes, I did."

"Never mind. Eventually he realized I meant what I said and here we are."

"Where? In a dilapidated terrace-house off Corporation Square?"

"It's where I want to be, Olivia."

"For God's sake, Victorine, you sound like mother."

"Well, we all have something of her in us. It just shows up more in Madelon—and in you sometimes. Didn't you know?"

I wasn't sure what she meant by that but now, as my anger softened and began to drain away, distress invaded me and I burst out, "Victorine—you don't know what you've done . . ."

"Oh yes, I do."

"No, you *don't*. Ideals and love and going to bed may be fine now but what about later, when you're older and have children to think about? Victorine, there are men who use women up. You know what I mean, men who live life so hard that it is too much for a woman. And don't tell me he's not like that, because he is."

"I can handle it, Olivia."

"Oh, for God's sake, don't be an idiot—nobody can handle it. It goes on for year after year, wearing you down, getting worse as you get weaker, until you're an old woman at thirty-five and he's still making speeches from a soapbox somewhere about liberty."

"You seem to know a lot about it."

"Yes, and so should you. There are types one learns to avoid. The Jean-François and the Max de Haans, and the idealists. Good God, Victorine, none of them ever pay their bills. And you can remember Junot. You know what it was like with all those creditors hanging around the stairs and how we had to put on all our dresses one on top of the other and run. And how they kept selling the furniture and giving false names and just moving on. A girl like Alys might think that kind of thing romantic until she had to live with it—or die of it, which would be far more likely. But you! Victorine—how could you do this to yourself?"

"I'll be all right, Olivia."

"Oh no—no you won't. You'll be in a sorry state before you're through."

She put on her gloves slowly, inch it seemed by inch, and got to her feet.

206

"Well, Olivia, what it comes down to is this. It's happened—a *fait accompli* with no going back. I think you should just make the best of it and wish us well."

"Yes, in your place I'd think the same. I am sorry. I don't feel up to it this morning."

She went to the door. Paused a moment, looking very solid, very blunt, and then, hoping for the best, said quickly, "I don't suppose you'll like this much, but there's a party—tonight at the Station Hotel."

"Your party?"

It sounded unlikely and I saw that for the first time since her arrival she was truly ill-at-ease.

"Not exactly. Max de Haan's party, I suppose. He's giving us champagne and all sorts of other nonsense, he thinks appropriate to a wedding. And mother is very keen on it. The thing is, Olivia that we'd be glad—both of us—Andrew and I—if you'd come."

She did not wait for an answer. I could not have made one, and in any case, it was unnecessary. She saw my face and knew. I watched her through the window talking to Robin on the garden path, saw him open the gate and walk along the lane beside her, accompanying her to the station or to the vicarage, perhaps, where she would have an invitation to deliver for Alys. And for the first time I hoped he would linger, would stay for luncheon, go to Bradeswick with Victorine, even take Alys for a walk; anything to keep him away from me until this fresh outburst of temper had cooled.

I would kill Max de Haan for this. I sat for half an hour at my parlor table indulging myself with the ways and means of murder, planning one hideous end after another for the man I knew was laughing at me. For Max de Haan would know exactly how I felt about this and why I felt it. But it did no good and when Robin returned I was still evil with offended pride, still ready to throw myself into the furnace if I could take my enemy with me.

"Olivia," he said, treating me once again with great care, "about the party . . . ?"

"What about it?"

"It rather sounds as if just about everybody is going to be there . . ."

"No, Robin, not everybody."

He lit a cigarette, inhaled once and then twice very deeply, the cigarette burning rapidly away between his long fingers which were stained, I noticed, quite heavily with nicotine. Why had I not seen that before? Did he really smoke so much? When had it started?

"Olivia, don't let's quarrel about it."

"There's no need even to discuss it."

"That means you won't go?"

"Robin—I wouldn't drink Max de Haan's champagne if it was the last on earth."

"Why should you feel so strongly about Max?"

Why indeed?

"I don't. But just tell me this. What is there to celebrate? How can I possibly raise my glass and toast the health and happiness of the bride when I know she won't be happy—couldn't be."

He lit another cigarette and stood for a heavy, thoughtful moment leaning against the mantelshelf, looking at me through the curling smoke.

"You can't know that, Olivia. No one can. They seem very fond of each other and, as it happens, I have a lot of time for Andrew. A lot of respect, in fact. He has the courage of his convictions, at any rate."

"Does he really? Then how can he reconcile his social conscience to all those magnums of champagne and the caviar and oysters and all the rest that Max will be splashing around the Station Hotel tonight?"

"Because he's doing it for Victorine."

"What sentimental nonsense!"

"Not a bit of it. Andrew doesn't want a party. He just told me so."

"It doesn't sound to me as though he even wanted a wedding. But when did *you* see him?"

"Just now. He was waiting at the vicarage for Victorine."

"How very cosy. Everybody gets together and talks things over except me. So Andrew doesn't want a party."

"Of course not. But your mother is very keen . . ."

"She would be. Her reputation can't stand a runaway marriage. She thinks a big party will add a coat of whitewash."

"Exactly. That matters to your mother and so it matters to Victorine. When Andrew understood how much, he gave in. I think you should do the same."

"I daresay you do."

"Olivia, this is very foolish you know. If you stay away you'll upset Victorine and your mother and we shall have Madelon in floods of tears, coughing her head off. But most of all you'll upset yourself. And since you'll make it up with them eventually, it may as well be now. What can't be cured, must be endured, you know, that's one of the maxims they teach at Hexingham. And no matter how bad you think her life is going to be, you can hardly want to make it worse. Darling—be generous."

What? I had spent my life being generous, with my time and my affections and with every penny piece I had ever possessed. I had withheld nothing from any of them. So now, let them cluster around Max de Haan and Andrew Rexford and Alys, and I would turn my energy inward and take care of myself.

"Why? They only want me there to make it look right. You go, Robin, and make my excuses. Say I feel sick, which is not far from the truth."

"I would prefer to go *with* you, Olivia," he said quietly and very seriously. "But, if necessary, then yes—I will have to go alone. I have already accepted Andrew's invitation and I wouldn't feel right about letting him down."

"How many more times do I have to tell you, Robin? *I am not going.*"

"Very well."

But it was not until I heard him ask the girl to lay out his pleated dress shirt and scarlet sash and the dinner-jacket which marked him as a man of fashion that I believed he really meant to go without me.

He was perfectly good-humored about it, chatting quite easily—too easily—through what seemed to me a long afternoon until it was time to dress.

"You can always change your mind, Olivia."

But I had already gone beyond that possibility. I had made too much fuss, given and received too deep a hurt and now a steely, unyielding stubbornness had encased my will so completely that, although a moment came when I knew I wanted to relent, I could do nothing about it.

"I'll be off then, Olivia, if you're sure . . . ?"

"I'm sure."

He took his hat and gloves, his coat, his long white silk scarf, handsome, incredibly beloved; a hundred miles away from me.

"Darling, do come. There's just time for you to change. It would please them so much—and me."

I shook my head.

"Olivia . . . ?"

If only I could. A part of my nature threw on an evening gown and ran down the road with him, laughing, hand in hand. But there was another part.

"No. Tell them I'm ill. They'll find it convenient to believe you."

"You are hurting yourself, you know."

I knew. Myself most of all. It made no difference.

I did not want to be here alone. I was not accustomed to solitude and had no skill with it, no liking for it, I wanted . . . ? The eternal, impossible longing for things to be as they were, to go back in time to the moment before one had spoken the unforgivable word, before one had taken the inflexible attitude so that there could be no retreat. To open dreaming eyes and discover myself—where? I didn't know. But not here, alone, while Robin made the journey to Brades-wick with Alys, and everyone else I cared for was sitting about the Station Hotel drinking Max de Haan's champagne.

There was, I knew, just one more train. Nothing prevented me from catching it. But even while I thought it over, leaning on the gate and planning what to wear, what to say, I knew I would not go. I would stand my ground as I always did. I would do as I had set out to do and would not deviate. And because I shared this stubborn pride with my grandfather I was thinking of him before I actually saw him appearing slowly through the twilight, leading a horse which had evidently gone lame.

"Good evening, Olivia."

"Good evening, grandfather."

"All alone, Olivia?"

"As you see."

He was all alone too. Why then could we not spend the time together? Why not? What prevented me from offering him a chair by my fireside, a glass of brandy, an hour of quiet conversation? Nothing, except the fear of his refusal. And I had suffered rejection enough for one day.

"Good night to you, then."

"Good night."

But if I could detain him just a moment longer, if, by some miracle we could begin to talk to each other, then even this dreadful day would have been worthwhile. If I could somehow make him listen to me, make him see me as myself, rather than an extension of my mother, a reminder of my father's bitterness, *then*—oh then, I might feel that my life here had achieved its true beginning. Grandfather—*please.*

Would he hear me? He peered at me a moment through the gloom, his eyes keen and shrewd, seeing through me and pinning me down as cruelly as Aunt Sibylla's husband spiked his butterflies.

"Have you lost your taste for weddings, Mrs. Esmond? Even Amyas has gone to your sister's."

"Has he really? I hope he enjoys it."

"I doubt it. Amyas is not a man for enjoyment. He does his duty and gets on with his work—as I do."

And nodding to me briefly he walked on towards his silent house, leaving me to mine.

"Good night, grandfather."

But my voice behind echoed and came back to me along the empty path. No one was there.

TWELVE

I sent the maid to bed and went upstairs myself, for it was my intention at least to look as if I had been sleeping peacefully when Robin returned. But my senses were too sharpened, too raw, for any kind of rest, my ears magnifying the sound of every creaking board, every rustle and scurry both indoors and out, every movement of leaf and root and nightbird beyond my window.

I heard the last train from Bradeswick come snorting up the hill, allowed the half-hour it would take for Robin to walk through the village and across the meadow and then, when the time to hear his footsteps approaching down the lane had come and passed away, I no longer pretended to sleep but banged my fists into my pillow and then my head and howled, as dismal and desperate as a lost, if still somewhat irritable, sheep.

Obviously he had stayed in town and why should I be surprised about that? The party would be far from over and why should he leave it to catch an inconveniently early train home to a wife whose attitude he considered unreasonable. He had gone as a matter of principle. Now he was probably enjoying himself. In a very neat but very painful nutshell, that was that. Had I gone with him, I might be enjoying myself too.

Alys, I supposed, would have spent the night at Aireville Terrace, an arrangement of which even her mother could not question the propriety. Robin would have found a room at the hotel, gone to his office, or simply sat up all night drinking and smoking those nervous cigarettes. Men did these things. It was all quite normal, reasonable, there was no need to be alarmed. I was not alarmed. Suddenly—oh God—I was terrified, heartbroken, drenched in a cold sweat of panic and self-condemnation. What had I unleashed upon myself? I had parted from him in anger, having given him a gala performance of the most unattractive side of my nature, and by allowing him to leave me in that frame of mind, I had made a gift of him to Alys or any other woman who had the wit to recognize his need for consolation—as I would have recognized it—and the will to supply it.

What a fool I was. What more could I desire than I already had? Nothing, except that it might continue, except that I might keep it intact. I had never learned the unique pleasure of asking pardon but I knew the moment had come for me to try. "Please forgive me." Surely that was all I needed to say? And he would forgive me gladly for he took no pleasure in storm and tempest, as I often did, but was a man for calm weather. Just let him come home to me safe and whole and willing to listen and I would be everything he wanted, for I had sense enough to know that the time for dazzling and overwhelming could not last for ever. Perhaps a relationship—like everything else—had need for change, movement, growth, in order to endure, and in that case the direction in which we must travel was to a level of quieter harmony, more suited to his nature, no doubt, than to mine, but to which *I* must adapt; since he could not so easily adapt to me. I was the stronger, I had always known that, and strength conveyed responsibilities upon its possessor. I knew that too. And therefore I, not Robin, must take the lead. I must give him tranquillity as well as adoration, friendship as well as passion, peace of mind as well as physical sensation. I must.

As the night drew to its close everything began to seem so very clear. I watched the light change from gray to rose-pearl, saw a cool, empty sky flush suddenly with the new morning and, lying there alone and presumably forsaken, I felt a fresh source of strength just beginning to stir inside me. But I had always been strong. Now I would be wise. My intentions had always been of the best. Now I would carry them out with more gentleness, more finesse. Now I would always remember to ask myself what *he* wanted, rather than what *I* wanted him to have. Just let him come and I would give my whole mind to loving him. Forgive me, Robin.

He came, striding up the lane in his evening clothes, at ten o'clock of a bright Sunday morning, considerably startling my reverend uncle's church parade, letting the garden gate slam shut to warn me, I supposed, to give me time to compose myself perhaps, or to pick up the hatchet—verbal or otherwise—which he would be expecting me to throw at him.

He was here. Safe. Grinning ruefully, boyishly, with a shade of real embarrassment since his scarlet sash and pleated evening shirt would already be the talk of Clarrow Fell. But he was home. I had known he would come. Of course I had. He was home. Thank God. Forgive me, Robin.

"Where the devil have you been all night?" I snarled at him through clenched teeth. "I've been frantic, that's all, frantic . . ."

"Well—perhaps I ought to be glad of that."

"Glad? Ashamed you mean—thoroughly . . ."

"No—no. Glad. You wouldn't have been frantic unless you were worried. You wouldn't have worried unless you cared. It follows, therefore, that you do care and I am fully entitled to be glad. That's logic, my dear, as they taught it to me at Hexingham."

I picked up something from the table, I didn't know what, something hard and smooth that I would probably grieve for afterwards when I had thrown it at him and broken it, and held it at the ready.

"Please don't," he said. "I've really been punished enough. It was no joke, I can tell you, walking up from the station past Clarrow in its Sunday best. Lord—if you had seen their faces! I thought the best way to play it was like Dottie Potterton—as if I was quite sure *everybody* must know it was the very latest Mayfair thing to wear a dinner-jacket in the village street at ten o'clock in the morning. Not that I fooled them, I suppose."

"Don't try to make me laugh."

"I'd rather thought it might be my only hope of salvation."

"Don't count on it."

But I had already replaced whatever it was I had clenched in my hand. He was home, not particularly contrite but not hostile either, hoping he would get away with it, I supposed, without too much trouble. Well—we would see about that. And remembering that rose-pearl sky of early morning and all my good intentions, I bent my head to hide a smile.

"Ah—what's this?" he said, the English schoolboy-gentleman again who had always charmed me. "There's a chance, then, that you might forgive me . . . ?"

214

"Possibly. Possibly not."

"Well—while you're thinking it over—is there at least a chance of breakfast? I don't mean to be a nuisance but I think I am about to die of starvation or very nearly."

"Didn't they feed you—in town?"

"Oh, sumptuously. But that was last night, you know— yesterday. And although I do seem to remember something called breakfast about five o'clock this morning, it was mostly champagne—*and* so long ago. A plate of bacon and eggs and sausages would probably save my life, Olivia. And mushrooms . . . ! There can't be much wrong with a world that grows mushrooms you know. That's what I think at any rate."

And since there was really no point in arguing with a man who had breakfasted on champagne, I sent the girl running up to Clarrow for new bread and fresh-picked mushrooms, gave instructions for hot water and towels and clean linen to be put in his room and realizing that I had eaten nothing myself since tea-time yesterday set two plates at the table.

It had been, of course, a splendid party, the whole dining room of the Station Hotel taken over for the night, masses of white roses and pink carnations everywhere, glorious hothouse blooms, Robin told me, his horticulturist's eye still glowing, a fortune in themselves strewn casually by Max de Haan at Victorine's feet.

"I had no idea he was so fond of her, Olivia."

"He isn't."

"Oh well—one assumes he has his reasons. But those roses! Every one had its own face, you know what I mean. I sorted out a few of the best ones to bring home for you but—well—you know how it is. I wonder where they are now? Pity."

The meal too had been magnificent, served at small tables set with pink and white lace cloths and decorated with all the sophisticated frivolity of moss garlands, tulle frills, pyramids of golden apricots and dark, dusty plums, silver-gilt candlesticks with apricot silk shades, the refinements of London and Paris brought by Max de Haan to Station Square. Certainly Robin had seen nothing like it before in Bradeswick. It had put *our* wedding breakfast to shame, there was no doubt about that. I believed him.

They had eaten turbot and grouse and black Beluga caviar. Crayfish in Chablis. Beef in red wine. Hothouse peaches and nectarines and those exotic bananas Max imported from Madeira along with his wines and his basket-work furniture. Well, of course he was an importer of tropical fruit and cane chairs and the Lord knew what besides. Didn't I know that? Of course I did. What else, I wondered sweetly? White slaves, perhaps?

"I shouldn't think so," said Robin with an air of perfect innocence. "Lovely black ones, I rather imagine—all polished ebony skin and gold bangles. Very fetching."

Quite so.

There had even been a wedding-cake, a real extravaganza three tiers high, covered with lovers' knots in pink and white satin ribbon and tiny posies of pink carnations done up in frills of silver lace. A marvel, in fact, which no one could imagine how Max had managed to get done in time.

"Money," I said, as blunt now as Victorine. For what else could Max de Haan possibly have to offer?

Indeed yes. Money, in almost visible piles of gold all over the Station Hotel. An aura of it hanging like a golden net above the petals of those perfect roses and the bloom of those exotic, out-of-season fruits; fronds of ivy that could have been garlands of ten pound notes around every candlestick, huge, important cigars that announced their own value, tiny crystal scent sprays for the ladies, each one containing a French perfume everyone had heard of and knew to be unobtainable in Bradeswick. An indication, one supposed, that Max was in the perfume-importing business too. There had been a river of sparkling, gold-flecked champagne on which my mother had floated— Robin knew no other word for it—a spray of orchids appearing to serve as the entire bodice of her dress, the skirt trailing behind her in yards of lace and fluted chiffon, her bare shoulders rather startling in the mother of the bride, her waist a mere nineteen inches, as everyone now knew, since Mr. Septimus Cross, the Banker, who could be frisky in his cups, had called for a tape and measured it. Nineteen inches!

"Like mine," I said tartly and her bosom—also like mine— was twenty inches more, the perfect hour-glass shape of high fashion. I sincerely hoped Mr. Cross had not taken it into his head to measure *that*!

"Lord no, for Mr. Greenlaw took it very much amiss and for a moment we thought it would be pistols at dawn until Max suggested they might care to have a go at battering each other with balance sheets and calmed them down rather. Your mother was very flattered and assumes she could be Mrs. Samuel Greenlaw any day of the week now."

"Not if his daughters-in-law can put a stop to it. And if she goes on like this then they soon will."

"Which would be a pity, since she gives those two old boys something to live for."

And how had the bridegroom—the progressive Dr. Rexford— reacted to this dinner for a couple of dozen people, the cost of which would have kept the inmates of Bradeswick Workhouse in nourishing broths and meat puddings for a twelve-month? Stiffly at first, Robin thought. But whatever one happened to think of Andrew Rexford's politics or his moral values, no one could accuse him of being small-minded, and having agreed to accept the evening as a gift from Max, he had done so with quite a bit of grace and dignity. Presumably, Robin supposed, he was shrewd enough to know that there would have been no way in the world of persuading Max to give the money to the Workhouse instead. And therefore, since it was bound to be squandered anyway, why not on Victorine? After all, no one expects the groom to pay for his own wedding reception.

And Victorine? Radiant, declared Robin. A cream silk dress with a high ruffled neck and floppy lace sleeves, a brown velvet sash that made her waist look not quite nineteen inches, perhaps, but smaller than one had supposed, her hair very neat and very glossy, done up in a single coil at the nape of her neck and parted in the middle. She had stood very erect, her head held high, her cheeks flushed with pleasure, the center of attention for perhaps the first time in her life, Robin wondered, and enjoying it hugely. Madelon, too, had been enchanted, dreaming no doubt of herself in the same situation with some Prince Charming who, at the moment, was wearing Ivor Naseby's face. Alys had been intrigued and captivated by the sheer audacity of Max's extravagance. Not condoning it, of course,— since she too would have preferred those meat puddings for the workhouse—but admiring its style.

While my mother had passed from a state of rapture to one of bliss and back to rapture again, knowing that the Nasebys and the Pottertons and the rest, although they had not been present, would hear all about it and, being quite capable of adding up the cost, would be bound to conclude that Lavinia Blackwood and her daughters were not easily to be disregarded. For no accusations of irregular or furtive behavior could be made against Victorine after this, no speculations as to whether she was really married at all or that, if so, she was ashamed of it, when her union had been announced so splendidly.

And then, when the older gentlemen and ladies like Miss Frances Grey who only cared to be excessive in moderation had departed, leaving, it seemed, only my sisters, my new brother-in-law, my mother, Robin and Alys, there had been a genuine, quite incredible cascade of champagne, the kind of thing one might expect King Teddy to do for Mrs. Keppel or Lillie Langtry or Sarah Bernhardt, but which had caught even my mother by surprise in Bradeswick, for Victorine.

Suddenly, when everything had seemed to be coming to an end, Max had called for wide-brimmed champagne glasses filled with sliced peaches and grapes and strawberries. No—Robin had no idea where Max had obtained strawberries at this season. Presumably he imported them too, packed in ice, from the South of France and, piling the glasses up, one row on top of another, into a fragile, beautiful, incredibly precarious pyramid, Max—with an arm they all thought incredibly steady considering the amount of claret and brandy he had drunk—had poured a continuous stream of champagne into the topmost glass, letting it spill over in a truly glamorous cascade until every other glass was full.

That had been breakfast, the grandest of grand finales, although Max had declared that one needed a warmer climate to do the job properly, a garden full of little nooks and crannies to stroll about in afterwards or an Italian lake where one could swim preferably among water-lilies and presumably naked. Robin had heard all about Max when he had been at Hexingham and evidently he had lived up to his reputation. Good luck to him, thought Robin.

"But you do see, Olivia darling, that although champagne and fruit salad are all very well, there's no substance to it. As breakfasts go I don't think it's likely to replace bacon and eggs—and mushrooms."

"I suppose you'll want to sleep now for the rest of the morning?"

"And for a bit of the afternoon too, I shouldn't wonder. I haven't felt quite so debauched since Cambridge."

"What did Amyas think of this cascade of champagne?"

"Amyas? Was he there? Yes, of course he was. That's the

trouble with Amyas, he just appears and disappears and one never notices—which suits him, of course, because for some reason or other, I'm quite sure he doesn't want to be seen. Funny chap, Amyas. Yes, he came and paid his respects to the bride, said everything that was right and proper, ate his dinner and went away. And until you mentioned him just now I'd forgotten he was there at all. If I'd been asked to supply a list of guests for the newspapers—or the police—I don't think I'd have included him. He left early because of Max, I suppose. I'd love to know just what there is between those two. So would Alys."

"Is there something between them?"

"Lord yes—something very deep and twisted. Alys and I have often wondered. But Amyas would never tell. We could never even find out just where he came from. We looked in all the family Bibles and read all the family letters we could find in Clarrow attic—oh yes, piles of them, all bundled up in ribbon just as letters ought to be, you'd love them—but we never even found a clue. Obviously he has to be a member of the family by some back road or other—somebody's love-child —but we could never quite fit him in. We decided at one point that the Squire must be his father and Alys still rather clings to that. But I have my doubts. The Squire's lady certainly didn't think so."

"You mean my grandmother?"

"Yes—so I do. She was a very adoring, very jealous wife, yet she was always kind to Amyas as I'm quite certain she couldn't have been if she had so much as suspected the Squire. And Lady Olivia would have done more than suspect, she'd have known. You have her name too—odd that I never realized . . ."

What? Was it this unknown grandmother, then, who had given first to her son and then to me our possessive, passionate, troublesome nature? A tantalizing thought, worth exploring in a quieter moment, when my mind was less preoccupied with the sorry task of counting how many times Robin, within the last few minutes, had mentioned Alys.

And, as always, I felt compelled to mention her myself.

"Did Alys go home with my mother?"

"Yes—and in style. Max drove them in his Daimler. Aunt Sibylla will be very miffed about it."

"She won't mind."

"You don't know her. Alys was supposed to go home on the

last train with Amyas. She even went to find her hat and gloves—which with Alys is always an uncertain undertaking, I grant you—but then Max said his little piece about caged birds and how the only thing that stopped her from opening the door was her conscience—you remember? He dared her to stay, in fact, and she did."

"Aunt Sibylla won't mind."

Take care, I thought. Talk about Victorine and Andrew Rexford or Max. Don't pick and pry into his feelings for Alys. Don't goad him. He *has* affection for her, you know that. Don't ask him to count it out for you, or analyze it, or compare it. Because it may be more than you can cope with, or more than he'd realized. Whatever it is, he has it in control, dormant. Let it sleep.

He stirred uneasily, a vague, uncomfortable image entering his mind.

"Why do you say that, Olivia?"

And wisdom was entirely overwhelmed by my destructive, irresistible compulsion to find out, to test him, to *know*.

"Because if Alys is with my mother today, there is every likelihood that she is also with Max. He will probably call this afternoon in his Daimler, and take them for a spin. Aunt Sibylla will be only too delighted."

"I am sorry, Olivia. I don't follow you."

But he did. I had deliberately presented him with the picture of Alys with another man. He had not liked it. Therefore—therefore? And as my carefully constructed world began, once more, to decay and crumble, my warm hearth to choke with cold ashes, panic to strike me, I said flatly, "Because Max is rich and Alys is single. Need I say more?"

"Not really."

But of course I had to. "It would be a very good thing for her."

He got up, pushed aside his plate, wanting to end it before it had really begun, by walking away. And knowing quite well that I should let him go, I nevertheless persisted.

"Well it *would* be good for her, you must admit. *Don't* you admit?"

He sighed. "Olivia, the only thing Max de Haan has to recommend him as a husband—as you well know—is money. Alys would not marry for money."

"Aunt Sibylla would."

220

"We are talking about Alys."

"We are talking of a girl whose mother is desperate to get her married. And, after all, the fastest way out of Clarrow vicarage is a husband."

"If Alys had thought so, then she could have married long ago."

"Guy, you mean?"

"Yes. I know he asked her."

"Did you ask her?"

Why—oh why—oh why, had I said that? Take it back at once. But one cannot retrieve the spoken word, one can only attempt to throw a screen of other words around it and leave it lying there, painfully visible.

"Never mind about that, Robin."

"I shan't. I didn't even hear it."

And then, hesitating at the foot of the stairs, on his way to bed and the sleep he visibly required, he said with some apology and gentleness, knowing, I suppose, how much it hurt me, "Olivia, one really can't talk about these things, you know. One *doesn't*, darling— that's all. You do see that?"

Yes. A gentleman did not discuss his dealings—past or present with a lady. A true gentleman, that is, like Robin or my grandfather or—yes, quite definitely—Amyas. Emil Junot, of course, and Jean François and Max would have told me anything I desired to know, graphically, with relish and color and great enjoyment. I would do well to remember that.

We spent a pleasant afternoon walking on Clarrow moor, purple September again among the heather, a smoky sky with the sun low and hazy along the horizon, leaves not yet on the turn but something in the air promising a fine, deep gold autumn.

"This is the time of year I love most," said Robin, inhaling the scent and taste of the changing seasons.

"You said that in April when the buds came and in June with the roses. You said it last December when you saw the first frost."

"Did I? How fickle I am."

"Yes."

"Not really, Olivia."

And it was possible now to smile, to take the hand he held out to me and walk home leaning contentedly against his shoulder.

A mood of ease and indolence had been created which carried us through dinner, no crayfish in Chablis, as I was quick to mention, but roast beef brought over in a hot dish from the main house, potatoes, cabbages and turnips from Clarrow home farm, Yorkshire puddings as light and crisp as only Mrs. Timmins could make them.

"You know, Olivia, you are getting just as ready to back a Clarrow carrot against the rest of the world as Aunt Sibylla."

Narrow, did he mean? He was smiling, teasing, evidently enjoying his plain English—Clarrow—food, but nevertheless, the comparison annoyed me slightly. Could I possibly have become so insular, so ridiculous?

The beef was replaced by an enormous treacle sponge, a deep custard tart fragrant with nutmeg and vanilla, a pint of thick custard sauce. "Now that," said Robin, "is exactly what I like."

I was reassured instantly, my humor swinging far too quickly from dark to light, and I smiled at him fondly, watching him eat with an almost gloating satisfaction, leaning across the table the moment his plate was empty to give him more.

"Am I a goose, by any chance, that you are fattening for Christmas?"

"I just enjoy your enjoyment."

"All my enjoyments?"

"Are you thinking of one in particular?"

"Of course I am. And I was rather hoping—well—an early night? Shall we?" We did. So early that even our little maid by no means famous for her quick wits noticed the implications and turned quite pink. And for an hour I gave my body, my inner being, my love unsullied by the flaws and fears of my daytime self, love that came pure and whole and direct and was given exactly as love ought to be, for no other reason than the pleasure of the giving.

I gave my body and would have given it again immediately, feeling, as I often did lately that I had not given enough, that there was still something inside me, something else, something more, some other level of sensation or emotion, I wasn't sure—but *something*. Yet for Robin the experience had been complete, exhausting, quite harrowing one might have thought by the groans and the perspiration and his helplessness afterwards, the precious moment of his collapse into my arms, breathless and defenseless and absolutely mine, pressing tight against me as if, having enjoyed me to the full, he needed to be comforted for it.

222

"They told us at school it was wrong you see," he said, laughing into my shoulder. "And every nanny I ever had said the same."

"They were telling you lies."

"They were keeping us under control. They had most of us thinking we'd go to the devil, or lose our hearing, if we so much as cast a sidelong glance at a female. Not that it worked with everybody. Certainly not with Max if one can credit even half the tales they tell of him at Hexingham."

I did not want Max de Haan's name spoken here in my bedroom, not ever and particularly not now in these fragile moments after making love.

"I don't want to talk about Max," I said, and then, because my resentment of him had been simmering all day, proceeded to do so at some length and most unwisely.

"I suppose you know that he gave that ridiculous party on purpose to annoy me? That wouldn't be his only reason, of course, because he's as tricky as a box of monkeys, but that was one of them—mark my words."

The delicately woven magic which had held us close together began to unravel, as always, much too soon and I sat bolt upright, furious again with Victorine in the first place for stabbing me in the back and then with Max for turning his own golden knife in my wound. For what else had it been but that? Why had he staged this spectacular extravaganza for Victorine, of whom he had never taken the slightest notice, when on hearing of my own wedding, he had simply thrown a bracelet and a pair of earrings at me with his curt permission to sell them whenever I should need to repair the roof of Clarrow Fell.

I knew.

"Why?" said Robin, running his hand the length of my back, not yet caring. "Why should Max want to annoy you?"

Yes I knew. It was crystal clear to me but strangely difficult to explain to someone as clean and straightforward as Robin.

"Because of Clarrow. He comes here every now and then like a carrion crow to see if my grandfather is any nearer to the grave. And last night was to remind me that when the time comes he has the money—and all the popularity and the power it gives him."

It had been a challenge, in fact, flung down with flamboyance and swagger but in great earnest nonetheless. He had the money. I

223

would have the house. Could I keep it? Or would he find a way to persuade me or force me to sell? That was the game.

Robin sighed and the hand which had been stroking my spine grew still.

"Yes," he said, his voice so neutral, so careful, that I knew he had been waiting for some propitious moment to speak and probably dreading it. "He did say something about Clarrow this morning when he drove me to the station. He put his cards on the table, in fact, and made me a very decent offer."

"Made *you* an offer!" I was incredulous. How dare he? He had absolutely no right!

"Well, I am your husband, you know . . ."

"Dear God—the arrogance of that man."

"Darling, not really. You must understand . . ."

"Oh no, I don't have to do anything. Not where the manor is concerned."

"Olivia—darling—stop clenching your teeth and growling and *listen*. It's not at all unusual that he should make his offer to me. Until twenty years ago a married woman had no property of her own. Everything she had or inherited belonged, by law, to her husband. Twenty years ago Clarrow Fell would have been legally mine, not yours, darling, and I could have sold it or knocked it down without even asking your consent. And even though nowadays the law does allow you to inherit the estate in your own right, old attitudes die hard and most men find it very difficult to approach a woman on a matter of business. That's what I do all day, darling, at Lawker & Lane—handle the business affairs of ladies who don't find it ladylike to handle their own. Even Frances Grey looks down her nose at her investments as if the mice had been at them. So Max was quite correct in talking to me."

"All right. I don't care, since he wasted his time anyway . . ."

And unable to endure the sudden silence, the thread of shocked suspicion it had aroused in me, I said quickly, hoping as I had never hoped for anything in my life before, that I was right, "You refused him, of course, and told him there would be no point in troubling you again."

What a question? A simple statement of fact? Or had I voiced a terrible doubt?

He got up, and sat on the edge of the bed, looking down, his face in shadow.

224

"Are you cold, Olivia?"

Oddly, I was, or must be since I had shivered, although the night outside our window was soft and warm.

"Not really."

And I waited, clasping my hands around my knees, naked and silent as if a moment of final judgment had come.

"I've thought about it, Olivia," he said, his voice slow and heavy, each word a great burden on his tongue. "There have been whole days together when I've thought of nothing else. And my answer to the problem is always the same. Olivia—I have to tell you . . ."

Don't, I silently cried out. Not yet. Let's wait a while. Let's hope the Squire goes on living until we're older, steadier—until we're ready.

"I'm not prepared to give my life to this estate, Olivia. For your sake I'd like to. But I can't. Darling—do you hear me?"

I heard, and drawing up my knees close to my chest, hugging them with fierce arms, I hid my face in the arc of my body, curling myself like a child in the womb, the position one assumes—it seemed—when face to face with the one conflict which cannot be resolved. So, I believe, I would have felt had I been asked to choose between the life of one dearly loved child and another, both equally precious. How could I sacrifice either one without tearing away one half of myself? Cruel, impossible choices. I could not choose. And so I took the only escape route open to me and refused to believe him. It was a mood, no more, and would pass. Just a mood, brought on by that damnable cascade of champagne, that false allure of Max de Haan's riches in which I had so little faith, his aura of exciting foreign places which, so very often, turned out to be dangerous, too, and hard. It was a mood. It had to be.

"Olivia, we never discussed it before we were married, as we ought to have done. And I know how much I'm to blame. I knew you had mistaken me for the ideal country gentleman—as you saw him—and I let you go on thinking that because—well—it was what attracted you."

"That's all right, Robin." Carefully now, but very quickly, I must choose the words to tell him how easily I could forgive him for that most forgivable of deceptions. He had shown me the side of himself most likely to please me because he had wanted to please me. I had done the same. I understood. But he gave me no opportunity to speak, feeling a great need to say everything he had to say as fast as he could, *while* he could.

"But I'm not really like that, darling. And isn't it time now you looked at me and *saw* me as I am, not as you've imagined me . . . ?"

How dreadful. That was all my mind seemed capable of holding, a sensation of absolute, impenetrable dread. I had been afraid of losing his love. But was he now saying to me something far worse—that he believed I did not know him and therefore my love could not really exist? How dreadful! How wounding. And since Robin did not inflict wounds lightly—did not, in fact, inflict them at all if it could possibly be avoided—I knew how long the need had been simmering inside him, how vital it was, how real.

"Olivia, I didn't choose to come to Clarrow Fell in the first place. It was just the most convenient address to send me. And I came back, after Cambridge, because my room and board were still available and because I'm—lazy if you like—a bit too much inclined to think tomorrow will do. But I never intended to stay. And certainly—absolutely certainly—I never meant to get stuck with Lawker & Lane."

And swiftly, with drowning hands, I clutched the straw he seemed to offer me.

"Then leave them. I wouldn't mind."

"And do what? Ride to hounds five days a week all winter like the Pottertons? Meddle with the tenants' private affairs like Aunt Sibylla? Or try to do what the Squire does and make an idiot of myself over it—because I don't believe in what he does."

"Robin!"

"Olivia, I am so sorry. I can't tell you how sorry and how conscious I am of letting you down. But I have to tell you—don't I?—because without honesty I don't see how one can live easy. The world is such a big place, Olivia, and I have seen so little of it. I've been to Bradeswick and Cambridge and to India . . ."

Where had I heard this before? Alys crying out, "I have been to Bridlington and Scarborough and once all the way to Eastbourne, how am I to bear it?"

"There's so much I've never seen, Olivia, so many other ways of life I've never experienced, never even had a glimpse of . . . And some of those ways must be right not just for me, darling, but for *us*. Clarrow isn't right for me. It's too narrow and too demanding. I'd have to give it my whole mind. Every scrap of energy I have—and every penny. There'd be no time for anything else and I can't just limit myself in that fashion. I've tried—very hard—to make myself believe I could. But what it boils down to is that I've only one life to lead, Olivia, and it just can't be here—it just can't be."

Yes, he had tried very hard indeed. I accepted that. I heard, too, the hint of tears in his voice, felt the strain of his nerves, knew how much it was costing him to hurt me.

"Olivia, do you love me?"

"Of course I do." It was a cry of anguish.

"Then be my wife."

"But I am."

"No. Be my wife. Live in the house I provide wherever I provide it. Don't weigh me down with five hundred years of tradition that I spent the biggest part of my life trying to get away from."

"You don't mean it. Not really."

I couldn't allow him to mean it. And as he watched the enormity of my distress—as once again I curled myself into that primitive, foetal attitude of helplessness—I felt his resolution waver. It takes a great deal of courage, after all, to hurt a woman one cares for and Robin had told me often enough that he was not brave.

"I mean it, darling. But I don't expect us to reach any decisions tonight. I just want you to know how I feel, that's all. So you'll know . . ."

I flung my arms around him, my mouth fastening upon his to stop the words, my body desperate for reassurance, as greedy for comfort as a frightened child, yet at the same time wanting to dominate, to make him desire me, to fill his mind with straightforward lust, if I could do nothing else to counteract its dangerous philosophy, to make something tremendous so that I could keep them both. And still it would not suffice. It was not enough to be the passive recipient of love-making, the patient, female earth waiting to be plowed and fertilized. I must now be the initiator, the aggressor, and so I took him, pinned him beneath me, lifted him to a groaning, quivering summit of joy that caused him to cry out as if I had stabbed him to the heart. And then he lay in my arms again, laughing weakly, his forehead beaded with sweat, a trace of moisture along his eyelids to which I put my mouth.

"Darling," he said, "I think you've just taken my virginity."

"I love you, Robin."

"Well, I should hope so, having ravished me in such glorious

Amazon fashion. Not that I'm complaining, don't think that. I'll lie still and promise not to scream should you care to do it again."

"I might."

"Please do. You really *have* conquered me, you know."

Yes. And we would heal the breach between us in our own separate ways. Robin would poke gentle fun at it. I would refuse to acknowledge there was a breach at all. Everything—with effort and persistence, with my love and his passion—would go well.

Yet when I woke an hour or two before dawn, my sleep penetrated by an uneasy physical awareness of night dangers, prowlers, specters, *something* wrong, it was to find myself alone, Robin at first only a deeper shadow among shadows, sitting by the window looking out, looking away, a tautness in the air around him warning that I must make no sound. I lay alone in my bed feigning sleep and watched him, the center of a slow whirlpool of misery, its ripples lapping outwards towards me and then drawn back again, by a visible effort of will, into the mind and body from which they came. In the morning he would turn a smiling face towards me. I would turn my smiling face to him. But now, at the very bleakest hour of night, he was suffering—as Hexingham had taught him a gentleman should—in silence and alone. And knowing myself to be the cause of it, accepting that the remedy was in my hands, I shuddered and closed my eyes.

Open the cage door, Max had told Alys. All that holds you is your conscience. And if the day ever came when I had nothing but Robin's decency, his integrity, his guilt with which to keep him at Clarrow, could I do it? Could I employ his own good qualities against him?

Dear God, let me find some other solution. Let me be different. Yet I wore the nature heredity and circumstance had blended between them and forced upon me. I was my mother's daughter and, like all her children, bore the scars of loving her; Madelon with her cough, Victorine who found security in flour and sugar, Luc in his magpie hoarding of shiny, durable things; where else had I acquired my own destructive need to possess the things I loved, the man I loved, my need to bind him because I dare not allow him the freedom he needed to love me?

I did not think, lying there in the dark, that I could feel greater misery. Yet I had still some way to travel before the truth, which as

228

truth often seems to be, was simple, cruel, easily visible. I had mistaken him, not for Guy, but for the image I had created of my stranger brother, and certainly, even in the days when I had dazzled his vision, filled his mind, so urgently aroused his senses, he had always needed Alys.

THIRTEEN

More than ever now I longed to conceive a child, but month after month through a hazy, amber autumn, a magical winter of cool sunshine and hard frost to another pastel springtime I was regularly and painfully presented with the evidence of my sterility. No easy cross to bear in the month of April when new life was stirring in every root and branch, and the hedgerows were teeming with new-fledged fur and feathers and the brave delicacy of wild flowers, the meadows dotted with lambs.

Yet the only doctor I knew who concerned himself with the reproductive dilemmas of women was my brother-in-law, Andrew Rexford, who, I felt, would have had no time to spare for me—since I had a roof over my head and four good meals a day—even had I cared to ask.

I asked no one. I clenched my teeth on my troubles and bore them, as Robin did, in silence. And as my complaints grew less so, by some natural process of leveling, his sympathy appeared to grow greater, allowing us to present an increasingly united face both to the world and to each other. There were no angry scenes between us for a long time after Victorine's wedding party, for at first we both knew that our relationship had become too fragile to bear them and later, when it might have been possible, the spark which had generated those grand explosions, those ecstatic reconciliations had somehow passed. We remained polite and sometimes loving with each other, quite often there was laughter, no tears which I allowed him to see. We both had our private pain to bear. But who has not? Robin was a man of integrity and decency, and great sensitivity who had known all along the strength of my feelings for Clarrow Fell. I was a loving woman who sincerely believed that his happiness as well as mine could best be found here. It was selfish of him to ask me to go, selfish of me to ask him to stay. One selfishness canceled out the other, requiring us to find a compromise. We had not yet done so. And in the meantime—because we *were* decent people—we behaved with far more courtesy and consideration for each other than we had ever done in the first blaze of love. We were, in fact, biding our time. Robin, perhaps on that dark, lonely night of brooding at our bedroom window, had accepted that unless he could present me with some viable alternative it would be impossible to ask me to tear up the roots I had fought so hard to put down. While I, to make his imprisonment easier to bear—and why, oh why, did that terrible word imprisonment spring so often to my mind?—began to make concessions; not bargains any longer—"You do this for me and I will do that"—but straightforward acts of surrender, without strings. When we received an invitation to a Potterton dance—"Just a small affair to celebrate the return of Felix, our dear nephew, to the County"—and Robin, wrinkling his nose, sighed "Not again," I at once declined without mentioning to him either my disappointment or Aunt Sibylla's avowed intention of seeing what could be done with Alys and the politically ambitious Felix Potterton who had evidently come North to try his luck with the constituency again.

"My daughter's interest in politics," Aunt Sibylla had said, "would appear less peculiar, in fact would seem quite appropriate if she became a politician's wife. Yes, we shall certainly attend the Pottertons' dance."

But instead of repeating this to Robin and assessing his reaction with a dry throat and narrowed eyes, I simply said, "We won't go."

When Mrs. Naseby called unexpectedly one sparkling late October afternoon, I allowed Robin to escape by the back door the moment her victoria was spotted on the drive, laughed and blew him a kiss as he vaulted the garden wall into the meadow, endured her myself and asked no questions on his return.

"Darling," he said, one Sunday morning not long before Christmas, a moment or two before it would be necessary to get out of our warm bed for church. "I've never gone to church from choice, you know." And he was speaking very clearly on impulse, a man seizing an opportunity, grasping a nettle, testing his ground.

"Have you not?"

"Never. The Squire forced me to it as a boy—then Hexingham. Now you. Can you let me off, I wonder? It's not my line—honestly—listening to old uncle Toby reel off those sermons Aunt Sibylla writes for him."

"Does she really?" I had wondered.

"Don't you recognize her style? All that rot about God having made the poor to be poor and the rich to be rich and wanting them to stay that way—etcetera, *ad nauseam.*"

"Does anyone listen?"

"If I were a farm boy sitting in the back pews I'd listen and I wouldn't be very pleased about it either. It might not give me a very good opinion of the Almighty, or of the gentry sitting at the front for that matter. Don't you see that, Olivia?"

Yes, indeed, for I knew far more about poverty than he did, and was far more concerned—at that stage of my life—with maintaining my own by no means certain place on those front pews than with the resentments of farm boys. But all I said, sweetly and to his visible surprise, was "All right, Robin. Consider yourself let off."

I went to church after that alone and left on my grandfather's arm, an attention he could no longer refuse me, standing beside him in the church porch after the service to share the hour he always accorded, after worship, to his tenants: my presence an acknowledgment that I was the nearest thing to a "young squire" they would be likely to get. And then, perhaps a grudging bonus but a sure one, we would walk back together through the village, pausing at this cottage and that to pay respects to the bereaved, console the sick or injured, admire the newborn—no easy task for me—and having ascertained where and what sort of assistance was needed would continue up the hill to the Manor where the traditional Sunday roast beef would be waiting. For the first time, although with very little of the satisfaction I had hoped for, since Robin did not share it, I sat at the head of my grandfather's table, the daughter of the house who knew the names and dispositions of the household staff, keeping up a pleasant flow of conversation with the Squire who would have preferred to eat in silence, and Amyas who would have preferred to watch and listen.

I bided my time, employing it skillfully I suppose and painstakingly, as birds construct their nests, to create an atmosphere that would change Robin's attitude to Clarrow Fell, weaving a net of small domestic spells about him to make his life easy and pleasant: working hard. He worked hard too, attempting to give me the correct response, throwing himself, for a while, with such unusual vigor into country pursuits that he seemed almost to be rehearsing the role of "squire," doing his best to make it fit. But it did not last and by the winter of 1903 to 1904—a notable sporting season—he "could not be bothered" with the steeplechasing, hunted so rarely that Dottie Potterton wondered out loud why his subscription was kept up; his time being largely spent in Bradeswick, at the offices of Lawker & Lane at least for an hour or two and then in the lively discussions on social and philosophical topics which went on eternally, it seemed, in the respective drawing rooms of Miss Frances Grey and Victorine.

I had made peace with my sister, of course. There had never been any real doubt about that and I was a regular visitor to her house off Corporation Square, built between a path of wasteland no one had ever named and a great criss-crossing of tram-lines, the meeting point of several routes where trams discharged their passengers all day, a constant raucous coming and going of brewery workers and ironworkers, women with market baskets and fractious children; more children, in swarms, who ought to have been at school, playing excitable, often dangerous games on that open patch of weeds, scrap metal and broken glass; young couples loitering there every night playing dangerous games of their own. A city landscape of gray streets and anonymous gray houses which did not seem displeasing to Victorine, a view of the backyards of Corporation Square and the unadorned rear of its public buildings from one of her windows, an uncompromising line of tramsheds from another.

The house itself was the last of a row of ten, a favored position since the yard was not only back and front but extended around one side; a proper garden, in fact, which Victorine soon planted with vegetables and herbs and salads, finding space—and time—for a hen-run, a rabbit hutch, a beehive.

"There must be peasant blood somewhere," my mother said, her nostrils visibly incommoded by the hens and rabbits, her whole demeanor uneasy about the bees. "In the Marriotts, that is, since there is not one drop of it in me."

But, once passed the dangers of fur and feather, Victorine's house was always warm in winter, always cool and fragrant in the summertime, rich and savory broths always simmering in her kitchen, her parlor always well polished, cheaply and cheerfully furnished with rainbow colored rag rugs, ill-matched armchairs in deep claret or crimson or a vivid green which did not please the eye but greatly assisted the comfort of the body. She had a cat and usually a kitten or two in a basket by the fire, a dog of pugnacious appearance and placid disposition and, that April, after only eight months of marriage, she had already conceived her first child, news which turned me cold when I first heard it and then sent me rushing to Corporation Square with flowers and chocolates and a flurry of good wishes.

My feelings about her situation were oddly and uncomfortably divided. I wanted Victorine herself to be happy. Yet, because I had opposed her marriage for reasons which still seemed perfectly valid to me, I did not want her to be happy with Andrew. When I saw that she *was* happy I was enormously glad and then just as enormously sorry since I didn't believe it could last.

Their life, of course, was far from conventional, for Andrew had no routines, no timetables, seeing patients and friends whenever they happened to call, turning out himself at any hour of the day or night to a sick-bed or a confinement whether he was likely to be paid for it or not. There seemed always to be someone knocking at Victorine's door, cheeky grinning lads from those mean streets behind the tramsheds coming to have their wounds stitched up after a brawl, men in cloth caps and neatly patched work-clothes who had somehow dragged themselves from the scene of an accident on broken limbs to save the doctor the trouble; little girls, themselves no more than children, bringing other children consigned to their care while the mothers were out at work, who had been scalded or bruised or had somehow fallen into the fire. Women miscarried their unwanted pregnancies quite often in Andrew's consulting room, having first visited the old woman at the corner of St. Saviour's Street not far away, who performed incomplete abortions for a guinea, relying on Andrew—now that her nerve and her eyesight were failing—to patch up her sorry results, usually free of charge. Other women came to him with bowed, anxious heads, a child carried on the hip, a child or two tugging at her skirts, a few more at home, asking in whispers for the means to limit huge families without anyone knowing, since contraception like orgasm was not supposed to be for decent women but only for whores. And from time to time a real whore would come too. Some of them old and pitiful and badly beaten up, usually on Thursday and Friday nights—wage-days—when there was money to drink and it might seem amusing, when a man had consumed the last drop, to beat up an old whore. Some of them young, frail, syphilitic, usually half-starved since whoring did not seem to pay in places like Bradeswick where the majority of working-men—except for those terrible families behind the tramsheds—had strong nonconformist moral values, and rich men were excessively discreet about their pleasures.

"What a terrible neighborhood," said my mother, on encountering one of these at the side gate.

But to Alys, who as a child had been told by her mother that babies came straight from Heaven and had been told nothing at all since she grew up, the attitudes of Andrew and Victorine were another breath of freedom. Her own first menstruation, coming at the vulnerable age of thirteen, had shocked her profoundly for the simple reason that she had no idea what it was. Had she contracted some terrible disease? Or, as her mother's attitude of frozen contempt seemed to indicate, had she committed some fearful crime for which she was now being punished? Would she bleed to death? Her mother, nostrils pinched with distaste, had walked away from that question and it had been her well-nigh non-existent father, the vicar, who had muttered a few embarrassed, scholarly words to the effect that she would very likely survive. Her own intellectual curiosity and an hour locating the relevant books in Clarrow library, had helped her to piece together the rest, yet her menstruation had never quite recovered from its furtive beginnings, had always been difficult and painful until Andrew Rexford, standing in the center of his crowded parlor, had informed her, quite loud enough for everyone to hear, that it was not a matter of which she had any reason to be ashamed.

"Am I ashamed of it?"

"Of course. The next time it occurs admit it and then forget about it. You are not unclean, you are functioning exactly as a woman should. And learn to call things by their proper names. My wife is not 'in the family way,' she is pregnant, the reason for that being that my semen has . . ."

"Andrew," said Victorine, patient, a little amused, immensely tolerant, yet definitely calling him to order, "*do* go and answer the door."

"My daughter is forever taking the train to Bradeswick," Aunt Sibylla seemed forever to be mentioning to me in her cool, supercilious fashion.

235

So was my husband.

"Shopping, of course, or exchanging her books at the public library—or so she tells me."

My husband, too, still liked to give the impression that he was going to his office.

"When I know quite well that she is spending her time with Victorine, which is quite bad enough, or with Miss Frances Grey in whose company she is unlikely to meet anything in the way of a suitable husband."

She would be quite likely to meet mine.

In Miss Grey's home, of course, one did not broach the subject of conception no matter how immaculate, her "*salon*," as it pleased her to call it, providing us all with a frequently diverting alternative. One went to Andrew and Victorine for full-blooded appraisals of life, the fundamental issues of feeding the hungry, sheltering the vagrants, healing the sick. One went to my mother for frivolity. One went to Frances Grey for intellectual stimulation of a fine, untouched-by-hand variety, the souls and psychology of the masses rather than their soup and bread and—increasingly—the issue of votes for women.

For over forty years now the Women's Movement had been little more than an occasional cause for laughter in the British House of Commons, a restrained affair conducted mainly by well-bred, mild-mannered females like my mother's aunts, their own ranks being seriously divided between those who believed all women should be given the vote, those who believed it should not be given to married women— whose interests would best be represented by their husbands—and those who believed it should not be given to "women" at all but only to "ladies."

But these old conflicts, Miss Grey assured us, could all be resolved if only by the processes of nature which were gradually leading their champions to the grave. The way would soon be open for new leaders. Miss Grey had no doubt that they would come forward to offer themselves in plentiful supply.

"I have a friend in Manchester," she murmured reflectively. "She and I were at school together in Paris—oh *rather* a long time ago. She was Emmeline Goulden then, and even in those days her personality was—well—*forceful*, I suppose. Although her ambitions, at seventeen, were straightforward enough. She just wanted to marry a rich Frenchman, and be a famous society hostess in Paris."

"I feel quite in sympathy with that," purred my mother.

"I daresay you do, Lavinia." Miss Grey looked amused. "But Emmeline's father, who was a very shrewd Manchester businessman, did not. He soon had her home again and by the time she was twenty she had married Richard Pankhurst. *Not* an obvious choice. Quite old enough to be her father and not in the least handsome. But so clever. Dear Richard, such a brilliant barrister, such mild manners and such scorching opinions. An idealist of the very purest variety, but so impractical that he could not even carve the Sunday joint of beef without mishap. Luckily Emmeline was able to do it herself. He died a few years ago, leaving her with four children to bring up, having positively worn himself out—as idealists do—in the service of others. And, of course, he had done most of it free of charge. Poor Richard. He promised his bride, on their wedding-day, that every struggling cause they encountered they would make their own—everything, Pacifism, Internationalism, Socialism, Suffragism—and it was a promise he certainly kept. He gave everything away, his talent, his energy, his money. Poor Emmeline."

At this point the lady had *my* sympathy.

"But she did not despair," Miss Grey went on. "She found employment as a registrar of births and deaths and has managed to put her daughter Sylvia through art college and to get her daughter Christabel qualified as a barrister—although the poor dear cannot practice, of course, because she is a woman."

And last October, the redoubtable Mrs. Pankhurst, in the middle of earning her living, educating her three daughters and her delicate son, had, from her modest parlor in a decent but not affluent area of Manchester, declared her intention of taking positive action against the British Government in order to obtain the enfranchisement of British women.

"Deeds," Mrs. Pankhurst had declared, "not words." The Suffrage Societies had been talking to Westminster for forty years. The dialogue had gone on long enough. Women must make themselves heard and seen, as men had always done in times of grievance. They must no longer ask politely, as women had been taught to do. They must *demand*.

"What do you think?" asked Alys, walking into the Gatehouse early one morning, a letter Miss Grey had received from Mrs. Pankhurst in her hand, clearly most anxious to talk it over at length with

Robin, although she tried to address her question to me. In the old days, I knew, they would have discussed it for hours and from all angles, sprawled out in the leather armchairs in the library at Clarrow, or sitting in the vicarage garden, their backs propped up against the chestnut tree. But today he had promised to take me into Leeds to buy silk for an evening dress and neither would listen when I said I was not particularly keen to go.

"A promise is a promise," said Robin

"It certainly is," said Alys, "and mother is expecting me home in any case '

We went to Leeds. I could not choose between apricot silk and white chiffon and so, at Robin's suggestion, bought them both. We had tea, browsed hand in hand along the crowded streets, booked tickets for the theater, took a later train than we had intended back to Bradeswick, missed our connection to Clarrow Fell and, arriving unexpectedly at Aireville Terrace, surprised Mr. Greenlaw kissing my mother most energetically in the back parlor.

"The old devil," said Robin, as we got into the best spare bed. "Do you suppose he was hoping to stay the night?"

"I'll put a stop to it if he is. I told her to keep him at arm's length until they're married."

He chuckled into my shoulder, his breath becoming a shiver of hopeful delight along my spine.

"What an absolute joy you are sometimes, Olivia."

"I do my best, sir, to give satisfaction."

"Then—unless you think you have some reason for keeping me at arm's length too—well—satisfy me, darling. Please."

We had tried hard—both of us—and had won a happy day. Perhaps if we tried harder tomorrow and the day after then, quite soon, it would no longer be necessary to try at all. But the next morning a note from Amyas, delivered to my mother's breakfast table, informed us that while we had been buying our silks and chiffons the previous afternoon my grandfather had taken a fall from his horse, a matter not to be treated lightly at his age. Should my mother know where to find me, Amyas wondered, would she be kind enough to send me home at once? And in the hour and a half it took me to get there I had ample leisure to contemplate the horror in Robin's face, as the crushing burden of the Manor grew near; all the time I required, to understand that what defeated him was his own decency, the kindness

238

of his own heart which made it impossible for him to withstand me. Explanations, words, *talk* of new ways of life were easy enough but, now that the weapon seemed about to be placed in his hand, how could he deal me so grievous a blow when he had promised to love and cherish me and a gentleman must not break his promises? The truth was that he could not and he knew he could not. He had struggled inwardly and very hard but it was over now and without being aware of it, I had won. He had come to the solitary conclusion that he could not hurt me and live at peace with the consequences. Therefore, what choice remained but to wear what seemed to him the strait-jacket of Clarrow Fell? None that he could see. He was resigned, as men are resigned to poverty, old age, to the gallows. Yet, when we arrived to find my grandfather already sitting up in his dim four-poster, considerably annoyed at his body's stubborn refusal to decay, Robin's relief was so intense that he strode out into the passage, leaned against the wall and shed tears of gladness—although they did not look in any way merry to me—at this blessed reprieve, this stay of his freedom's execution.

And as I watched him, feeling helpless, guilty and sick at heart, I understood that I could not accept this sacrifice. For the essence of love, after all, is *self*-sacrifice, the giving not the taking, and I could not hurt him either. I opened my mouth to say "Don't worry, Robin. I don't want to keep the Manor," but the words died on my tongue. I would tell him tomorrow, later, when I was steadier, when my grandfather was up and about again and it was no longer an urgent matter.

"Your husband is looking very tired of late," Aunt Sibylla told me a week or so later.

I, too, had noticed it.

"Is he under some strain, perhaps?"

Yes indeed. Great strain and I had the power, the intention, if not yet the desire, to remedy it.

"Nor do you appear to be your usual sparkling self, my dear," went on my aunt, having called to tell me about Alys's progress with Felix Potterton and discovered that I—by the look of me—might have something to tell her.

Nothing at all. I doubted if I would ever explain myself to anyone, even to Robin. I was the stronger. I was the one who loved the most. I was the one who had been determined to make him love

239

me and had so drastically altered his life. The error of judgment had been mine and now I must pay for it. When the time came I would sell my house and my land and I would live in the house he provided, wherever he provided it, as he had asked me to do. I would impose no burdens upon him. I would not crush him. But the prospect so appalled me that I could not bring myself to speak of it, could not even form the words in my mind which would have so instantly and mercifully eased his fears. I had decided to sell the Manor but I could not tell him so. When the time came I would simply do it. And by the look of my grandfather it would not be long.

FOURTEEN

My brother Luc came home from school for the long summer holiday, a polished, young Englishman of fourteen with fluid foreign hands and eyes, a combination which went instantly to the head of my mother's parlormaid. And he at once informed me that he had no intention of returning to Hexingham.

"Just not my scene any more, Liv—honestly, old girl."

"Liv!"

"Well, Olivia, then—dear sister, if you like—although it's rather the thing, you know, right now, to use pet names. All the chaps do it."

"What fun."

"A crashing bore, actually, like the rest of that mausoleum. So it's settled then, is it, old sport—that I'm not going back, I mean?"

"Luc . . ." And the tone of my voice warned him that whatever I was going to say next, I meant it. "You'll go back to Hexingham if I have to drag you there by the scruff of your neck."

He smiled, using an amount of charm that would have dazzled me had I been anyone else.

"Do you know, Liv, I wonder—these days—if you're up to that kind of thing. I've grown, you see, quite a bit."

"It makes no difference, Luc. You may be taller, but I'm fiercer you see—quite a bit."

Yet his calm insistence that he would not return to school persisted through July and into August, worrying Madelon whom he tormented with wild schemes of expeditions to Equatorial jungles,

Arabian deserts, New York—knowing she was the only one who would believe him—and certainly getting in my mother's way.

"Talk to him," I asked Robin, but he lifted his shoulders with what, for him, was exasperation.

"I should think I'm the very last person to convince him. I wouldn't send a stray cat to Hexingham, much less my brother."

"Talk to him," I urged Mr. Greenlaw, who had brought up two sons of his own and ought to understand. But Mr. Greenlaw did not hold with these "damn fancy schools" where they taught a lad anything but how to earn a living and he had nothing to offer but a possible situation at the Ironworks which was totally unacceptable to Luc.

"Could you—do you think you could possibly talk to him?" I asked my grandfather, with bated breath, the hope that he might one day extend just one hand to me still flowing strong. "He'd listen to you, grandfather."

"I fear not, my dear. We have no language in common."

And when I opened my mouth to ask again, persistent to the last, his face tightened with its habitual spasm of distaste and he said curtly, "He is one of your people, Olivia, not mine. You must accept your responsibilities, as I do."

"Am I not your responsibility, grandfather?"

We were standing in the library at Clarrow, the August day entering through the long windows in shafts of amber and gold, showing me the dusty crevices of his face, the stoop of his shoulders, the veins and knuckles piercing the brittle skin of his hand as he tapped irritable fingers against the windowsill.

"That might well be a cry from the heart, Olivia. If so, I regret that I cannot answer it."

"Oh yes you could if you . . ."

He raised the hand which may have lost its grip but in which authority still remained.

"That will do, Olivia. You will serve no purpose by distressing yourself. Yes—I owe you far more than I have given. In fact, you have the distinction, I believe, of being the only person I have ever deliberately failed. That may or may not console you."

"It doesn't."

"Then—it does not. I am not a capricious man, Olivia. I have my reasons. Should you meet Amyas on your way out would you be good enough to ask him to come and see me?"

242

Amyas? But no, Luc would not listen to Amyas, Hexingham having taught him to recognize his social inferiors. While Andrew Rexford's opinion of public schools was even lower than Mr. Greenlaw's. There was Max, of course, who was often in Bradeswick now, keeping an eye on my grandfather but I would not have cared to ask Max for a drink of water had I been dying of thirst in the desert, much less his advice on the best way to handle my wayward brother. Yet, as luck would have it, Max was present on the morning I arrived in Aireville Terrace to find Madelon in tears, my mother biting her lips and frowning—a bad sign, in her, since frowning, which could permanently crease the forehead, was usually to be avoided at all costs—to be told that Luc had run away.

"Run where? Has he any money?"

"Well, of course, his letter didn't say, but I rather think he has—just a little. Madelon's pin-money and a few pounds I keep in the kitchen drawer to settle the butcher's bills."

"He stole?"

"Well, of course, dear. You can't imagine that I would have *given*?"

"He didn't steal from me," whispered Madelon. "It was lent to him, and it wasn't much anyway. But then he won five pounds last night from Mr. Greenlaw at cards, while you were at the theater, mamma."

"So," said Max, very much amused. "We know he has the train fare to London. And *I* know where I'd be heading, at his age."

Of course. My brother's route and his intentions were equally clear to me. The early train from Bradeswick to Leeds where he could pick up the London express. And then a life of adventure and squalor following in his father's footsteps, seedy hotels, shady deals, turning a quick and usually short-lived profit on anything that came to hand, a card-game, a horse, a gullible woman. I would not have it. I would go now to Leeds and put a stop to it.

"I see nothing to be done," sighed my mother, her resignation suggesting that she had found him rather too much for her of late.

"We shall never see him again," sobbed Madelon.

Oh yes we would. He would come back regularly enough, if only to borrow Madelon's pin-money again and whatever he could scrounge from my mother when all else failed; turning up on their doorstep—*my* doorstep, really—at odd hours, remaining for odd intervals, his creditors not far behind. I would not allow him to live

243

like that. But in order to stop him I would have to catch him first and as quickly as possible, preferably in Leeds before the departure of the London train. And since this was no longer a personal matter of dying of thirst in the desert, but of Luc who must not be allowed to reach the anonymity of a capital city, I turned to the person who could help me most.

"Max—that *is* your Daimler standing outside?"

He nodded, betraying by not one flicker of an eyelid his perfect understanding. "One may safely assume so, since there are only two or three other motor vehicles in Bradeswick, none of them Daimlers."

"Could it get me to Leeds in time for the London train?"

"It could. If I happened to be going there."

He wanted me to plead with him, of course. But—knowing him, knowing me—that was only to be expected and I would not think kindly of myself afterwards if I lost Luc because I had been too stubborn to say please and smile.

I smiled, therefore, with all the false brilliance of Luc himself, lowered my eyelids for good measure and gave a lingering little sigh. "Max—I would be so grateful."

"I very much doubt it."

"But you will take me?"

"Naturally. I wouldn't miss the fun and fireworks for the world."

I had had no dealings with motor cars since just before my marriage when Robin had borrowed a vehicle *he* had thought very thrilling, to take me driving and flirting on Clarrow Moor. And despite the greater luxury of Max's claret-colored Daimler, the first half-mile was quite enough to convince me that I still did not entirely believe in this new method of transport, having no faith at all in either its performance or its future. The noise and odor of the engine still seriously incommoded me. I felt exposed, vulnerable, increasingly sick and instead of the exclamations of wonder and delight which most motorists seemed to think their due, I could do nothing but tie on my hat, grit my teeth and *endure*. An attitude which was difficult enough to sustain through the quiet suburbs of Bradeswick, but well-nigh impossible as we roared into the center of Leeds where considerably more than Bradeswick's three motor cars coughed and choked and jockeyed for position among the haphazard traffic of these industrial streets, the patient, ponderous shire animals dragging their coal-carts and wagons heavy-laden with raw wool or finished pieces; broken-winded hacks between the sinister shafts of the cabs one preferred not to hire since one never knew what drunken or infected persons had gone before; the nervous dancing hooves of thoroughbreds drawing showy private carriages; a sudden, solitary bicycle darting through the *mêlée* like a swallow; the constant ebb and flow of men and women on foot, ambling between the vehicles at will, in blissful ignorance of the fact that the motor car, which accelerated easily enough, was far more difficult to stop.

"You are not at ease, Olivia?"

"On the contrary, Max—perfectly easy."

"Why do you tell me so many lies, my darling?"

"They are not lies. They are called good manners."

"Your cousin Alys adores motoring."

"She had better not let her mother catch her."

"My dear," he said, narrowly avoiding—or so it seemed to me—the passengers who were swarming like harassed bees around an already overcrowded tram. "Sibylla Blackwood would be only too delighted to catch me with her daughter anywhere preferably in circumstances delicate enough to bring on an attack of wedding bells. You should know that."

"Yes. But you wouldn't, would you, Max? I mean, you wouldn't succumb to that sort of attack . . . ?"

Could he, indeed, succumb even if he would? For I had always tended to believe not only that his wealth was of the kind to melt away just when one needed it most, but that he already had a wife.

"I don't know, Olivia," he said, turning into the station-yard by the simple process of driving in front of everything that stood in his way. "What would you advise? If I settle in the neighborhood, as I may well do, if I set myself up with a good house and a good stable then I would need a hostess—a resident companion—who in this provincial society, would have to be a wife. And Alys is an *original*, one must give her that. It might be interesting to see what the right clothes and jewels could do. If one displayed all that silver hair and ivory skin to advantage, one could make her an ornament fit for any man's table."

My table, I thought, my house, Alys taking my place at Clarrow as had always been intended. I was not resigned to it. I would simply *do* it, when the time came, would take Max's money and hand over the keys and hope, with all my heart, I would bear no grudge, not even for one bitter moment, against Robin.

"So you will sell the house to me, Olivia?"

"What makes you think so?"

He stopped the car and, smiling, helped me down as if I had been a princess alighting from a silk-lined carriage drawn by a team of white horses; which was, in fact, the way I most liked to see myself.

"Because I usually get my way with women."

"How very monotonous for you, Max."

He laughed, gave his light bow, looking at me with the concentrated enjoyment I had seen in him at the card-table.

"*Touché*—at least for now, Olivia. Shall we find your brother?"

The station was full of steams and vapors and hurrying, anonymous faces, the London train standing in proud silence with half an hour yet to go before the start of its majestic, slightly condescending progress South.

"Where would he be?" I asked Max, meaning "Where would you be in his place?," not liking the resemblance between them but unable to ignore it.

"Drinking a brandy in the hotel, having eaten an excellent luncheon."

"He can't afford it."

"Olivia, my pet, you must know a little thing like that wouldn't stop him. And in a moment or two I imagine you'll see him sauntering along the platform to his compartment—first class, of course."

Of course; a handsome, elegant young gentleman from a distance, nonchalant and altogether at his ease, unless one happened to know that he was fourteen years old and had nothing in his pockets but Madelon's pin-money, sadly depleted, one supposed, after luncheon with wine and brandy at a Leeds hotel. An Emil Junot to the life, with a whisper of my mother's subtler fascination and the surface polish of Hexingham. A potent blend indeed, displayed to full advantage as he gallantly assisted what looked like a governess and a family of very personable young ladies into a first-class compartment and then joined them. And as we watched him through the open carriage door, reclining elegantly in his seat, engaging what seemed already to be an audience of adoring females in ready conversation, Max lit one of his thin black cigars and, his eyes narrowing speculatively through a veil of smoke, murmured "The young devil. Shall I give him a hundred pounds and see if he can make his fortune?"

"I believe you would."

"Yes, I believe so too."

"Don't be stupid, Max."

"All right. I shall stand here then and watch, with considerable interest, just how you mean to go about extricating him from that train."

"Oh—I rather thought that you . . . ?"

"Oh no. He is fully my height and something like twenty years younger. *Your* game Olivia. Absolutely yours, my pet."

I had not thought of this. The urgency had been to get here before the departure of the train and now, having achieved that much—having risked life and limb in that abominable motor car to do it—I had no intention of standing tamely on the platform and waving a tear-stained handkerchief as my brother sped away. But what? I walked down the platform, no doubt looking brisk and bold but without a single constructive notion in my mind. Something would come to me. It would have to. For unless I handled the matter skillfully he would only run away again tomorrow.

"Ah, Luc, there you are," I called out in English, beaming brightly, and then, in rapid French so that his female companions—and hopefully Max—would not understand, I informed him in no uncertain terms that before I lost what patience was left to me, he had better come home.

"Olivia—must you meddle?"

Another voice had spoken those words to me several times. Robin's. And my answer remained the same. "It is for their good." This time I was in no doubt of it.

"Yes, Luc. I must. And there are two ways of going about it, darling. You can make some excuse to your friends, and saunter away—with me—to Max's car, and they can spend the journey to London in a flutter about what a delightful young man you are. Or I can tell them that you're fourteen, that you've run away from home, having cheated your sister out of her pin-money and stolen from your widowed mother. Well, she *has* been widowed once or twice hasn't she and it's not very grand, you know, to make off with the widow's mite. These girls would laugh their heads off about that and you never know just who they might tell, or when you might meet them again—do you, Luc? Or just who might be listening in the station-yard when I start to tell the tale, because I'd raise my voice very loud and I'd have to break down and cry, of course, and wring my hands quite a lot—you know?"

He knew.

"You wouldn't, Olivia." But he was nobody's fool and already, beneath his horror, I could sense the grudging beginnings of mirth.

"Don't be an idiot, Luc. You know quite well I would."

"I won't go back to Hexingham."

"We can talk about that—all right?"

"All right—but don't assume that you'll get your way."

"Would *I* do that?"

He grinned, his resistance collapsing so suddenly that I won·dered if he had been staging a protest rather than taking flight and had perhaps been rather more pleased to see me than he cared to acknowledge.

"My apologies, ladies," he said, in his impeccable Hexingham drawl, "I fear our delightful journey is not to be—not today at any rate. For this person—my sister's French governess, actually—has been sent with a message that I'm needed at home."

And making his bows, accepting from these pretty, totally deceived young ladies, their wishes that the news was not bad and their hopes of meeting again, he raised a courteous hat and descended from the train.

"Have a cigar, old chap," said Max.

"Thanks old chap, I will."

And they walked off together, two men about town, two *boulevardiers*, smoking their leisurely cigars, glancing in cool appraisal at every woman who passed by; leaving their French governess to follow after them a step or two behind.

It was quite in accordance with my mother's character that she had not waited for us, having, after all, her social engagements to fulfill—her public who could not be let down—and she had gone out as usual, leaving Madelon, who was much better at it, to weep and worry and rejoice when we brought Luc home. Mother would be back for five o'clock tea accompanied by "friends," but Luc's crisis was solved long before that by an invitation in the late morning post to spend a fortnight with a schoolmate of his in Harrogate, a wealthy boy whose family had thoroughbreds to ride and a car to drive. Within ten minutes Luc no longer desired to take the London train. He wished to go to Harrogate to ride Tom Whitaker's Arab mare and have a look at the Whitaker sisters who played tennis and danced and were a great deal livelier than Madelon who, unable to cope with stress so easily as mother, had started to cough.

I put her to bed with the hot milk and honey Victorine had recommended, sent Luc to pack his bags for Harrogate, had a note taken round to Robin's office asking him to meet me here in time for the afternoon train home, and returned to the drawing room, surprised to see Max still there.

"Are you waiting to see my mother?"

"Should I be?"

"Oh, don't be clever, Max—just a simple answer to a simple question is all I need."

Suddenly I was very tired. I had stumbled through these domestic crises all my life, always managing—by trial and error, hit and miss, sheer stubborn refusal to give in—to find a solution. I had waded through murky water on many occasions, carrying one or another of them on my back, and I had never yet failed, if only just, to reach the shore. I had reached it again today, without disaster but without much satisfaction either. The day which had been so hot and heavy had exhausted me, the drive to Leeds had strained both my stomach and my nerves. The thought of Max as the new squire of Clarrow Fell with Alys as his lady appalled me, infuriated me, hurt me far more than I could admit. Yes, I *would* sell to him—for Robin—yes—yes— I would *do* it. But until it became absolutely unavoidable, until my grandfather was dead and buried, I held the decision locked inside my body like a disease with nothing showing, as yet, on the surface. But I was tired now and irritable and wanted Max to go away. He ought to know that. He *did* know it. But he wanted to stay and, as was to be expected, his own desires were more important to him than mine.

"So what happens next, Olivia?"

"About what?"

"Well, about young master Luc for a start. How do you rate your chances of getting him back to Hexingham?"

"Excellent."

"You mean he'll do as he's told."

"Yes, I do."

"He's quite right, you know. Hexingham *is* a crashing bore."

"No, it's not."

"How can you know that? Because it turns out honorable gentlemen like your husband. It produced me too, you know. So beware. And Luc doesn't want to be honorable."

"I daresay. That's because he's young and doesn't realize . . ."

"Realize what? That dishonor doesn't pay?" He raised his arms, displaying the impeccable London tailored suit, the pearl stick-pin in his gray silk tie, the diamond on his hand. "But it does, my pet. It does."

"It may appear so."

He leaned forward, nearer than I liked, an undeniably attractive odor of expensive cigars and a richly spiced *eau de Cologne* in my nostrils, enveloping me in the aura of ease and luxury and pleasure; for which purpose such costly fragrances are intended.

"Olivia, do you still think of me as a walking masquerade? Really? You have known me for three years at least and whatever I may lack it must be clear that I am never short of money."

I shrugged, not in the least impressed.

"I knew a man called Emil Junot much longer than that and there were times when he appeared to be as rich as you."

He made an impatient gesture with his scarred, jeweled hand and clicked his tongue, dismissing my mother's third husband—my second stepfather—rather as a top-flight courtesan, secure in the possession of powerful lovers, enduring beauty, a bank vault full of pearls, might dismiss the efforts of a common street-walker, plying her trade for pennies along the waterfront.

"Oh yes—I have heard all about the famous Emil Junot. Your mother remembers him tenderly. But he has never come my way nor is he likely to. We have nothing in common."

"You play the same game."

"Yes. I win. He loses. As I just said—"

"Nobody wins every time."

But I had sounded truculent, mulish; and smiling, he got up and crossing to the sideboard began to make free with my mother's decanters and glasses.

"Sam Greenlaw keeps your mother supplied with an excellent brandy. Will you join me?"

"At three o'clock in the afternoon? Certainly not."

But he put the glass on the wine table beside me and after a moment or two I picked it up irritably and drank, the bouquet returning me to the cafés along the boulevard Saint-Germain, into an identity which, whether I cared to admit it or not, had been more truly mine.

"Smooth as velvet," he said, enjoying in its entirety this moment of drinking, the act of tasting and of inhaling this rich aroma and knowing the exact cost of it, turning his glass to the light so that his eyes, too, might have their share of pleasure in the deep amber and gold gently swirling around cut crystal.

"Beautiful." And I nodded morosely, the spirit sending hot little tentacles spreading through my body, removing me a significant distance from Bradeswick.

"I am financially sound," he said suddenly, abrupt as a whip-lash.

And just as abruptly I replied "I don't believe you."

"Why?" He was not in the least offended. "Because I have no premises—no factory with a thousand employees like Sam Greenlaw, no smart suite of chambers in the city with a mahogany desk and a Turkish carpet? You should know better than that. All I need are my wits and a convenient telegraph office—occasionally a fast train."

"And a pack of cards."

He laughed and threw out his hands in the swordsman's wide gesture of surrender.

"Marked cards, did you mean to say? No, my pet. No longer. I'll tell you how it is with men like me, should you care to know?"

"I know."

"I wonder. First of all one makes money, any way one can. Africa, in my case, took care of that. And then one uses that money to make more. Believe me, there's nothing so effective as one gold piece when it comes to attracting another. Or so it's always seemed to me. Any kind of gold piece, anywhere one happens to be. I'll turn my hand to anything, Olivia. Wherever I see a need, I'll find a way to supply it at a profit. There's always somebody in some corner of the world who wants something he can't make or can't grow and who'll pay my price. I ship hot-climate fruits to cold-climate countries; French perfumes and silks to the Australian outback where they've got plenty of rich women and no rue de la Paix. I ship goats to Corfu because somebody told me about a breed from the Scottish Highlands that would do well there—and it does. I deal in exotic feathers for women's hats and when the fashion for feathers is over I'll know about it—because I'll have kept my eyes and ears open—and I'll be ready with whatever the designers are wanting next. I deal in chinoiserie, carved ivories, hand-woven carpets, lacquer cabinets, fans, screens, cloisonné vases . . . "

"Beads to the natives," I said sourly, "and guns."

"Well, not precisely, although I've sold Ashanti spears to Brit-

251

ish Officers who liked to think they'd won them in battle. And I used to fetch cartloads of Zulu beadwork down from the interior at one time for all the young English ladies at the Cape."

I had not wished to show interest, had tried hard to stop myself from feeling it but now, a series of colorful images chasing each other through my mind, I could not hold back a laugh of real enjoyment.

"I'm sorry. I just can't imagine you on a mule-cart or an ox-cart or whatever, and then squatting down in those native villages haggling for beads—in a bush hat and a dirty shirt and no decent brandy . . ."

But in fact I could imagine it very well.

"Olivia," he said, quite seriously, "I would go anywhere if there is a profit to be made. Absolutely anywhere. And one takes a hip flask, my pet, and an African servant or two to swat the flies and load up the cart and keep the witchdoctors and the missionaries at bay—and a sharp lookout for the headhunters and the husband hunters, both black and white. A good life—for a young man—although one knew plenty who didn't survive it. Olivia, dear, I do believe I have won your attention. I must tell my African stories more often. They have a mesmerizing effect on Alys too."

Yes, and the fortune he had made there—if it *really* existed—in Africa, Madeira, Corfu, the Australian outback, here in Bradeswick from the death of the Queen, would purchase Alys my inheritance, my hopes, the place in life for which I—as surely as my grandfather—had been created. Did I begrudge it to her more than to another? I hoped not. I was going to lose it in any case and if my loss should be her gain I would at least try to be glad. As she had done when I had married Robin.

The afternoon spread around me, sultry, lethargic, the house very quiet, Luc having dashed off to town to spend what remained of Madelon's money, Madelon herself asleep, I supposed, the maid out somewhere gossiping, telling my mother's secrets; the garden where Victorine had planted her careful rows of lovage and marshmallow and marjoram, wilting and colorless with the heat. There was no sound, no breath of air reaching me through the open windows, not even the busy, somehow comforting ticking of the drawing-room clock which no one remembered to wind since I had moved away. Would I ever live in this house again? I had been so certain of the future once—in a time that seemed a moment and a hundred years away—that I had begun to think it inevitable. Now—who knew?

252

"So, Olivia—are you going to sell to me?" he asked, reading my mind easily since the question was always between us.

"No." But it was no more than a token resistance and without even waiting for his answer, I said quickly, "Why do you want it, Max?"

"Ah—I believe we are making progress. Because I want it. That is the only reason that matters. You can agree with that?"

Yes. I got up and walked about the room for a moment going nowhere. Trapped. By whom? Myself? And how could I escape such intimate captivity? The truth was—and I *must* face it—that I could not.

Yes, Max, I will sell.

But the words remained locked in my head, a bitter iron weight upon my tongue.

"All right, Olivia. I will tell you a little more about it. I came to Clarrow as a young child—you may know that much about me— a very alien child—far more so than you. My mother is half Spanish and half Dutch and I was born in Morocco. Don't ask me what my parents were doing there. My mother hardly remembers herself— except that she did not enjoy it and there was no money."

"Is your mother alive?"

"Excessively. She lives in my house in Funchal and we get on well enough—now that I no longer need her. When I was five years old she took no persuading to give me away to the Squire. I am not an emotional man—far from it—but just the same I feel a certain rancor. Wouldn't you?"

Of course. But the feeling uppermost in my mind was fascination, intense curiosity, the beginnings of something like recognition—for who had more appreciation than I of the scars so casually left by cheap lodgings, absent fathers, careless mothers?

"Yes, I suppose I would be bitter—although they say you were a handful."

He shrugged, dismissing anything "they" may say as hardly meriting his consideration. "Well of course I was. I was alone in a foreign country among strangers. The only Englishness about me was my father and no one would talk about him, except Amyas. He'd do anything for me in those days, good old Amyas, but he couldn't tell me how my father had died or where my mother had run off to, because he didn't know. I believe I had a crazy notion that my father was dead just because the Squire refused to talk about him. And so I gave him good reason—or rather bad ones—to keep on talking about me. I wanted his attention. I got it. I even kept it until I was old enough to know he didn't really have the power to make me disappear by ignoring me. I think you'll understand."

I nodded.

"Now I want his house."

"*Exactly* why?"

"I want it, Olivia."

"It's not particularly grand."

"No, nor even in a particularly healthy condition. But it has something, nevertheless. What would you call it?"

"I don't know. I try to ignore it."

"Do you succeed?"

I shook my head, finding that we had come face to face on the hearthrug a few inches apart, drawn together by this attraction—ridiculous, unfortunate, illogical, so very strong—for a heap of bricks and mortar, considerably in need of repair in places, which was powerful enough to overrule the plain fact that we did not trust each other.

"I want it, Olivia. I don't much care to analyze exactly what it means to me. The wanting is enough. You want it too."

"Yes."

How wonderful, at last, to make that admission, to open that closely guarded door within myself and release such a soaring lark-rise of emotions.

"Yes—I want it."

"Badly?"

"Badly." And I took another step towards him, knowing that this was a kind of lovemaking, a dangerous indulgence in a shared passion which—because we were male and female and both of us handsome—was rapidly building into a moment of sensuality.

Step back, Olivia.

I had heard of high priestesses in ancient mythology who had made love as an offering to their temple, a form of consecration. Yes indeed. Or was that merely an excuse to enable them to make love with a clear conscience, to acknowledge that women too could feel desire without tenderness or any lasting affection, as men have always been allowed to feel it?

Olivia, do take care.

254

"How badly do you want it, Olivia? Tell me." And his voice was itself a caress, an invitation, fully understood and deeply felt, to shake off all restraint, to be—if only for a moment—my real imperfect self again; to give free rein—just for one wild gallop—to the facets of my nature I had thought it wise, here in Bradeswick, to conceal.

"Tell me, Olivia."

"Very badly."

"And it hurts you?"

"Yes. It does."

"Then you should have waited, shouldn't you."

"For what?"

"For me, my pet. And then you could have had it all."

I knew, of course, that he was going to touch me. I knew I was playing with fire and did not care. I wanted him to desire me, not love me, and none of it had anything to do with Robin. The woman who stood here a breath away from Max was not Robin's wife, not Lavinia's daughter, or anyone but the raw essence of myself. For the first time in my life I was aware of my own nature in isolation, entirely separate from all influences but my own, and I was intensely curious about it. *This*, then, was freedom. No one to consider but myself. How very odd. How fascinating. And, while this strange sensation lasted, I could say nothing, do anything I chose.

"Did you want me to wait?"

"I would have married you if you had. But one doesn't let a little thing like marriage ruin one's appetite. I want the house and I want you. I shall get the house, Olivia—all I need for that is money. And when I have it, I won't care if the woman who shares it is married to me or to another—so long as she pleases me."

"And I please you?"

"Yes, you do. Like the house pleases me—and pleases you . . ."

And so we came together, a purely physical meeting, as slowly, I thought, as if I had walked into him in a self-induced trance, his first kiss direct and none too gentle, his body hard, experienced, exciting, a *body* to which in that same entranced fashion I responded. I had believed Robin to be the personification of Clarrow Fell. How terrible—truly how terrible—that it should be Max.

"I sent you a message," he said, his mouth still on mine. "Did you understand?"

"What? What message?"

"Victorine's party. *That* message. It could have been for you. It still can. Yes, Olivia?"

"No."

"Yes—oh yes, I do think so. You've never had a lover, have you, and it's time now, darling. The house you can't bear to part with and money to go with it—a lot of money. Yes, Olivia?"

But my sanity returned as quickly as it had left me and I broke free.

"Good heavens—what on earth are you doing?"

"Rather well, it seemed to me."

"Don't ever do such a thing again."

He laughed, neither flustered nor disturbed, nor even out of breath.

"Olivia, what a ridiculous thing to say. Couldn't you really see the ideal solution? You had the house, I had the money. If you hadn't gone rushing into the arms of young Master Esmond . . ."

"That's enough."

"—so fast that *he* didn't know just what had hit him . . ."

"That's enough."

"—then you wouldn't now be in this sorry state—"

"Shut up."

"You'd be rich enough to please *yourself*, not Dottie Potterton and Bessie Greenlaw. And at least the poor chap would have his peace of mind."

I struck out at him hard and encountering nothing but a raised elbow which hurt my hand, struck again, resorting to a wild flurry of blows none of which came even near to breaking through his guard.

"Damn you, Max de Haan—absolutely damn you to Hell."

He caught my wrists in a grip I thought would break them, and dragged me towards him, his intention to kiss me again very plain, my intention to get my teeth or my nails into him just as pressing, until—his eyes flickering around the room, remembering to check his security and guard his back even in a moment of passion I saw wariness, speculation, some spark of warning enter his face. And, spinning round, following his narrow gaze to the open window, I saw Robin on the path beside the herb-garden, watching us and hearing us, the expression on his face neither anger nor hurt, but a tremendous relief.

I could not fail to recognize it. I could never come to terms with it. Nor could I ever forget it. My husband had caught me in the arms of another man and he was glad.

256

FIFTEEN

"It's all right," he said, "honestly, Olivia. It's all right."

But reality had somehow slipped out of focus and I had no faith whatsoever in my ears or my eyes. Was it the heat, the brandy? Or a distorted dream? A silly dream in which he kept on saying "It's all right" in that reassuring fashion, when this was the worst thing that had ever happened to me in my life. No, Robin. It's not all right. But I was voiceless. Or he could not hear me.

We could not communicate.

"Don't worry, Olivia."

Worry! I had to *explain*. I had been caught in the most classic and most ridiculous of situations and I had to get to him, on the other side of that window and tell him—what? Not to be angry when he was standing there smiling as pleased as punch; not to be hurt when he looked—what was it?—as if a *burden* that was it exactly—had just been lifted from his shoulders? Tell him what?

I ran out into the garden in time to see the gate close behind him and, more by instinct than by premeditation, I ran back into the house, scooped up my hat and gloves and chased after him down Aireville Terrace.

"Robin—please wait."

He waited.

"Robin—just listen . . ."

He appeared to be listening but what could I say, what ought I to say? Why—oh why—was he still smiling?

"Robin—it meant nothing. I don't know what you saw or heard

257

but it was just Max being stupid and you must know that I wouldn't—
that I couldn't possibly . . . Whatever it looked like then it wasn't—
really—it just *wasn't* . . ."

It was late afternoon, a busy time of day, women hurrying
home with heavy baskets, ladies with keen eyes and sharp tongues
passing by in their carriages, lace curtains twitching at every window
in Aireville Terrace as my mother's neighbors told each other that
one of my mother's daughters was in trouble at last, which they had
known would happen all along.

"It's all right, Olivia."

"No. It's not." And what was so wrong about it was that air
of tolerance and gentleness when he ought to have been furious or
frenzied, when I would have given anything—absolutely anything—
to have him beat me and drag me down Aireville Terrace by the
hair.

"Robin—please listen."

He put a warm, steady hand on my arm, a touch that was both
reassuring and affectionate.

"Not now. Could you give me the time to really think it
through? Let me go back to Clarrow alone. Stay at your mother's and
I'll come and see you in the morning."

But nothing on earth would have induced me to do that. He
would go straight to Alys, I knew it, and in any case, how could I
possibly face Max?

I shook my head.

He sighed. "It would be best, Olivia."

"No. I can't."

I would follow him wherever he went like a bloodhound if I
had to, until he agreed to listen, to talk, to have things out and put
them right. I could not wait. He understood that, sighed again and
smiled, still patient and tolerant, still with that strange and terrible
air of relief.

"Well then—we'd better hurry or we'll miss the train."

The station was unusually full for this was the glorious week
of Bradeswick's annual holiday when both the Ironworks and the
Brewery were shut down, releasing their grateful employees—who, in
effect, were faced with the task of living for two weeks on one week's
pay—to dress up in their Sunday best and take the train to moorland
villages like Clarrow Fell or Appleburton, just beyond it, where an
August fair was held.

"What fun," said Robin. "I went to Appleburton Fair every year before Cambridge made me too grand for it."

How could he even *think* of Appleburton Fair or anywhere else? How could he speak so calmly, so easily, when my throat was so tight that every word that I managed to force through those restricted muscles, that dry tissue, cost me pain?

We found an empty first-class compartment. He shut the door. We sat down facing each other, my hands clenched into fists, my stomach aching.

"Robin . . ."

And once again he smiled.

"Please don't worry."

"Please stop saying that."

"But you *are* worried and there's no need. I know you've done nothing wrong."

"Yes, I have."

"I don't think so. It all looked very—very natural, somehow."

"Robin!" I was aghast, so deeply shocked that its impact frightened me and I could have burst into tears and whimpered like a child, had I permitted myself the luxury. And then because it was vital to know, I said, "How long were you there?"

"Oh, quite long enough to—well, to understand. I walked round the back to see how they'd been looking after Victorine's herbs— pretty badly, it turns out—and since the window was wide open . . . You were telling each other how badly you wanted the Manor and meaning something else, it rather seemed to me. At any rate, one could see where it was heading and no mistake. And it did. I do realize Olivia that you meant it to go no further and would have stopped him whether you'd been interrupted or not. He saw me, by the way, a full minute before you did."

What had Max done or said in that minute? What had he made me say, knowing that Robin was listening? What did it matter? He had made his mischief and Robin had not been deceived by it. But he had heard my passionate declaration of love, not for the man but for the Manor and how could I defend myself against that? I had told no one but Max of my decision to sell and Max would not help me. Would Robin believe me if I tried to tell him now? I closed my eyes, took a deep, drowning breath. "Robin, I decided ages ago— when the Squire had his accident—that I was going to sell. To Max, of course. That's what it was all about just now, really."

"I don't think so," he said quietly. "And in any case you mustn't sell."

He was looking out of the window, that terrible smile hovering at the corners of his mouth, looking I thought wildly, as if he might suddenly start whistling a tune or burst into song. And I felt a scream, a great piercing wail of rage and fright start to push its way out of my lungs and through my chest.

"Robin, I can't bear this—I can't. Don't you care . . . ?"

"Very much."

"Then why don't you *do* something—show some feeling. If I'd caught you with—with someone—I'd have wanted to kill you."

"Yes, I know you would," he grinned, boyish, charming, the whimsical schoolboy-gentleman of our first meeting. "But none of that is going to be necessary, is it? I mean . . ."

"What do you mean?"

He shook his head, not because he wanted to make a denial but rather in amazement that what he was about to say had not occurred to him before.

"I mean that we don't have to hurt each other. I thought there was no other way, that we were set forever like flies in amber—I'm sorry that's not a very pretty comparison but it's the one that occurs to me—and now I see it's not so. Things have been wrong between us for such a long time, darling—so very wrong that we were afraid even to discuss it because there seemed to be no solution. *I* could see no solution at any rate."

We had left Bradeswick behind, traveling fast through one long, gray, anonymous suburb to the next, voices raised in laughter somewhere along the train, a giggling, flirtatious girl, a man with his holiday-club money in his pocket heading for Appleburton; strong sunlight slanting in through the window, dazzling my eyes so that I was not obliged to see.

"What on earth are you talking about, Robin?"

Whatever it was, he could not force me to believe it. What it would amount to in the end would be a contest of wills and mine was still the stronger. I would convince him, by the time we reached Hardenrigg Junction, four miles away, that I really did mean to sell the house; that however much I loved it, I loved him more. I would make him see that. It would be all right.

"I believe I am talking about freedom."

At a subconscious level I had suspected it and my mind froze, a great many vital things inside me becoming suspended from their function as they were encased, perhaps mercifully, in ice. For how else could I have remained calm and, therefore, capable of defending myself, of doing battle for what remained of the love which I must not lose. For if one shred of it could be retrieved, one bare thread, then it would be something on which to build.

"What freedom?"

"Olivia, I'm not sure this is the place to go into it. Perhaps we should wait until we get home. Darling, it is bound to hurt you."

It was a declaration of freedom in itself. He was going to hurt me deliberately, because he believed it to be necessary, perhaps even for my own good. He had never had that kind of courage before. Always, in the past, when truth became painful he had shied away from it, preferring to suffer the pain himself rather than inflict it on another. But now—yes—he was like a man to whom some great spiritual secret had just been revealed—*that* was it—a convert, a devotee, dazzled by his first glimpse of some white, eternal light. And while he remained mesmerized by that flame, ready to cast off everything and anything—in the way of converts—and follow it to freedom, then I knew my danger.

"You're so strong, Olivia."

Yes. Strong but not indestructible. I would not break, perhaps, but I could bleed.

"And so absolutely splendid."

It was the word I had heard him use many times to describe his father, the Squire, the riders of the Imperial Yeomanry; a category he found worthy of respect but in which he did not place himself.

"I do so much admire you."

And it was a death knell, for what man desires with passion that milk and water entity "an admirable woman?" Not Robin.

He was going to leave me. Panic came first, a blind swirl of it, for a moment obscuring everything. Then a quick burst of fury soon gone, soon burned away. A pang of raw pain against which I clenched my hands, contracted the muscles of my abdomen, held myself together, somehow, inside that blessed casing of ice.

"I am going to leave you," he said. "Not necessarily for very long. I just feel that I have to get away, alone somewhere. I don't know where or how much time I'll need. Perhaps not a great deal."

Lies. Bitter lies. He was going forever. He knew it.

"Olivia—is it such a shock? Yes, I suppose it is when one considers how I've spent my life walking around hurdles or pretending I couldn't see them—anything, in fact, but get down to it and tackle them. Today has changed that—don't you see?"

Because of Max? I must ask him, must unclench my jaw, my teeth, the rigidity of my throat and ask. But my teeth began to chatter as if with cold, my jaw to escape my control and tremble, so that I was forced to clench it again.

"Because of Max?" My voice sounded strained and small and rather offended but at least I had managed to speak.

"Yes, indeed—and how strange that is, since he probably means nothing to either of us. And isn't worth much anyway. Yes—because of Max."

I shook my head fiercely and leaning forward he took my knotted hands in his and held them, still smiling that eager, hopeful, initiate's smile.

"Olivia, when we first met I was so hopelessly in love with you. You filled my whole mind—just wiped everything else clean away. There was nothing else in me . . ."

And my own mind, assuming a separate identity from my tight-clenched body, cruelly translated: "I was infatuated. Blinded. I didn't know what I was doing."

"I think we just didn't get to know each other well enough, Olivia, didn't give ourselves time."

But that pitiless brain of mine knew he was saying: "When infatuation faded, as it soon does, I looked at you and found nothing else."

"I was to blame, Olivia. You made no secret of the kind of life you wanted. And I let you believe I could supply it. You wanted a young squire. I played the part for you without too much trouble because I know the lines. Lord, I *ought* to know them. And some of them are great lines except that they're not mine. And how could I let you sell the Manor for my sake, Olivia? How could I live with that? And how could you have done it without bitterness? It would have been too great a burden, darling, for both of us. A burden for me knowing that I'd have to find the way to compensate you for your sacrifice. And a burden for you, surely, pretending I *was* compensating you when it would have been no such thing. And so, because—I'm not sure how I can tell you this . . ."

I already knew. My whispering, punishing brain could have said it for him: "Because I thought you loved me madly, obsessively, to a point where you could love only me. And having inspired such a grand passion, I felt responsible for it. I believed I had to stay with you no matter what the cost, until this afternoon, looking through your mother's window." But I would not help him to crucify me. He would have to do it all himself.

"I know you loved me too, Olivia. I know I represented some kind of an ideal—something that was hard to live up to but which I *would* have lived up to, somehow or other, for as long as you needed it, because I'd promised . . ."

"I do need it."

"No you don't. Darling—that's just what I saw this afternoon. You don't need me. I don't know what Max means to you and it's not really important. But you were *natural* with him, Olivia. You were yourself as I first knew you, far more than you ever are with me, which means . . ."

"No it doesn't . . ."

"That I am not the right man for you just as you are not . . ."

"Don't say that . . ."

"Just as you are not the right woman for me. It's no one's fault, darling. We were both mistaken. That's crystal clear to me now. And it would be senseless to spend the rest of our lives punishing each other. We have to separate."

I gasped as sharply as if he had struck me and wrenched my hand loose from his, the ice cracking a little so that now, to stop myself from falling apart, from shrieking and fighting and—worse than that—pleading, I would have to *concentrate*.

You are not the right woman for me. Yes, he had said that. Was it true? Yes, that damnable, callous, free area of my mind whispered to me. Quite true. But what mattered was the way to convince him otherwise. If only my teeth would stop chattering and my jaw would obey me.

"Most men—most women—could say that, at some stage—these things come and go—bad patches."

"No, darling." He had thought it all out carefully, repeatedly, during his midnight vigils at our bedroom window and he was sure. "It's more fundamental than that. We don't know each other. That's at the root of it. Perhaps I don't know myself. That's why I have to go away—to discover just what it is I'm on this earth for."

Excuses. Excuses. The things men say to spare their own feelings when they break a woman's heart.

"There'll be no problem about money, Olivia. I'll see you have enough to go on looking after your mother and Madelon and keeping Luc at Hexingham. I know what that means to you. And afterwards—when we've sorted ourselves out—we might find we're *friends*. I'd like that. Friendship means a lot to me, you know. It's the emotion I'm most comfortable with."

Alys. It meant a lot to her too.

"It's Alys, isn't it? Is that what you're telling me?"

He shook his head, sighed, frowned and smiled at the same time. Just as she did.

"Olivia, I don't know. It's possible. What I need now is time alone—time to look and think and breathe. It's what I've always needed. I have one life as you have, darling. You know what you want from yours. I don't. I *must* find out, Olivia. And now I can find out. I'd given up hoping but now—don't you see—*now* I can go . . ."

Open the cage door and fly away. All that detains you is your own conscience. Max had opened Robin's cage already. And when Alys saw him soaring away from the petty captivities, the cloying conventions of Clarrow Fell—the escape they had surely planned together all their childhood long—she would be a fool if she did not follow him.

Jealousy, in that ghastly moment, was the least agonizing of the many emotions which assailed me and I seized upon it almost as a weapon to shield me from the rest.

"Words, Robin—words—excuses. Max is an excuse. The estate is an excuse. You've made a mistake and now you want to get out of it—that's what it amounts to. You don't deceive me. *Men* don't deceive me. And don't talk to me about courage, because only cowards run away. And that's what you're doing, or trying to do. Evading your responsibilities, breaking all those promises they taught you never to break at Hexingham—being *weak*, because it takes strength to stand your ground, and hard work to build marriages, just like houses—but you wouldn't know about guts and hard work—you and Alys . . ."

"No, darling," he said gently, kindly, giving me his permission to call him any dirty name I liked if it eased me. And because it did not ease me, because it was undignified and unjust and completely undeserved, I jumped to my feet and stood leaning against the window shaking from head to foot, my knuckles showing white as they gripped the window frame, hot, sooty air rushing past my face, scorching me.

"I don't know very much about anything, Olivia. That's what I've just been saying to you. And if one makes a false start, as we have, is it right that there should be no way of correcting it? We could go on together for the rest of our lives—because I haven't got enough of those guts you speak of—and at the end we could look each other in the eye and admit it has been a mistake. And what a waste, my darling. What a tragic waste. I've always known the world to be as full of hopes and opportunities as Clarrow meadow is full of daisies in springtime. I just never felt able to pick myself a handful until today— or that I'd ever get the chance of it . . ."

". . . that you'd ever allow me to do it," my rogue mind again translated, picking up the vibrated longings of *his* mind and murmuring them to me: "Set me free, Olivia. Don't cling to me, or overpower me. Don't arouse me to a passion that is insufficient in itself. Let me breathe. Let me go."

My decision to sell the Manor had brought me face to face with the element of self-sacrifice in love. I had recognized it, obeyed it. Must I now face it again at an even more profound and painful level and admit to myself that the best gift I could offer would be to release him? I loved him. Therefore, I desired only his happiness. And if I had become an obstacle to his happiness, should I not remove myself from his path as effectively as I would have removed anything or anyone else which troubled him? And, furthermore, should I not take my leave carefully and sweetly, without reproaches, wishing him well? That—surely?—would be a true act of love. Be generous, Olivia. Since he is going in any case, send him away with tender memories, not bitterness. I wanted to be generous with all my heart but even in that moment of sincere liberality, of unstinting desire to sacrifice my own good for his, an inner voice whispered that even generosity could be turned to advantage. For if I made it easy for him to go, he would also find it easier to return. "Leave a door open," the voice said. "And Alys, who may seem mysterious now and desirable as you once did, will be less so when they are wandering the world together, getting lost together; feeling the cold."

He could hardly set off on his voyage of self-discovery before morning and so I had the whole night before me. I *would* not despair.

I leaned out a little further, Hardenrigg Junction just a moment

265

away now, nothing in its rows of dingy houses and littered stretches of wasteland to distinguish it from anywhere else; the lights of another train approaching in the twilight, heavy-laden, like ours, with iron-workers and brewery workers on holiday, rather more sedate families, these, I thought, who—in place of a gay evening at Appleburton—had spent the day out on the moor.

I had no premonition of disaster. My whole mind was absorbed entirely by my own loss and my refusal to lose it, by ways and means to get it back again.

"Robin—" I turned round to face him and at that precise moment my ears were assailed by the most terrible sound I had ever heard.

"Robin . . . ?"

The wood, the metal, the whole train was screaming.

"Robin!" I was screaming too and leaping towards me, flinging his arms around me, he seemed to be pushing me downwards into the heart of that dreadful sound which swallowed me, consumed me, and then emptied me into blackness.

I was not afraid. I was asleep and there was no need for fear since nothing that happens in sleep has any reality. One simply wakes up at the end of it and the terror goes away. And Robin was with me, lying arched, somehow, on top of me, his body covering the whole of mine, so that whatever was behind him—and I knew *something* was there—could not touch me. Deep, empty sleep again. And then the noise, not so terrible as before, of cold metal scraping against metal, unwelcome, malodorous, waking me to a dark void where it seemed that something was burning. Suddenly I could not breathe. My nostrils had clogged with earth and grit. Something had moved me, heaved me over. Where was Robin? Blind panic. Pitch dark, as I reached out, desperate, sightless, clutching at shapes, tormented by raucous cries and shrill bird voices. Robin! But whatever force had moved me had taken him too. I couldn't see him. I could see nothing through the dark. I began to fight for breath as if I were drowning, to struggle for vision, to flounder—I thought—like a fish stranded in air, scorching on hot, dry sand. And then there was Victorine, her face a startling white circle surrounded by blackness, and somewhere behind her the voice of Andrew Rexford saying quite clearly, "She's concussed, Victorine. She can't hear you."

"Oh yes I can," I thought I said. And how typical of clever

266

Andrew Rexford, who had stolen my sister, to be so wrong. "Of course I can hear." But no one answered.

"Where's Robin?"

"She's concussed," said Victorine to someone else.

"Where's Robin?" I pleaded with her. "Where am *I*?" But—with her face only an inch from mine, my head, I supposed, held in her sturdy, pregnant lap—she did not hear me.

"Victorine!" I realized with horror that I had not actually made a sound. Searching inside myself I gathered together every scrap of energy and will, every vital thing my body still possessed, directed the whole of it into the single act of speech and still could not bring forth a single word.

"Victorine," I tried again, terrified now, appalled, beginning to understand. "Victorine. Where's Robin?"

"She seems to recognize me. I think she's coming round."

"Idiot," my mind yelled, savage with panic. "Where's Robin? For God's sake—where's Robin?"

I was in a field of battle. I knew quite well that it was the scrubby little field just before one came to the gasworks at Hardenrigg, yet battle had been there nevertheless, the bodies of those two holiday trains grotesquely concertinaed together, a reeking dust rising from them into the hot twilight, a pall of disaster hanging low and pervasive as factory smoke over that little space of weeds and sparse tufts of grass where the injured lay on the hard ground as they had done in Africa. And where, a yard away from me, my brother-in-law, Andrew Rexford, blood-streaked and filthy as a demon, severed a man's limb to free him from the wreck.

I lost consciousness again and came to in a corner of the field where others like myself huddled in shock or lay in separate, silent pits of grief. For it had been a holiday excursion, after all, one set of families going to Appleburton, another coming back, and there were children and grandmothers, best Sunday hats, broken toys as well as broken limbs scattered about this battlefield, lost wailing children, little yapping mongrel dogs who could bleed like everything else, men and women staggering in hopeless circles, searching the abominable litter on the ground—as I must begin searching—peering, in sick horror, to make certain that that particular bundle of rags was not—could not be—a husband, a child, a lover.

Yet these employees of the Ironworks and the Brewery and the few small textile mills still operating in Bradeswick, these patient, competent, tough-grained working people, were far more resigned to the facts of physical disaster than I. They had always known that tragedy of this magnitude could and very likely would happen to *them*. Until now I had believed that such things happened only to others.

I had no judgment of time. I sat for what may have been two minutes or two hours hunched against my knees, struggling to focus my eyes, to combat dizziness and nausea, the buzzing in my ears that threatened to fill my head and sweep me off again into oblivion.

It was dark now. How strange! But there were lights down by the trains, and the terrible tap-tap-scrape of metal against metal engraving itself upon my memory, the sound of men lifting twisted iron to release torn flesh, breaking open those cozy, suburban trains—special cheap-day returns for Bradeswick's holiday—to lift out the dead and lay them down in neat rows like the corpses of the Boer women and children in the Transvaal.

My senses swam away from me again but I clenched myself around them and held them back, forcing myself to look at individual faces—all strange to me. Where was Robin? Who could tell me? Victorine? But Victorine was busy down by the trains, bandaging and stitching, helping her husband. A woman came up to me, a housewife from one of those mean, gray streets in Hardenrigg, coming, like all the other women in her neighborhood, to do what she could.

"Now then, Missus . . ." But the broadness of her speech, that persistent buzzing in my ears, obscured everything in her meaning but its kindness and when I did not answer, she patted my shoulder and moved on.

The woman beside me was holding in careful arms a child I suddenly knew to be dead, rocking it to and fro and crooning something, her face placid and entirely blank. There was blood on her tranquil, tender hands, blood on me too, not mine I quickly ascertained, scrambling to my feet and crying out.

"Hush," said the woman and I understood she was asking me not to wake her baby. Where was Robin?

It was Victorine who found him and took me to him in the end, supporting me across the rutted road to the row of cottages where the worst of the injured had been taken. It was a small, single-roomed dwelling, the doorway so low that I had to bend my head to enter— I remember that very clearly—that, and the soiled mattress in the

268

chimney corner with the man who, already, was not altogether Robin, lying in complete stillness and solitude upon it. I had known for perhaps two minutes that he was dying, for Victorine had thrown the words at me curtly, like an accusation, and then burst into tears.

"He's dying, Olivia."

Yes. I think my body had known it all along, had been grieving for him, mourning him, while I had been stumbling from one group of injured to another, calling his name, until the hope had drained out of me like my lifeblood, leaving a dry-eyed bitter shell face to face with his death, and with Victorine.

"Andrew says there's nothing to do now but—just be with him."

And then, appearing suddenly in the night, Andrew was there himself, gruff and grim and considerably out of breath, hating death, I realized, ready to bare his teeth at it and snarl whenever his science failed him.

"There's nothing I can do, and that's that. Even if I had the means to get him to hospital, he'd never survive the journey. I did as much as there was to do, lassie."

Yes. I believed him. More, even than most men would have attempted.

"Thank you, Andrew."

"I'm sorry—damn sorry. Just be with him."

And so I knelt down on a muddy floor that could have been an army tent in Africa and looked at a face the color of a wax candle, hollows scooped out already beneath the cheek-bones as the wax melted, black smudges around the eye-sockets as the candle began to gutter. An anonymous, dying face with Robin's living eyes, Robin's spirit still there inside it, quick and urgent and as eager for adventure and experience and the excitement of self-discovery as it had been a few hours ago. He knew, with atrocious clarity, that he was losing his life in the moment of finding it. I saw that knowledge within him and it pierced my heart. I knew too that by using his own body to shield me he had probably given his life for mine, obeying an instinct of gallantry which now—because I also knew he did not love me—I believed he must regret. And I could not, in any way, cope with the blind injustice, the waste, my frenzied guilt, my grief for him, his own despairing grieving for himself. I could not cope with it.

I had always recognized the existence of hatred in the world.

I had simply never understood its real power. I understood it then. And in that moment I hated with a full and murderous loathing the witless destiny which had done this to him.

I could not speak to him. I hated. I burned and shook with it, the poison entering my soul where the dregs remained. And if later those poisonous traces took their toll of me, I believe they saved me, that night, from going mad.

Just be with him, Victorine had said, and what more could I do than that? What could I give him now? Nothing. Of what use was my grief or my love? No use at all but to remind him that tomorrow I would still be alive to grieve and to love, and he would not.

How healthy I must have looked to him, kneeling there with not a scratch on my well-nourished body, *his* blood, not mine, on the skirt of my dress. How vital and strong and inescapable. How loathsome. It seemed to me that he shuddered and then, managing a faint smile, he turned his head to one side and closed those desperate, living eyes, shutting me away.

But I had seen what lay within them. There *was* something he wanted, and even now, as he lay dying, he could not bring himself to wound me by asking.

"Robin?"

He did not answer. I knew he would not speak to me again. I had dazzled his vision, obscuring the true purposes of his life. His sight had cleared. He knew now exactly what it was he wanted, and that it had always been within his grasp. He was dying in bitterness and because I was not the woman he wished to have beside him, he had chosen, by closing those tortured eyes, to die alone.

I understood.

"Olivia," a voice from the doorway, and seeing Max there I got up and went across to him.

"Yes?"

"What can I do for you?"

There was only one answer but I hardly recognized the strangled voice which made it.

"Nothing for me. But go to the vicarage—quickly—and fetch Alys."

He glanced at Robin, nodded curtly and a moment later I heard the roar and snort of his engine going up the hill. I closed my mind until I heard it come back again. I saw her enter the room and

270

I knew the exact moment that he became aware of her. I saw his eyes shoot wide open and the incredulous joy which suffused his face. I saw the love and the need in him, and the frenzied attempt he was making to condense it now into minutes instead of the years they could have had together. I saw him reach out for her. I saw him offer her the true essence of himself. His loving friendship. I saw her take it. And then I went out into the street where Max was waiting and leaned, in silence, against the cottage wall. On the wasteland in front of me I could see the lights still flickering up and down, could hear sudden shouts of warning or command, but in the main a great silence had now fallen, the aftermath of battle when the wounded and the dead have been separated and counted and it is time to pack the supply wagons and go away.

"Are you cold?" said Max.

I had no idea. Certainly I was shivering and could not stop.

"There's a rug in the car."

He brought it, valuable of course, and put it around my shoulders, a huge mink blanket which covered me from top to toe and did not warm me. And there, leaning against the derelict stone wall, wrapped in sumptuous furs and shaking inwardly from the bones with a bitter chill, I gave the last moments of Robin's life to Alys like a macabre and tragic wedding-gift, waiting in absolute silence until she came, a chalk-white specter, to say he was dead.

SIXTEEN

I wore heavy black crêpe and the anonymity of a mourning veil at his funeral because these were the garments laid out for me by Aunt Sibylla and Mrs. Long. I had not forgotten his dislike of mourning clothes but, since I had failed him in everything else, it could make no difference now if I failed him in this. And it was left to Alys to appear in what she declared to be a shade of blue he had always preferred. I could not remember hearing him express any particular liking for that color but if she said it was his favorite then I assumed that she would know.

The funeral service was at Clarrow Church, the villagers, to whom his life or death made no difference, attending for sentimentality or curiosity or because Aunt Sibylla had let them know it was expected of them and the names of absentees would be noted. My uncle, the vicar, preached, in his beautiful, empty voice, the empty sermon Aunt Sibylla had composed; Aunt Sibylla herself "receiving" the mourners as if they were dinner guests, explaining to all those whose rank entitled them to explanations that my hard stare and the granite set of my countenance might reasonably be attributed to shock and the blow I had received on my head.

Dottie Potterton came, advising bravery, which was, after all, she declared, not far removed from good manners. Mrs. Naseby, whose health permitted her to be with me only in spirit, seemed to think it a pity that the laws of England would not allow me to burn myself on his funeral pyre as she believed was often done in India. My mother, twice widowed herself that we knew of and perhaps three times since we had heard nothing lately of Emil Junot, did not attend although

272

I think the Squire would have relaxed his ban on her presence at Clarrow for this one day. Victorine and Andrew stayed close beside me. Madelon coughed and cried and gasped so painfully for breath that she had to be taken out of the church by Amyas. Luc was grave and courteous and correct, a perfect Hexingham gentleman. Alys, in her blue dress, her pale hair which she had bundled underneath her hat, escaping in stray wisps and tendrils down her back, knelt in the vicarage pew, her head unbowed, paying not the slightest attention either to her father's polished performance or her mother's annoyance over the blue dress.

I did not shed a tear. My eyes had burned dry in their sockets. My head ached, and my throat and my chest. I could not cry. I could not sleep. I could not speak a civil word to anyone. I hated. That was the sum total of me. Hatred, venom, impotence. Where was Robin?

We took him out into the churchyard and buried him in Clarrow earth where he had not wished to be and then walked up the hill to the Manor, my grandfather stamping ahead of me, angry too, but at the sheer perversity of death in taking this young man when he—the Squire—had let it be known that he was ready.

Amyas was there before us, having consigned Madelon to Mrs. Long who had put her to bed and we were taken into the hall where, on the table beneath the window, the funeral feast had been set.

"Come along," said Aunt Sibylla, "for I imagine no one had time or appetite for breakfast and the weather is on the turn—exactly the time of year when a proper diet is essential to ward off the cold. Victorine, dear, remember you are eating for two. A little of this game pie would not go amiss, unless your clever husband should consider it too rich."

But she had little real fault to find with Andrew Rexford now that he had done her the favor of marrying Victorine instead of Alys and, after bestowing a liberal helping of pie on his plate too, she attached herself smoothly but firmly to Dottie Potterton, wishing to know when we might expect to see her nephew, Felix, at Clarrow again.

The squire took a glass of claret, went off without a word to the Justice's Room and closed the door, leaving Amyas—as always—to act as his substitute. Victorine, four months from her time and enormous, sat down by the fire and placidly occupied herself with the task of eating for two or even for three by the look of her.

"Are you all right, lassie?" Andrew Rexford asked me keenly, knowing I was no such thing. But funerals were extremely common in Bradeswick that week and I had not had to pawn my furniture and my Sunday boots to pay for this one, like the twenty or thirty new-made widows in Andrew's practice. I may well have lost my appetite but at least I had food on my table, a roof to shelter me which belonged to my own family rather than to the Greenlaws or the Nasebys who would serve eviction notices on Bradeswick's widows the moment their husbands' places were filled at the Ironworks or the Brewery.

Because of a signalman's error, scarcely a family around Corporation Square and those mean streets behind the tram-sheds remained untouched by bereavement, the whole town still resembling, in spirit, the camp of an army in miserable, mud-clogged defeat, its citizens trailing the streets with the apathy and dejection of refugees. Young men had been killed in their prime or maimed beyond the possibility of employment, canceled out as wage-earners and, therefore, in a very real and cruel fashion, rendered useless for life. Children had been left motherless which, in Andrew's Bradeswick, meant virtually defenseless. Mothers who had thought themselves overburdened by their children now stood in their empty doorways, sunken-eyed, idle-handed, desolate. The signalman, whose mistake had caused those two holiday trains to collide, had gone home and hanged himself that same night, leaving a young, frightened wife and three small children.

A fund, of course, had already been started by certain Bradeswick ladies to help the needy, just as money had been raised, by the same charitable, energetic individuals, to assist the men who had limped or had been carried home from Africa. Our friend, Miss Frances Grey, had been among the first to join the Disaster Committee and would—until the next thing came along—devote her efficiency to the cause. The Greenlaws would go to great lengths to make sure of giving at least a hundred pounds more than the Nasebys and vice versa, although the eviction notices would suffer no delay. Andrew would stitch wounds, dry tears, would be called in, perhaps, to cut down the next man who hanged himself. Miss Grey and her committee would disagree—in their refined manner—about the best method of spending their fund and in the end would probably erect a totally useless monument to the dead in Bradeswick Park.

"Yes, Andrew—thank you—I'm all right."

"Good," he said, preferring to believe it, and retired to the library with my reverend uncle to discuss comparative religion, tariff

274

reform, and what appeared to be the true love of the vicar's life, his butterflies. Madelon was busy upstairs nursing her cough. Luc, I realized, was no longer there.

They all had their lives to lead. I understood that. But my life had reduced itself now to the level of things which are to be endured and already, I could feel myself drawing away from the rest of them, separated from their eager capacities to hope and to enjoy by an encircling moat of murky, empty space. But my misery, my savagery, was my own affair and, irritated by their voices, their appetites, their substance, I left the room without excusing myself to anyone and walked back to the Gatehouse down that magical quarter of a mile which had once meant so much to me. What did it mean now? The burning behind my eyes, my hollow, aching bones did not allow me to answer. If I could only lay myself down somewhere and rest. But when I tried, my bones seemed to pierce the skin, my eyes to burn drier; sleep—such as it was—being no more than a shallow dream, haunted by Robin's living, grieving eyes.

My grandfather should have invited me to spend those first dreadful weeks at the Manor but he did not. I had a mother in Bradeswick who could not refuse me bed and board, he supposed, since I paid her bills. I had sisters, acquaintances, who should be able to distract me; or, should I care to take a holiday—a change of air, he had always heard, being considered most beneficial to widows— Amyas would arrange it. But I did not wish to be distracted and was not yet ready for Bradeswick and the warm turmoil of my mother's life.

"Come and stay at the vicarage. It is not good for you to be alone," said Aunt Sibylla, meaning that my solitary prowlings around the Gatehouse garden might seem odd to the Pottertons.

"No thank you, aunt."

"Well then—Alys is going to Bridlington with her father and would be glad of your company."

And since Alys was the nearest I could get to Robin I nodded, "Very well."

I spent the remainder of August and three weeks of September in a small seaside boarding-house where we were the only guests, the vicar setting off early every morning to indulge his new interest for observing the ways of seabirds, returning just in time for supper each evening, having made copious sketches and notes and to his evident satisfaction not spoken a word to a single soul all day. And alone with each other in the quiet town, the summer visitors all gone away, we spent our time walking along the shore, this English seascape of white and gray being new to me and strange, leaving a memory of damp, ribbed sand, gray mist hanging low over gray water, the sun an occasional red haze in the far distance. From a sultry midsummer, the year had plunged deep into autumn, a sharp wind dislodging the first sad, slow falling leaves of this sad season, each turn of the tide bringing a drizzle of fine rain.

I borrowed from our obliging hostess a long hooded cloak as serviceable as any army blanket, and went out walking just the same, the heavy garment growing heavier and unwieldy as the rainwater soaked it through, walking solitary miles without the least idea of direction or purpose unless it was to see how much punishment my body could take, how long before exhaustion felled me into a sleep deep enough to obscure the nightly visitation of Robin's blue, living eyes in the dead candlewax of his face. I walked and would not stop until the vast, painful issues of his death, my life, the multitude of recriminations, became submerged by the basic need to force one leg to follow the other and get back to my lodgings without falling down.

There was a week of heavy gales and fierce, wild waters, a mighty elemental uprising which communicated exactly with my humor. I stood on the cliffs in the shrieking air and dared it to topple me over, gritted my teeth and fought it because it was easier than my silent, dry-eyed battle with grief and guilt and with the insidious, whispering voice inside my head, telling me over and over again the tale of my own failure, asking me "What now, Olivia?"

I was not ready even to contemplate the future. I walked in lashing rain and wind, drenched my body and my spirit in cold air and cold water and—as a life—it suited me.

Victorine, too pregnant now to make the journey to see me, wrote long letters concerning neither my trials nor her own—if indeed she had any—but about the repercussions in Bradeswick of the accident. For a great many of the injured had been decent working men, of those low-income groups where it was possible to feed, house and clothe a family—admittedly at a very basic level—provided the wage-earner remained in full employment every working day of the year. Such families, particularly those with young children who were years away from earning wages of their own, could not afford to put a penny-

276

piece aside or even to pay the subscriptions to a sick club or a trade union; were, in fact, totally vulnerable, crushable, chaff in the wind of even a moderate disaster. And when the wage-earner lost an arm or broke a back or was otherwise rendered unfit for labor and had no adult children to care for him, it was the responsibility of no one but the Poor Law Relieving Officer to pick up his pieces and stow him away in the workhouse.

Victorine's message to me was clear. I was not the only one who had suffered. I absolutely agreed with her. It made no difference.

My mother waited three weeks before arriving with Madelon to spend a day and a night with me, caressing and careful in her manner, truly sorry for my agony, but nevertheless, very concerned and wanting to concern me about Bessie and Hattie Greenlaw's latest plan to remove their father-in-law from her grasp.

"They wish to send him to Bournemouth—well not precisely send him since he's very partial to the place and had quite made up his mind to retire there before we met. They want him out of the business, of course, so their husbands can arrange matters just as they please. And Bessie wants him out of the family house so that she can do it up to her liking. And of course, there is a lady in Bournemouth, a widow like myself, except older and plainer and very rich. They wouldn't mind *her* as a stepmamma, I need hardly add. Well—I could relinquish him gracefully, of course, for he is not the grandest passion of my life by any means. But on the other hand, one grows accustomed . . . He is rather agreeable and most obliging when it comes to losing at cards. What do you say, Olivia?"

Presently, mother, I thought. Presently.

"Ivor Naseby has come home again," Madelon suddenly whispered, breaking the long silence in which we had been strolling along the seafront. "I saw him in Bradeswick Park last Sunday and—well— he *looked* at me and raised his hat—you know. And then he was at Miss Grey's on Monday evening—so pleasant and so *interested*—you know—asking how I had been spending my time since we last met and had I made any new acquaintances—which I thought, and mother thought, meant that he wanted to find out if I was fond of anyone— you know, Olivia. And then, at Mrs. Greenlaw's on the Wednesday, Mrs. Naseby would hardly speak a civil word to me, as if I had done something *dreadful*—which mother thought rather encouraging. Do you think so, Olivia?"

277

She would need help, I knew, with Esmeralda Naseby. My help. Presently, Madelon.

My brother, Luc, still only fourteen but looking twenty, sounding twenty-five, arrived loudly and without warning at my lodgings, accompanied by his friend from Harrogate and two young ladies of nineteen or thereabouts: shop girls, I thought, or even parlormaids out on a spree whose acquaintance had been made in a manner I dreaded to think. And since Luc's notions of entertaining young ladies, even at that age, were very grand, where was the money coming from? Did my mother even know his whereabouts much less what he was up to? Of course, she did not. Had anyone but me given a thought to the possible consequences of the champagne picnic he was planning on the beach with this pretty little girl who very clearly lacked the sense to deny him anything.

"Well, I know a fellow's not supposed to boast, but it wouldn't be the first time, Olivia, you know."

"Luc? I thought Hexingham was supposed to give you standards. You do realize what could happen—to the girl, I mean."

"I realize it could happen to the girl," he said cooly, "and she doesn't even know my real name."

I put a stop to that, of course. I sent the girls away, escorted the two completely unrepentant young men to the station and put them on the train for Bradeswick, my temper so high that, for the hour it lasted, I was very nearly my normal self again.

"Why does it shock you?" said Alys, shrugging a cool shoulder, her attitude taking me by surprise. "It is the way of young gentlemen. All females of inferior social status are fair game to them. I thought you would have known that better than I."

Yes, far better, and in a manner she could only imagine since, for the first twenty years of my life, I had been considered fair game too, by the sons and fathers and even the grandfathers sometimes of the families who had employed me. But my own brother should have had more integrity, more compassion, and if Hexingham could not turn him into the true gentleman of my ideals—like Robin—then some other way would have to be found.

"Not all men think like that, Alys."

"No. But enough—far too many. The local people would not send their girls into service with Dottie Potterton when her sons were at home. And whenever Clive Potterton comes back on leave from

278

India there is trouble in the village; another little Potterton left behind for someone to feed—not Dottie of course—and Dottie looking down her nose at the fuss because in her young days, when her brothers were doing the same thing, the girls thought it an honor to be ruined by the young squire—or so she imagines."

One could well believe it of the Pottertons.

"And Guy," she said, not looking at me. "One of the tenant's daughters had to be sent away because of Guy, who accepted no responsibility for it. The Squire paid, of course—which is more than the Pottertons have ever done—just as he always paid when it was Max's father—or Max. They all took what pleased them because it pleased them, regardless of the consequences to others. And because it was a matter of sexual gratification no one blamed them. Even my mother takes the view that men are simply made that way. And she positively adores Clive Potterton. She would marry me to him tomorrow if he would have me, which, fortunately for me, he will not, since he is not interested in marrying integrity or even virginity, only money. So your brother is merely following a long tradition of callousness. One law for the women, another for the men."

"Not all men, Alys."

"I know that. Not Andrew Rexford. Not my father. Not Robin. I have met no others as yet . . ."

We walked together that evening on the beach, the capricious season having turned balmy and soft as a Mediterranean summer, and kneeling down on a flat green rock while Alys hunted for shells, sifting the coarse sand through my fingers, inhaling salt spray and filled with restless longings aroused by the vastness of the sea, I said, without meaning to say it, without hoping for anything in particular, just releasing a need: "When I went to him in that dreadful little cottage, he turned his head away from me."

She made no answer. She simply *stopped*, everything, her movement, her breath, the blink of her eyelids coming to a halt, waiting while I, with lunatic persistence, continued to sift the sand through unsteady hands, watching it fall as relentlessly and heedlessly as an hour-glass.

"He was going to leave me, Alys. Did he tell you?"

And I watched the motion return to her slowly, with the heavy grace of a woman swimming underwater, long mermaid hair, pale mermaid limbs quietly floating.

"Yes."

"Would you have gone with him? Please—I think I have to know."

We did not look at each other. I watched the sand running between my hands like time uncaring, listening to the wind getting up again far out at sea, heralding the return of winter.

"I think we would have made our ways separately yet still have been together. Do you understand?"

"Yes. So you *were* in love with him."

"Not as you understand it, Olivia."

And then, standing slightly on tiptoe, leaning forward as if she might suddenly take flight and simply no longer be there, she said without the slightest hint of cruelty, simply speaking the truth, "But it was the way Robin understood it, of course. We had been friends all our lives, you see, and perhaps we both expected that friendship to grow and mature with us, to acquire its share of things like love— and passion—as we ourselves became aware of them, but to remain friendship, just the same. Yes, I am quite certain we both expected that, and so we believed we had plenty of time. We never talked about getting married. It never seemed necessary. We assumed we would, I am sure we did, because it was the only way we could live together. But there was no urgency about it. And no one else appeared to be aware of it. Not until Guy came back from Cambridge and took it into his head to fall in love with me. I don't know why he did that. He had known me forever without a glance, and then suddenly he was asking for things I could never give. My mother has never forgiven me. I know I was the cause of great disappointment to the Squire. When Guy was killed I felt responsible. It was the wrong moment for Robin and me to be together. And in any case there was still so much we both wanted to do. Then you came. I understood that, you see, because for just a while, when Guy first loved me, I was attracted to him too. I knew I could never feel as he felt. I could never feel so intensely about anything, nor do I wish to do so. And if I *did* I would not care to let it show. But Guy's feelings were huge and explosive and overpowering and although I *knew* I could never bear to be over-powered, I was intrigued by it. I hesitated, which he mistook for encouragement and that is why I felt such guilt about his death. You should not feel guilty on Robin's account, Olivia. I am as much to blame as you. I waited too long. And when I saw what was happening

280

between you I made no move to dissuade him, as I could have done. Perhaps I thought you were the punishment for what I had done to Guy. But it is far more likely that I was just not ready. Well, at least *that*—being ready or not ready—is irrelevant now."

Silence flowed for a moment between us.

"I am sorry," she said, and now, through the twilight, I saw the tears pouring from her eyes, the relief which was still denied to me. What had she told me? I understood only that she would have gone away with him and that they would have been happy together, that she, who had loved him tranquilly and easily all her life, was far more truly his widow than I, who had shared three passionate, hectic, mistaken years with him.

I neither liked nor disliked her for it. I accepted it.

"I shall have a great deal of trouble, now, at home, you know," she told me, smiling through her flow of tears. "For I have no one else, you see. I am alone now, Olivia, as I think you have never been. And how on earth, I wonder, am I to manage my mother?"

I was in Bradeswick for the birth of Victorine's son that December, a beautiful, healthy, noisy miracle who did not long prevent her from the work she had undertaken in Andrew's practice. The infant Matthew being wrapped in a blanket shawl and carried peasant fashion across her hip while she not only distributed soup to the needy but gave them instructions on how to make their own from the cheapest butcher's leftovers and such gleanings from the vegetable market as might be available. Children were dying, she declared, not only from poverty but from ignorance. And if there was little she could do about the poverty, the ignorance came well within her province.

Victorine was concerned neither with politics, religion nor morality, only with results. She could do nothing to prevent the men of Bradeswick's twilight areas from drinking their wages on Thursday nights, or from annually impregnating their wives. But she could point out to these women that the stunted growth, bad teeth, poor eyesight and bandy legs of their children could be corrected to some extent by proper feeding.

Her territory was small, just those few streets behind the tramsheds, but she could be found regularly in one or the other of these, doing what her husband described as "her rounds." The woman on the corner who had no proper stove, and whose culinary skills had never progressed beyond the bread and dripping variety, needed in-

281

struction on how to cook in one pot over an open fire the tasty stews and herb dumplings which had nourished our own childhood. It must be pointed out to the woman next door, that instead of spending money on patent medicines and powders or the even more dubious, occasionally lethal preparations from the old woman at the end of St. Saviour's Passage, she might easily cure her constipation by an infusion of dandelion leaves—always easy to find—while a clove of garlic simmered in milk would do wonders for her husband's cough. And as for the woman at the end house, Victorine could not tell her often enough that the milk for her baby should not be more than a day old and *must* be boiled.

"My wife's preventive medicine is taking my living away," said Andrew gruffly, very proud.

"In a less tolerant age," murmured my mother, "my daughter Victorine might well have been burned at the stake."

"My prevention," said Victorine stoutly, "is better than anybody's cure, for the simple reason that it costs less. And if you would tell your cook to save me the outer leaves of your cabbages instead of putting them in the dustbin, I would be very obliged to you, mamma. You could also ask her to save me the water in which your vegetables have been boiled. I am not sure why, but it has a decided effect on the scurvy."

Both Alys and I accompanied her occasionally but I was too impatient and had no domestic skills to impart in any case, while Alys, although her intentions were of the best, her spirit the most willing in the world, found herself weak in the flesh, most particularly in the stomach, when it came to the intimate details of unwashed children, the sore eyes and running noses and grubby, clutching fingers, the stinging odor of baby linen which, on wet days—of which there are many in Bradeswick—had simply been hung up in front of the fire for the urine to dry.

"I have the utmost admiration for you, Victorine," said Alys, "but I do believe I will be obliged to save humanity in some other fashion." And thereafter she increased her visits to Miss Frances Grey.

I spent Christmas again at the Manor, entirely alone this time with my grandfather and Amyas, as silent and as grim as them, waited upon by the inscrutable Mrs. Long who, if she was the mistress of Amyas as Mrs. Timmins insisted, gave no sign of it whatsoever as she calmly accepted his instructions about refilling the punchbowl, serving the claret and making up the fire in the Justice's Room where my grandfather, who had suffered severe pains in the leg and the hips since his fall, was now sleeping.

He left us immediately after dinner and, sitting in the library with Amyas, I felt the house closing down around me, coming to an end. Already the upper floor was in disuse, the Squire's old butler had been pensioned off and not replaced, Mrs. Long attending to the silver and the wine herself, Amyas to the carving, the Squire making no secret of his unsteady hand. One of the farms—one of the best I rather suspected—had become vacant and no new tenant was being sought. My grandfather believed he was dying at last and wanted his house, as he had known it, to die with him.

"Shall we drink to the New Year, Amyas?"

He smiled quietly.

"It is not quite time, Olivia."

No, but very nearly, for death had already crossed the threshold of the Justice's Room, I was well aware of it. And what would Amyas do then? What would I do? I was not yet certain—but whatever it turned out to be I would prefer to have Amyas with me, not against me. I raised my glass and smiled at him.

"I shall be quite ready for it, you know—the New Year—when it comes."

"Mr. Hird!" Mrs. Long's voice said, a little too sharply, from the doorway, "the Squire is asking for you."

And as she began to light the lamps, her taut body beneath its housekeeper's black silk, bristling with what looked very much like indignation, I realized how seriously the sight of Amyas sitting in the dark, drinking claret with me, had upset her.

The year ended and re-opened: the same days and nights and seasons with a different number. I was not Queen Victoria whose sovereignty permitted her to nourish her grief for forty morbid years, but Olivia Heron with her mother's extravagance to curb, a young brother who might easily get into debt and would certainly get into trouble if I did not watch him, a young sister who had fallen in love and felt entitled to her share of the energy and ingenuity I had applied to the affairs of everyone else. And so grief became a private matter, concealed by the hustle and bustle, the social and financial pressures of everyday. I knew what I had done and failed to do. I knew what I had lost, misconstrued, damaged. It was no one's affair now but mine.

My sister, Victorine, conceived another child that summer,

deliberately, she insisted when I raised pained eyebrows and inquired the reason for her haste.

"Why not?" she said, "I'm good at it. I'll have this one and then, if it's a girl, no more."

"Why should you want a girl?" said Alys. "Who'd be a girl? This world was made by men to please men. And what seems to please men most is the burying alive of women."

"Oh no," said Madelon, "you're wrong, Alys. It's absolutely glorious to be a woman."

But Madelon, as we all knew, was still at the first rapturous stage of love where all that mattered was seeing Ivor Naseby without any thought of the consequences, listening to his voice without really registering the words he was speaking, dancing every dance with him in a trance of bliss as she had just done at the Pottertons' latest ball and then weeping all night because his mother had refused to speak to her afterwards.

"You will never make a suffragette out of Madelon," said Victorine. "There are women who want to be dominated, Alys, you know."

Alys did not know nor did she believe it. Nor did Miss Frances Grey who, from the refinement and perfect safety of her "*salon*" kept us accurately informed as to the progress of the Women's Social and Political Union, under the leadership of her friend, Mrs. Pankhurst.

"Formidable, in fact," said Miss Grey, "but then, there has always been something formidable about dear Emmeline."

She had caused a disturbance at Westminster in the May of that year when, attempting to hold a protest meeting at the entrance to the House of Lords, she had been moved on, none too gently, by the police.

"How—how very provoking," said Alys, wondering, I knew, how she would endure it if any rough-spoken constable should ever raise his voice to her.

But Mrs. Pankhurst, accustomed to voices raised in anger, had gone on to spend the summer touring the traveling fairs which visit every town in the counties of Lancashire and Yorkshire, her speeches on the wrongs and *rights* of women soon drawing the holiday crowds.

"How very *enterprising*," said Alys, "how brave." Hoping, should the opportunity ever arise, that she too would have the courage to walk into a busy fairground ringing a muffin bell, stand on a soapbox and submit herself to the jeers and ribaldry of strangers.

Mrs. Pankhurst's next move was to send her daughter, Christabel, to a public meeting to demand of the principal speakers, the Liberal politicians, Sir Edward Grey and Mr. Winston Churchill, whether, if a Liberal government should be elected, it would give the vote to women. Miss Pankhurst, far from receiving an answer, was roughly handled by the crowd and thrown bodily into the street where, in order to get herself arrested, she committed what she, as a qualified barrister, knew to be a technical assault. She spat, in what she afterwards insisted had been a most ladylike fashion, in a policeman's eye—her arms being pinned behind her back—thus securing for herself a week in jail and more press coverage than the suffragist cause had ever dreamed of.

I saw Alys turn pale at the news, her fastidious soul recoiling in horror as she imagined herself forcibly ejected from a public place, coarse hands twisting her arms, coarse breath mingling with her own, incarceration in a prison cell in close proximity, she supposed, with the possibly gross personal habits of others.

"How absolutely splendid," she said. "I can't tell you how much I admire her."

"Yes," murmured Miss Grey, "Christabel was always Emmeline's favorite child. Well, well, this promises to be an interesting general election, for it seems that dear Emmeline is finally coming to the boil. She has been simmering all her life, you see, and now—well, I think we must keep our eyes and ears wide open in the direction of Manchester . . ."

"I would like to go there," said Alys, her chin quivering.

"Then go," murmured Max de Haan, who had arrived unexpectedly that evening as he always did, after an absence of several months. "Go. I have my brand new Mercedes outside. Shall I take you?"

She smiled, recovering her composure and shook her head, giving the same truthful, sorrowful reply as always.

"My mother would not permit it."

"Then don't ask her."

"You know very well I could never do that."

He arose, a glass of Frances Grey's excellent brandy in his hand and stood on the hearthrug, the natural dominant position of the male in a gathering of women.

"It occurs to me," he said, his eyes wicked with mischief, "that the world is a terrible place for women."

"Of course it is."

"And that you are your own worst enemies in it."

"How is that?"

"Quite simple. For if your own instincts don't trap you, ladies," and he raised his glass to include all of us, "then my instincts certainly will."

"He means," said Frances Grey unnecessarily, not liking to see Alys so much the center of attention, "that even if a woman is not naturally inclined towards matrimony and maternity, etcetera, then some man will find a way to persuade her to it, for his own convenience."

"We know," said Victorine, blunt as she liked these days now that she was beholden to no one.

But Max was looking quizzically, speculatively at Alys. And Alys, through a worried frown, was blushing: and smiling.

The anniversary of Robin's death came. And passed. I mentioned it to no one. Neither did Alys. I locked myself away inside the Gatehouse. She sat in the churchyard with her book "being with him." And when evening fell she went away.

I felt cold and distant for several days thereafter, so numb and so oddly lethargic that I wondered if anything again would ever really move me. But one fine, frosty morning in the middle of November, having spent an hour or two in the saddle, my grandfather came back to the Manor and dismounted awkwardly, Amyas thought, so that Amyas was ready, when he stumbled and sagged at the knees, to get him to the Justice's Room where I—who had been visiting Mrs. Timmins in the kitchen—came running.

He was on the narrow army bed they had made up for him, the room airless and acrid with sickness and old age and bad temper, Amyas kneeling by the bedside, haggard and horrified, the visible emotion in this hitherto emotionless man shocking me far more than the proximity of death, which I had been expecting.

But my grandfather, perverse to the end, did not want to be with Amyas, who loved him: perhaps *because* he loved him, and, as I entered the room was already waving him away.

"Where's that girl?"

"I'm here, grandfather."

"Yes, I thought you would be." And he spoke the words in agony, his body hunched grotesquely on one side, his lips blue.

We kept watch beside him, Amyas and I, the doctor flitting in and out, doing little but wonder why it was taking so long. Somewhere very far into the night as I bent over him, thinking him very still, his long gnarled hand closed with the suddenness of a trap over mine and gripped, not hard perhaps, but with a strength that startled me because I had expected no strength at all.

He began to say something, his voice weak, more breath than speech and, as I leaned nearer, he squeezed my hand again, believing, I think, that he was holding me fast although I could easily have escaped him.

"You were too much of a risk, Olivia."

Had I heard aright?

"What risk, grandfather?"

I saw him gather what remained of himself together, saw the iron clamp of his will force the air through his lungs for a moment longer, saw the mighty concentration of effort required for the simple transference of words from the brain to the tongue, the pain it cost him to open these cracked, sunken lips.

"Risks with everybody—always took them . . ."

Sweat was beading his brow in large cold drops and gingerly—because I had never before touched him—I wiped it away.

"*Risks*, Olivia. That's what people are—risks—bad ones mostly."

And then, on an abrupt and final surge of strength—the very last of him—in a voice which after that hoarse whisper sounded fierce and loud he said "My son, your father, was a poor fool. And all those lads—none of them—not one—worth an ounce of the trouble. Guy worst of all. And my wife was not all she seemed. Risks—bad risks. You were too late—damn you."

He never spoke again.

The whole village turned out to mourn him, needing no prior instructions from my aunt, his tenants weeping openly in the church, Dottie Potterton who considered it bad manners to weep in public, energetically blowing her nose; even my uncle, the vicar, displaying faint signs of emotion since—like all the other tenants—he had lost the security of his living. Aunt Sibylla appeared to be and probably was quite broken-hearted, while Alys wept so copiously and with so little restraint that I concluded these were the tears she had not dared to shed for Robin. Amyas alone, his grief rock-hard and silent in a way I recognized, might have moved me, yet did not. My grandfather could have loved me. I could have loved him. We had been cast in the same mold and ought to have loved each other. It had not occurred.

"Damn you," he had said. I understood. It had been too late. There had been nothing either of us could do.

I went back to the Manor to preside at his funeral tea and there—a little later—seated in his chair in the Justice's Room where I had watched him die, I saw him again, faintly in the gloom, his hard mouth cynically smiling, his hard eyes watching me as, through the living agency of the lawyer, Mr. Lawker of Lawker & Lane, he dealt me his final hand. The Manor was mine, of course, nothing could be done about that. But the capital he had painstakingly accumulated through a long, frugal life, the cash in Bradeswick Commercial Bank, the shares in Mr. Greenlaw's Ironworks and Mrs. Naseby's Brewery, so vital to the maintenance of the house and the land, had been bequeathed—perhaps to purchase her freedom—to Alys.

SEVENTEEN

The legacy was accepted at once by Aunt Sibylla on her daughter's behalf and, by the following morning, her version of my grandfather's meaning and motives was in circulation throughout Bradeswick and Clarrow Fell. The Squire had intended Alys to marry Guy, everyone knew that, and this was simply the dowry which, had Guy lived, would automatically have been hers. There was nothing in the least odd or even surprising about it. The African War had deprived her of one husband. Her cousin Olivia—although this was only very discreetly implied—had deprived her of another. The Squire had simply desired to put matters right. And for the benefit of those who, when her back was turned, might shake their heads and declare it hard and unfeeling of the Squire to will his money away from the Manor, which badly needed it, my aunt—with her gracious smile and a glint of steel in her eye—felt bound to add that the old man had tended to regard Alys as if her marriage to Guy had actually taken place, thus making her a first and evidently favored grandchild.

I think that Alys herself, in theory and in principle, would have liked to give the money back to me, knowing that without it I had no hope of keeping the Manor. Yet in reality her choice was between a lifetime of suffocation at Clarrow vicarage or a breath of fresh air, which I perfectly understood to be no choice whatsoever.

We could share it, of course. She offered that, walking from the vicarage to see me, looking cold and strained and still sickened by her mother's jubilation. But I shook my head, knowing that Aunt Sibylla would go to any lengths to prevent her from parting with a penny-piece.

"No, Alys. It belongs to you. And half of it wouldn't make any real difference to either of us. It wouldn't be enough to keep the wolf from the Manor door, just put off the day of reckoning a little. So keep it."

"It won't be enough to attract Felix Potterton either."

"No. But it will pay the train fare to Manchester, won't it, or London—or anywhere else you fancy."

"I wouldn't want to quarrel with you, Olivia—about money."

"You won't."

That much at least I could do for her. Were you listening, Robin?

I walked up from the Gatehouse to the Manor and stood for a while in the hall beneath the great window watching the reflections of the November sun on the jeweled glass and then, slowly, carefully, walked from room to room touching walls and doors and the carved oak frames of chairs, stonework and woodwork and ironwork, marble mantelshelves and polished marble hearths, the surfaces my brother and father and grandfather had touched all their lives long; possessing with my eyes and nostrils and with the pores of my skin this beautiful breathing house which had always been home to me, joining with it, adding myself to it while I still could.

And when the pilgrimage was over and I had covered every corner, every tread of the stairs, every musty, unlit passage, and explored the murky treasure trove of every attic, I went to the Justice's Room, sat down in the Squire's chair, placed my hands palms down on the Squire's table and remained there, deep in thought and silence—like the Squire—until the room darkened with twilight and Mrs. Long came tapping sharply on the door asking if I meant to dine here: hoping I did not.

I wished to decide why my grandfather had done this to me. "You were too late—damn you." I would never forget that. I had been temperamentally far closer to that tough-grained, sour-tempered old man than I had ever been to Robin. He had known that too. But, although men do not always love their own reflections, why—since he had not appeared to care what happened to the Manor—had he taken these cruel, crafty steps against me? Had he indeed been motivated by simple affection for Alys, a straightforward desire to liberate her from her mother's clutches? Had the money been intended merely as an escape route from Clarrow vicarage, an alternative to accepting one of Aunt Sibylla's arranged marriages which, until now, had been her only chance of getting away? No doubt, the Squire had thought of that, had considered with grim amusement the prospect of Aunt Sibylla's discomfiture when she realized how greatly the legacy would diminish her maternal authority. But I thought it unlikely that my grandfather's reasons—like my own—could ever have been so simple. Far more likely that he had sat here night after night in the gathering dusk just as I was doing, patiently and sardonically constructing for me the final hurdle, the final knot which he did not expect me to unravel.

You are a schemer, Olivia. Scheme yourself a passage through the maze I have left behind me. Open the doors I have closed tight shut. If you can. Why, grandfather?

He had defeated me, and I did not take it kindly. Or had he? I feared so, truly I feared it, for I could, in that bleak hour, see no loophole, no loose end, no leverage of any kind. He had won. I would probably—in a day or two—bring myself to accept it but if, in the meantime, something should occur to me, something should cross my mind—well—we would have to wait and see about that. I had been in trouble before, many times. I was no stranger to insecurity, sudden swings of fortune both good and bad. And what I did believe in, ardently and devoutly as a religious creed, was that when life shattered and splintered as it often did, the great test, the great division, was between those who could pick up the pieces of themselves and start afresh and those who could not. And having rebuilt myself before— once or twice—then, somehow or other, I would do it again.

The heart of my dilemma, after all, was money or rather its lack, and I was used to that. My allowance from the estate—Guy's allowance—had ended with the Squire's death. My allowance from Robin's father had ended too, Colonel Esmond having indicated very clearly that, with a new young wife of his own and a new baby son to keep, he could accept no further financial responsibility for me. And how else could I keep a roof over my mother's head than by selling this one? How else could I pay the ten pounds a term which Hexingham, like Eton, cost me, if not by selling the estate and investing the money to provide myself with a small but regular income, independent of the whims and fancies of a benefactor? How else could I retain a toe-hold in Bradeswick so as not to lose sight of Victorine and to give Madelon her now much reduced chance of Ivor Naseby?

I would have to go back to Aireville Terrace, a widow with no expectations, nothing with which to fool the world that I might one day be a person of consequence and, therefore, must be treated with respect. While Madelon, who might have been acceptable to the Nasebys—and then only just—had she become Miss Marriott of Clarrow Fell with all the prestige of the Manor behind her, would have her work cut out to be accepted now. Or, rather, I would have mine. Damn you, grandfather.

And if I sold to Max there was always the possibility that he would bring Alys here with him. How could I bear that? As stoically, I supposed, on the surface as she had borne her own sorrows.

But who knew? Who *really* knew what might suddenly be encountered at the next bend in the road? Not even my grandfather, from the vantage point where he had placed himself to watch me, could be certain of that. There was not much hope, of course—not much—but at least my eyes were constantly alert to catch its faintest glimmer, my ears straining to detect its footsteps hurrying away from me so that I could follow.

We'll just wait and see, grandfather? Shall we?

It was, of course, ironical that Max who had watched and waited so long had been called away from Bradeswick two days before the Squire's death and could not be found.

"My dear," my mother said, "*who* could one possibly ask?" And since no other buyer seemed likely to present himself and there was no telling when Max might appear again, I allowed myself a breathing space, a thinking space, and—to the great annoyance of Mrs. Long—closed the Gatehouse and moved up to the Manor, alone, defiant, already making plans. I was harder now than before and had never been gentle. For an hour or so my grandfather had entirely crushed me but it had always been my custom, in times of trouble, to hold my head high and I arrived to take up residence at Clarrow Fell not only looking like the new young Squire—which I undeniably was—but as if I had an army of decorators, painters, tilers, upholsterers, behind me, coming to make my Manor fit for a king.

I took the large front bedroom which had belonged to my grandmother, Lady Olivia, further annoying Mrs. Long by my insistence that the bed curtains should be changed, fires lighted daily not only in my bedroom but in several others so that they would be well aired and cozy in case of guests. While I required the ground floor at all times to be warm and bright, a great pile of logs glowing and crackling in the hall, lamps left burning in all the passages—upstairs and down—to dispel the gloom, great bowls full to the brim with pot pourri to take off the odor of damp.

And since I *was* in residence and had always disliked doing anything by half, I had my breakfast brought to my room on a tray with my correspondence—mostly letters of complaint from Luc at Hexingham, and a few stray bills of my mother's—took my luncheon in the small dining parlor, five o'clock tea in the drawing room, dined in the hall beneath the window, alone or with Amyas, drank brandy by the library fire afterwards and then retired to the newly swept and dusted Justice's Room where Amyas would attend me, reporting to me as accurately as to the Squire the business of the day.

"If you would care to look at these estimates, Olivia—the matter of the fencing at Clarrow Cross—the drainage problem at Pasture Cottages . . ."

I barely understood what I heard. He knew that. But he had loved my grandfather. So—damn him—had I. And it eased us both to continue the ritual until the return of Max de Haan should bring it to a final close.

There were no servants left in the house now except Mrs. Long, Mrs. Timmins, our talkative, indifferent cook, and a trio of maids, their wages all paid to the end of the year. The Home Farm was staffed and functioning at a minimum, the farm at Clarrow Bottom—the best we had—stood empty, while the tenants of the other farms waited, as I did, for Max.

His card was brought in to me ten days after the funeral, pure white and very glossy, printed only with his name in bold italic letters in the manner of men who have no permanent address; an expression of sympathy and a convenient way of letting me know he was back in the district, to which I replied by sending a note to the Station Hotel inviting him to dinner.

The way had always been clear. As Emil Junot had often told me, there is always an alternative if one has the wit, the stomach, the determination to take it. I had simply wished to make quite certain that no other solution would be likely to cross either my path or my mind. I went down to the Gatehouse garden, stripped bare by winter, and stood for a while in a biting wind, taking shelter by the bare wall which would be covered, next year, with clematis and honeysuckle.

Next year. Last year. I forced myself to think in both directions, to go back for a final time to the past fragrances and laughter of this garden, to acknowledge its present emptiness, and then to leave it, letting the wind take the gate and slam it shut behind me. I did not think I would come here again.

I walked back to the Manor, went straight upstairs to the attic and emerged an hour later, dust and straw on my skirt, cobwebs in my hair, grimy treasures in decaying, acrid-smelling wrappings in my arms, my course of action finally decided. My plans laid.

"Mrs. Long—a word in your ear if you please—and in yours too Mrs. Timmins. I am giving a dinner-party tonight."

I had them decorate the hall for a gala occasion, cyclamen and fuchsia, vast arrangements of ferns and dried winter grasses standing everywhere in gleaming copper bowls, candlelight and firelight turning the panes of the great window to jewels. The long table set for two places only but with as many of the family heirlooms as I had retrieved from the treasure house above stairs; a standing salt of rock crystal and silver-gilt with large silver herons perched on its lid; a silver-gilt wine service of two jugs made like Greek urns with fluted handles, and goblets carved with what appeared to be a group of sadly lascivious nymphs and shepherds; silver filigree spice boxes; a tremendously ornate table candelabrum of silver leaves and branches garlanded with crystal. I had spent all morning cleaning these marvels myself, using the tops of old cotton stockings for polishing rags as Victorine had taught me, gloating—there was no other word for it—as the precious metal came alive beneath my hands. And then, going foraging once again in those tantalizing chests and boxes to which I, and I alone, now held the keys, I uncovered a precious hoard of glass packed away fifty or more years ago by some careful housekeeper and forgotten; frail-stemmed goblets enameled with white flowers or engraved with a fine cobweb tracery, claret jugs of clear crystal flashed with ruby, opaline jugs and beakers delicate as eggshell, in pale misty mauves and blues and lilacs. I carried them to the kitchen myself, blew the dust lovingly from each one, washed them, rubbed them with lemon juice, washed them again, ecstatic as a child on a birthday morning, as I discovered in each one its buried sparkle.

"You'll be finding a skeleton up there next," said Mrs. Timmins sourly, disliking the confusion I was creating in the kitchen almost as much as the menu I had asked her to prepare. Not crayfish in Chablis, of course, which was decidedly not in her repertoire, but a more interesting sauce than usual on her beef and something to perk up the blandness of her eternal green vegetables. Wine. That was not in her province she was happy to say. Mr. Amyas Hird would see to that. But Amyas had gone to York for the day and I was forced to rely on Mrs. Long's selection of clarets and brandy. But by eight o'clock that evening the hall, at least, looked just as I had always imagined it and I—the mistress of the house, the lady of the Manor—was waiting, wearing a gown of black lace molded very tight around a waist that was still only nineteen inches, cut very low on a bosom that was exactly twenty inches more, the bodice slipping from my shoulders in the way of my mother's evening dresses, a necklace of seed pearls and garnets, discovered upstairs in a bureau drawer, worn high around my neck, the bracelet Max had given me as a wedding-present clasped around a bare arm. I had done my hair in a tail of Empire curls, rouged my lips just a little and painted a faint blue line along my eyelids. I was ready. I may not succeed in my undertaking but, if not, then I would fail in style. And if I had to leave this house, then every single one of the forgotten treasures in those boxes upstairs would go with me. But I did not intend to leave. For I had come to the conclusion during those long evening hours sitting alone in the Justice's Room in the twilight, that it would be far safer to invest my love and loyalty in the Manor, which could be rescued from decay by the practical medicine of money than in frail and often fickle humanity, which decayed all too fast.

I heard the, to me, still unpleasant sound of Max's motor car, saw the swirl of his long black fur coat as he tossed it at Mrs. Long, felt the satisfaction in him, the alert pleasure of the hunter, the gambler, the adversary, as he came into the hall, immaculate, expensive, a gardenia in his buttonhole, entering the Manor of Clarrow Fell for the first time in over twenty years.

"Max—how nice."

"Yes, I believe it is—truly delightful." But his attention in those first moments was for the house, his eyes rapidly checking and assessing everything from the heraldic emblems on the window to the portraits on the walls, the heavy oak chests and sideboards whose scars and stains I had covered with my bowls of flowers, the glory of my table, the shower of sparks released suddenly as a smoldering log burst into flame in the hearth.

"Well, Max? Is it to your liking now that you see it again after so long?"

And I wondered what I would do, which way I would turn, if it proved to be less than he remembered it, a boy's dream which now, when it was at last attainable, did not suit the man? What a disaster! Yes, but I had rather more than a nodding acquaintance with disaster and if it happened, I would have to look elsewhere, scheme another scheme, make haste to devise another plan.

But, although he had come to buy and, therefore, could not afford to let his enthusiasm show, I recognized his will to possess, saw that his keen cool eyes, still flickering everywhere, were not so much questioning the availability but considering the price.

"It is a sad ruin, of course, Olivia, in an even worse condition than I had supposed. I am glad to see you have managed to make yourself a warm corner."

I smiled, very bright and terribly innocent.

"But I am very comfortable here, Max. Felix Potterton was quite surprised, I think, to see just *how* comfortable. In fact he seemed quite impressed."

"Felix Potterton?" And although his voice—since he was so excellent a card player—had not sharpened a single note, his expression of polite interest never wavered, he had played into my hands just a little by asking the question at all.

"Yes. He rode over the other day to have a look around. I couldn't think why, since I am barely acquainted with him. But then it struck me that if he wins the election he will need somewhere in the constituency to live—won't he?"

Felix Potterton, of course, had not been within ten miles of the Manor that I knew of, but Max could not be sure of that. And if Felix did succeed in becoming the Honorable Member for Bradeswick with Clarrow Fell, then, although it was not likely it was not absolutely *impossible* that he might make me an offer for the Manor.

"Really," said Max. He did not think it likely either, but just the same . . .

We drank sherry in the library until Mrs. Long, in her best black silk, came to tell us that dinner was served and then, when we had taken our places at my wonderful table, proceeded to serve it, smoothly, a shade scornfully, just possibly wishing that it might choke us to death. The beef was overcooked, the *Chasseur* sauce too thin, the vegetables tedious, the conversation easy and of no consequence, the wine excellent. I talked about Paris, the possibility that next season's hats would be larger than ever, my mother. He talked about the forlorn, forsaken island of Lanzarote scorched by the hot wind which blew over from Africa sixty-four miles away and where he might just possibly engage in a venture to grow vines out of soil which amounted to little more than volcanic ash. He talked of osprey feathers, the annual pigeon shoot at Monte Carlo, his last year's visit to Singapore when a tiger had been shot under the billiard table at Raffles Hotel, my mother. We agreed that although Mr. Greenlaw would be more comfortable with the lady his family had chosen for him in Bournemouth, he would die happier in the arms of his Lavinia. We even talked of Aunt Sibylla. Not of Alys. He remarked that the silver-gilt salt which I had correctly placed at the center of the table was very old and probably worth a fortune. I agreed that he was probably right and made no mention of where it had come from, sticking with great determination to my resolution that whatever the eventual outcome, the contents of the attic would be mine. We remained in the hall for our coffee and brandy and, when Mrs. Long had left us, Max rose to his feet and stood for a moment quite still, allowing the house to see him, I think, and feel him, the alien child who had been brought here against his will returning now as a man of substance and sophistication, to make himself—if it suited him—its master. And then, with a smile of complete satisfaction, he raised his glass not to me—not yet—but to the portraits on the walls, giving every dark-complexioned, heavy-lidded Heron squire and every squire's lady a separate and wholly cynical salutation.

"Your health, sir. I believe you did not expect to see me here again."

They had not expected to see me either.

"They are all dead, Max. They can't hear you."

"I can hear me. *That* is what matters."

"Which one is your father? Nobody ever told me."

"My dear—the handsome one, of course. That one next to the Squire as a young man. He was a fool, my handsome father. He played the games I play and lost—like your friend Junot—which gives me every right to despise him. He was not efficient, my father. Take his courtship of my mother. He got her to marry him by persuading her he was a rich "milord," which is fair enough. But what he didn't trouble to do was check her story first. *She* had convinced him that her father was a Spanish merchant prince instead of the bankrupt old roué he turned out to be, with a crumbling slagheap of a castle near Seville in an even worse condition than this. You'd like Seville, by the way, Olivia. So—they woke up on their wedding morning, my mother and father, to discover that neither one of them could pay the hotel bill. Very careless. And the gentleman over there to the left is your father, by the way—did you know that?"

"Oh—I am so glad, since *he* is really the handsome one. I wanted my mother to come and explain them but she says that until she can bring herself to believe that the Squire is really dead, she would rather not. Is that really the Squire as a young man? I believe he looks like Amyas."

"Possibly. But you'd be wrong to draw the obvious conclusion."

"You know about Amyas then?"

He nodded.

"Will you tell me?"

"My dear—you should know that a Hexingham gentleman could never divulge . . ."

"All right, you won't tell me. Then what are you offering for my house and my land?"

"Are you ready to sell?"

"Until I have an offer who can say?"

"I can. What game is it, Olivia? Are you trying to force up the price or is it something else?"

"Oh—I think we can safely say it is a matter of money."

"Good. You are looking very well tonight, you know."

I knew.

I had drawn my chair up to the hearth and he came to stand beside me, one polished pointed shoe tapping against the fender as he lit a cigar and threw his match into the fire.

"Shall we begin again, Max? What are you offering for my house and my land?"

"Nothing for your land. My interest is solely with the house, the woods at Clarrow Bottom and the moor."

"And what do you suggest I do with the farms and the cottages?"

"My dear—whatever takes your fancy. Get rid of them as fast as you can, I'd say, before they start costing you money in repairs."

"You don't really want to be the new Squire, then —the feudal lord?"

"Absolutely not. I have not the least intention of burdening myself with the duties of a landlord and a patriarch and a father confessor. I will tell you what I want, Olivia—a life of pleasure and privilege while I still can."

"You mean before your money runs out?" I fired at him anxiously, needing to be absolutely sure about it.

He laughed and shook his head. "I am truly sorry to disappoint you, my pet, but I mean nothing of the kind. I mean, very simply, that I intend to take my pleasures while the pleasures themselves endure, not my ability to pay for them. I will tell you what it is, Olivia—I have the great good fortune of living in an atmosphere, an era if you like, which suits me perfectly. It was not always so. It may not remain so forever. If that self-indulgent old reprobate of a king of ours had resembled his sainted father, or his mother for that matter, it would not be so today. This atmosphere he creates of ease and plenty and good weather is exactly the one in which a man like me can flourish. But one must constantly bear in mind how easily it could change. Edward is not young. One hears that his son is a narrower man, closer in temperament to his grandfather, Albert the Good, than our wicked old Teddy. And if there should be a depression, or a religious revival, or a war, then these very pleasant times would definitely be over. So I must enjoy them while I may, my dear Olivia, do you not agree with that? And since I have a fancy for a sporting estate, I will begin by offering you a reasonable price for yours, the best you will get—in fact the only one you will get, I imagine—since both the woods and the moor need re-stocking with game and the house in its present condition, is not worth much. Fortunately for you I can afford to be sentimental."

"Max—my house is beautiful."

And so, in the flickering firelight, surrounded by my treasures of crystal and silver, was I.

"Olivia—your house is falling down."

"But you want it, Max. I know you do."

"Yes—at a price."

"You want to restore it and bring it to life. You want to own it because it once rejected you."

"Do I indeed?" he said, his eyes narrowing keenly, the con-

299

centrated alertness in his face—the expression of a card player watching the cards, working out his own next move and mine—telling me that he understood we were no longer talking solely of the house.

"Indeed you do. You want to be Master of Foxhounds instead of Georgie Potterton and have the hunt meet here instead of Dawney Park. You want to give shooting parties and murder your hundred grouse a day with a hundred shots like your father. You want to keep the best cellar and the best table in the County. You want to live graciously and easily like a butterfly until the winter sets in . . ."

"How very profound and how very poetic. But not a butterfly, Olivia—and not a grasshopper either. A hawk—how about that? Curling high and bringing down all these sparrows and perhaps one very pretty bird of paradise."

"You *do* have the money, don't you Max? I mean a lot of it—all the time?"

"Yes, Olivia. A great deal of it. Don't fear to wake up one morning and find it gone."

"I am not going to sell the Manor, you know."

"I do know. You are going to ask me to marry you, I rather think."

And, my nerve faltering just a little, I heard my voice declare, sounding indignant, "Well, you said yourself it would be the natural solution. I have the house, you have the money. That's what you said . . ."

It had, of course, occurred to me that he would turn me down. I had even worked out a scheme by which, at the slightest hint of a rebuff, I would turn it into a huge joke. "Good heavens, Max, you can't possibly have taken me seriously. How very entertaining." But watching him now, his face carefully without expression, deliberately giving me no clue, I felt a desperate unease, a suspicion that I might burn with the remembered embarrassment of this moment for the rest of my life. Max, if he felt so inclined, would see to that.

Slowly he lit a cigar, the Spaniard very evident in him as the firelight put shadows into his face, darkening his eyes and his skin; his silence so prolonged that, my nerve snapping altogether now, had to break it.

"Well, it was your idea in the first place, you know—not mine. I would never have thought of it. You did say you wanted me—didn't you?"

"Yes—some time ago. And if it turns out that I've changed my mind what will you do? Go and offer yourself to Felix Potterton?"

I picked up my brandy glass to throw at him but he caught my wrist, his hand moving so fast I did not even see it coming, the brandy spilling over my bare arm and the sleeve of his jacket, the glass shattering on the stone flag.

"My glass . . ." I muttered, trying to pull away, remembering how lovingly I had washed it this morning, how carefully I had held it up to the light, had almost given it a name.

"My sleeve—" he said, holding me fast and kissed me very hard, a display of superior male strength rather than passion, taking my breath and my dignity away, crushing me.

"Yes, Olivia. I'll marry you."

I could think of nothing to say.

I could only recall how different, how utterly different from before. Yet with Robin too the intent and the will had been mine. I had deliberately created a situation in which he—a Hexingham gentleman—had been bound to propose. But there could be no fear that *this* Hexingham gentleman would ever be dazzled or overwhelmed by me, that desire for me might blind him to the true purposes of his life and imprison him. No fear of that. He wanted my house and my body. I wanted my house, his money and was by no means repelled by his body. It was straightforward enough. I understood it. I could do very well with it.

"Yes—and I believe I'll take a little something in advance, if I may, Olivia," he said, his hands on my shoulders, the tips of his fingers sliding between my skin and the froth of black lace to my breasts.

I understood that too.

We went upstairs together, sealing a bargain, to the large, well-aired bedroom which had been my grandmother's, and when I had undressed, slowly at his direction, he made love to me very thoroughly and comprehensively, taking possession, moving the lamp nearer to the bedside to check that my body was as he had imagined it, that my waist's minute circle was a real one, not the fierce restriction of a corset, that my hips and breasts did curve naturally and softly away from it, smooth and firm and exactly—it seemed—in the way which suited him.

"Very nice, Olivia—*very* nice—just dip that breast into the lamplight, my darling—*there*—exquisite."

And he brought me to a thundering climax, uncomplicated by any of love's nagging little anxieties—does he really love me? Will he love me tomorrow? Does he love me as I love him?—which might have detracted from the quivering, growing, expanding threads of physical pleasure and their glorious explosion.

"Very nice, Olivia."

"Do you know," he said a little later, easy and smiling, now that he had arranged matters entirely to his satisfaction, "your breasts once preyed on my mind for a whole summer. You were playing croquet, or trying to, and one or two eager young men were showing you how to handle your mallet with positive hunger and thirst written all over them at the sight of those breasts."

"Well—why didn't you show me how to handle my mallet? I suppose you must know the way?"

"I know better than to compete with the young and hungry in public." And once again he took complete possession of my breasts, and then of the whole body which had responded with healthy, impulsive, mindless sensuality to his stroking hands and caressing lips, the hard brown length of his own body entering, lingering, entering, totally *enjoying*, wholly intent on the refinement and prolongation of his pleasure and—since refinement demanded it—of mine.

I got up soon afterwards, indicating that I would like him to leave before the presence of his motor car outside my door at this late hour should come to the notice of my aunt, or his own presence in my bed to the attention of Mrs. Long. And as I glanced out of the window the lights of the vicarage, in the far distance, gave me a sudden, uneasy pang.

Open the cage and fly away. My grandfather had given her the money to do it, yet so far she had still not taken flight. Could Max de Haan be the reason? Had the threads of our lives twisted and tangled yet again?

Naturally I ought not to ask. But knowing what I ought to do had rarely stopped me from doing what I pleased, and lightly, airily, as if it really could not matter less, I trilled out "Do you know, Max, I thought at one stage that you were going to marry Alys."

And the answer came in a low, wicked chuckle from the comfortable depths of my grandmother's bed.

"My dear, so did I—at one stage."

"What changed your mind?"

"She did, my pet. I asked her—oh, not so very long ago—and she turned me down."

302

EIGHTEEN

We were married a few days before Christmas, quietly if one judged by the number of guests, luxuriously if one counted the cost of the diamond solitaire and the long pale furs he gave me. I had gone to church on my first wedding-day in a blaze of happiness which had lifted me far and foolishly above the heads of ordinary humanity. On this second occasion I was so far removed from bliss that, as I stood in the church porch waiting for the organ to strike up the bridal hymn, it would not have astonished me had some officer of the law appeared to inform me that Max was to be arrested for fraud or debt; or some woman claiming that he was her husband and, therefore, could not be mine.

But I could detect no bailiffs closing in across the wintry fields, could hear no horses clattering up the frozen cobbles of the village street, and so I entered the church on the arm of my brother, Luc, seeing no one but my mother and Madelon who were very pleased with me, Victorine who was not: and Alys. The ceremony was conducted by my uncle in his usual absent fashion, his mind on his seabirds and his butterflies, while Aunt Sibylla had used the excuse of a slight head cold to absent herself altogether. She had had high hopes of Max for Alys and now that I appeared to have thwarted her once again, she quite simply could not bear to watch. And it was not until later that I realized Amyas had been absent too.

We drank champagne in the hall, distributed Christmas presents of satisfying value to my family and, climbing into the Mercedes, set off to spend the winter in Madeira, the destination for which Max had been heading when the Squire's death had called him home.

My new husband had left behind him a battalion of tradesmen who, in our absence, were to undertake a vast and detailed program of repairs and renewals, the installation of bathrooms and new kitchen equipment, the extending and improvement of the stables and the construction—well concealed, I had insisted—of a garage block. While I—and I had no idea whether Max knew about this or not—had given just one order of my own; that every box and chest and canvas bag from Clarrow attic should be removed to the Gatehouse so that, on my return, I might have the leisure and the privacy to assess their worth. For if there should be some treasure of antiquity among them, then I intended—simply and cooly—to conceal it from Max, holding it as security against the day when his creditors, his enemies, his own flawed judgment, his extravagance—*something*—might bring him down.

We stayed a few days in London spending money, an occupation I found most congenial when it concerned Doucet gowns in supple fabrics and pastel colors, strands of pearls and strands of gold, a negligee with an ermine trim, another diamond; and then set sail for the port of Funchal, a favorite landfall, I knew for British officers and merchant adventurers on their way to Africa.

The voyage out—the first and therefore the most exciting of my life—began with heavy seas, an intense cold, a thin film of ice covering the decks as we moved through the gray waters of the Channel. The ship was larger and far more luxurious than I had imagined, the dark mahogany and red plush interiors of a grand hotel concealed beneath the functional lines of a seasoned, ocean-going vessel. There was cut crystal, violin music, *tournedos* flamed in brandy in the dining-salon; the comfort of deep crimson carpets and leather armchairs in lounges where soft-spoken Portuguese stewards served hot *bouillon* at mid-morning from silver trays. There was a library, a card-room, a roulette wheel, a smoking-room for gentlemen, a small *salon* for ladies only where one could gossip and drink tea as in an English parlor.

I walked on deck in my long, pale furs or sat, shielded from the wind, on a *chaise-longue* with a blanket around my knees sipping brandy against the chill and chatting to the English majors and colonels on their way to rejoin their regiments in various parts of Africa, gentlemen of the Colonial Service back from leave, impressive, large-bosomed dowagers taking daughters or nieces out to the Colonies to find them husbands; one or two elegant, beautifully preserved women traveling alone who glanced speculatively at Max until I put my ungloved hand on his arm, not to show them my diamonds which would have made him even more inviting, but my wedding ring.

I had heard of sea-sickness, of course, and quite naturally did not intend to be troubled by it. But the treacherous winds and currents of the Bay of Biscay, which Max had crossed so many times that he had quite lost count, took me entirely by surprise. I spent a day and a night in my stateroom—the best on board, I assumed, since Max had booked it—lying flat on my back unable to move while the ship groaned and shuddered and was tossed like a cork from one mountainous wave to another.

"One expects this kind of thing at this time of year," said Max, casually dismissing my insistence that both I and the ship were about to break asunder.

I had not expected it.

"If you had told me, then I might not have come."

"Of course you would." He was quite right, and leaving me to the deferential care of the steward he went off to the card-room and won the price of our passage several times over.

But with Cape Finisterre behind us the days began to lengthen and to lighten, the sky to become more luminous, far more reluctant to mellow into evening, the wind in our faces softer, bringing us our first taste of the South. Just beyond the horizon there was sunshine. I could feel it.

There was a day when I stood poised between two seasons, summer in front of me, winter at my back and then, imperceptibly, the division was over, there were porpoises playing around our bows, leaping and splashing in blue water, and a few hours beyond them, the island of Madeira looking dark and volcanic at first in the far distance, and then an enchantment of high, black cliffs and rich green hillsides as we slid into the harbor of Funchal. I supervised the disposal of my hat-boxes and my cabin trunks, said goodbye to the colonels and their ladies who still had a long way to travel, wished the young husband-hunters good luck and stepped ashore, on the arm of the man I still could not really think of as a husband, into a fragrant, permanent July.

There were women in wide peasant skirts and aprons waiting on the quayside with baskets of orchids and mimosa and white Madonna lilies. As we drove through the steep, red-roofed town, I saw tall, scarlet poinsettias growing wild at street corners, golden and red

305

hibiscus in profusion, hedges of blue hydrangea lining the roadside while every garden we passed had its delicate pink and white oleander, its lily-of-the-valley tree, its camellia, every wall its flamboyant covering of bougainvillaea or Cape Jasmine, every open courtyard shaded by a trellis of vines.

Max's house, which lay in a narrow street behind the small, brown and white cathedral, had a tiled courtyard with a fountain surrounded by geraniums in stone pots. The interior was cool and dim, shuttered windows, polished brown tiles underfoot, white walls adorned with jeweled dark-skinned Madonnas in gold frames, orchids of every exotic color and variety arranged in bowls of antique ruby glass. The furniture was heavily varnished and richly inlaid, the atmosphere hushed, in need of air; an enclosed world where my new mother-in-law, Mrs. Rosella de Haan, appeared to spend her time very much as my own mother did, playing endless games of whist and serving sweet Madeira wine, instead of Bradeswick's favorite China tea, to friends.

She was small and thin and sallow, spoke Spanish or Dutch or Portuguese to Max, wore a great many rings, and had no interest in me whatsoever. Ten minutes of her company, I at once concluded, would be an excess but fortunately her interest in Max himself extended no further than the presents he gave her, his company and presumably his affection being so irrelevant to her that she made not the slightest claim on either.

She had no room ready for us. It had not occurred to her that we might wish to stay in the house. It had not occurred to Max either and therefore to my great relief we were able to spend two months in the opulence of Reids Hotel, perched on its blue-green cliffside above the harbor, its gardens sweeping down towards Funchal like a tapestry woven with exotic, intensely colored blooms and polished tropical foliage, its terraces offering me a dazzling expanse of blue air and dancing blue water, the constant excitement of ocean liners sliding majestically below me into their moorings.

We drove out together through plantations of squat banana trees and sugar-cane. I wandered alone through the streets of Funchal on the many occasions when Max, who had his business to attend to, would simply toss me his wallet and tell me to indulge myself, riding home with my parcels in the curtained ox-sledges, at which my fastidious mother-in-law turned up her nose, declaring the patient, plodding animals would give me fleas. I spent my mornings in bed or taking the sun, my afternoons gorging my appetite on embroidered linens and fine fringed shawls for my mother and sisters, trinkets, bric-a-brac, or just simply giving money away to children with eyes like black velvet who handed me flowers in the streets. And every evening I bathed and perfumed my skin, dressed my hair very high, put on a low-cut gown—mindful of my husband's partiality for my breasts—and with my own diamond sparkling on my hand, diamonds in my ears—new ones, these, which Max had one day casually tossed into my lap—I dined luxuriously and very late with Max and whatever courteous, olive-skinned, supple gentleman he might bring back with him.

It was a time of sensuous ease and pleasure to which I surrendered completely, an interlude composed entirely of bodily enjoyments which muffled my sources of reason, guilt, judgment, like swathes of soft satin. I drank wine in quantities which amazed me, made love with a variety and an abandon I had never imagined, sinking afterwards into hours of silent sleep from which I awoke hungry and thirsty and easily aroused to sensuality. It was the life of the harem, the courtesan; my body always warm, always in a state of being caressed or waiting for caresses, orgasm always hovering in my mind or in the pit of my stomach ready to start, my limbs growing supple and languid, boneless almost in these leisurely, slow-building, exquisite processes that were Max's skillful, almost professional approach to love.

"How clever you are, Max."

"And how wanton you are, my pet—although I rather suspected it."

"You made sure of it, you mean."

"Of course. I had no intention of tying myself to a cold woman."

"We *are* tied together then—are we? Legally, I mean." It was not entirely a pleasantry and, lighting a cigar, he leaned back on the lace pillows and smiled, looking very Spanish again in the dim light.

"Are you by any chance suggesting that I might have another wife somewhere?"

"No, of course not. Have you?"

He chuckled, a decidedly wicked sound.

"No, Olivia. No wife. No *legal* entanglements of any kind except a self-centered mother and you."

"And the illegal ones?"

"Do you care?"

"Well—it is none of my business, I suppose."

"None whatsoever."

"Quite. So I will not ask—except that my mother once said that in Corfu you . . . ?"

"Don't listen to her, Olivia. She knows nothing about me."

"Neither do I." And my voice held an unmistakable note of indignation.

"Then learn to know me as I am now. Enjoy the life I can give you. Spend my money. Indulge yourself."

"And don't ask questions?"

"That's right."

"Very well. I won't. Max . . . ?"

"Yes, my pet."

"What *is* that scar down your back?"

He sighed. "What would you imagine?"

"A knife wound I rather thought."

And in spite of myself I was—certainly not impressed—but interested, for not even Emil Junot had actually been stabbed in the back that I knew of.

"Yes, Olivia. Quite correct. But that's the small one higher up. The one which so intrigues you is a whiplash."

"*Max!* I don't believe it."

"*Olivia!* I remember the occasion well and I do assure you."

"But how?"

"In prison."

"Where?"

"In Pretoria."

"Why?"

"You will have heard of Jameson's Raid?"

"Of course I have. But that was a political matter. They don't whip political prisoners—surely?"

"Not for supporting the raid. For objecting to the man who stabbed me in the back—when I'd recovered sufficiently, that is, to make my objections felt."

"Why did he attack you in the first place?"

"There was a woman I was fond of. He expressed certain views about her color. I expressed views of my own about his character."

"Oh yes—I see. What did you do to him afterwards?"

308

"Olivia—my dear Olivia—whatever it was I am unlikely to do it again. If that disappoints you then I must beg your pardon, since I know how attractive violence can be to women."

"Not to me—not at all."

"Ah—you are a little turtle dove are you?"

"I don't want to hurt—or to be hurt either." And although I had not intended it, I had released a cry from the heart.

"Olivia—I shall not hurt you, you know."

I knew; for unkindness could not be to his advantage, nor to mine either. And since deep wounds can only be inflicted by those we love and trust and truly cherish, Max and I were safe from each other.

"I am not interested in pain, Olivia—only in pleasure. You ought to know that and be glad I can tell the difference. There are a great many Hexingham gentlemen who like nothing better from a woman than a good thrashing, you know. Yes, of course you know, since the French call it the English vice—well don't they? Just be thankful my vice is luxury. And if you would care to get up now and walk over to the table—there, in that path of moonlight, arching your back for me—and bring back what you find there . . ."

I went, having already seen the jewelry case, and came back slowly, walking as I imagined a harem dancer might walk, since I had never seen one, an oriental collar of rubies and pearls in my hands, heavy and pagan and magnificently attuned to the slumberous, sensuous atmosphere this island had created.

"I see that luxury excites you too, my darling. I am so glad."

"Yes." Why not? I would have gone barefoot—once—and thought myself happy and privileged, to make the sacrifice. But now, since my nature craved excess in one direction or another, and neither love nor sacrifice in this hazy, harem world could possibly apply, I might just as well devote myself to luxury. And if these stones proved real—and I would find a jeweler in Leeds to tell me that—then they would be a useful addition to my squirrel hoard of treasure, concealed in the Gatehouse. My insurance against that inevitable stormy day when *someone*—if only myself—would find Max out.

"Put it on," he said, but the jewels and the precious metals cobwebbing them together were so pleasing to my skin that I let them slide between my breasts, trailed their precious coolness along both arms and then both legs, clasped them around my ankles, decorated

309

my waist, arched and coiled myself this way and that until I had bathed my whole body in the luxuriance of rubies, the wantonness of satin sheets and perfumed lamplight.

"*Very* nice, Olivia."

"Yes, Max—they're beautiful—thank you."

"I didn't mean the rubies. But yes, they are beautiful. And they're *reliable*. They'll never stab you in the back or run off and leave you for another woman. They'll be there when you want them, absolutely in your control. They don't feel the cold. They're not subject to disease. They don't wither. They don't cost you a penny to feed. And they hold their price. If the worst comes to the worst you can sell them and they won't even give you a reproachful glance for doing it, like a horse or a dog. They won't care."

"Yes, Max." I had thought of all this already, for myself.

But the lazy, mindless life of the seraglio could not last forever and at the beginning of March we set sail for home, Max with the purchase of horses and guns, roof-tiles, bathrooms, fixtures and fittings on his mind; while I was anxious to begin the task of marrying my youngest sister to the Naseby millions.

I was by no means unhappy. I had married money and money—at the moment—was in ample supply. I was by no means happy either. But I recognized happiness now for what it was, a most unstable emotion, whose lack did not greatly concern me. If I had known happiness once it had been very briefly, my first wedding-day and a few ecstatic moments thereafter. And where had that led me? Better by far, I decided, to pitch myself at this lower—infinitely safer—emotional key.

I came home as the undisputed mistress of Clarrow Fell, wearing my long pale furs and a French hat like a gray velvet cartwheel decorated with gray satin roses, to find—as Max had fully expected but I had not—the very latest system of central heating already in operation, the hot-water pipes concealed by decorative grilles, the gloom and the mystery of the corridors and back passages banished forever by the steady but unromantic miracle of electric light. To the left of the hall, opposite the Justice's Room, a pair of decaying and decidedly sinister store-rooms had been knocked together and were in the process of conversion to a billiard room; electric lights here too, hanging low over the green baize-covered table, black leather armchairs grouped companionably around a carved stone fireplace Max had purchased

310

from a derelict castle, boxes of cigars and decanters of brandy readily to hand, portraits of heavy-eyed, slumberous nudes on green velvet walls, an air of tasteful, well-bred wickedness.

The same corridor led on to the gun-room, a simple storeplace for weaponry no longer, but an additional smoking-room, the guns displayed behind glass; leather armchairs and leather-covered wine tables once again circling a cheerful fire, an outer door with a wrought-iron boot scraper strategically placed on its step, giving direct access to the stable-yard, the new tack-room and harness-room and the row of new loose boxes not yet compelted.

The staircase, opposite the billiard-room door, had been widened to give easier ascent to the medieval tower where the bedrooms which had once belonged to Guy and Robin, to a younger Amyas and to Max himself, had been done up to suit the accommodation of visiting bachelors. An arrangement which enabled them to stagger upstairs from their cigar-smoking and brandy-drinking sessions, their eyes glazed, no doubt, from staring at all those pink, painted nudes and fall into bed without inconveniencing anyone else.

The main upstairs corridor was now brilliantly illuminated by electric Swan lamps in wall brackets festooned with crystal, my bedroom redecorated like a bridal posy in peach silk and white lace, the dressing-room which separated me from Max having become a bathroom with a blue and green tiled floor, mosaics of mermaids and exotic fish on the walls, a giant bathtub encased in dark mahogany with heavy gold fittings. I had a Chinese carpet of peach blossoms and pastel-tinted clouds on my floor. Max had the handsome dark reds and browns of Persia. My bed curtains, drawn up into a gleaming brass crown, were of the finest, lightest silk, exquisitely draped and tied back with lace ribbon. In his room—which had been my grandfather's—Max had removed the dull, earthmold-colored tapestries and replaced them with crimson velvet, thrown a black bearskin across his bed, another in front of the black-veined marble hearth, decked his walls with the spears and shields and tribal masks of African warriors, his cabinets with spectacular pieces of carved ivory and Chinese jade: so much barbaric splendor being necessary, perhaps, to conceal the memory of the Squire.

The downstairs rooms, at my request, had been *almost* left alone. The chandeliers in the dining room and drawing room still had their flickering candles setting the crystal rippling and dancing as those perfectly steady Swan bulbs could never do. But the gas brackets had all been taken away—Max disliking their odor and the yellowish tinge they imparted to a woman's skin—and electricity was there too, whenever it should be needed, discreetly concealed behind heavy shades which would soften it, they told me, although I was still not certain that I wished to see my dinner guests quite so clearly.

The Regency chairs, upholstered in that same earthmold color so beloved of my ancestors, were—after a sharp argument and a little shrewd bargaining between Max and myself—to be re-covered in pale green watered silk. Pale Chinese carpets, in exquisite shades of apple green and pink, their texture like velvet, which Max had shown me on our way through London, stacked high in a dock-side warehouse which appeared to belong to him, were to cover the highly polished, eighteenth-century floor. Chinese lacquer cabinets and a great deal of porcelain were to be sent up from London for my inspection on the understanding that should I be less than enthusiastic Max would send it all back again.

The dining room remained English oak and pewter and brass. The Justice's Room I would allow only to be cleaned and polished. The hall, which had been extremely bare with only that long refectory table beneath the great window, would acquire—little by little—armchairs and sofas, fur rugs thrown here and there on the stone flags, a grand piano covered by an antique shawl, a map table for the setting out of newspapers and sporting magazines, a heavy oak writing desk for the use of the guests I would clearly be expected to entertain.

I went outside, my first morning home, having successfully ignored the additional height of the water tower and the apparatus which appeared to be manufacturing our electricity, to discover a garage block under construction behind the new stables with rooms above it to accommodate a chauffeur, an arrangement not much to the liking of Mrs. Long who appeared alarmed at the effect this new male presence and the highly exciting nature of his occupation might have on the diligence and possibly the moral fiber of her laundry maids.

"They are obliged to cross the yard, Mrs. de Haan, to hang out the linen and there has been trouble enough in the past with the grooms. If there is to be a chauffeur, and a mechanic, and presumably a boy, then it would be helpful to know to whom they are answerable. Inside staff, house-maids, parlormaids, footmen and the like, tend to know their place and to keep it. Stable staff and garden staff are considerably harder to control since they have far more opportunity to misbehave—as do laundry-maids who are sometimes inside and sometimes out. Therefore, Madam, it becomes necessary to know whether this new department is to be classed with stables and kennels and coachhouse and placed under the general jurisdiction of the butler? Naturally there is to be a new butler . . . ?"

"Oh—naturally."

"And I would be most grateful, Mrs. de Haan, if you would have a word with Mrs. Timmins. Her kitchen is being torn to pieces before her eyes, and strictly between ourselves, madam, I am of the opinion that she has not the least idea how to operate these new stoves, much less prepare the dishes madam is likely to require."

Mrs. de Haan. I was not accustomed to it yet. Not here, at any rate. And closing my mind swiftly, as I had taught myself to do, against useless guilts, unprofitable sorrows, I nodded quite cooly to Mrs. Long and went off to discuss the problem of Mrs. Timmins with Max.

"Pension her off," was his solution. "The sooner the better. I have a chef coming up to see me from London next Tuesday and if he's suitable he can get to work straightaway. By the look of that old harpy I'd judge her capable of putting arsenic in his tea—or mine—so get rid of her."

"Max—she's been here forever."

"All the more reason to pension her off. There must be an empty cottage somewhere?"

"I daresay. Well, Amyas can see to it."

"I suppose he might. But I wouldn't rely too much on Amyas in the future, darling."

"Why ever not?" I was shocked, quite scandalized, having fallen into the general Clarrow habit of assuming that Amyas would see to everything. And if there should be any suggestion of replacing *him* I would not hear of it.

"Because—my pet—Amyas will not work for me. I am quite certain."

Instantly I bristled, angry and offended as a cat, determined to make my position very clear.

"Max, this house belongs to me."

'So it does."

"Amyas is in *my* employment."

"Yes, my pet, so he is. But he knows as well as you—as well as I—just who pays his wages. He will not take them."

"Will you tell me why?"

"No. He may tell you himself, should he wish you to know—when he comes to give you his notice."

"Max, have you never heard that a husband should have no secrets from his wife?"

"Olivia—*really*." He took my hand and kissed it, laughing. "I have heard that a wife should have no secrets from her husband. But I know of no society anywhere in the world which imposes such limitations upon its gentlemen. Do you—my pet?"

No, I did not. Nor did I truly believe, or wish to believe, that Amyas who was as much a part of Clarrow as the Squire, would uproot himself now because of Max—because of me—and leave. Could I, indeed, manage without him? The prospect appalled me. Amyas will see to it. Amyas will know. And so he always did, efficiently, unobtrusively, his presence so quiet that I had not realized how much I had come to depend upon it until now.

"Amyas." I came upon him in the hall talking to Mrs. Long and, since Max had driven off to Appleburton to look at a horse and I could never leave well alone, I called him to the Justice's Room and, sitting at my grandfather's place in the room where Amyas and I had watched my grandfather die, I asked him "Is everything all right, Amyas?"

"I believe so. The farms at Holme Meade and Clarrow Cross are to be bought by their tenants, as you know, and although there is no interest as yet in Tarn Brow, we are just entering the buying and selling season. About the Home Farm, nothing was decided before you left, that I know of . . . ?"

I sighed, impatient and saddened by what I had to tell him.

"Max wants to use it as paddocks for his horses. He insists that we don't need a farm. Apparently there is a butcher now in Bradeswick and a milkman and a baker with motor vans who can deliver daily at this distance, so there is no point any longer in growing our own."

This, Max had told me, was the direction in which "the times" were moving and he saw no reason to go through the laborious and risky processes of home baking and brewing, slaughtering, curing, and

314

the Lord knew what other acts of agricultural barbarity, when it could all be done at a discreet distance by professionals and brought to our door fresh every morning.

"Ah yes," Amyas said, apparently accepting that Max was not really a countryman. "The dairy herd is to be sold then?"

He sounded interested, almost keen, as if he already had a buyer, and I heard myself blurt out with an unmistakable note of grievance and of sadness, "I didn't want to sell the land, not a yard of it, Amyas, you know."

"Yes. I do know. But there is a certain logic to it, Olivia. Land was once the only acceptable form of wealth. One had land and was a gentleman and a gentleman lived on his rents and only on his rents. Very few can do that today. With cheap corn coming in from America, meat and wool from New Zealand, our farmers are often hard-pressed to make ends meet and so rents cannot be increased to meet the expenditure of the estates which depend upon them. Many estates are falling into decay. In order to survive these days, a gentleman is obliged to diversify, to involve himself in things which he has been brought up to consider ungentlemanly—commerce and speculation, *cash* instead of acreage. The Squire knew that and chose not to participate. Unless Lord Potterton can bring himself to admit it, I imagine we shall see the end of Dawney Park within a generation. So your husband is right in advising you to sell while you can command a decent price."

But Max had not advised me. He had simply told me "get rid of the farms" and refused to discuss it. I realized that Amyas would understand how deeply I resented that.

"Yes, I suppose he is."

"You do not sound very sure."

"No. I see the logic but I feel—well, quite differently."

"Times change, Olivia."

They were changing too fast for me, running always a step or two ahead of me so that every time I caught up with whatever I wanted it seemed always to be in the process of becoming something else. And, because I always preferred to ask for the truth, however unpleasant, rather than wait to be told, I said, my voice curt with anxiety, "You will stay, won't you Amyas?"

He smiled, very quietly.

"No, Olivia."

"Oh—Amyas—!" Incredibly my eyes had filled with tears and

I felt myself sway forward a little until my movement was sharply impeded by the desk which lay so solidly between us.

"I am a land agent, Olivia. When the land is gone how could you employ me?"

A hundred ways, I felt sure of it, yet could name none of them. I needed him. That was the reality of it. How it had come about, or why, or to what extent, I had no time just then to question. I simply knew that I trusted him. That he was the only man I knew—had ever known—on whom I was willing to rely. And the fact that it was illogical, ridiculous, ill-advised, did not detract one particle from its truth. I needed him.

"Where will you go?"

If it was to Dawney Park and the Pottertons I would be consumed with fury—and jealousy. It would break my heart. Heavens—how nonsensical. Truly. Yet it was the exact extent of my feelings.

"Not far—with your agreement, that is."

"What agreement?"

"The farm at Clarrow Bottom."

"Yes?"

"It became untenanted some months before the Squire died and I left it vacant—with his permission of course. It was not in his power to sell it to me. Would you object to doing so?"

I sat down again in the Squire's chair, my hands palms down on the desk, as he had often placed his hands, regaining my calm; Amyas sitting before me, careful, attentive, unobtrusive, "bloodless" my mother called him, "deep" declared Victorine. "Amyas will see to it. Amyas will know." Yes, he knew. Everything I felt about the house and the land, the chain of service in which I believed myself merely a link, all this Amyas knew and understood. Somehow, by some back entrance, some clandestine encounter, Amyas and I resembled each other far more than I had resembled my brother Guy, my cousins Alys and Max—and Robin. In spirit, as well as in blood and bone, we were both the Squire's children. Dare I ask him why?

"Amyas—I would, give you the farm, gladly—believe me—if I could . . ."

And it was hard to admit that although the land was legally mine, I had no real power over it. For, like Amyas—as Max had said—I could not forget who paid my wages.

"I believe you, Olivia, and thank you. Although of course I would not take it from you as a gift."

316

"No. I suppose not." But had I possessed any true authority, I would have found a way to be generous.

"I may proceed with the purchase then?"

"If that is what you want."

"I want it very much."

A part of Clarrow Fell. Yes, of course he did. I merely wished to be certain that he was doing the right thing.

"But Amyas—what you said, a moment ago, about farming?"

"That applies mainly to the large estates. You could no longer support Clarrow and your various dependents on the rents of four farms and a few cottages. But each farm, if properly handled, can support its own family in decent comfort and make a reasonable profit. I will also be very glad to take your dairy herd off your hands—should that suit you—and some of the Home Farm machinery which will not be needed for the paddocks."

"Of course. Anything you need."

I believe he hesitated, although his speech and manner had remained so neutral that it was difficult to tell.

"There is one other thing I should mention, Olivia, and which may cause you a certain amount of inconvenience—for which I apologize. Mrs. Long will be coming with me."

"Oh—I see." It was none of my business, absolutely none at all, and I had no right to interfere. But when had that ever stopped me? And what I did see very clearly was her taut, unbending, unloving body, her tight lips and sharp, suspicious eyes. She was handsome, of course, when one looked at her closely, efficient, upright; utterly boring. He was my kinsman, at a very deep level, and I wanted better than this for him.

"Are you going to marry her, Amyas?"

He smiled.

"That would not be possible."

"Why not?" Was she married already? I doubted it for the title "Mrs." was commonly given to housekeepers and cooks as a matter of courtesy to enhance their prestige and authority.

And now he hesitated very clearly, closed his eyes a brief moment and then, having made up his mind, leaned towards me a little, his manner converting what had already been a private matter into something so difficult for him to speak of that I felt a dryness in my own throat, an unwilling weight on my own tongue.

"Amyas—if you would rather not say . . ."

"Indeed, I would rather not. But it strikes me that you ought to know. Once we set up house together there will naturally be gossip and yes—I would prefer you to know the truth."

He paused and I found myself swallowing hard, my mouth parched.

"Olivia—Maria Long is my sister."

"Oh—oh, indeed." Was I relieved? Disappointed?

"Or rather my half-sister, since we had the same mother."

"I see." But not quite, not altogether.

"Yes—which makes my relationship to her the same as my relationship to Max, since he and I had the same father."

Vivian Heron. Of course. I should have thought of it, indeed I should, and of all its implications. And what now? Had my eyes filled with tears again because I had been hoping, in some foolish recess of my mind, that he might turn out to be the son of my own father's early, wayward youth? Another brother? How reassuring and comforting that would have been. How wonderful. I should have known that life did not arrange her scandals so neatly as that.

"Amyas—I am so sorry."

"Why? Because I have been inflicted with a brother like Max?"

It was the first time I had ever seen him grin, his flash of humor astonishing me and then communicating with my own, so that it was in a state hovering between laughter and tears that I held out a hand to him and said irrationally, "I'm so glad because I always knew you were a part of the family—related."

He did not take my hand.

"No, Olivia. Quite on the contrary. I am not a member of the family."

"Of course you are. You are my cousin and my brother-in-law and . . ."

"No. If we are to be specific what I *am* is a bastard."

"Lord—what of it? So is my sister, Victorine, or was until my mother and her father bothered to get married. So is my brother Luc, I rather imagine, for none of us can ever quite remember *that* wedding-day. What difference does it make?"

"It has made an enormous difference to me. Think about it for a moment."

I thought, swiftly, emotionally, putting myself entirely in his place and having done so I brought my hand down flat on the desk top and suddenly rapped out "Why were you so good to him?"

318

It was not the question he had been expecting. For an instant he looked startled and then, as he understood, he gave me once again his brief, quiet smile.

"The Squire? He was good to me."

"Was he? He sent the rest of them to Hexingham and you to the Grammar School in Bradeswick. He made you sit in the middle of the church every Sunday behind the family with your sister behind you. How could you bear it?"

How? Was that why he had become so unobtrusive, reducing his personality to a deliberate minimum, a kind of self-destruction, so that no one should notice him sitting there in the lesser pews, walking always a step behind, sitting always well below the salt, humiliated and suffering?

"He could have let me go to the workhouse, Olivia," he said calmly, "as his brother would have been perfectly ready to do. In which case I would have received no education to speak of at all and my sister, Maria, who is less robust than she seems, would not have survived."

"Will you tell me?"

"What? My banal little tale? I wondered if Max had already told you."

"No. I asked him because I realized he knew and he said he supposed you would tell me yourself if you wanted me to know. And now, Amyas, since you have begun . . . ?"

"Very well. My mother was a young widow with one small daughter—Maria—when she met Vivian Heron. She had come to Clarrow Fell to keep house for the vicar who had the living before your uncle, an old bachelor who was a distant relative of hers. Vivian Heron was here, one imagines, to borrow money from the Squire. One may safely assume that he was bored. The fact that she appears to have believed his protestations of affection proves that she was not clever. By the time she knew of her condition he had gone off to marry Rosella de Haan who, within a few months, was expecting Max.

"The rest is really no more than standard procedure. My mother's relative, the vicar, couldn't expose himself to gossip. After all, he was a bachelor, remember, which made him particularly vulnerable and if he'd allowed her to stay at the vicarage somebody would have started the rumor that the child was his. Unfortunately she had nowhere to go. That is usually the case. She spent a night in the waiting-room at Bradeswick Station and then, when the stationmaster came to move her on, decided that rather than be picked up for vagrancy she'd kill herself. Her idea was to throw herself and Maria under a train—which, I suppose, seemed obvious and final enough. Happily Maria refused to be thrown and hung on screaming until the guard separated them and called a constable.

"In the end the Squire found them a cottage at Appleburton where I was born and spent my first year or two. But my birth did my mother no good. It made her melancholy, very prone to sitting in the dark and staring at nothing—Maria remembers—not eating or washing very much. Neglecting herself, in fact, until she died.

"The Squire brought me to the Manor and sent Maria away to school somewhere—the kind of semi-charitable foundation where they teach the domestic skills to deserving young girls in unfortunate circumstances. The Squire found her a position in service in London after that and we had very little to do with each other until she came back as housekeeper ten years ago."

"So the Squire was well paid for his charity. Mrs. Long as housekeeper and you as his agent."

And once again, to my astonishment, I was rewarded—and it truly seemed a prize—by his grin.

"That is what Max used to say, Olivia."

"Was Max unkind to you?"

"Oh—I don't think Max is ever really unkind to anyone, is he? I don't think he cares enough to be unkind—which, of course, can be hurtful in itself to anyone who happens to care about him."

"Did you? Do you?"

"I did. I do not."

"Why?"

"Olivia—it is very complex and quite painful in places."

"It would mean a great deal to me to know."

"Would it?" He looked at me for a moment with his eyes full on my face, their expression so intent and searching that I almost turned away. "Then I suppose I must tell you. The Squire had many disappointments in his life. Perhaps Max was one of the greatest. He blamed himself badly for the way Vivian had turned out. They had been orphaned young, the elder brother had brought up the younger, and he believed he had failed. By the time Max arrived he was beginning to think he had failed with your father too, and he may have welcomed Max as a second chance. And whatever Max may tell you, the Squire did welcome him—or tried to."

320

"What was he like then?"

"Max? A little fighting cock, all beak and claws. Small for his age, which made him wily and devious at first and then lethal when he suddenly grew bigger. He barely knew a word of English when he came and it took a good few years before he acquired the accent he wanted."

"Did you know he was your brother?"

"My dear—of course not. I thought he was just another waif and stray brought in from the muck-heap like myself, except that he was smaller and stranger and got kicked out of the way rather more often by—well, by such members of the family who didn't much care for waifs and strays. Your father, as a matter of fact. While the Squire, of course, was stricter with Max because he wanted to make something out of him."

"You protected him?"

"I suppose I did. Not that he really needed it. He just let me do it because sometimes it was easier than doing it himself. Max always *took*—always won. There was never any cause to worry over him. When we discovered our relationship he expected me to be resentful. Perhaps I was. He found it amusing to persecute the Squire. I did not. He thought me a great fool to stay here. I saw it as my duty. That amused him too. He hurt the Squire atrociously."

"And you too."

"It is a very long time ago, Olivia."

"Yes. And I suppose what hurt him most was that out of all the young men who came under his tutelage—Vivian and my father, Max and my brother Guy by the sound of it, and Robin—the only one who resembled him and who could really have followed in his footsteps was you."

He looked down very quickly and kept his face decidedly in shadow for a moment, before telling me very gravely, "I do not think there is anything to be gained by even considering that, Olivia."

"I just wanted to be sure you knew it."

"My dear, I know it very well. So did the Squire. He gave me what he could."

"He was unjust to you and to me."

"Did that stop us from loving him—which is, of course, what he intended? I think it did not."

"Amyas, you *are* my cousin, you know."

"Yes, of course I am."

321

I came round the desk towards him and this time, rising quickly to his feet, he took my outstretched hand and kissed me very lightly, the briefest most fleeting touch of a closed mouth on the corner of mine.

"Clarrow Bottom is not far away, you know."

"You will do splendidly with it, Amyas."

"I shall do my best. And if I can be of help to you at any time—then—well, I would be most distressed if you did not turn to me."

"Thank you."

"Is that understood?"

"Yes it is. Amyas?"

"Yes?"

"I do wish you well you know, with all my heart."

"I know. I know a great many things about you, Olivia, believe me."

Once again those foolish tears were stinging my eyes but now the dark little room with its tiny mullioned windows was turning shadowy with twilight and I could only hope he did not see.

"I will make all the necessary arrangements then about the farms."

"Yes. Thank you, Amyas."

He went out and I sat down again at the desk, my hands palms down on its scarred polished top, taking comfort from the grain and the solidity of the wood, letting the evening gather round me, thinking it through. With some considerable effort of will I convinced myself that I had no idea what had really happened between us, or what had so moved me. For the first time in my life my mind closed itself inwards, scurrying with commendable speed behind a protective shell, without even the least desire to peep, much less to poke and pry into so many things which were better left unsaid, unfelt, severely alone. Nothing had happened. And like Amyas I had my work to do. I picked up a pen and wrote one after the other a series of carefully composed notes to my mother, to Esmeralda Naseby and to Madelon.

NINETEEN

The most contented woman I knew, my sister Victorine, gave birth to her second son in the new maternity hospital maintained by private charity and some small, none too willing, assistance from the Town Council. But which had actually come into being as a direct result of her husband's campaign for conditions in which Bradeswick's mothers might give birth without exposing themselves to even more disease, damp, and indifference than was to be encountered in their own homes. The struggle had been bitter and prolonged, Bradeswick's middle-classes, on the whole, preferring to contribute to some charity such as war-widows or lifeboats which could be discussed openly in their drawing rooms, rather than Dr. Rexford's constant and somewhat delicate harping on about how many women were likely to die in childbirth in the mean streets behind Bradeswick's tramsheds where registered midwives at twenty-one shillings a delivery simply did not practice, and the old woman who did was losing her eyesight. But finally, at a whisper from Miss Frances Grey, a committee had been formed, money made available, two tall old houses knocked into one and given the title St. Winifrede's Hospital for Women. The opening ceremony had been performed by a local countess and all had gone well until Victorine on her admittance had decided to take off her wedding ring and give her maiden name in protest at the policy, firmly insisted upon by the founders, that St. Winifrede's pristine facilities must be used only to deliver the babies of women of good character.

"Are you a married woman?" had inquired the matron, an

astringent spinster whose main qualification for the position seemed to be that she was a second cousin to Bradeswick's Lord Mayor.

"I am a pregnant woman," Victorine had replied. "That should be quite enough for you." And it had taken the timely arrival of Andrew—bluff, proud, highly emotional—to smooth the ruffled feathers and get Victorine into bed.

"This woman is my wife, matron."

"Then why did she not say so?" And as Andrew began an impassioned explanation of the rights of man and the wrongs of women, the nature of the ideal brotherhood—and sisterhood—of humanity, the quality of the responsibility one human being should feel for another, Victorine had been left to get on with her labor alone.

But her point had been made and she had returned home with her healthy new son in her arms in a state of mind that was decidedly triumphant and just a little smug.

"How very unwise," said my mother. "Supposing they had turned you away?"

"That is exactly the point I was making, mother," insisted Victorine, safely installed now in her own bed, a bouquet of red roses from her husband—a romantic in spite of all his good intentions—arranged beside her. "They did turn a girl away only a week ago who ended up having her baby in a toolshed in Commercial Street. It is girls like that who need St. Winifrede's. Girls who are neither paupers nor vagrants nor promiscuous either—just young and perhaps not too clever and who have been seduced by somebody old enough to know better. By some frock-coated, silk-hatted gentleman, often enough, like the ones who sit on the hospital committee."

"Well, at least he is a very pretty baby," said my mother who had given him no more than the briefest glance, exhibiting not the least desire to touch.

"Very sweet," said Alys automatically, not looking at him either.

"Very noisy," said Victorine proudly, "and much bigger than Matthew. Well—they say they get bigger every time but I shall only do it once again. In about two years I think I shall try for a girl and then no more."

"Your confidence," my mother murmured just a little wistfully, "amazes me. In my day, in such matters, a woman was simply in the lap of the gods. One learned to take what came."

"Nonsense, mother," Victorine declared robustly. "You had the choice between abstinence and abortion which are still the most widely used contraceptives—in many cases the only ones—available today."

"Victorine, dear—must you?"

"Yes, mother, for one must learn to call things by their proper names. Abortion is the only remedy most women—certainly most working women—know of, or are allowed to know of. And when they are desperate enough, when they simply cannot feed or clothe or house any more children without taking bread from the mouths of the children they already have, then they will use it. They will go to that old woman down St. Saviour's Passage who makes a tidy living out of infanticide. Or to the druggist in Bradeswick Place who sells lotions and potions at his back door that will poison the foetus and quite often the mother as well. But I have a few remedies of my own, of a much more scientific nature, and I am about to declare a war to the knife against those two charlatans when I am up and about again."

"My daughter—the witch of Corporation Square," murmured my mother faintly, her nostrils wrinkling with distaste.

"How absolutely splendid, Victorine," said Alys, meaning it most sincerely, but not quite able to cover her embarrassment.

I looked down at the child curled in his wicker basket, their voices receding, just a shower of words washing against my ears, not touching my mind. His brother, Matthew, born so soon after Robin's death, had barely moved me but my arms and my breasts were aching already for this one, my nostrils full of the warm powdery odors of the newborn, my ears delighted by the stirring and the snuffling of his apparently impenetrable slumber. Timothy Rexford, my nephew, a tiny marvel made up of secrets and surprises and potential, perfect in every detail except that his mother would have preferred him to be a girl.

I had never thought about daughters. I had regarded children as sons, miniature copies of Robin, little boys with his face, his whimsical, diffident humor, his wholesome, honest sweetness. Robin all over again, three, four, half a dozen times. Robin, not Max. But what of daughters? A copy of myself; or a little girl as appealing, as adorable, as Madelon had been? Could this miracle happen now? Why not? Oh heavens—*please*—why not? And the desire which I had believed to be dormant or burned out, like so much else, flooded over me without warning, overwhelmed me so that to my own surprise and alarm and considerable chagrin I burst into tears.

"Pay no attention to me," I snapped.

"I won't," said Victorine with her accustomed bluntness. "If your sterility still bothers you then you should have a word with Andrew. It can sometimes be remedied."

"Oh, I wouldn't do that, dear," my mother said lightly, archly, her tone and her quick glance at Victorine's bountiful breasts and ample shoulders seeking to remind me of the unfortunate manner in which maternity affected the figure.

"Oh, I see," said Alys, still looking slightly puzzled, "you want to have a baby." And although she was full of sympathy once the cause of my distress had been pointed out to her, I understood she would never have thought of it herself.

"I should like to have a dozen," said Madelon, waking momentarily from the trance into which anything even remotely concerning love and marriage always threw her.

"Would you *really*?" said Alys.

"Alys," said Victorine, remembering how bravely her cousin had attempted and failed to help with those lousy heads and runny noses behind the tramlines, "does not have maternity on her mind."

"Clever girl," said my mother.

But Alys's mind was fully occupied in other directions for, a few days later, opening her cage door its first and vital fraction, she drew a certain sum of money from her bank and, without her mother's chaperonage and most assuredly without her blessing, went first to Manchester to pay to Mrs. Emmeline Pankhurst her shilling membership of the Women's Social and Political Union and then to London where the movement had established its headquarters at Clement's Inn.

Christabel Pankhurst, the young and undeniably beautiful young barrister, who had gone to prison for spitting in a policeman's eye, was the principal organizer, the orator, the evangelist. Her sisters, Sylvia and Adela, played their subordinate and sometimes arduous roles to Christabel's star performance. But the warrior queen, the Boadicea, the Joan of Arc of the Movement, rushing first into every battle with a flaming torch in her correctly kid-gloved hand, remained their mother, Mrs. Emmeline Pankhurst herself.

"Her tactics are perfectly simple," Alys told me when I met

326

her on one of my frequent shopping trips to London. "And what alarms everyone is her absolute singleness of mind. To Mrs. Pankhurst the issue is Votes for Women and she sees nothing else. Perhaps that is what constitutes a great leader. The elected government of the day, which happens to be Liberal, has refused to help us and so she intends to bring the government down—just that—and the next one, and the one after until our demands are granted. And what is so extraordinary is that she is so very elegant and refined in her appearance, extremely concerned with matters of propriety and of dress. A lady, I suppose one calls it."

"I hear she does not always behave like a lady."

"Why, Olivia?" Alys looked at me blandly, calmly. "Because she stands up in public, at political meetings and rallies, and in a perfectly proper manner asks whatever cabinet minister happens to be speaking if his government will grant votes for women? That is all she does, Olivia. That is all her supporters do. They ask one, polite question.

"It is hardly Mrs. Pankhurst's fault that none of these eminent gentlemen—neither Mr. Asquith nor Mr. Lloyd George, nor Mr. Winston Churchill—can bring themselves to answer. It is always the same. The ministers take their places on the platform and make their speeches. Some man jumps to his feet in the audience and puts a question about tariff reform or non-secular education or National Insurance Acts and the minister is graciously pleased to answer. Another man gets to his feet and contradicts the opinion of the first, and the minister just smiles and acts as a kind of avuncular referee.

"The audience listens intently and no one so much as suggests that either of these men is causing a disturbance or attempting to obstruct the proceedings. But then a woman stands up and makes her inquiry about votes for women. Suddenly Mr. Asquith or Mr. Church-ill has gone deaf. She asks again. No reply. The stewards appear, take hold of her by the elbows and start to drag her off. She resists. And you would be amazed, Olivia, how eagerly those respectable bank clerks and shopkeepers in the crowd set about her, how they pull her hair and pinch her and hurl abuse at her. When she lands on the pavement the police are usually waiting. Naturally they are accustomed to removing prostitutes or drunkards, women of low character who are accustomed to foul language and rough handling. When the Suf-fragette objects to it she is arrested for causing a breach of the peace."

"Alys," I said considerably shocked. "Surely *you* have not . . . ?"

"Not yet," she said, her face suddenly turning white at the thought of it. "So far I have been a spectator. But eventually one supposes . . . An acquaintance of mine was arrested last Tuesday and charged with assaulting a policeman."

"Heavens, Alys, I remember reading something about it in the press."

She gave a pale, tight little smile.

"Quite so. The truth is that the man, in the course of a scuffle, had deliberately ripped open her blouse and fondled her breasts. She was—well—considerably outraged and said so. His reply indicated his belief that this was the kind of thing she had been looking for and that her present behavior was caused by the lack of it. She protested and went to prison for seven days."

"Alys!" The cool tone of her voice, her prim, little phrases amused me, their content caused me a great deal of indignation and alarm.

"Indeed. And, of course, at the Opening of Parliament this year, when it was learned that the issue of the women's vote was not to be included in the King's Speech, a positive army of mounted police were turned loose on the women who went, in a perfectly peaceful procession, to the House of Commons to protest. A great many were ridden down by the horses. A great many were punched and kicked and molested in a manner which—well, which could only be employed against a woman. And fifty-seven of us were arrested."

Why so much violence?

Max, who had joined us by then, raised his elegant shoulders.

"One could possibly put it down to weakness."

"Weakness?" I would have called it brutality! But he smiled and shook his head, inviting us to observe that there was no sign of weakness in him.

"No—no. *Weakness.* For I have a notion that men who are really strong feel no need to be brutal with women. And as for these others, well perhaps they are just paying off old scores.

"Because women can seem very powerful, you know, in child-hood. Perhaps these poor chaps had a wicked nanny once, or a sarcastic mother, or a sister who was brighter and quicker and had no mercy when it came to making a fellow feel small. Perhaps, when they aim a blow at a Suffragette, they are remembering the girls they couldn't get, or the girls who teased them and cost them money. Or the wives

328

who have those convenient little headaches at bedtime. Or perhaps they are just afraid of the competition. Strong men, of course—clever men—have nothing to be afraid of."

But, whatever the causes, a goodly proportion of the male population continued to react to Suffragism with violence, while there seemed no doubt that our senior statesmen, however charming they might be with "woman" in the singular and in private, had not the faintest notion how to cope with "women" enraged and *en masse*.

"Woman's place is in the home," declared the British Government, the Church, the Metropolitan Police, my Aunt Sibylla.

"Rise up Women," invited Mrs. Pankhurst, to which a rapidly increasing army of female voices flung back the ritual answer *"Now."*

"What stirring times are these," murmured Miss Frances Grey, who had not yet moved from her own elegant drawing room and perhaps would not do so until, the battle won, a cooler head and a more calculating mind than Mrs. Pankhurst's should be needed to dictate the peace.

"My daughter is in London visiting friends," said Aunt Sibylla, very pinched about the mouth.

And when would she return, one wondered?

"Shortly," declared my aunt, her faint air of surprise implying how could anyone doubt it.

She came, looking pale and strained and resolute, but was soon off again, returning throughout the spring and summer every three or four weeks for a day or so, just long enough for Aunt Sibylla to maintain the fiction that her daughter was still "marriageable," still "a young lady at home."

"My daughter is becoming such a gadabout," said Aunt Sibylla superbly. "Quite the social butterfly, flitting here and there from one invitation to another. One must hope she will not wear herself out with her enjoyment . . ."

"Are you all right, Alys?" I asked her, speaking the words for Robin.

"Oh—I don't know about that. I'm doing what I *should* be doing, that's quite certain."

"Good." Robin, I knew, would have been glad of that.

"Intriguing," said Max. "One wonders just where and just how she will fly. One might even make a little excursion into suffrage circles every now and again to see."

"If she intends to bring down the Liberal Government," said

Andrew Rexford, with his gruff humor, "I would be obliged if she would wait until they have introduced their Old Age Pensions Bill."

"I daresay we might *all* be over seventy by then and able to apply," said Victorine, up and about again, one sturdy child at her skirts, another strapped to her side, red-cheeked and sharp-tongued as she stirred her barley broth and camomile tea.

"Over seventy!" said her mother, her expression as pained as Aunt Sibylla's at the mention of sex or filial disobedience. "My dear— one would simply never admit it."

The repairs to the Manor were gradually completed, a chauffeur-mechanic and his apprentice installed in the rooms above the garage, new grooms appointed—presumably to the delight and peril of our laundry-maids—to school and exercise the tall, nervous thoroughbreds with which Max soon populated the stables. Clarrow woods were re-stocked with pheasant, young birds to be hand-reared by a gamekeeper all spring and summer so that they might be driven in flocks before a walking line of guns every autumn, and shot down. Clarrow Moor was burned, much to the disgust of Lord Potterton who could not be convinced that old heather was an inadequate food for grouse, our new crop soon nourishing a multitude of birds, likewise destined to be slaughtered by that walking line of guns. We acquired dogs, retrievers, spaniels, terriers, a pair of fragile, fastidious greyhounds; and kennels in which to keep them, Max having no conception of animals as pets although I did allow the greyhounds inside from time to time when no one was looking, to lie on the fur rug before the fire in the hall.

At the same time we acquired a butler, as suave and disdainful as the head waiter of a grand hotel, a tiny haughty chef who was not quite so Parisian as he appeared, smart new parlormaids, a lady's maid who believed she knew far more about fashion and fabrics and the value of my jewelry than I knew myself. And when Mrs. Long indicated to me her intention of "taking service with Mr. Hird" at Clarrow Bottom, I wished her well without expressing the slightest curiosity, disclaiming all knowledge of her true relationship as Amyas had asked me to do, and engaged a Mrs. Charles, an efficient, anonymous woman who kept the maids in order and did not trouble me.

"What did I tell you," chortled the ever malicious Mrs. Timmins, when I called at the cottage I had found for her in Pasture Row. "Not that I ever thought to see even Maria Long run after a man so fast. Brazen, I call it. And he won't marry her, you know."

"I know."

"Good heavens," murmured my mother across her whist table, "Amyas and Mrs. Long! Should one be charitable do you think and assume that she *is* just his housekeeper?"

"I fear one must assume the worst," declared my aunt, hoping— one supposed—that a scandal so close to home would obscure the London scandal of Alys.

And when Victorine called at the farm, not socially, of course, but to interest Amyas in her scheme to supply milk to the infants of St. Saviour's Passage—since he had a dairy herd after all and she believed he could always get a motor van from somewhere or other— Mrs. Long's possessive attitude towards Amyas appeared ample confirmation of everyone's suspicions.

"Amyas," I carefully inquired, "would it not be better to let people know the truth?"

But he shook his head and smiled.

"How—without revealing that Maria's mother bore an illegitimate child or that Max is my brother which could be awkward for us both? I see no gain and the possibility of harm in stirring up such an old scandal. Maria and I learned long ago how to live with it. Please do the same, Olivia."

"But you might want to be married one day—surely . . . ?" I blurted out, wishing desperately before the words were off my tongue that I had not said them.

"I don't suppose so."

"Don't you? Then she, perhaps . . . ?"

"No. She was married once very briefly. Never again, she says. Olivia—what happened to our mother affected Maria very keenly. She is older than I. She remembers—not only the tragedy but the disgrace. And the fear, I suppose. One should not forget that for the first ten years of her life she must often have been afraid—of the workhouse for instance and the absolute insecurity of people who are not respectable. It has made her tense, and rigid of outlook, unbending, perhaps, and such people are far more likely to break than those of us who sway with the wind or keep out of it altogether. She prefers that the secret should be kept—as the Squire did—and I think you and I must abide by that."

"Yes, of course, Amyas."

I had sold him Clarrow Bottom at the figure he had suggested, his life savings, I supposed, and my dairy herd at its exact market value. But I had also refused a very reasonable offer for the small farm at Tarn Brow whose fields bordered Amyas's fields, knowing that in time and with good fortune he would want to purchase it.

"Just a ramshackle old barn and a few scrubby acres," I told Max. "Who could possibly want it?"

"Certainly not I, my pet." But he said nothing more and Tarn Brow was soon added to the list of my secret treasures, as neglected and outwardly unproductive as the grimy packing-cases stacked three and four high in the Gatehouse kitchen, yet capable—like them—of yielding me a ripe harvest of independence and security. And an opportunity to be generous.

Did Max know about my squirrel hoard? Very likely. Did he know that I had inquired the authenticity and the value of every piece of jewelry he had given me? I thought he very probably did, although it in no way discouraged him from buying me more: nor did it incline him to curb my own very favorite pastime of lavishing gifts on my nephews, my mother, and Madelon.

I paid my first visit to Esmeralda Naseby the week after my return form Madeira, arriving in the chauffeur-driven Mercedes, wearing a blue velvet hat adorned with ostrich feathers, a blue velvet coat-and-skirt with a pearl gray chinchilla collar, a high-necked blouse of fine Venetian lace, my diamond on one hand, a cluster of sapphires on the other, a smile of notable brilliance on my discreetly rouged lips.

"Mrs. Naseby—how very nice to see you again."

"Yes," she said nervously. "Quite so—Mrs. de Haan, I suppose I must call you now."

"Perhaps *you* should call me Olivia."

And giving her no time to drop some stinging little hint about the speed with which I appeared to change my name, I settled myself down in her slightly darkened drawing room—an indication that her nerves or her head were troubling her or that she expected them to do so—and took the reins of conversation in my own firm hands. For an hour I talked exclusively and deliberately of prestige and wealth, of the alterations we were making to the Manor, of Max's property in Funchal and Lanzarote, the hats I had ordered for the Races at Ascot and Longchamps, the notion my husband had taken to play polo at Hurlingham, the decline of the Pottertons who were hard-pressed, one heard, to replace their ageing carriage-horses these days much less invest in polo ponies and those terrible longlegged thoroughbreds they had been so glad to sell to Max. Why yes. Had Mrs. Naseby not heard? The Pottertons' prize bays, their black mare and that spectacular chestnut stallion they had made so much fuss about were all in our stables now. And if Dottie hoped to hunt next season she would either have to borrow a decent mount from us or make do with whatever old Dobbin she had left. Sad, of course, and one could only presume the pack of foxhounds would go next since, the way things were, they could hardly support twenty couple hounds eating their heads off or pay the wages of a kennel man and huntsman for that matter. Yes, no doubt, Max would buy them and in that case, no doubt he *would* be invited to take over the mastership of the hunt in Georgie Potterton's place. Such an appointment was of small interest to me, but Mrs. Naseby, with her greater knowledge of country life, would understand—I felt certain—the nature of the prestige involved, the hunt balls at which I, not Dottie Potterton, would be forced—such a bore!— to preside; the position of first lady of local society which would be positively *thrust*—oh dear, how tedious!—upon me.

Good heavens! Dinners and dances and houseparties with people up from London and abroad, titled people some of them and all of them interesting and wealthy since Max only seemed to know that kind. No doubt I would rise to the occasion, and must certainly engage a secretary to write out those hundreds and hundreds of invitation cards. For what a social catastrophe it would be to anyone whose name should inadvertently be missed. And I reserved for the moment of my departure my single reference to her son.

"Is Ivor keeping well?"

"Oh no," she said sounding very much out of breath although she had barely spoken a word. "Not well at all. That boy grows more and more delicate. The lungs you see—the chest . . . Never strong. I believe I must send him off to Italy again."

But he was no longer of an age to be sent anywhere and when she returned my call—curiosity and the safeguarding of her own social position proving stronger than maternal solicitude—he accompanied her, his presence causing her less anxiety than it might have done since I had let her know, through my maid who could be relied on to gossip to her maid, that Madelon would not be there. But, in my beloved attic, I had discovered a portrait of my mother, painted I supposed in the early days of her marriage to my father, when her beauty had possessed the same fragile, spun-glass quality as Madelon's, her slender body the same air of untouched purity, false no doubt in her case but making her look in her freshly dusted frame on my drawingroom wall so like my sister that Ivor Naseby most gratifyingly lost all appetite for his tea.

"Ivor, dear, you *are* unwell," his mother told him, visibly triumphant.

"How are things in Bradeswick, Mrs. de Haan?" he said, not even looking at her. "Does that rum old girl still give her lectures about women's rights and wrongs in Aireville Terrace? Strikes me I might look in on her this evening."

He went, spent an hour whispering and giggling with Madelon in a corner—to the considerable annoyance of Miss Frances Grey—and thereafter, throughout the summer and the hazy approaches of autumn, they met regularly both in Bradeswick and at the Manor, Madelon never more enchanting in the tea gowns of white organdy and spotted Swiss muslin lace we had chosen together in London, or the evening gowns of floating, pastel chiffon which had sent her into a trance of delight.

"Olivia—how beautiful. Can you really afford it?"

"Yes. Take the blue as well. And then we will look at hats and a feather boa, I think, and something to put in your ears. Pearl drops? Or coral? Or both."

"*Olivia.* Do you know, I feel so spoiled and special and—well— I think I can put up with it very well."

"You are making her very vain," declared Victorine, having spent a day with Madelon during which she had talked exclusively of perfumes, silk stockings and romance; topics which, in Victorine's opinion, might be pleasant enough but had few real practical purposes and were unlikely to endure.

"I am giving her what she wants, Victorine."

"How do you know? You would have married me to Rodney Clough if I'd been so obliging as Madelon. And there's no need to glare at me and set your jaw because I know quite well you mean everything for the best. But you should be careful with Madelon because—well, Olivia, you ought to know it—she hasn't much character of her own. She *reflects.*"

"Victorine—what *are* you saying?"

"Just this—she is very sweet, our Madelon, very eager to please and very worried that she won't please and so she reflects the person

334

she happens to be with. She takes on other people's characteristics, adapts to *their* values and requirements because she's been too confused all her life—by mother's flights of fancy mostly, I suppose—to work out any values of her own. And she's far too timid to have requirements. So she'll become exactly what her husband wants her to become—or what she thinks he wants. So—how well do you know Ivor Naseby?"

Well enough, I thought. And if I had a reservation at all it was that there seemed little enough to know. He was handsome, rich, spoiled, could be aroused to peevishness by his mother's increasingly desperate cosseting. But I had seen him touch my sister's hand as if it were made of a substance fine enough to shatter beneath his finger tips. I had sensed the private communication between them, the words silently conveyed from his mind to hers across a dinner table, penetrating noise and distance and the blundering insensitivity of their fellow guests. I had seen them stand inches apart and had realized that, even with his mother's venom and everybody else's eager curiosity between them, an almost physical contact had been made. I saw my sister give herself wholly to love and I believed myself privileged to watch it. I had myself once experienced a similar emotion, not with this entirety, not with so pure a heart and such total surrender of the mind, but I had come close enough to it, had held it just long enough to recognize the miracle I had missed. I wanted Madelon to have that miracle, to spend her life on the precious height from which I had so quickly descended. For what else could compare with it?

"Nothing," sighed my mother mistily. "I have been in love like that *so* often."

I very much doubted it.

"What do you think of Ivor Naseby?" I asked Max, knowing his judgment would not be charitable.

"Ah yes—Esmeralda's little angel. I imagine he must be every matchmaking mamma's dream come true."

Very well. I was no one's mamma. But I had Madelon and if she wanted Ivor Naseby then his cloying, clinging mother must not be allowed to stand in their way. There must be an end to the sick headaches which prostrated her, the allegedly near fatal flutterings of the heart which occurred every time he slipped his lead and went to Bradeswick. The emotional blackmail, the deliberate arousal of his guilt and with it his temper, must cease.

I drove over to her house and told her so, finding—as I had

rather expected—that, when faced with an adversary who cared not a fig for the state of her health, she became very healthy indeed.

"You are an interfering woman," she hissed at me when I had made my requirements perfectly clear.

"And you are a selfish woman."

"I do not want my son to marry the daughter of a woman who is little better than a whore."

"You do not want your son to marry anybody. And my mother is a better woman than you are, Mrs. Naseby. Whatever else she may be she is not a cannibal. She does not try to eat her children alive, like you."

More venom followed—a great deal of it in fact—as was only to be expected; but in the end I was able to convince her that if she persisted in her opposition—which apart from everything else was making my sister cough—she would lose two things, her social position which I personally and very effectively would destroy, and eventually her son.

"I will never forgive you for this, Olivia Heron—or whatever your name is."

"Then don't forgive me, Esmeralda Naseby. Just come to dinner tomorrow evening at eight o'clock and smile."

She came, looking brave, an invalid sinking beneath the shadow of death and attempting to conceal it for good manners' sake, her smile very wan but at least a *smile* as she greeted my other guests, Victorine, my mother, my brother Luc on his winter holiday from Hexingham, her eyes sharp enough to notice that neither Aunt Sibylla nor Alys who had been expected home the day before, were present.

"Dear Alys," she sighed, "I do so adore her. I had hoped at one time . . . Ah well!"

She had hoped no such thing.

"Dear Alys—if I had had a daughter, I have often thought she may have looked like Alys."

But no one was listening to her, our attention totally held by Madelon, a fairy princess in pearl-trimmed white tulle, an enraptured bride already in spirit so that when she disappeared for a while with Ivor and they came back hand in hand, two blissful, birthday party children coming to tell us, as if it were the greatest secret in the world, that they were in love, their engagement and marriage and ecstatic future were so firmly in our minds that the announcement might well have been made a year ago.

336

"Well done," Max told me later, highly amused. "It strikes me that you might care to take a little holiday, to recover from your exertions? Monte Carlo, I always think, is pleasant at this season. And by the way—where *was* Alys? It is not like your aunt to cancel without explanation. But I expect you will be going down to the vicarage in the morning—won't you?—to break the news about Madelon."

I went, with no real news to break since Aunt Sibylla could have had no serious hopes of Ivor for Alys. But anxious nevertheless. She had certainly been expected last night at dinner. *Something* of a fairly grave nature must have occurred. But whatever it was, it did not appear to have affected the vicar who, walking up the garden path with his field-glasses around his neck and his picnic hamper in his hand, greeted me as always with an air of not quite remembering my name; clearly on his way out to enjoy a day of birdwatching and solitude.

Aunt Sibylla was in her kitchen giving instructions for the mammoth house-cleaning operations, the washing of walls and ceilings, the emptying, dusting and re-filling of cupboards, the re-lining of pantry shelves with which she always approached the Christmas season.

"Oh, Olivia—yes, dear. I will be with you in a moment. I must just get them started on the linen. And the mending. And I believe I have a notion to whitewash the cellar."

"Aunt—I wanted to tell you that Madelon and Ivor . . . ."

"Oh good. A spring wedding then? Quite delightful. I suppose I need not remind you to be very specific in the marriage contract about the amount of pin-money she is to have? And a proper dress allowance, of course, and *exactly* what she would receive as a widow's portion. But you know all that. Of course you do."

"Yes, aunt."

"Well, then—since I have a loft full of apples to be made into pies . . . You will be busy too, I daresay—with all your great undertakings . . . ?"

"Yes, aunt."

"So—I will see you presently. And by the way, dear, whatever plans you are making for an engagement party—a ball perhaps?—it might not be possible to include Alys."

"Oh—really?"

"Indeed. For we had news yesterday that my daughter has been arrested and sentenced to three weeks in Holloway."

TWENTY

Her first task as a member of the W.S.P.U. had been entirely suited to her nature. For weeks on end she had sat at a desk in Clement's Inn putting together the facts—collected by others—of the underpayment of women in sweated industries, the filthy, over-crowded conditions in which they were forced to labor. But the W.S.P.U. had a great many elderly or infirm members who could undertake this work and Alys could not ignore the knowledge of how badly young, able-bodied women like herself were needed in the field. She had gone to her first political meeting with her little purple, green and white suffrage banner neatly folded inside her handbag and a ton weight of dread pressing on her heart. Good manners were so essential a part of her nature that she had always taken the greatest care never to interrupt even in private conversation, never to raise her voice, *never* to draw attention to herself in public and what she had agreed to do was abhorrent to her. But, unfortunately, it was necessary. She had made up her mind long ago about that and when she finally jumped to her feet and forced through her dry throat the classic suffragette demand "Will this Liberal Government grant votes to women?" she was not so much asking a question as offering herself as a sacrifice.

She was set upon as she had expected, both arms pinned behind her back, hustled between rows of jeering and, in some cases she thought, lascivious faces, and thrown out into the street where to her intense embarrassment she was violently sick. But she had survived. A barrier had been broken. She had crossed a threshold of experience and the next time—surely?—it would be easier to bear.

It was not. She understood, after several political rallies and several by-elections, that she would never grow accustomed to violence in any of its forms, could never walk calmly—as many women did—into any assembly which wished her ill, could never catch even a spark of the fiery exultation which drove Mrs. Pankhurst and her eldest daughter so splendidly and so often into battle. For Alys the work would always be hard, just a painful hair's breadth short of the impossible, but it was *right*. She was entirely certain of that. And so she saw no alternative but to force herself to it, sick with apprehension and disgust at every call to arms but stipulating only that her activities as a militant should be conducted at least fifty miles from Clarrow, since her mother could not stand the disgrace.

She had taken "rooms" in Cheyne Walk, modest ones we assumed, accepting here too another challenge since it had never before even crossed her mind to wonder how her linen was washed or her dinner cooked, how beds were made, fires lit, and what exactly it was that one did about dust. Yet her skirt and shirt were very adequately pressed, her gray coat well brushed on the November night she accompanied a certain Mrs. Peel, an elderly, retired colonel's lady, to the meeting of a Liberal minister at whose home Mrs. Peel had been a dinner guest a few evenings before.

And when this elderly and apparently frail lady had been ejected from the meeting hall, and began to hold a meeting of her own on the pavement outside, a cheerful crowd collected, both men and women, who were not all pleased when the police arrived to move her—and Alys—on.

"Leave the old girl alone."

"Show a bit of respect mate—she's old enough to be your granny."

"It's a free country ain't it? Let her have her say."

But Mrs. Peel's "say"—and the few timid words Alys could bring herself to interpose—were becoming audible and considerably annoying to the honorable gentleman inside the meeting hall, some of *his* audience starting to drift outside to see what the noise, and the fun, was about.

"Move those women on," the honorable gentleman scribbled curtly on a scrap of paper that was hurriedly conveyed from the speaker's platform to the by now somewhat harassed and irritable police.

"Now see here, just get along with you, there's a good lady."

"Votes for Women" was Mrs. Peel's strident reply.

"Votes for Women," quavered Alys, compensating for her parched whisper by unfurling her surprisingly well-ironed purple, green and white banner.

And in the ensuing scuffle, during which Mrs. Peel was knocked to the ground Alys, finding herself clasped in a uniformed embrace which, to her complete horror, she suddenly realized to be amorous rather than restraining, began to struggle, to kick out, claiming her right to defend herself not against the law but as a woman against the sexual opportunism of a man.

"Assault," said the constable, looking pleased about it.

"Twenty shillings or three weeks in the Third Division," said the magistrate next morning, looking agitated and out of sorts and much inclined to take early retirement or colonial service or anything else that would spare him the sight of another Suffragette.

"I will not pay the fine," said Alys, following the suffragette creed to the letter. "I *choose* to go to prison."

She was not even aware of the significance of serving her sentence in the Third Division, or of the vast gulf separating one level of prison population from another. Certainly she must have heard of it, since Suffragettes by then were being locked up, it seemed, whenever and wherever officialdom was given the chance. But, like embroidery and bakery, it had never penetrated beyond the surface of her mind. Prisoners in the First Division were allowed to wear their own clothes, have their own food sent in by friends or order it from their favorite restaurants. They could write and receive as many letters as they chose, could be attended at their own convenience by their legal advisers, doctors, secretaries and could be supplied with all the materials and facilities they considered necessary to carry on their business or professional activities from what might be thought of as hotel rooms rather than cells.

Prisoners in the Second Division were obliged to wear prison dress and subsist on a prison diet which, although meager, did include meat two or three times a week and a little fat bacon. And, from the start, they were permitted to write one letter a month and to receive one letter in reply.

But those who were sentenced in the third degree were simply shut up and were barely heard of or seen again, until their term expired, having no right to letters or visits of any kind for the first two months, by which time they were usually—if perhaps only temporarily—free.

340

It was the category reserved for harlots, vagrants, drunkards; and suffragettes.

"Be brave, dear," said Mrs. Peel who, as a previous offender, had been given three months. "You will encounter nothing worse than a few fleas. Although indeed it is the vermin which have broken some of our most resolute spirits. I have seen them march off to prison as courageously as you, ready to endure any brutality, and enduring it too, gritting their teeth and doing well until a dose of head lice entirely brings them down. Remember, dear, one does not die of fleas."

She was taken from Cannon Street Police Court to Holloway in the notorious "Black Maria," a species of cattle-truck for human beings in which men and women were indiscriminately bundled: a journey which Alys passed in a state of frozen disbelief, sandwiched between the sweating, tattooed hulk of a seaman who stank—her nostrils would never forget it—of beer and vomit, and a thin, hollow-cheeked girl, no more than fifteen, who was hugely pregnant.

And closing her eyes she decided that, in order to survive, she would also have to close her mind, to remove her senses—particularly her sense of disgust and humiliation—from her body until the nightmare was over. Her body would suffer. There was nothing she could do about that. But, with rigid control, severely maintained self-discipline, then the mind, which was after all the best part of herself, would remain untouched. It was the only policy she could possibly pursue and she held fast to it, clutching it around her as the prison gates clanged shut and she was thrust for safekeeping, until she could be properly examined and labeled, into what seemed like a vertical coffin. Just a bare, dark cubby-hole, in fact, with nothing in it but a lavatory without a seat where she was obliged to stand for hours until she could be attended to, her nostrils shrinking from the odor of ancient plumbing, her body aching with fatigue, her mind—still, if only barely, under her control—refusing to allow her to sit down on that insanitary receptacle and encounter the contagion lurking—she could almost smell it and hear it—around the brim.

And when her nerve began to crack and panic started to whisper that she was entirely alone and helpless and at the mercy of strangers, what steadied her was the reminder that if her friends might not know of her terrible plight then neither did her mother. She was here. It had happened. She would not resist.

Very well. She must offer her body for humiliation with dignity, proving by her behavior that she was not a criminal but a woman of integrity and social responsibility, the representative, in this dreadful place, of other women like herself. For these raw-boned, grim-faced wardresses were women too and must be given no reason to despise the suffragette cause because of her.

"Undress," bellowed one of them, taking her into a room full of other women in various stages of nakedness, where Alys who had been brought up to undress behind a screen in her bedroom at the vicarage to avoid the observation of her own maid, took off her clothes, saw them ticketed with her name and packed away, and then submitted herself to the rough appraisal of a prison officer who searched her body minutely, scornfully; her first experience of intimate contact with another human hand which made her skin crawl, her stomach heave.

But at least, since nothing could be worse than that, the worst was over. There was worse to come. The bathroom. Just a shed with half a door so that one could see below and above it, the bath discolored, abominable, half-full of the same tepid, dirty water in which five other women—she knew because she had counted—had bathed before her.

"Get in."

"I can't," she said. "Please . . ." And it was the whisper of a trapped animal with the hounds in full cry behind it, a chasm before.

"Get in," thundered a wardress, a big, angry, probably weary woman at the end of her shift who, for one sickening moment, Alys believed to be a man in disguise.

"I can't." For at least one of those other women had had sore patches all along her back and none of them had been clean. But when one is a prisoner in the Third Division, with no right to communicate with the outside world, no possible outlet for complaint, no help, one can do, or can be made to do, anything. She got in, and out again, and was sent to join the other "washed" prisoners who were pulling and tugging at a heap of garments on the floor, putting on what they could grab regardless of fit. Old, stained underwear worn by a hundred strangers, coarse brown serge dresses, ridiculous white caps tied under the chin, clothing which would probably not be changed until the end of Alys's sentence, everything marked all over with the emblem of shame, the broad arrow, white on dark colors, black on light.

She was given a number "27" and a cell containing a plank

bed, a slop pail, a shelf with a tin mug and a flaking wooden spoon which had been used by every other "27" before her. And here, three times a day, she was served one pint of oatmeal and water and six ounces of brown bread, supplemented twice a week by a small slice of unsweetened suet pudding and eight ounces of dubious potatoes.

"No thank you," said Alys, most fastidious of diners politely handing back the oatmeal gruel.

"Eat it," she was told, "or you'll be fed."

"I can't." But she was a prisoner in the Third Division who could do anything, absolutely anything, she was told. Twice a day she was permitted a brief dash to the lavatory in the corridor, twice a week she was taken to the exercise yard for half an hour to walk in single file and in strictly enforced silence. For the rest of the time she was made to scrub her cell floor, or simply left alone, locked up in that terrible solitude to brood, to pine, to wither, as she chose. Open the cage and fly away. But this new captivity had a purpose. She accepted it. She would endure.

She was, of course, more fortunate than many others. She kept on reminding herself of that. She had no sick husband at home like No. 42 who believed she would be met at the prison gates in six weeks' time by the news of his death. She had not left two infants locked in a lodging-house attic while she went out into the streets to ply her trade, like No. 58, who seemed in the process of losing her mind with the worry of what had become of them. She had not given birth to a child in a prison hospital cell like poor, hollow-eyed No. 71 who had neither husband nor home nor anything very much in the way of hope for the future to bestow upon her son.

She was cold, of course, bitterly cold all day, all night, and nauseous, her stomach, her skin, every physical part of her wrinkled with disgust so deep, so engraved upon her that she wondered if she would ever be able to eat, inhale, touch, taste, perform any physical function with enjoyment again.

Her body felt parched, hollowed out, elongated by strain. Her head ached—and *itched*. The last occupant of "27" had left menstrual blood on the mattress. There would be rats somewhere, she thought. And, when the cell door was locked for the night and the uncertain gas jet flickered out, she dared not close her eyes.

"I could go to London," suggested Max, who knew something of prisons, "and pay her fine. In which case they would release her?"

Would Robin have done that? No. I shook my head. "She chose imprisonment. She should be allowed to abide by her choice."

"Very well. Then I must find out how one goes about smuggling in champagne to prisoners in the Third Division."

"*Max.*" I was astonished, a little exasperated, rather impressed. "You can't, Max—not even you—it's not possible. Is it? How?"

"My dear—*money*. What else? I find it will do the trick every time."

"I don't think she even likes champagne."

"Maybe not. But she'll appreciate the gesture. Wouldn't you?"

"Very likely."

"And if you were a Suffragette and someone arranged for you to be transferred to a higher Division, would you accept the transfer? Or would you prefer to stay and suffer with your sisters-in-arms?"

"I wouldn't suffer *anywhere*, Max, if there was a way out. Can you really arrange prison transfers and influential things like that?"

"I know people who can. And if I didn't, I'd make it in my way to get to know them. And by the way, darling, if you should be thinking of arranging a little celebration, or even a big one, to welcome her home, then yes, I absolutely agree with you. Certainly her mother will have need of it. I'd even endorse flags at the station and a brass band."

We did not go to quite those lengths, but very nearly. On her release from Holloway she was met, as had become customary, by a deputation of Suffragettes who presented her with bouquets of flowers, took her out for a celebration breakfast and bestowed upon her the brooch, the tiny portcullis and broad arrow in purple, green and white which had become the medal the W.S.P.U. awarded to those who had seen service in Holloway.

The task which lay before her now was very clear. By allowing so many literate, articulate women into its prisons the Government had unleashed upon itself rather more than it had bargained for and it was now the duty of Alys and others like her to tour the country explaining to the electorate the vile conditions its elected representatives condoned there.

Her physical conditon was weak and uncertain. She was still plagued by that strange elongated feeling in her limbs, the terrible sensation that *something* was crawling all over the surface of her skin. But she would have set off at once had Max not appeared in Clement's Inn to beg leave of absence for her from her leaders. And even then she would have refused it had he not convinced her of the necessity of seeing her mother.

I went to Leeds in the Mercedes to meet their train, Alys looking thin and nipped by cold even with Max's wolfskin coat around her shoulders, and drove her back to Clarrow where for the entire Christmas season I took her everywhere with me, holding a special dinner in her honor as if she had been a French *marquise* released from the Bastille. I was the lady of the Manor, after all, and if I welcomed her home as a martyr, a heroine, then everyone else would be well advised to do the same.

"My daughter has made several most interesting friends," said Aunt Sibylla, her mouth smiling, her eyes looking as if they ached. "Lady Constance Lytton, for instance, and Mrs. Cobden-Sanderson, the daughter of the great Richard Cobden who gave us free trade—and a Mrs. Solomon whose husband, as I suppose you are well aware, was once Prime Minister of the Cape. Exalted circles, indeed."

And Alys, wearing her little purple, green and white brooch shaped like the broad arrow, listened to us and smiled.

I had been Max's wife a twelve-month now. The house which had brought us together was finally ready to endorse the life of ease and pleasure we had fixed upon, and instead of the traditional roast turkey and plum pudding, our Christmas dinner that year—produced by our peevish little chef, Monsieur Clement, in order to prove his expertise—consisted of oysters served on crushed ice, fresh caviar, clear turtle soup, sole poached in Chambertin wine, venison cutlets with Madeira sauce and truffles, spit-roasted quails, *parfait de foie gras*, frosted tangerines, sweet omelette stuffed with mincemeat and flamed with rum, an almond *soufflé* crowned by a complicated design of crystallized violets, cherries in claret.

"Exquisite," said my mother, glancing swiftly over her shoulder to make sure the Squire was not somewhere behind her in the shadows, listening. "Exactly as *I* would have done things had I remained here."

"Jolly nice," said Luc, who had been taught at Hexingham to curb his enthusiasm.

"Well done," said Victorine, "and I can use up your leftovers very nicely tomorrow at the street party in St. Saviour's Passage."

"Thank you," said Alys.

While Madelon, her hand in Ivor Naseby's hand, her mind entirely enfolded in his, said not a word.

"Gentlemen," said Max, raising his glass of old and valuable

Château d'Yquem, "Shall we be honest with ourselves and drink a toast to the bravery of women? For when they *are* brave—dear God, then what one sees is real, raw courage. Who can deny it?" And rising to his feet followed by Andrew and Luc and Ivor Naseby and my mother's portly Mr. Greenlaw, he raised his glass once more to each of us in turn, to me, to Alys, to Victorine sitting with her elbows planted on the table four square and eternal, to Aunt Sibylla whose smile, throughout these trying weeks had never wavered, whose head—no matter how much it ached—had continued to be held high.

"Yes—to the bravery of women—not forgetting all their *very* delectable frailties."

Alys returned to London in the New Year, our lives separating yet still tenuously held together as they had been for so long. "You will come back and stay with us when you can?"

"Yes indeed." But she had given herself to the suffrage cause as she had been unable to give herself to a man, with the same dedication of the whole heart and mind with which Madelon had given herself to Ivor—with which Alys, perhaps, in time *would* have given herself to Robin—and it was with his voice that I wished her well.

Spring was a scented, gilded promise that year—and the year after—summer a lavish pleasure-barge on which we drifted through hot, blue weather from one ripe, floral landscape to another.

For Madelon's wedding in April, a marquee like the interior of a sugar pink cloud was erected on the lawn where we served a spendid buffet of galantines and *terrines* and *pâtés*, roast baron of beef, dishes of cold quail and salmon, ices in unlikely colors and exotic flavors, baskets of nectarines, peaches, melons; more than half of these delicacies finding their way, the next morning in neatly packed hampers to St. Saviour's Passage.

"I am the happiest woman in the world," said Madelon.

"I must dash off to Manchester," said Alys, "where Winston Churchill is fighting a by-election. For now that Asquith has become Prime Minister we shall have our work cut out."

"I'm going to Rome—and Venice," said Madelon, "with Ivor."

"I am expecting another baby," said Victorine, "from *choice*, mamma—because I enjoy making things grow. And before you bring Asquith down, Alys, you should thank him for introducing his Old Age Pensions Scheme. Although five shillings a week for men over seventy, provided they can prove themselves to be of good character, is not over-generous."

"If I could get to see him," said Alys, "I would tell him, Victorine. But you must know that Asquith is a declared opponent of the women's cause. For years he has turned his back and closed his door to us. Now that he is Prime Minister we fully expect him to do worse."

"Olivia," murmured my brother Luc, giving me a highly professional little boy's smile, "if you could let me have five pounds until pay day—or even—look here—I don't suppose you could make it ten? At least that ought to stop me bothering you again next weekend."

I entertained extensively because Max took it for granted that I would and, indeed, having gone to so much trouble to secure the Manor, it would have been nonsensical not to use it to the full. There were tennis parties and tea-parties on the lawn every day the sun shone, huge hats like upturned saucers of whipped cream, spotted muslin gowns and parasols, exquisite flowered china on lace tablecloths, cucumber sandwiches, scones and strawberry jam, cakes the consistency of swansdown feathers. There were houseparties, visitors to be met at Bradeswick Station, the huge roofed leather trunks to be sent on to Clarrow and picked up in a horse-drawn van but the guests themselves driven over in the Mercedes or the Rolls which soon succeeded it. They were, for the most part, acquaintances of Max's about whom he gave no explanations, suave, fluent, supple men, middle-aged for the most part and invariably prosperous with whom I felt perfectly at ease, although I would not have cared to inform myself in any great detail as to the source of their fortunes.

"Guns—or white slaves," I suggested to Madelon, the young Mrs. Naseby, who having spent three honeymoon months curled up in a cocoon of bliss had emerged just sufficiently to show a measure of curiosity about the outside world.

"And their wives?"

"Oh—retired madams I should imagine, grown rich and turned respectable."

"*Olivia!* How very interesting. Do you really think so?"

No. Not really. Simply women of experience, I supposed, who understood the value of the rings on their capable, well-manicured, if not always well-shaped fingers, wives of long standing and immense tolerance accustomed to meet each other in any corner of the world where the financial speculators, the *entrepreneurs*, the manipulators of stocks and shares might choose to congregate.

I made no close friends among them but they were easy, even pleasant company, so accustomed to traveling and visiting that they thoroughly understood the duties of a guest. They were punctual and polite, requiring no special diets, appearing perfectly pleased to see each other every morning at breakfast. They were never bored, never cross or out of sorts, conversing with knowledge and wit—their low, sometimes guttural voices passing easily from English to German to French and back again—on the safe topics of fashion, hotels, ocean liners, restaurants, telling tales in amusing not unkindly whispers of the amorous escapades of their own and each other's husbands.

And if adultery was committed under my roof occasionally it was done so discreetly that I had no need to be aware of it; these impeccably mannered, beautifully dressed husbands and wives appearing all to be so fond of each other that it was indeed difficult, sometimes, to tell them apart.

All morning, throughout the autumn, every armchair in the hall held its lady in her expensive town-made country clothes, reading, chatting, flirting mildly with any man—my brother Luc proving very useful for this purpose—who had not gone out with Max to shoot.

Luncheon would be served at noon, a light meal in the Regency dining room, a heavier one taken out in hampers and hot metal boxes to the sportsmen, several ladies usually driving out to drink a glass of wine in the coverts and watch the first drive of the afternoon. Tea would be served at little tables around the fire, at the cozy twilight hour of five o'clock, the display of elaborate tea gowns delighting Madelon who was at her best in billowing mauve, lilac or apple-green chiffon that slid from her shoulders, I noticed, exactly as my mother's dresses used to do before Bessie and Hattie Greenlaw had obliged her to be a shade more respectable.

After tea there was bridge or whist, a serious business this, occupying both our male and female guests—and Max—until dinnertime, which was rarely earlier than nine o'clock and always a gala performance of Worth and Doucet gowns, gold embroideries on white silk, silver on black, cascades of Venice and Brussels lace, sequined tulle, at least one diamond on every hand, a pearl choker at every throat, rubies and emeralds according to taste, all enticingly displayed.

The meal never less than ten courses long, would be superb,

348

the conversation civilized although difficult for Ivor Naseby and any others—Alys, even, when she came briefly but fairly regularly to perch among us—who could not speak two or three languages at the same time. And afterwards there would be whist again, sometimes baccarat, billiards, more talk of grand hotels, *haute couture* and *haute cuisine*. Sometimes a word or two on music and literature and painting about which they knew far more than one supposed.

And in addition to this I festooned the hall with holly and mistletoe at Christmas, with daffodils and branches of forsythia in spring, with summer roses, autumn fruit and ferns, deep brown and pale yellow chrysanthemums and, to celebrate the turn of every season, I gave a ball.

"Do you ever feel the Squire watching you?" asked Max.

Oh yes. He was there, now and again, looking out of his frame, his dark face and heavy-lidded eyes reminding me more and more strongly of Amyas; despising us, no doubt, every bit as much as he had expected.

I invited Amyas on every occasion but, apart from a brief appearance at my big Christmas dance, he never came. I offered to invite Mrs. Long with him, no longer caring what anyone thought of me and would have been perfectly prepared to accept her into my house as his supposed mistress if she still insisted on concealing the truth. He smiled and shook his head. I asked him to sit beside me in Clarrow Church in the family pew as I believed him to be fully entitled. He shook his head and smiled about that too. But quite soon he was able to buy the land at Tarn Brow which I had been holding, increasing his property to one half of the Clarrow estate.

"Unfortunately it will never make me a rich man."

"So long as it makes you happy."

"Yes—of course, Olivia."

I met him by appointment in the offices of Lawker & Lane to sign the necessary conveyance but when I suggested that, having cause to celebrate, we might open a bottle of champagne and eat a few oysters at the Station Hotel, he replied, once again, with that quiet smile, that courteous but definite shake of the head. It would not, he thought, be wise—for his sister Maria would be waiting and would have a meal ready prepared for him.

I understood. Maria Long, after a great deal of wandering in the wilderness, had found a refuge for herself and would tolerate no intrusion. Clarrow farmhouse was her home. Amyas—although I discounted the possibility of any physical relationship between them—was her man. Like a cat guarding her territory she would do her taut, tight-lipped best to keep me—or anyone else—away. But Amyas had asked me to turn to him when there was trouble and although I had no trouble—not really, nothing that mattered—there were times when I felt less cheerful, less confident, not quite so much in control as others. Nothing terrible, nothing I couldn't cope with, but just the same . . .

How many times this month had Luc wheedled money from me and what had he done with it? Had he really returned to Hexingham yesterday or had he gone off on his travels again as he had done last spring? Would I be likely to receive a letter from his headmaster in a week or two—as had happened twice already—inquiring his whereabouts and then a telegram from Luc himself, stranded in Cannes or St. Moritz or Baden-Baden? Would he even need me now, or want me to rescue him when I had introduced him to so many sophisticated women who had apartments in Paris and villas in Monte Carlo and might be only too pleased? What was I making of him?

And Madelon? She was happy, there was no doubt about it, frenziedly so it often seemed to me. Was all this feverish gaiety really good for her? How often had I seen her lately, swaying towards me across the lawn in the middle of the afternoon, champagne glass in hand, squinting in her enchanting fashion through the strong sunlight, casting so engaging a spell—that misty, fragile sorcery of the child-woman, the startled nymph—that like everyone except her mother-in-law I had smiled fondly, happy to indulge her in anything.

And what of these new friends of hers, that brittle, young couple she and Ivor had picked up somewhere, and with whom they were forever dashing off in motor cars with just a toothbrush, a bottle of perfume and a bottle of champagne, bathing naked in rivers which did not particularly trouble me, and gatecrashing parties of which I could not at all approve. High spirits? My mother said so. It was quite natural that Ivor, in control of his fortune and free of his mother at last, should let it all go to his head for a while and that Madelon—still busily "reflecting" Ivor—should do the same. And no matter how spendthrift they became, no matter how many motor cars Ivor ran into ditches nor how often Madelon lost her jewels which she kept on doing—having just "put them down somewhere," often enough in the long grass while she went for those intoxicated midnight swims—

350

there seemed no danger of their money running out, considering the healthy condition of the Brewery and the shrewdness of the managers Ivor's father had left in control. It was Esmeralda Naseby's fault, of course. She had ruined him. Was he ruining Madelon? Victorine thought so, and said so, blaming me of course, quite rightly.

"Nonsense, dear," soothed my mother, exceedingly pleased with the little luxuries two of her daughters were now able to put her way. "Wild oats, no more. I have sown my share. And they are happy—even Victorine doesn't deny that." Of course they were. They were in love, like children perhaps playing with toys that were too costly, just a shade too dangerous for games, but with a radiance that touched the heart.

Yet, there were times when *something* gnawed at my peace of mind and, although I never confided in Amyas or asked his advice, an hour of his company, in the farmyard or the open fields, invariably steadied me. We talked of nothing that I could afterwards remember; sometimes hardly at all. I watched him at work with his young stock. We walked, always for some specified agricultural purpose, across the plowed fields. We stood in the yard and observed the weather, the good health of his draft-horses and his officious, bustling sheepdogs, while his sister—who kept the long, low farmhouse as if it had been the Manor, serving him his claret every evening at dinner—peered out of her mullioned windows and resented me.

"Thank you, Amyas."

"My dear, for what?"

"Because you do me good."

I was playing, just a little, with fire, indulging myself only a whisper—with possibilities neither of us would ever explore. But those long, golden summers through which we lived, those slow, pleasant seasons blending so hazily one into the other, were ripe with indulgences. Days of good temper and good weather and luxuriant ease, of basking in every indolent ray of sunshine without the least suspicion of change. We were *here—now—forever*. Fixed in amber. Yes, I remembered who had once said that to me and I knew that he—like Alys—could not have lived like this.

Light days, iridescent days, a giddy eternity which—as it drew to its close, would turn my sweet sister Madelon into a tipsy, amorous butterfly and my brother Luc into a jewel thief.

TWENTY·ONE

On Friday, 6th May, 1910, that gallant *boulevardier*, King Edward VII, died in his sixty-ninth year, the chief mourners at his funeral including his eldest nephew, the German Kaiser, eight other kings, President Theodore Roosevelt of America and King Edward's stiff-legged and visibly dejected fox terrier led by a servant in Highland dress.

I was in Monte Carlo at the time where I had just discovered the *Ballet Russes* and the new Oriental gowns, hand-painted satins in all the glowing colors of a peacock's tail, crimson silks laced with gold thread, the opulence of Schéhérazade which these Russian scene painters and choreographers and costume designers had made so popular. And I had little thought to spare for departed kings.

"Oh dear," I said. "How sad." The featherlight grace of those Russian ballerinas, Pavlova and Karsavina, whose performances I had just enjoyed so much on my way through Paris, being far more real to me than anything King Edward had ever done.

"So good old Teddy is no more," said Max, lighting an after-breakfast cigar on the balcony of our hotel.

"Do you expect to make a fortune out of it—as you did with his mother?"

He shook his head. "There is no fortune to be made out of mourning these days, my pet. Even widows are discarding their weeds after a month or two. The times are changing, I fear."

"Are they?" I could see no evidence of it. Certainly I did not fear it, could detect no threat to my own well-being either from society

352

in general or from my own nearest and dearest in particular. But Max, although by no means afraid, seemed less optimistic.

"I know you rarely read the papers, my darling, but it strikes me that unrest—unease—is rather becoming the order of the day. And not just in the Balkans and in Ireland. The Lord knows we are used to that. But it cannot have escaped your notice that Sam Greenlaw's foundry workers have been out on strike this past month and more, since your sister Victorine has organized a soup kitchen to feed them when the strike pay runs out."

I smiled, remembering Bessie and Hattie Greenlaw's indignation and my mother's embarrassment. But how did it affect us?

Max shrugged and lit another cigar, leaning on the balcony and looking down at the leisured, fashionable scene below.

"Only as an indication that things are coming to a head. Even the Suffragettes are learning to defend themselves. They appear to have discovered that they cannot be so easily removed from a public place if they take the precaution of chaining themselves to something fairly solid—a lamp-post, for instance, or the grille of the Ladies' Gallery at the House of Commons. The idea being, of course, that even Prime Minister Asquith can hardly go on ignoring the existence of militant women when there is every likelihood of his finding one padlocked to the railings of Number Ten. Unfortunately, I do not think he will appreciate the joke."

"Then he should give us the vote and have it done."

"My dear," said Max, laughing. "How can he possibly do that? He is a Liberal. He imagines you will vote Tory. And there are a great many of you, you know."

But none of this, however much it might inerest me or even concern me, disturbed the crowded, often hectic patterns of my life, and Max's life, which ran not closely together perhaps—not even very regularly together, since he was often away from home, and I was not always there when he returned—but *smoothly* along the same broad, tolerant, well-oiled lines. Nothing directly harmed me. Nothing threatened me, or at least nothing I could not tackle, not even the sudden appearance of Luc in the Casino one night on the arm of a woman who understood that his attentions would not be free of charge. Not even the news that Madelon, who had given birth to a tiny wisp of a daughter three months ago, had abandoned the child to a nurse and gone off with Ivor and their fast young friends, the Lasonbys, on a jaunt to India, of all places, where Patrick Lasonby had just inherited property. Not even the news that Alys, who had been jailed twice last year, was in Holloway again.

I took Luc aside and told him I would withdraw his regular allowance unless he sent this irregular source of income back to her husband. I fretted a little—perhaps even a good deal—about my new little niece, Natasha, and then I cabled Victorine to keep an eye on her until my return. I assumed that if anything could be done these days to ease the lot of a militant suffragette in Holloway, then Max would do it—or have it done—for Alys.

And I believe it was Luc's casual remark that he supposed Alys would be on hunger strike by now like the rest, which brought us back to London a week or two earlier than we had planned.

"It is all Asquith's fault," I declared, quoting Alys. "He has refused time and time again to talk to the women. Whenever they try to approach him he turns his back. Whenever they try to deliver a petition to his door his only answer is to set his policemen loose on them like a pack of dogs. They have tried to do everything through the proper channels and he has ignored them. Is it any wonder that they have started to pick up sticks and stones and iron bars and defend themselves?"

"Don't blame Asquith too much," said Max, his skill as an *entrepreneur* enabling him to see, quite simultaneously, everyone's point of view. "He has other things on his mind, you know. A whole policy of social reform, for instance, which the House of Lords are blocking. And Irish Home Rule must be giving him a headache or two. It's a bad moment for him to have a bunch of articulate women in Holloway claiming the status of political prisoners and thinking up this hunger strike of theirs to twist his arm. I don't think he can let them get away with it."

But they *had* got away with it, for the first group of Suffragettes who had refused not only to eat prison food but to wear prison dress and to obey the prison rule of silence, had been released long before their sentences had expired.

A new weapon had been found, or so it seemed, and the next time Alys was sent to jail she stood shoulder to shoulder with her comrades, arms linked, their backs pressed against the wall when they were given the order to undress and, like the rest, was forcibly stripped and thrown bodily into her cell where she passed her sentence naked under a blanket. She was released five days later—three weeks before the end of her sentence—having taken no food. And although she looked no thinner when I went to see her in Cheyne Walk, there was a certain strangeness about her as if she were looking at me through a veil, hearing my voice from a distance, with no more than a surface layer of her mind. She had encountered, so many times now, the unendurable and had endured it. She had set herself to do what her nature had decreed to be impossible and had performed it. Yet she was still prone to that odd elongated sensation in her limbs, a feeling of being stretched, drawn out into a fine, taut line which, to be kept intact, needed the full concentration of her will.

"Olivia—how kind of you to come. Did you hear that our women marched to Holloway and blocked all the approach roads in protest at our solitary confinement?"

"Did it make you feel less lonely—locked up inside?"

"One doesn't feel the loneliness, Olivia. One doesn't think about it—that's all. One doesn't think about food either. And of course after a day or two there are no hunger pains. One gets a little light in the head and one *sees* things, I'm afraid. Things that aren't there, I mean, which is rather distressing, especially if one realizes one had been talking to—well—to thin air in fact. But I was fortunate this time. Some of our women were kept handcuffed for twenty-four hours in Stangeways, you know."

But far worse was to be done to "our women" than that.

"It was only to be expected," Alys told me, years later, in the cool, quiet voice she always used when speaking of horror and tragedy. "I suppose, in the Government's view, we had been getting out of hand. One or two bricks had been thrown through one or two important windows by then, you will remember. One of our women had even flown over the House of Commons in a balloon waving our banner. And when we started our hunger strike and seemed to be getting away with it, Asquith may have thought we were laughing at him. Perhaps we were. And that night in Birmingham, when it all began, the women did go rather wild. The police had sealed off the whole area around the hall where Asquith was speaking. But the women knew that would happen and they'd taken lodgings inside the barricades the day before. Naturally they couldn't get into the hall itself because it was ticket-holders only. But what they did was climb onto the roof of the building next door, prise up the tiles and throw them, just as hard as they could, onto the roof of the meeting hall. Poor Prime Minister Asquith. There he was trying to explain to the gentlemen of Birmingham how he was going to curb the veto of the House of Lords, and all that could be heard was clatter and crash. That is what started it."

The women were brought down from the roof, taken away to jail, and there, after several days of hunger strike were forcibly fed by means of a rubber tube pushed up the nostril and into the stomach, down which liquid food—presumably prison gruel—was poured.

It was, of course, not only a brutal procedure but possibly a fatal one for the dangers of suffocation, of damage to the heart, of puncturing a lung, were clear enough. And, in case they were not, one hundred and sixteen surgeons wrote at once to the Government to point them out. "Hospital treatment," the Government replied, "intending to preserve order in His Majesty's Prisons and to save lives." Not so. It was a procedure which had been used without success in asylums for the insane, so barbarous—medical opinion insisted—that persons regularly exposed to it might not only choke to death but could be driven to madness.

Torture, then. And more than that. It was rape. Every woman who experienced it, who was held down on her bed by alien hands while a stranger inserted two yards of hose into her helpless body, followed by warm liquid her body did not wish to take, knew she had been raped. Every woman who got up afterwards and staggered from the prison hospital to her plank bed in the punishment cell, retching, dizzy with shock, half asphyxiated, *knew* that she had been sexually molested and invaded. Yet, just as they had submitted themselves to a more straightforward violence, they submitted themselves to this, aware, perhaps, that no Government which went on raping its women could hope to survive.

Alys?

Would she undergo this horror too? I never doubted it. Nor could I doubt how patiently and proudly Robin would have waited for her at the prison gates, "being with her," as he was with her now—I understood and was glad—in those merciful hallucinations in her cell.

"It would be a great embarrassment to one and all if any of those women should die in there," said Max, glancing speculatively in the general direction of Holloway. "So if a prison doctor should declare her to be at death's door, I believe they would release her."

"Can you arrange it?"

356

"Let's see, shall we?"

He had asked her to marry him once, or so he said. I had never wanted to think about it. I did not want to think about it now. What mattered was getting her back to Clarrow Fell where she spent two slow summer weeks sitting beneath the chestnut tree in the vicarage garden, watching the dappled sunlight through the leaves, breathing, inhaling the wholesomeness of grass and foliage, tasting clean water; so separate, her reality so far removed from ours that even her mother did not question her.

Yes. She had been forcibly fed. It had happened. She supposed it would happen again. Unfortunately she had rather lost her taste for food, her stomach refusing anything but bread, it seemed; crusty and fresh, yes please, how lovely—and a little cheese. No—no thank you— no soup, nothing liquid or warm—oh dear. "I beg your pardon," and bent double by a spasm of nausea she was obliged to hurry from the room.

But she would not stay. She was officially engaged now by the W.S.P.U. as an organizer at a salary of two pounds a week, rather more than Mr. Greenlaw paid his foundry men, although they, of course, were not required to risk their lives. Victorine did not agree. Had we not noticed the change in Bradeswick, the men walking with that dejected slouch of the hungry and the unemployed, along the streets, or sitting listlessly on their doorsteps with nothing to do and no money coming in now that the strike pay had run out? Would the suffragettes feed them from their war chest?

"No," said Alys, "we will get the vote and bring in legislation for higher wages so that they can feed themselves."

"Will you?" said Victorine. "Your friend Miss Frances Grey is opposed to Lloyd George's National Insurance Scheme—or didn't you know? She feels that the payment by the State would ruin the caring relationship one often finds—she believes—between a mistress and her maids."

Alys smiled. "Ah yes. But I have yet to meet Frances in Holloway."

I drove her to the London train at the end of the fortnight's convalescence she had allowed herself and then hurried back to the Manor to prepare for guests, finding myself unable to respond with anything approaching enthusiasm to the menus Monsieur Clement had left on my desk or even to the quiet competence of Mrs. Charles.

Dinner would be magnificent. It always was. The guests—and Max—would be charming, witty, attentive, immensely civilized, as they always were. The weekend would be a success, exactly as Max expected and wanted. Exactly as *I* wanted. Surely? This was the life I had chosen. I was *here* at the Manor, where I had so urgently longed to be. And I had not the slightest complaint to make of Max. He had never hurt me, never so much as raised his voice to me, he had not lost his money. Pain, as he said, did not interest him, only pleasure and we had pleased each other. Max liked me—at least I thought so and hoped so. I liked him. And if he was unfaithful to me now and then, when he went abroad alone—as he was going to Madeira, I suddenly remembered, next week—then it would only be casually and it had not even occurred to me to be unfaithful to him.

What ailed me then? Why—when there was nothing in my life I intended to change—was I suddenly plagued by so many vague dissatisfactions, an odd, irrational feeling that life, which was probably half over, had not really succeeded in getting started at all. What did I want? Nothing I could put a name to. What worried me? Madelon's was the first name that sprang to mind. She should not have gone junketing off to India and left a three-month-old child. When Esmeralda Naseby had said much the same thing I had flown at her like a spitting cat in my sister's defense, but *I* could say it. For however astonishing, however distressing, it was the truth. And there was Luc, of course, who had left Hexingham last year in nothing even remotely resembling a blaze of glory and had seemed content ever since to lounge around my house or my mother's house or Madelon's before she went away, taking his monthly allowance twice over, I supposed, from each of us.

But Luc and Madelon and my mother had always worried me. It was more than that. What did I want? *When* was it going to start?

"*Very* nice, Olivia," said Max, watching me slip into an Oriental tunic of crimson satin painted with gold peacocks and chrysanthemums, worn knee-length over a long black satin skirt.

"Thank you, Max." I had gold earrings and bracelets, an ebony cigarette holder mainly for show since I had tried hard, but without much success, to learn to smoke. I had assurance, poise, a ready flow of conversation. Like Max, I did not care enough about the people assembled in my dining room to be hurt by any one of them. They were pleasant, rather more decent and vulnerable in some cases than they liked to appear, a little greedy of my hospitality sometimes but making no claims on my affections, never disturbing my peace of mind. No harm could come to me through them, or so I believed, until the next morning after breakfast when an apologetic but slightly alarmed woman, who had spent the evening flirting with my brother Luc, came to tell me that she had lost a diamond ring.

It was the situation every hostess must dread.

"Is it possible you have put it down somewhere, *madame?*"

But her fingers were big knuckled, tenacious, not likely to lose their rings.

"I'm afraid, Mrs. de Haan, that I remember distinctly putting it away in my jewel case. And my personal maid has been with me for years. She is entirely to be trusted. I am sorry, *madame.*"

I believed her. She was a hostess of some experience herself and fully understood the implications, the awkwardness. But just the same, one could not take the loss lightly and if I had a thief in my house—among the staff of course since clearly no one had broken in—then for my own sake I ought to know about it. And unfortunately the ring in question was of sentimental as well as monetary value, a present from her first husband before he had died in South America. I would, therefore, understand the delicacy, and that although she knew, whatever happened, she would be adequately reimbursed financially, by her insurance and by Max, what she would really like was her ring back again. Her present husband—as I had surely noticed—was older than herself and, while we were on the subject, she had better tell me—in case there *should* be an investigation—that although her husband had slept alone last night, or so she imagined, she had not. Naturally she would not wish to reveal the gentleman's name—not to her husband at any rate—but, if it became absolutely necessary, he could confirm that she had put her jewels away, since he had watched her do it.

Dear God! My stomach lurched and froze. Please—not that. But it was *that* exactly—what else? Luc with his magpie hoard of shiny, sparkly things on the night of my mother's attempted suicide. Luc now, substituting those old crystal buttons with diamonds. Oh, God help us. I drew a deep breath, knowing I should have seen it coming for a long time.

"I understand, *madame.*"

"Yes. I am truly sorry."

We searched the house and the grounds, of course, Mrs. Charles very tight-lipped, the maids nervous and scared, looking guilty every one; finding nothing. What next? Drawers and cupboards to be investigated in the staff bedrooms, mattresses to be turned over. And then, unless Mrs. Consuelo Forrester's elderly second husband would settle for substantial compensation from Max, the police. I could not allow that.

"Max!"

"Yes—my pet?"

Help me, Max. You help Alys often enough. Now help *me*. How could I ask him in such a manner that he would understand the urgency and not suspect the cause?

I had no need.

"Perhaps we should adjourn," he said, "for an hour or two. Perhaps *someone* may benefit from a little time to think. And luncheon, of course, in the library. Consuelo, my darling, a drop of this venerable brandy might take just a little of the evil taste away . . ."

I followed Luc up to his room, giving him no time to bolt his door, and, rushing at him, hit him a stinging blow across the head.

"I say—steady on, Olivia." But he was scared, almost glad to be caught since it meant that now *I* would have to get him out of the mess. And having no time to tell him how despicable, how low he was, how atrociously he had let me down, no time to threaten him with reprisals, I hit him again, a whole flurry of blows to the head and the chest, hurting him as much as I could.

"Leave off, Olivia—don't mark my face."

"Oh—you think it's your fortune do you—you tuppenny-ha'penny little gigolo. You despicable little toad. Just give me that ring."

"All right. All right." And as he opened his wardrobe, took the ring from the pocket of his dinner-jacket and put it in the palm of my hand, my temper faded, leaving me sick at heart.

"Why, Luc?"

"Why not?" he said, turning sullen. "She doesn't need it. She has a dozen more. What are you going to do?"

"Find it. She knows you took it of course. Obviously she doesn't think you were worth it. I don't blame her."

"What then? When she's got it back, I mean?"

"You can go to Cambridge—or get a job."

360

"You won't tell Max?"

It was the last thing in the world I intended to do, so much so that when the door opened and Max came into the room I slid the ring into my pocket and said in a startled, foolish, extremely unnatural fashion, "Oh Max—hello."

I had never seen him angry before. Sarcastic, yes, and in a finely tuned state of alertness, competitive, wary, keeping his nerve. Perhaps, in the normal run of the cards, he did not care enough about anything to be angry. He was angry now, in a manner far removed from my own heated explosions, his temper cold and accurate and of the kind that would feel no remorse later, as I so often did.

"All right, Luc." And ignoring me entirely he held out his hand.

"Sorry Max—I'm not quite with you."

"Consuelo Forrester's diamond, Luc."

"Well—there's a rum thing. Olivia had the same idea, but she's had a good look round and she knows I haven't got it. Tell him, Olivia."

I had lied for him often enough before. It was natural that he should expect it now. But he ought to have seen—as I could see so clearly—that it was no use. Max had known from the start, as I had known, and there was nothing I could now do to cover Luc's tracks. Did I even want to cover them or think that they should be covered? His dishonesty had soiled my house—Max's house—and Max was fully entitled to take any action he pleased about that.

"Luc—shut up!" I said, as he began a fatuous, Hexingham muttering about the dishonesty of "serving wenches" and how good old Consuelo had probably flushed her jewels down the w.c. But I was too late. Max had already struck out, rapidly, viciously, and Luc was staggering backwards, his hand held tight across his eye.

"Max—oh don't," he gasped, plainly terrified, younger and a little taller now than Max, but collapsing entirely as Max moved in accurately and precisely and hit him twice more in the mouth, drawing blood. And I obeyed an instinct that was entirely female, entirely from the heart. I defended the child against the man, irrespective of who was guilty, who was to blame.

"Leave him alone—that's enough."

He stepped back, transferring his cold gaze from Luc to me, evidently finding nothing to his taste in either one of us.

"Can you really defend what he has done, Olivia?—even you?"

Of course I could not defend him. It was just that I could not bear to see anyone else attack him. I had struck myself a moment ago and would probably have done so again had Max not interrupted us. But I could not watch anyone else strike him. He was entirely in the wrong. I could find no justification for him, no excuse. He deserved to be punished. Just the same, he was my little brother.

"Don't touch him. He's scared to death of you. He's only a boy."

"Really? When it comes to getting into bed with my friends' wives or their maids, or your maids, he doesn't call himself a boy. Although when it comes to work, of course, then yes—I absolutely agree with you—he's just a child who can't be expected to pay his way—not *ever*, it seems to me. And now he's a thief. What are you, Luc? Tell me."

And when Luc, appalled by the sight of his own blood on his hands and staining his shirt frill, did not reply, that hard lean hand shot out and hit him again, knocking him over onto the settee.

"I said don't touch him."

"I heard you."

"Max—please stop. It does no good."

"Ah—you know how to handle him then, do you? You know how to make a man of him? I doubt it, my pet—believe me, I do. So I'll take him off your hands. He goes to the Cape at the end of the month and he can sweat for his bread—as I had to do."

We spoke both together my brother and I—one voice. "No."

"Yes," said Max.

"You can't make me."

"Yes, Luc. I can. You'll be out of this house bag and baggage by the twenty-third."

"It's my house, Max."

"No, Olivia. Not really. We both know that. I can tolerate a great many things, most things in fact. Not a thief. He goes."

"Just where?"

"I'll make the arrangements. I have business interests out there—associates who can put him to work."

"He'll get into trouble . . ."

"Of course he will. He'll do that anyway. Better Cape Town than Clarrow Fell."

But I could not have Luc running around a vast, dangerous

place like the African continent, getting up to Heaven alone knew what—except that I had a very good idea—with no one to turn to. I could not abandon him to strangers. No matter what he had done—and I had no illusions and very little hope of his improvement—I could not do that. My brother was a thief. My blood froze and my skin burned with shame at the thought of it. But Africa! Yes, he was a thief. I kept reminding myself of that. But instead of the smooth, callous young philanderer—the tuppenny-ha'penny gigolo I had just named him—I saw the child clutching his small shiny gleanings for security. And I remembered how I had taught him to depend on the ingenuity and the generosity of older women.

"Max . . ."

He turned towards me, rapid, contemptuous, hard as iron, classing me now, I could see, with Luc and my mother, with Emil Junot and probably Madelon.

"Yes, Olivia. You would do well to keep out of this, you know. In fact *out* altogether would be a good idea. I'd like just a moment or two alone with him."

"Why?" Instantly I bristled with alarm. "What are you going to do?"

"Nothing he'll die of. He's been to Hexingham so he's had a good thrashing before. If you please, Olivia . . ."

He held open the door for me and I went out into the corridor and stood with my back to the wall, my eyes closed, my position entirely false, since Max was within his rights in punishing Luc, I was completely wrong in my urge to protect him, *wrong*—so wrong—in allowing resentment to boil up inside me so that when Max finally reappeared it was plain to see. How dare he say the Manor was not really mine, even though it was not? How dare he send Luc away? Did he not realize how hard I had struggled to keep my family together? How could he expect me to discard a lifetime of loyalty to my brother, no matter how undeserving he had turned out to be? But Max was loyal only to himself and did not understand the complicated emotional process by which it seemed possible, at the same moment, to condemn and to forgive.

"The ring," he said curtly, snapping his fingers as he held out his hand. "You have it, I suppose."

"Don't snap your fingers at me, Max de Haan."

"Why not? You take my wages, don't you, like everybody else."

"Is that what I do?" I was appalled, the breath driven out of me as if he had struck me a foul blow. Indeed, he *had* struck me. "Is that what I do?—What you think I am?"

"Just give me the ring, Olivia. Do you care what I think of you? So long as you have your brother and your sisters and your mother and somebody to pay your bills, do you care about anything—unless it's that cartload of junk you keep at the Gatehouse that I'm not supposed to know about? You'd better go down there tomorrow and take stock, in case your precious Luc has helped himself to a piece or two."

I was trembling badly, but since I could not conceal it, I would make him think it was with anger, not with anything else I might be feeling.

"I might do that. Is Luc all right?"

"Intact you mean? Reasonably. He has blood on his shirt which seems to upset him—silk, I suppose. I imagine you'll buy him another."

"I imagine so."

I had clenched my fist around the ring and now I opened it, he put his hand beneath mine and I dropped the diamond and emerald cluster—not the best one I had ever seen–into his palm.

"Thank you, Olivia."

"What are you going to do with it?"

"Find it. What were you going to do with it?"

"Find it."

"Quite so. What a pity we just couldn't see a way of finding it together."

"I suppose that remark must be very profound."

"Very likely—so we had better forget it hadn't we?"

"As you please, Max—since this is *your* house, after all, and I am just—well—I don't really know." Wounded, I thought, but I would die of those wounds before I would let him catch a glimpse of them. And, in any case, he was still too cold and too angry to notice.

"You had better go to your brother. I am sure he needs you."

"He always has."

"If that is supposed to move me, Olivia, then I'm sorry to disappoint you, for it is altogether beyond me. I have never needed anyone, *never* at any time in my life. It is outside my range of feeling—which is where I intend to stay. So if your brother needs you or you need him, or anyone else, I can be neither sorry nor glad nor very much interested at all. Where need is concerned you must do as you think best."

Nodding curtly, he put the ring in his pocket and walked away.

TWENTY·TWO

Consuelo Forrester, her elderly husband and our other guests left on the Monday morning after a weekend of scrupulous politeness, no further mention being made of the stolen ring or one word of surprise expressed by anyone at the sudden nature of its recovery; only Consuelo herself having any reason to doubt that Luc's black eye and cut lip were the results of a disagreement with his horse.

He had made love to her at her invitation and if she believed he had taken the diamond as payment he considered to be due, she was probably not far from the truth. She was returning now to London with a husband twenty years her senior who played bridge every evening and then fell asleep, and who had married her for her family connections in the textile trade. But she was smiling, affable, poised, utterly carefree as we arrived at Bradeswick Station, kissed me goodbye, hoped to see me again, waved to me from the window of her train, her husband engrossed already in his copy of *The Times*.

Poor Consuelo: to depend—at forty or was she forty-five?—on any chance snippets of thrill and fantasy she could snatch from men like Luc. Yes—poor indeed. I got into the Rolls—similar to the one which would be waiting for her at King's Cross—and drove home, lethargic in the August heat, realizing that for perhaps the first time in my life I had nothing very pressing to do, no one's affairs to put in order but my own. Max was leaving next week to check certain of his interests abroad and had been far from specific about the date of his return. Luc's passage to the Cape had already been booked. Madelon was in India, whence came tales of picnics offered by Indian princelings with rubies as big as pigeon's eggs in their turbans, regimental balls, of *fun*, such fun—goodness, she had never realized the world was such a *jolly*, such a marvelous place. Alys was in London, Aunt Sibylla so busy with her parish and her domestic duties that she had never a moment to spare. The vicar was collecting butterflies. My niece, Natasha, was reposing in her cradle, looked after by an indifferent nurse and her grandmother, Esmeralda Naseby, who although she did not herself care for children quite so young as that, was determined that *I* should not have her. While my mother—Natasha's grandmother too—who could not really have been refused regular access to the child, was about to set off for London to equip Luc, at Max's expense, for his colonial journey. And although Victorine, with three little boys now to her credit, had no plans for leaving Bradeswick, she was too critical and too shrewd to be good company in the present depression of my spirits.

The summer promised to be long and hot and lonely. The prospect of parting from Max for an indefinite period in these strained circumstances filled me with vague alarm. Not that I expected him to do anything drastic or final or even anything unusual at all. He would behave, I supposed, just as he always did, which was exactly as he pleased, returning in the autumn for the shooting with presents and anecdotes and gossip, guests arriving by the next train, a horse on its way from Tattersall's, a new car, a bale of Indian silks, a bale of Chinese rugs. He would be good-humored and easy, looking forward to the season's sport and would probably never mention the incident of Consuelo Forrester again.

But it had happened. I had reacted emotionally, wrongly, had not explained myself, would be unlikely ever to explain myself now. He had spoken harsh words to me so coldly that I could not even pretend they had been spoken in temper and not really meant. He had expressed contempt, dislike, not for the whole of me perhaps but of more than enough to shatter the smooth surface I had achieved and stir up a gnawing, persistent unease. That same evening at dinner he had behaved as if nothing had occurred. The next day, both in public which I could understand and in private which I found difficult to accept, he had been absolutely and in every way his usual self.

I was less civilized than that. When I was hurt I required time to heal. When my feelings were wounded they bled and would not stop, conveniently, because it was dinner-time or because a partner was needed for whist. I needed to have things out. I needed confrontation, consolation, *time*. I needed . . . ? What did I need? Would I recognize it if I came upon it in the street? When would life begin? And why—*why* did I keep asking myself that foolish question when the answer was clear? It had happened, gone, and I had been running too fast to notice. I would do well now to compose myself—preferably at once—and be the lady of my Manor, as I certainly desired, take care of my village, or the few cottages which still belonged to me, and live my days reasonably and pleasantly, one at a time. Max? Max used me. Very well. I had done the same. I was *here*—*now*—living as I had chosen. I would do well to get on with it and forget this nonsensical obsession with beginnings.

I took luncheon alone and then walked the mile to Clarrow Bottom through blue, cloudless weather, carrying a basket of roses for Maria Long; a gift to provide me with a reason for coming and which I knew she would not want.

"Mrs. de Haan, how very obliging of you to call."

"I have just brought you these few flowers . . ."

"How kind."

She took them from me and put them on her kitchen table where I rather imagined she would leave them to wither, ceremoniously escorted me into her parlor and seated me in a chair of state, the room closing in on me as it always did, obsessively clean and polished, the windows heavily shrouded with net so that no ray of sunlight could slip in to attack the carpet, a heavy dark red curtain across the door; an impression, I always thought, that the room had been sealed off, Amyas and Mrs. Long sealed *in*.

She knew, of course, that Amyas had told me of their relationship but she had never, by word or deed, acknowledged it. The fiction to which she clung *must* be played out and it was as a salaried housekeeper that she stood rigidly in the doorway and informed me "Mr. Hird will not be back for some considerable time."

"Oh—where has he gone?"

"I really couldn't say. But he will not be back. He is so busy just now."

"Is he really? I thought farmers had nothing to do in the summer but wait for their crops to grow."

"Mr. Hird—madam—is a dairy farmer."

"Yes, Mrs. Long, I do know that—and there he is, I believe—surely that is his horse just coming into the yard?"

And to her intense mortification I twitched aside her net curtain, opened her window—to which, she in her role of housekeeper, could make no objection—and called out "Amyas—don't come in. I'll come out to you."

"Mr. Hird will be wanting his tea, madam. He has had a long ride."

"Not yet. You may serve in an hour, Mrs. Long, or thereabouts. And tea with lemon for me, these days, if you please."

She would have strangled me—quite naturally—if she could. She could not. Yet her dislike, her jealousy—for what else was it but that?—pursued me as I went out into the farmyard, her spare, dark figure watching at the window as we walked away.

"I believe I have upset your sister, Amyas."

He smiled. "You always do. She always recovers."

"Does she make you suffer for it?"

"No."

"But she suffers?"

"Alys would say that that is what women are made for."

We walked a fair distance, saying little. He had had a long ride, perhaps he *was* tired, perhaps a pot of his sister's excellent tea would not have gone amiss. But her taut presence dominated the house, drained the atmosphere entirely of everything but her obsessions and her insecurities, her unhealthy determination to shut herself away with him, and had I allowed him to go inside she would have done everything in her power to detain him. But now—plagued once again by that odd impression of time either not yet begun or running out—I said suddenly, startling myself, "Amyas, do you know you are leading a very odd existence?"

And he replied without pause or hesitation, as if I had made some commonplace remark about the weather, "Yes—as it happens—I do."

"With Maria I mean."

"I know what you mean."

"Doesn't it overburden you?"

"A little. There is no physical side to it, you know."

"Heavens—of course not . . ."

"Why should you be so horrified? It is not uncommon between a brother and sister who first met as adults. Maria is simply not a physical person—not in any shape or form."

Dare I ask him about himself? Suddenly he told me.

368

"I am not celibate, Olivia, if that is what you were wondering. It is possible to enjoy a sexual relationship from time to time which is neither romantic nor entirely commercial."

"Is that enough for you?"

"Yes."

"It can't be, Amyas."

"I think it has to be."

I had quickened my step, needing to get as far away as possible from the house and the woman inside it—who would be shielding her eyes, I imagined, to check the direction in which we were heading—and I was breathless when we reached the point at which I knew we were out of her sight.

"Has anything happened to you, Olivia?"

"Lord, no—what could happen to me?"

We were on high ground, the land sloping away from us in a patchwork of greens and browns, healthy fields doing exactly as they should, neatly divided by gray stone walls; and suddenly there was a breeze, rising straight up from the moor above us, bringing the scents of heather and bracken and coarse, dry grasses.

Nothing stirred. I had been here once before in this high blue solitude with Robin, never with Max, who only came to the moor with a gun in his hand. Max who could bring down his eighty birds with eighty shots any and every autumn morning. Max who took and won. Amyas who did not. I knew exactly what he had meant by his encounters which were neither romantic nor commercial, widows of his own age in reduced circumstances, some of them pretty enough, I supposed, glad of his kindness and his advice and whatever presents he might feel inclined to give them or their children at Christmas time. Women who might miss him more than they had intended when he went back to his sister.

It was not enough for him, could never be enough. The aridity of his life in that clean, dark house overwhelmed me with such force that I seemed to live it for him, felt it parch me and choke me, submitted, for a horrifying moment, to the demands Maria Long made not on his emotions but on his conscience, his capacity not for love but for pity. I wanted more than that for him, much more—for he was *worth* more than that, worth more than a hundred of me.

"Amyas . . .!" There was something urgent and vital I had to say to him, something, anything, to prevent this self-immolation, to convince him that no matter what Maria Long had suffered she was not entitled to this. Yet, my throat and my chest were tight with tears, and I could not find the words I needed: could not speak at all.

And it was then that one of the most momentous events of my life happened to me. Amyas took my hand. Just that, his fingers sliding along my wrist and closing around mine firmly, quietly; a simple hand-clasp to tilt the horizon and the earth beneath my feet so that I could never look at anything from the same viewpoint, never tread the same ground again. He held my hand; and it was as if the whole of myself reposed there in the hollow of his palm, sheltered, at peace. At home.

It was marvelous and terrible. Life just beginning and at the same time running out, since there was no hope anywhere, not even the faintest glimmer, that it could be allowed to last.

"I love you, Olivia—does it offend you to know it?"

But I had known it for a long time already without acknowledging it to myself, had come to him so often for warmth, for air and moisture, to lean on his calm strength. Amyas will see to it. Amyas will know. I would trust my life to Amyas.

"My dear—don't cry," he said. Was I crying? Yes, and strangely, no sobs, no laboring of the breath, just water trickling from my eyes quite silently.

"Why are you telling me?"

"Because I have succumbed to the temptation. There is no other reason. I would not insult you by . . ."

"I would not be insulted."

"Olivia, you are married—to my brother, as it happens, although *that* relationship hardly matters. And I have a commitment of my own. But when I see you dejected and unhappy as you are today—however much you try to conceal it—then the feeling I have for you wants to be heard. Just now I failed to hold it back—that is all. There is nothing I expect you to do, nothing I would be prepared to ask. Please don't cry."

But I could do nothing to stop the tears that were pouring down my cheeks, released now, in this unlikely place, by the realization that I was indeed loved as I had always wanted to be loved, in the way that I had always wanted to give love, that this was the mind and the spirit which matched my own; Amyas, who had always been at my side, quiet, unobtrusive, invisible.

• • •

'I didn't see you," I cried out. "You didn't let me see you."

"I had nothing to offer. I was your grandfather's land agent. Vivian Heron's bastard son. And your eyes were dazzled by other things. I met you at the station in Leeds when you first came here— you may not remember . . ."

"I remember."

"I had never seen anyone so brave and so beautiful as you were that day, Olivia. I began by desiring you, I suppose, since one does not really fall in love with a stranger. But desire alone would have soon faded had there been nothing more. It never has. I watched you that evening and the day after and the day after that, taking on the world all by yourself; except that *I* was there, watching—even if you didn't see me—absolutely at your side. I have been watching you, my darling, with delight and anxiety and pride sometimes, ever since. I am not humble, Olivia—just realistic. I have never had anything to offer you—except the knowledge that you *are* loved. If that is of use to you then I shall be glad."

Of use to me? For the whole of my conscious life I had yearned to inspire such devotion and to give it, to exchange total loyalty for total loyalty, to take on the vast commitment I had always known real love to be. My nature had been formed expressly for that purpose, to *feel*, with the courage to give myself entirely and the strength to receive, in his entirety, the man who loved me. I had been made for this one absolute emotion which would have led me—or anyone else privileged to feel it—towards a warmer, purer humanity. It was a revelation of truth. What now?

Nothing. Or so it might have seemed to any casual observer walking his dog on the moor. We stood inches apart, just his hand still holding mine, those tears still seeping from my eyes. Nothing: except that I gave myself without moving a step, wholly and absolutely. Spiritually, essentially, with everything that concerns the will, the aspect of myself which I had learned, without too much understanding, to call the soul, we joined together. We made love. Truly and perfectly so that nothing remained in me that he had not touched, possessed, gently returned.

"My dearest love—God keep you . . ."

My body wanted him too. But I knew he would have to be tempted indeed to take that.

He wished to walk with me back to the Manor but I refused.

What kind of woman was I to inspire love which did no good to anyone, and he was tired, had probably eaten nothing since early morning. No. I set off alone, walking fast, hoping by exhausting the body to quiet the mind. But the turmoil would not subside and when I entered the hall every nerve was still tingling, my head full of the clamoring, racing thoughts of a feverish dream.

I saw Max's hat and riding gloves on the hall table, glanced at the clock, and running upstairs—my intentions still incoherent, impulsive rather than resolute—I tapped at his bedroom door and went in.

He was standing by the window, doing something to a dueling pistol which had probably been his father's, a decorative, showy thing no longer fit for firing. But the sight of a gun in his hand startled me into the flippancy with which I often covered my alarm.

"Lord—don't shoot me."

"Why? Should I? What have you done?"

"Nothing."

"So—then you're safe, aren't you."

No. Very far from that.

"Max . . ."

"Yes?"

"I just wanted to say . . ." But there was nothing I could say. I needed to act, not speak, and making a physical appeal to a physical man I threw my arms around him, found his hard mouth and kissed him, offering—for everyone's sake—the desire which had been aroused by Amyas.

"What's this—at four o'clock in the afternoon?"

"Never mind what it is. Take advantage of it."

"I believe I will."

"I just thought we should make peace—that's all."

But I was not peaceful. I had never felt so urgently the need to be physically possessed, to be taken, held down by arms that were stronger than mine, crushed by hard shoulders and entered with the force of an impalement, ravished. And, although it was not the way Max habitually made love, his sensual experience was varied and full and having sensed the need he knew how to supply it.

But exultation was succeeded by a great wave of misery and self-disgust so that, as he got up to dress, I turned my face into the pillow and howled, "Oh God—why don't I conceive!"

He glanced keenly down at me.

"You want my child? How touching."

"I want *my* child."

"Of course. You will agree that I do everything in my power to oblige."

"I know—I know. It's me. I'm a barren woman—oh *Christ!*"

"Don't take it so much to heart. And how's my brother by the way? I was out on the moor a little while ago and I glimpsed you in the distance."

"He's very well."

"Good. Tell me—do you and he always walk hand in hand?"

"Why not? He's my brother-in-law isn't he? And those fields are very uneven."

"So they are." He was almost dressed now, choosing his shirt studs and tie.

"Max . . . ?"

"Yes, my pet."

"When you go off, wherever it is you're going, next week, would it be an inconvenience if I came with you?"

The light from the open window was behind him and I could not see his face, was simply aware that he did not answer at once, his silence alarming me. Did he suspect me? And of what? I had done nothing that could even remotely be called adultery. At least, not in the way Max would understand it. I closed my eyes.

"No," he said, "no inconvenience at all. It would be a pleasure."

We traveled down to Maderia with Luc on the first leg of his voyage to the Cape, and were met in Funchal by the suave gentleman who handled Max's affairs in South Africa. He would keep an eye on Luc, he promised me, a practiced eye in fact, since he had sons of his own and knew what pitfalls to look out for.

"He'll be all right, you know," Max said on the night they sailed.

"I have my doubts about that. I just agree that it had to be done."

"You did the best you could for him, Olivia."

"Oh—thank you kindly, sir. Obviously it wasn't good enough."

"And I was brutal to him, which I do not in the least regret and brutal to you, which may have been unnecessary."

"Are you actually apologizing, Max? I can hardly believe it."

"Ah well—I may not go so far as to say that. But what I will say is that I am glad we have remained—well—very much as we were. I have a reason to go over to Agadir and, since you have never landed on the African coast, I thought it might interest you. And then, if I make the profit I expect to make, we can go and spend it in Casablanca."

And on my bedside-table that night there was a suede box containing an emerald rather finer than the one he had given, on the day of our arrival, to his grasping, indifferent mother.

We went from Casablanca across sparkling blue water to Cádiz where I bought lace and pearls and met a great many of Max's Spanish relations who seemed, mostly, to be employed by him at the warehouse he seemed to own at the old port. We went on to Genoa, then Athens where Luc had been born and where I inquired, very casually, at breakfast one morning, "Are we going to Corfu?"

"No, darling," he said, without turning a hair, "I am going to Corfu." And he left me alone—admittedly very comfortably installed and well provided for—while he attended to whatever business awaited him on the island.

Had he a child there as my mother had once suggested? Hardly a child now, I supposed, any longer, since my mother's remark had been made nine or ten years ago. Did I have any right to inquire? I inspected ancient monuments, climbed the Pnyx, twisted my ankle on the hot, stony slope of the Acropolis, wondered what to do in case he did not come back for me. For even now I did not discount the possibility that he might suddenly find himself bankrupt, clapped in irons and bundled into some foreign jail, set upon in a dark alley one night by old enemies and never seen again: stabbed in the back by a jealous woman.

He appeared a week later, smiling, immaculate, bringing me turquoise and coral in barbaric settings of beaten gold; ready, he said, for Venice, Paris—the only city I knew better than he did—London, and home. He would be too late for the grouse, which he liked to take at the start of the season, but the pheasant would be plentiful, the air frosty already and crisp, which would be a welcome change to this eternal sunshine. Had it been a good trip, I inquired? Oh yes. It had adequately covered our extravagances of last year and the extravagances we would be likely to make during the year to come.

We had been away for almost five months and not one cross

word had been spoken between us. It had been light, superficial, yes, and as unsatisfying, in the long term, as a diet of sorbet and whipped cream, but so pleasant, so easy, *safe*. And how very far—in physical and spiritual miles—it had taken me from Amyas. It would have been my mother's notion of paradise, Victorine would have found it wasteful and dull, Alys would have been enchanted by landscape and architecture and history, by the thrill of being abroad, and embarrassed by the cost of fine food and wine, the casual profit and loss at every turn of the card, the jewelry.

And Madelon? I had heard nothing from her since Cádiz when, in a note which had taken a very long time to reach me, she had scrawled in her hectic appreciation of the Raj, "I think I shall stay here forever, unless, of course, it is China next as they are talking of. Not that mandarins are likely to be a patch on rajahs—although one never knows . . ."

And so, on our last night in London, sitting in the restaurant of the Carlton Hotel, after a sumptuous dinner of oysters and caviar and quails, I was taken completely by surprise when I heard a trill of familiar laughter interspersed by a sharp, nervous cough and, looking up, saw coming towards me a woman slender enough to seem almost transparent, pale hair in a wild tumble of curls and gold ribbons, her dress, which was not much more than a few gold sequins and a swirl of gold-spangled chiffon, slipping from her shoulders, the movements of her brittle, nervous, fragile body clearly visible beneath it.

"Madelon!"

She looked quite naked and utterly enchanting, a wicked, affectionate, engaging little wisp of thistledown, no substance about her anywhere but her huge excitement, an intense exhilaration erupting from her like the sparks of a Catherine-wheel, her body feeling hot, her bones as tiny and breakable as a bird's when I put my arms around her and kissed her.

"Madelon, indeed," said Max, rising to his feet, looking amused and appreciative as he drew out a chair, "and *not* Madelon's husband, I see."

I had seen it too, or rather I had seen *him*, her husband's friend, Patrick Lasonby, who was supposed to be going to China, here now, very much at her side.

"Madelon—where's Ivor?"

She put her elbows on the table, dislodging a great deal of

silver and glassware, her chin perched on her hands like the mischievous, three-cornered face of a kitten.

"I only wish I knew."

"Darling—how long have you been in England?"

"I wish I knew that as well."

And, squinting at me through the candlelight, her eyes by no means in focus, she went off into a trill of laughter like a scattering of high notes in music, broken very charmingly here and there by her cough.

"Madelon!" I warned, although Patrick Lasonby and Max were both laughing with her. And, sitting up straight, playing the child at school, she said, "Yes, Olivia. I will behave. I will even try to remember."

And she was off again, laughing, taking a sip from everybody's glass, waving to acquaintances she saw, or thought she saw, across the room.

"Max—I always thought you were a good host. Why don't you give me a drink?"

I shook my head but he shrugged, ordered more champagne.

"You haven't said how pleased you are to see me."

"Of course I'm pleased."

"And pleased to see Patrick—since he seems to be all I have in the world at the moment."

I shot a glance of alarm at Max but he shrugged again and, until we had shaken hands with Patrick Lasonby, she would say nothing more. And then, when the courtesies had been observed, with a comic attempt at discretion, she sent him away, offering him a regretful, little wave of the hand as he went to wait for her in the foyer.

"Well then—it's like this—we came home instead of going to China because—well, I don't know, but it sounded reasonable at the time and I must have agreed to it. Anyway, we stopped off at Suez and then sailed the Med, which was heavenly, except that Lois was sick—then Paris. And then we headed for the coast and went beachcombing near Calais waiting for a ship—which was fun except that Lois was sick again—too many *langoustines* that time, I think. Yes—so we had two cars, you see, don't ask me who they belonged to—me and Patrick in one, Lois and Ivor in the other—and we were racing for the steamer. Well, I suppose we won, because Ivor and Lois weren't there. They must have missed it and taken the next one, which probably means they'll be safe and sound in Clarrow Fell by now."

376

"Really?" said Max. "In that case, my sweet angel, why aren't you in Clarrow Fell yourself—since you took the steamer before them? When *was* that, by the way?"

"Oh dear," she said, heaving a huge, comic sigh. "Well—I'm afraid it was Tuesday."

"And today's Thursday."

"Is it really?"

"It is—that makes three nights—little angel—that *someone* might ask you to account for."

"Heavens!—Well, I suppose there's no guarantee that Ivor has gone straight home. I should think probably not."

"Well," said Max, "just in case, perhaps I should send a telegram to the effect that you are with your sister who will be bringing you back."

She beamed brightly and then, putting her hand on his arm, erupted once again with mirth, "Oh, darling, how clever—you have been reading my mind, haven't you? That's just about the best solution I could think of and I didn't even have to ask you. When are we leaving? Please don't say tomorrow."

"Monday. Where are you staying?"

She put her mouth to his ear and breathed an address.

"All right. I'll collect you at ten o'clock Monday morning— or somebody will. Be ready—and be *there*, my sweet. You have enough trouble already."

"Lord yes." But she had decided not to let it worry her, not yet at any rate. Monday evening would be soon enough.

She got up and dropped a quick light kiss on my cheek. "Thanks, Olivia. I do love you, you know."

I nodded. "Yes, I love you too."

"Monday morning, then."

She tripped away, scattering smiles and kisses as she went, coughing a little behind her hand, pausing in the doorway to throw her arms around someone; a man I seemed to know yet could not, at that moment make the effort to identify.

She had not once mentioned her daughter. But how long would my mother have remembered her, or me, if we had had to compete with the lure of fast motor cars, Patrick Lasonby, and India?

First Luc, then Madelon. And I could no longer pretend that I was close to Victorine. Suddenly the winter cold touched me and I shivered.

"She'll be all right, Olivia," said Max.

"Yes. I know. She understands the game. She watched my mother play it long enough."

But I had not wanted her life to be a game. I had wanted it to have meaning and purpose and direction. I had wanted her to have the one pure absolute love I had craved for myself and continued to miss. I had believed in her love for Ivor Naseby and it was painful now to see how easily it had evaporated, that it had been nothing, after all, but a reflection.

"I have been in love like that *so* often," my mother had said, and I had scoffed. She had seen clearer than I.

Max slid his arm along the back of my chair and put his face against my hair to inhale its perfume, a tender gesture which was unlike him—with me, at any rate.

"Don't worry. Her husband is probably on a jaunt with Lasonby's wife somewhere and will never miss her."

"I know. That doesn't make it right, does it?"

He smiled and sniffed at my hair again.

"I'm not qualified to judge. I think I must be glad—considering your upbringing—that you have turned out so virtuous, although less so than Victorine, thank God."

A schemer, my grandfather had named me, yet nothing had turned out as I had planned. No one had followed the courses I had so carefully mapped out. What else could go amiss, I wondered? Who else might be likely to let me down?

And it was then that I remembered, or thought I remembered, the man who had been embraced so enthusiastically by Madelon on her way out of the restaurant, and who had—I now realized—accompanied her. Was it possible? Oh yes, God dammit, the way my luck was running, was there really any point in doubting that it had been Emil Junot?

TWENTY·THREE

We returned Madelon to her husband who, having only arrived home himself the night before, seemed rather more inclined to forgive and forget than his highly indignant mother.

"I am not deceived," she hissed at me as we were leaving. "I know what that flibbertigibbet is doing to my son—even though *he* is too good-hearted to see." But a few days later, Mrs. Naseby's tables were slightly turned when her good-hearted Ivor was discovered in compromising circumstances, in Madelon's bed, in fact, although not with Madelon and not with Lois Lasonby as might have been expected, but with a red-haired girl called Polly who had come up for the weekend from Cheltenham. Lois Lasonby, who *was*, after all, Ivor's official mistress, had hysterics very publicly in Mrs. Naseby's drawing room, while that good lady, more than slightly hysterical herself, retired to her bed with what she declared to be a heart attack at the very least. Not to be outdone, Madelon—"I *am* the betrayed wife after all, well aren't I? since no one has actually *caught* me yet with Patrick"—decided to leave her husband, arriving at the Manor with a few "essentials," a trunk of evening dresses, her feather boa, her perfumes, the *lingerie* Ivor, or was it Patrick, had bought her in Paris, and settled down quite happily to enjoy our shooting parties and dinner-parties until Max decided that her flight had lasted long enough.

"My dear little angel," he said, his arm around her, Madelon leaning the whole of her breathless, brittle body against him as she did now with all men. "Much as I enjoy your company—and would have enjoyed it even better, I daresay, ten years ago—I do feel that your place is with your husband, whose stamina, shall we say, is greater than mine."

She pressed her flushed, pointed face against his shoulder. "Darling Max, are you absolutely sick of me? I don't blame you. Or is it that you just want to be alone with Olivia? How sweet. You'd better watch out, Olivia, for he's clearing the decks all around you. I can read the signs. First Luc off to Africa and then me back to poor old Ivor who probably doesn't want me a bit, now that he can't seem to make up his mind between Lois and Polly. Ah well . . . !" And she held out her arms, wrists together as if for handcuffs, "I am ready. Lead on."

A second honeymoon began. Lois Lasonby went back to her husband, Polly to hers. Ivor shed tears in Madelon's arms which—as she told me and anyone else who wished to hear—she had found most exciting. Esmeralda Naseby, her condition now approaching shock, went to Eastbourne to recover, taking Natasha and her nurse. I quarreled with my mother. Madelon quarreled with Victorine. Victorine, whose husband had decided to stand as a Liberal Candidate—the Party of old age pensions and national insurance—now that the Government had finally decided to pay Members of Parliament salaries like other professional men, quarreled with Alys. And when Alys came North and created a disturbance at a meeting where Andrew was speaking, Victorine slapped her face. Max had sharp words—of all people—with Amyas who, after suffering repeated attacks on his poultry, had shot several foxes; for which heinous crime of vulpicide he was taken severely to task by the Clarrow Hunt.

Ridding the land of foxes was the privilege and pleasure of gentlemen as Amyas Hird, a former land agent ought to know. And no clod-hopping farmer with a gun must be allowed to deprive those gentlemen of their sport. No tenant of the Pottertons—or so the Pottertons said—would dare to behave in that fashion. But Amyas was no one's tenant, no longer obliged to watch his fences and crops ridden down by the County's sporting landlords with their hounds and their horns and their brave hunting cries. He owned his land outright. He intended to protect his stock and had every right, whenever he found a fox among his chickens, to shoot, no matter how many meetings of the Clarrow Hunt he might be depriving of their prey. He said so. Max rode over to Clarrow Bottom on his tall, black mare, very much the Squire, to call him to account for it and I had every reason to believe that the confrontation had been bitter and sharp.

Nor did it end there. Max de Haan—said the Pottertons—had done no service to the community by selling his wife's ancestral lands for money instead of preserving them for the pleasure of his colleagues and his peers, as the Pottertons were preserving theirs, no matter what the cost. It might even be said—and Lord Potterton, his nephew Felix and his son Clive, did not scruple to say it—that Max de Haan, in the interests of financial gain, had been guilty of disloyalty to his class. And there was trouble about that too.

I would be glad, I thought, when the winter was over.

I had, of course, brought up the subject of Emil Junot.

"Why yes," said Madelon, "the sweet old thing. He wouldn't come across to you that night at the Carlton because of Max. He's heard of him, you see, and wasn't sure of his welcome. It was mother who asked me to look him up. He wrote to her, ages ago, giving an address in London and she said that if I was ever passing, I might like to go and have a look at him and tell her the worst. Well, I was passing, I remembered, and he's not all that bad. You'll see when he comes to stay—if he comes. I *did* ask him but the way things are between me and Mamma Naseby it might not be easy. If you won't have him then—well I suppose it would be too shocking wouldn't it if he stayed with mother?"

I went, at once, to Aireville Terrace.

"And why shouldn't I write to him?" inquired my mother, unusually flustered, "since, after all, he is my husband—Luc's father— which must count for something."

"Mother, I am sure you never married him."

"Oh, didn't I? No, of course, there was no ceremony as such, I admit. But we did live together for—well, I can't say how long— but quite long enough to be considered husband and wife. And when he had money he was always generous."

"Presumably he has none at the moment."

"I daresay."

"Neither have you, mother. You can't afford him."

"Olivia, I must ask you not to speak to me in that way—to lay down the law so very—very *brusquely*—as to what I must not do or what I can or cannot afford."

"I know what you can afford, mother, because I pay for it."

"Oh yes—quite so. You do. And I am grateful. I *have* to be grateful. But what you do not take into account—and why should you when your own life is so hectic and gay—is that I am lonely sometimes—yes—so I am, for there are whole days when no one comes near me for hours together—when I am simply left to *molder*—yes, indeed I am. You *were* away five months last year, Madelon longer. And don't talk to me of Victorine. She has no sympathy to spare for anyone who gets enough to eat, and in any case she bores me."

"*Mother!*" Victorine, I knew, could be irritating and irritable too but I did not like to hear her criticized. "Mr. Greenlaw still comes to see you—surely—every day."

"Oh yes. To tell me about his aches and pains and his bad chest—to *wheeze* in my ear instead of . . ."

"Don't tell me you were thinking of giving him up, mother—after all this time and effort?"

"Certainly not. What else is left to me? And I am very fond of him. Goodness, I ought to be, since we have practically lived together these past ten years, no matter what his sanctimonious daughters-in-law choose to think. And I am quite determined to have some legal acknowledgment for it in the end. I am not greedy. I don't expect *all* his fortune, and Heaven knows there is quite enough to go round. Just a comfortable widow's portion and I am quite prepared to earn it. I will take him down to Bournemouth out of their way and give him his cough syrup every three hours and rub his back with that foul ointment which brings tears to my eyes. And I will do it very cheerfully, because—as I said—I *am* fond of him. It is just that sometimes—not quite always yet—but *sometimes* he is such an *old* man."

"You are not quite seventeen yourself any longer, mother."

She paused, biting her lip, tapping her long pointed nails against the mother-of-pearl lid of a cigarette box someone—Mr. Greenlaw I supposed—had just given her.

"Do you know, Olivia," she said, not looking at me, "I believe that is the trouble. I *am* seventeen. Yes—yes—I know the body ages. Lord—who knows that better than I, for there are mornings when I cannot face myself in the mirror. My hair is getting thinner, my skin is passing beyond my skill to repair—I know. But underneath—how terrible—I am *seventeen*. So is Madelon. I should not have had to live so long."

I was appalled and said so. She burst into tears and told me I need not trouble myself to come and see her again—since she realized how great a nuisance she must be to me—if all I could do was cause her pain.

"Just leave me to sit here with Sam Greenlaw and decay."

And then came the fall-out between Victorine and Madelon.

It was difficult to quarrel with Madelon but Victorine managed it. How, she inquired, did Madelon reconcile with her conscience the fact that half the working population of Bradeswick were eking out a miserable existence on the starvation wages paid them by her husband's Brewery? While the Brewery itself seemed to exist for the sole purpose of supplying Madelon with French hats which she left out in the rain, silk stockings and *lingerie* which she never wore more than twice, parties where the favorite parlor-game—all Bradeswick had heard about it—was to spray one another, French gowns, dinner-suits and all, with champagne. Such extravagance was criminal at any time, but when it was achieved as a result of the underpayment of decent men, when children were walking the streets on legs crippled by malnutrition, or dying from preventable, curable diseases because their mothers could not afford a doctor's fee, well then—one could better understand the fate of Marie Antoinette. And should a guillotine ever be erected in Corporation Square she would be saddened but not surprised to see her sister first into the tumbrils.

Victorine, of course, was right. She usually was. Only the bluntness of her reforming zeal—her tendency to accuse rather than to explain—was slightly off-key. And Madelon so careless of her possessions that she would have given them to anyone was distressed and horrified, attempting to defend herself with Ivor's brash and convenient philosophy that it was the allotted task of the over-privileged to explore their privileges to the full.

"Rubbish," snorted Victorine. "You've been poor yourself. You ought to know better than that."

But Madelon had escaped her poverty by being pretty and winsome, by her ability to please over-privileged men like Ivor and Patrick who never made her feel wicked and cruel no matter what she did to them. She would never come to Bradeswick again, she vowed, where everyone hated her and where Victorine—virtuous no doubt but *fat*—could do nothing but glare and grumble. She went home, crying all the way, vowing that she had never meant to do any harm to anyone, drank a great deal of champagne after dinner and fell in Clarrow River, to be rescued by Clive Potterton, on leave from India, who wrapped her in his coat and carried her very gallantly not to her home, of course, but to a cottage on the Potterton estate where they spent the night.

She had discovered older men, military men accustomed to

take command, who could put strong arms around her and shield her from Bradeswick's spite.

"I do so adore him," she whispered to me, "I have never felt anything like it. I thought I loved Ivor, and Patrick, of course, was so much like him—just an extension really. But Clive . . . !"

And she looked as ecstatic and vulnerable and pure-hearted as in the early days of her love for Ivor.

"What shall I do," I asked Max, "if she goes back with him to India?"

"Nothing. India may be very vast geographically, you know, my pet, but socially it is very small. I have—associates—there who would probably be able to get news of her. And I doubt if there is any need to worry. You will probably find that he cannot afford her."

"So you will take care of it, will you Max?"

"I will. You are not the only one, you know, who was accused by the Squire of being a schemer."

"And you are not shocked, of course, by all these wanton goings-on?"

"Are you?"

Yes, I rather believed I was, for it was getting nowhere, it was unproductive and wasteful and it was making her cough. And what of Natasha? But when Dottie Potterton came marching up to the Manor one day with the evident intention of taking it—and me—by storm, I marched out to meet her and, giving her no chance to complain of Madelon, told her, in very certain language, that she ought to be ashamed of herself for having raised a son who would take such shameless advantage of a married woman half his age and with not a fraction of his amorous—or lecherous—experience. And when Esmeralda Naseby came scurrying back from Eastbourne, hoping for the worst, I told her in equally explicit terms that her precious Ivor was entirely to blame, that *he*—because of the criminally indulgent upbringing *she* had given him—had led my sister astray by his own infidelities and that he must have done something very dreadful, or very peculiar indeed, to have driven her into the arms of Dottie's middle-aged, well-worn Clive. Just what it was, of course, Madelon was too good-hearted to say, but if I heard another single word against my sister then *I* would begin to talk, would investigate every one of Ivor's fads and fancies and who knew—did she?—what I might discover? She would do well to take care.

384

"Do you feel better for that?" asked Max, when I returned home still breathless, still ready for a fight if he, or anyone else, had one to offer. "And more to the point, does Esmeralda feel worse?"

"All right—I take your point. It will probably make no difference in the end. But it's easy to point a finger at a woman like Madelon—too easy—because one can see what she does wrong. She doesn't hide it with good manners like Dottie, who'd give Madelon and Clive her own bed to sleep in if Madelon had any money to bring with her. And that damned sanctimonious Esmeralda Naseby has just no right to throw stones at anybody. She got a rich man to marry her because he wanted to sleep with her—although God knows why— and then made out she was too delicate to do it, my mother says, or not very often anyway."

"Ah yes," Max said, "just one of the pitfalls of being a rich man, I fear. One feels bound to sympathize."

And finding no comment I wished to make about that, I hurriedly muttered, "I don't care what they say about her. I don't care about causes either, like Victorine or Alys. I just care about looking after my people—is anything wrong with that? Well—is there?"

But among "my" people, Luc appeared to have settled down well enough in a decorative rather than a commercial capacity, at the Cape. Victorine had had no need for me for a long time. While my mother, once it had been pointed out to her that Emil Junot could not be less than sixty and may well need his back rubbing too, seemed ready once again to settle for cough medicine and a fair degree of comfort in Bournemouth, whenever Mr. Greenlaw should say the word. Who remained to me but Madelon and Alys, both intent, it seemed, on destroying themselves? Madelon burning herself out with these false, feverish loves, her constant, headlong chase, not after sensuality, I felt sure of it, but affection, not orgasm but security. And Alys who, three times now, had offered her body to the legal rape of prison doctors.

She came to stay with us at the Manor a few weeks before Christmas, her conscience forcing her to Clarrow Fell each year at this season but her relations with her mother being now so tense that the vicarage had become unendurable. She spent a day or two moving quietly on the fringes of my existence, making a polite effort to interest herself in the routines of everyday living and, despite her good intentions, finding them, at best mildly amusing, at worst trivial. She had never cared for such things. She had now reached a stage where it was totally beyond her understanding how anyone could care for them. She took solitary walks on the moor, not for pleasure, I suspected, but because the fresh air was good for her. She ate careful, ample meals for the same reason, repairing the damaged fibers of her body and her spirit as patiently and impersonally as a fisherman mending his nets in the sun.

One evening a note was sent round to her from the vicarage and taking it up to her bedroom I found her dressing for dinner, standing by the mirror in her plain white petticoat so that I could see both her wafer-thin body and its reflection, the hollows and angles of her brittle bones, the small, still childish breasts and the bruises which covered them, black patches like inkstains that were turning green and yellow at their edges, appearing again on the insides of her arms.

"Alys—*Good God* . . . !"

She made no effort to cover herself, simply standing there, not displaying but allowing me to look at these marks of violence, her expression perfectly calm.

"Oh, Alys . . ."

She smiled, and shrugged, apparently taking for granted, these days, both the facts of violence and her own nakedness which would, not so long ago, have seriously embarrassed her. Yes, she had been badly beaten. So had many others. And I might stare at her, if I chose, for as long as I chose. Having passed through the hands of so many prison wardresses and prison doctors, so many "innocent by-standers" who came out on Saturday evenings just to see the Suffragettes having their blouses torn and their corsets pulled off, she was quite accustomed to it.

"What happened, Alys—this time?"

She shrugged again. "Nothing too unusual. I was going, with some others, to the House of Commons, hoping to present a resolution—all correctly drawn up, of course, and advance warning given of our intentions. We did not expect to be received. We did not even expect to reach Westminster ourselves. What we did expect was to be rounded up, as we usually are, thrown into the prison vans and locked away before getting within earshot of our Honorable Members of Parliament.

"Some of us would get away, of course. Some of us would be

man-handled by the crowd. We knew that. But most of us would be arrested, would hunger-strike, and would probably be force-fed. We had prepared ourselves. But we are on the eve of a general election, remember. And I suppose no government can take the risk of going to the polls with its jails full of educated women, whose husbands and brothers all possess the vote. The police had been ordered to turn us back, but not to arrest us. It took six hours, I believe. And they had brought in a special force from Whitechapel and other rough districts to do it. It became not only brutal, but sexual. Many of us were stripped to the waist—as you can see—and many of us required medical treatment for breast injuries the following morning. It is feared that Mrs. Pankhurst's sister, Mrs. Clark, will not recover. It was last Friday—the 18th—Black Friday, they are calling it."

"Alys, why are you doing this to yourself?"

She smiled, very quietly. "What else should I do, Olivia? When one truly believes in something then there is nothing else." And then, tossing her long, fine hair over her shoulders to cover her bruises, her smile deepened, became almost impish. "But one thing I am sure of. Breaking windows, for which one is certain to be arrested at once, is beginning to seem far safer than taking a walk to the House of Commons. I should not be at all surprised to see hatchets and hammers being issued as standard pieces of a Suffragette's equipment in the New Year. How sad."

"Would you carry a hammer, Alys?"

"Oh yes, my dear. So would we all. Can you just imagine it? All our elegantly dressed ladies strolling along Regent Street or around Knightsbridge wearing their French hats and then suddenly opening their handbags, taking out their hammers and demolishing the plate-glass windows of Harrods and Libertys and Marshall & Snelgroves? I imagine that Mrs. Pankhurst will reserve for herself the windows of Downing Street."

"Are you serious, Alys?"

"Terribly serious."

Her prophecy was also correct.

I managed to gather my family together for just one day that Christmas, to eat a festive dinner at my table and share my letters from Luc; my mother sulking just a little because I had not included Emil Junot who had turned up after all, admittedly at his own expense, and was staying at the Station Hotel; Victorine firmly on my mother's side about Junot—no longer "boring," I noticed, but altogether my mother's favorite child—telling me that Junot had been very good to us once and was welcome at *her* home any time; Victorine's children asking too many questions, some of them of a very personal nature and teasing the dogs; Andrew, who had been up all night at a confinement, falling asleep after dinner and starting to snore; Max visibly irritated by the children; Madelon pining for Clive who had been "confined to barracks" as he put it, at Dawney Park by his mother; Ivor, who had suddenly turned jealous, watching Madelon pine with a disturbing blend of satisfaction and agony. Alys had returned to London. Aunt Sibylla was in bed with a cold. Esmeralda Naseby had presented a dozen reasons for not bringing Natasha.

Happy families.

Victorine, who had worked hard all year, fell asleep in her turn at the opposite side of the fire to her husband. My mother began to lay out a restless game of solitaire. Madelon sat on the hearthrug, drooping, utterly dejected, coughing a little and, from time to time, heaving a sigh. Ivor bit his lip and stared at her. Max sent his dogs to their kennels and Victorine's children out into the stable-yard, where, if they misbehaved, the grooms would not be gentle.

"I suppose they could hurt themselves—couldn't they?" I suggested.

"Yes," he said, "I'd thought of that. Although not fatally, I fear. Would it trouble you if I went down to the Station Hotel for an hour or two? This Emil Junot of yours might be able to give me a decent game of cards."

"Would it trouble you if I came with you?"

"No trouble. Get your coat."

"Take me," said Madelon, appearing suddenly between us. "Anywhere. I'll come."

"You'll go nowhere—you'll stay with me." And there was Ivor who perhaps had no real right to be jealous, bleached white with jealousy, sick and shaken with it, his thin hand fastening on her arm like a talon.

"You'll go with me—when I say—where I say."

She pulled away from him and seizing her by the shoulders he began to shake her hard, wanting and needing to hurt.

"No," said Max, anticipating the move I was about to make in her defense, his arms coming around me like a steel trap. And when I struggled he rapped out, "It's not your affair, Olivia. Leave it to them."

"Darling," she moaned, "oh, darling." The attack had become an embrace. Ivor was about to weep in her arms again, his surest weapon, it seemed, in these love games they played.

"Darling—take me home."

"The dear child," murmured my mother, as their car roared away. "They have had a happy ending again. I am so glad."

"For how long?" I said sourly. Two days and then, at some chance remark of hers, Ivor was shaking once again with jealous rage, and striking out. Esmeralda Naseby was having something approaching a fit—the maids gave a graphic account of it—while Madelon went running outside not quite barefoot but in very thin evening shoes, and in a sufficient state of disarray to look—and feel—like a woman cast out into the storm. Although Ivor, of course, would come after her quite soon to fetch her back and shed those delicious tears again. Dawney Park was not far away. She was seen shivering along the road—coming to the Manor, I supposed—by the Pottertons' game-keeper who rushed to inform Clive. And within the hour she was in the housekeeper's room at The Park, wrapped in a blanket and sipping brandy; Clive Potterton who was over forty and had never been in love before, ready to lay himself, his undistinguished military career, his debts in the officers' mess and, in the course of time, his crumbling ancestral mansion, at her feet.

"I need you," he said, absolutely believing it.

"Not under this roof," declared his mother, who needed above all things a rich daughter-in-law.

"Then we will leave at once."

Events had moved too fast for Madelon. She had not intended to come to Dawney Park. She had not really intended anything.

"She is going to get a divorce, mother, and I am going to marry her."

She had surely not intended that. But she did love Clive—indeed she did. The last two days with Ivor had been quite special, of course, but Ivor was so moody, so strange sometimes, whereas Clive was so wonderful and wise, always there when she needed him, and unlike Ivor, had even spoken sharply to his mother for her sake. He had very little money of course, nothing really except his army pay—and she had not the least idea what a cavalry major might be likely to earn—and although India had been fun, she was not keen to go back there. But if that was where Clive wanted to take her then—yes—there was no doubt about it, she would do anything for Clive. He bolted the door and she surrendered at once, not to orgasm of course—for she had never achieved that, not yet, did not really believe in it, she had told me—but to the sheer dazzling enchantment of pleasing, of being wanted. Clive needed her and she had no words to tell him how grateful she was for that.

The Pottertons' housekeeper was sent to retrieve such items of clothing as Esmeralda Naseby saw fit to release. They spent the night at the Station Hotel, caught the first train to London the next morning, leaving a note with the hotel receptionist for Ivor saying it was all for the best, and a note for my mother asking her to "explain to Olivia."

"I am sorry about Natasha. But what use would I be to her? What do I know?" She was saying it was not good for one child to be brought up by another.

Ivor Naseby got drunk, wept in the arms of Lois and Polly and Lois again, and then went off to the South of France, taking Lois and—to my immense chagrin—Natasha with him. Esmeralda closed up the house and returned to Bournemouth. Within weeks, the Nasebys,who had been a part of Clarrow Fell and Bradeswick since I had first known it, were gone. And Dottie Potterton, when I met her in the village, snubbed me.

Not that I cared for that or for anything but the whereabouts of my sister.

"It is my life all over again," murmured my mother wistfully.

"She has a great capacity for inspiring affection, that little one," said Emil Junot who, in the turmoil had managed to get himself a seat in my chimney corner.

"It won't last," I said bleakly, torn between anxiety and a most bitter, a most grievous disappointment.

"I daresay," said Max.

"And Clive Potterton is worth nothing at all."

"True. But Madelon thinks him very wonderful and wise—although one would not have to be *very* wise, I admit, to appear so to Madelon. She may even convince him of his own worth and end up as Lady Potterton one day. And she'll have fun trying—that's certain."

390

'Yes—and with the next one. And then she'll be old.'

I saw my mother wince.

I would have given a great deal to be able to walk down to Clarrow Bottom and stand a while with Amyas in the farmyard, not saying a great deal, perhaps, just being with him. I made up a fourth at bridge instead with my mother and Junot and Max, a game at which they all excelled and on which I could not be bothered to concentrate.

"Dear God, Olivia," said Max, slamming down his cards, my mind so thoroughly elsewhere that I had not the least notion what crime I had committed, or why it should matter.

"It's just a game, Max, that's all."

"Exactly—like everything else. And there is only one reason for playing a game, my pet—to win."

Max was away on and off throughout the sleet-ridden, soggy month of February, away again in March, returning at the very end of the month for the Clarrow steeplechase, an event in which as it turned out he did not compete, his horse being seriously startled the day before on a trial run when Patrick Lasonby's bright red and very noisy roadster came tearing out of a gate. The horse reared, screamed, bolted, and Max, thrown to the ground in a bad fall, was taken to the nearest house—the farm at Clarrow Bottom—where Maria Long attended him very distantly, he said; and Amyas—whether in silence or not, he did not tell me—eventually brought him home in the gig.

"Very good of you, Amyas, in the circumstances," he said.

"Yes," said Amyas, smiling, "I think so too." And raising his hat to me he drove off.

Max limped into the house supported by two menservants, prepared to be brave, of course, but not sweet-tempered; downright disgruntled, in fact, when Andrew—who came as soon as he could—told him he had got off lightly with a few torn muscles and a strained back. Rest was the only medicine—and time. But he was in a great deal of pain, nevertheless, and made it clear, at once, that he expected the undivided attention of the entire household, including mine.

"After all, my pet, what else have you to do but look after me?"

I wondered. Because of the recent uncertainty of his movements we had no guests. Luc and Madelon might worry me—did worry me—but they were both physically beyond my care. My mother, although very glad to see Junot again, had been discreet—and if anything *had* occurred between them, then either Mr. Greenlaw had not noticed it or did not care. And now that Mr. Septimus Cross, my mother's other admirer, was so prone to falling asleep after dinner, there was no doubt that Junot made a very useful addition to her card-table. Victorine remained Victorine. Natasha—no, I could in no way dispute Ivor Naseby's right to take his daughter where he chose. And I had even received a letter from him, heavy and sentimental, vowing to devote himself now to Natasha as she was all that was left to him of Madelon; an attitude which proved him to be rather more his mother's son than I had suspected.

No; the house was quiet. My family had dispersed. The local gentry, taking the part of heart-broken Dottie Potterton, were not, for the moment, on visiting terms with me. No one disturbed us but the postman, ringing the doorbell four times a day to bring letters mostly for Max, which he would occasionally share with me, usually not. We were alone, the house settling warmly around us, the weather, which had turned unseasonably cold for April, firmly shut out, high winds and spiky showers of rain utterly defeated by the ancient solidity, the deep engrained peace of the manor.

Max lay on the library sofa, logs piled high on the fire, a decanter of brandy, a decanter of claret, a box of cigars to hand, newspapers in several languages piled around him, irritable sometimes since the torn muscles in his shoulder made the act of writing an ordeal about which he saw no reason to be patient.

"I could write your letters for you," I offered, remembering that I had once earned my living in that way.

"Ah yes—but then you'd know my secrets, wouldn't you?"

"Have you so many?"

"A few."

But when his letters had been taken to the post, his newspapers read and their information cross-checked, when the chauffeur had been sent yet again to Bradeswick with telegrams and when more telegrams had been received, when—with much moaning and groaning—he had been propped up on cushions to eat his dinner and had found it "very edible" or "What the hell does Clement think I'm paying him for?" then he was quickly bored.

"Entertain me, Olivia."

"How."

"Well yes—my injured back does rather rule out the first idea that springs to mind. Cards?"

"Oh no. I'll get into a muddle and you'll shout at me."

"Darling—would I do that?"

"Yes you would."

"What's left? It rather looks as if you'll have to talk to me."

"All right. Do you think that Junot . . . ?"

"Yes of course I do."

"What do you mean? You don't know what I was going to ask."

"I can well imagine. I believe your mother has finally drifted into the situation she's always been looking for—where she can have her cake and eat it too. Junot is a very agreeable fellow, very sprightly—exactly what is needed to brighten up a dull evening in Aireville Terrace or Marine Avenue, Bournemouth, or wherever. And Sam Greenlaw is a long way past lusting after anything more strenuous than gossip and a decent game of whist, you know. Whereas your mother . . . Obviously it suits them all, because Sam Greenlaw's no fool and he wouldn't part with a penny piece unless he thought he was getting good value. So—if they want a *ménage à trois*, at their age who could possibly object?"

"His daughters-in-law, if they knew what it meant."

"Then we won't tell them. So—if you have any more problems for me to solve, feel free."

He reached out towards his cigar box, winced with pain, and kneeling down by his sofa I gave him a cigar, struck a match, moved the ashtray to a more convenient angle, refilled his glass. What else? Well, another log on the fire would not go amiss, and if I could do something about these cushions which had slipped sideways again—and the footstool just an inch or so that way.

"Is that better?"

"Yes, *very nice*—for the moment. I think my convalescence might be rather long, you know."

"Yes, I rather thought you might be thinking that. Don't imagine I'll sit here forever arranging cushions and lighting cigars and . . ."

"Being a ministering angel to a man who needs you. I thought all women longed for that."

"But you don't need anybody. You said so."

"And of course you believed me."

"Max—really—I believe every word you say."

"How very obliging. And *I* believe you have maneuvered me

into a position where I could appear churlish unless I apologize for well—certain remarks of mine made in anger."

"Max, if I have maneuvered you anywhere, then it is only because you wanted to go."

"Yes, that *is* true, of course."

And smiling he leaned a fraction towards me, moving without any show of pain I noticed when it suited him, and put a hand on the nape of my neck.

"Nevertheless, my pet—whatever I may have said to the contrary—this house *is* yours, in the sense that it would be unimaginable without you. That has always been my opinion."

I felt my skin turn hot beneath his hand, the flush spreading to my immense consternation into my cheeks, covering me with a most unlikely and infuriating confusion.

"Olivia," he said, with evident delight, leaning closer still, "I have made you blush."

"Yes. And I see it has done wonders for your back."

"Ah—well—so it has. Which only goes to show—what?—the healing powers of a good woman?"

"Max—what nonsense."

"Far from it. For that is what you are—a good woman. Misguided and wrong-headed at times, of course."

"Just as you are unbearably smug."

"I daresay—but *wounded* which means you are bound to forgive and spoil me."

"You are spoiled enough."

"No," he said, speaking seriously for a moment, "I am not. I am *self*-indulgent. Who else indulges me? It became my aim, many years ago, to put myself in a position where I could cater to my own whims and fancies, whatever they happened to be. I have achieved that. But if it turns out that there should be pleasure in needing someone—you, for instance—then why should I pass it by? If it should turn out like that. Life goes in cycles, after all, I find—one enjoys what one can, suffers what one must, balances the profit and loss, and then the world tilts to another angle and one moves on. When we are ready—if we are ready—to pass on to another phase of experience, why not do it together?"

He was looking at me in a way which always made me uncomfortable, the narrow-eyed concentration of the card player, his

Spanish face, like the ones I had glimpsed in the bullring in Cádiz, lean and dark and wary, watching me, assessing me, a far more astute and powerful schemer than I.

"Tell me, Olivia, do you still think my fortune likely to evaporate?"

"Possibly."

"And if it happened would you give me those treasures of yours from the Gatehouse, to keep me solvent or out of jail?"

"I might."

"I wonder if that means you have decided to belong to me?"

"Yes. It does."

"My word—such immediate surrender."

But I had taken the decision long ago, at a time when I had been planning not only for myself but for Luc and my mother and Madelon, for Victorine; even for Natasha who *might*, by some miracle, have been left to me. None of those considerations now applied. The decks had been cleared around me. Max had sent Luc to Africa, had encouraged my mother to throw in her lot again with Junot, leaving us here, together, in this beautiful old room in the firelight.

Could I imagine myself anywhere else? Or him? And how easy it was to be charmed by him, when he wished to be charming, how easy it had always been to desire him. What an adventure it might be—what a challenge—now, after all these years of verbal swordplay and evasions, all these clever, sophisticated games, to break through his guard, to let him break through mine—and discover what lay behind his self-indulgences. We had always been able to talk to each other. What prevented us now from speaking the truth? Another phase of experience. Yes: for a long time now I had been ready for that.

"Why have we never spent such a pleasant evening before, Olivia?"

Truly: I wondered.

TWENTY·FOUR

The spring gales blew themselves out, leaving a clean pale blue sky, delicate sunshine, the odor of damp earth burgeoning with daffodils. Max got up from his couch, having exploited the advantages of invalidism to the full, and we did—what?—sat in our house, walked in our garden, ate dinner, I hardly know what else except that it was easy and delightful and my mind was full of it. He set himself to charm me and I was charmed. He set himself to seduce me, as if my body was quite new to him; and I was seduced. We were having a love affair, entirely outside our marriage. I had never had one before and yes—as my mother had always told me—it was glorious. I was his mistress. How ridiculous. How marvelous. What *fun!*

"Shall we go to Monte Carlo in the morning?"

"Yes."

"Shall we go to Rome?"

"Let's."

"Shall I take you to Hongkong?"

"Yes. In the morning."

But in the morning we stayed in bed, gossiping, laughing, making love, being together: a time of hovering deliciously on the brink of a hundred minute but vital discoveries, deliberately light-hearted, even flippant. Froth and glitter with possibly something precious at its core—possibly not. But it began to seem likely. Very likely. And then it ended.

We had reached the early days of June. A bright morning. Sunshine flooding through my bedroom window so that, looking out

I saw the postman making his first delivery, a heavy bag which meant that Max would be late for breakfast.

"Invitations," he said, appearing at last, handing me several envelopes, "and bills."

"Have I been extravagant?"

"I hope so. I have to go to London today, by the way."

"Oh—just you?"

"I'm afraid so."

It had happened a hundred times before. I had never questioned him. He had never seen the need for explanations. And now when I inquired, with some hesitation, "Is something wrong?" it was his poker face, his Spanish face, which looked up from his newspaper and said, "Darling—why ever should you think that? I really don't suppose so. And if anything should be wrong, then I expect I'll manage to put it right."

He had said that to me before too.

"Will you come to the station?"

That request was entirely new, and as I dressed and put on my hat I could have told no one how much it worried me. But we had not yet—not quite—made the transition into that new phase of experience he had talked of, and had I thrown my arms around him and begged him to stay, or take me with him, or to tell me what troubled him, then I believe I would have embarrassed us both.

We got into the car and drove to Bradeswick.

"I won't be long, darling," he said, and I realized that his usual, rakish "Well then, my pet, I'll be off," would have given me more comfort.

"Will you see Alys in London?"

"Would you like me to?"

"Yes—if you can. I've been worried about her lately."

"Have you, darling? Why is that?"

Surely, I began to tell him, he must know. But the train was about to leave. He kissed me. "Max . . . ?"

But what can one ask or explain in that moment when whistles are blowing and doors slamming? I clutched back my alarm, smiled, waved my hand and walked back to the car.

"Aireville Terrace please, Stevens."

But, as we approached my mother's door, I realized that her company, her permanent, amorous card-party of Junot, Sam Greenlaw and little Mr. Cross, would be impossible in my present humor.

"I'm sorry, Stevens. Would you take me home."

The house seemed absolutely empty. I went upstairs, changed my shoes and walked down to the vicarage, hoping that Aunt Sibylla would be obliging enough to pick a quarrel about my mother or Madelon or the Pottertons, any quarrel would do, to distract me. And it struck me once again that Max must have been preoccupied indeed to have asked why I was worried about Alys, with the Suffragette Movement in its present dangerous state.

Demonstrations, mass meetings, legalized torture in His Majesty's prisons had not been enough to sway public opinion. Window-breaking had posed an insufficient threat. And so, in this final, terrible phase of the struggle, letterboxes were set alight or the mail destroyed by pouring acid and tar through the slots, telegraph wires were cut, golf greens destroyed, cricket pavilions, station waiting-rooms, art galleries, warehouses, church halls, stables, damaged by fire. Lloyd George's new house at Walton Heath was blown up by a bomb: this last ambitious effort being the work of Miss Emily Wilding Davison who, at the beginning of this present month of June, had rushed in front of the King's horse at the Derby and sustained a fractured skull from which—I had just seen in Max's paper—she had died.

No other lives, so far, had been lost, the Suffragettes' avowed aim being to damage property and, when unavoidable, themselves, not other people. But nevertheless this destruction of private property, as opposed to Government property—particularly the letter-burning which affected everybody—had won the Movement no new friends and had alienated some old ones. Street crowds, who might once have protested at the rough handling of women by the police, were becoming more inclined to join in. Wholesale arrests continued, the Government having lately unleashed its new weapon against the hunger strike, the Act of Cat and Mouse by which a woman, when her health deteriorated to a dangerous level, could be released, sent home until she recovered and then picked up again.

Ample reason, I would have thought, to be worried about Alys.

But Aunt Sibylla was not at the vicarage. She had left that morning for Bridlington. I had just missed her. Surely I had known she was going? Yes, of course, and I had meant to come and see her before she left. But I had been—what?—too carefree lately, too happy, and it had slipped my mind. I walked home via the Gatehouse to check as I had done so many times, how much the Heron heirlooms

398

would be likely to fetch at auction. And then there was my jewelry, and furs, the silver plate, the bloodstock. If Max needed it, then it was all here. Of course it was. Would it be enough?

I clenched my teeth, drew myself together and settled down for a long, uneasy time of waiting. But he came back, most unexpectedly, two days later. And Alys was with him.

Something was clearly, badly wrong and no attempt was made to conceal it.

"Alys is far from well, Olivia, as you can probably see. If you have a room ready I daresay she might like to rest before dinner?"

Of course there was a room ready. I took her up to it, made conventional affectionate murmurings, to which she gave affectionate exhausted replies. Certainly she was not well. I went downstairs to the library where Max, wreathed in cigar smoke, was standing, tapping a foot against the fender, and told him so.

"She's not well."

"No, she's not."

"Do you know what ails her?"

"Yes. I do."

"And . . .?"

"I shall have to tell you."

"Is it bad?"

He shrugged and threw his cigar into the empty hearth where it smoldered a while and then, imperceptibly, went out.

"Yes. You will think so. I think so—possibly for different reasons. But yes—very bad."

Although not entirely unexpected, he supposed in these days, when women were going out, night after night, into an atmosphere of hostility and resentment and violence. For when men where laying their hands on young, attractive women in overheated conditions like that, then—dear Christ, he made no excuses—but it had been bound to happen to somebody. It had happened to Alys.

She had rung her little handbell once too often and attempted, with several other women, to explain their grievances to a crowd that had grievances of its own. Stones had been thrown, presumably by men—and women—who had had their correspondence burned, by shop assistants who had lost wages from closures due to all those broken windows, golfers who objected to seeing "Votes for Women" burned onto putting greens. These people—he was quite ready to admit—did not care whether the women's case was just or not. All they cared for was their own inconvenience. Didn't everyone? There had been a scuffle, Alys had been separated from the other women, seized upon by three or four youths, sixteen or seventeen years old, she thought no more, and dragged into a side-street where, in an outhouse of some kind, she had been raped by each in turn. A procedure which he—himself a potent and predatory male—found horrible to contemplate.

He would have done murder had he been on the spot. I saw that in him very clearly. But Alys, he said, had borne it with considerably more fortitude than one would have supposed. Her body was used to violence. She had, in a sense, been raped before, every day for fifteen days on one occasion by that damnable feeding tube in Holloway, and she had discovered that if one made no resistance, then the pain and the danger of suffocation was less. She knew that hands on her throat or pressed over her mouth and nose to stifle her cries could be fatal, whereas one did not die—as she had learned in Holloway—of disgust. Therefore, she did not cry out but feigned unconsciousness, while one clumsy, drunken stranger after another plowed through her virginity. And she lived.

He would leave me to imagine her condition when she had finally found her way back to Cheyne Walk. Her mental condition, that is, since physically she had far less to show for it in the way of bruising than after a protest march to the House of Commons. And bruises heal. So did pregnancy, of course—in time. Yes. She was carrying a most hideously begotten child. She had just realized it and was still, he thought, in shock.

I sat down, bowed my head, closed my eyes, allowing it to enter my mind and take shape there, first the brutal facts and then their ramifications, spreading around the central atrocity like waves of murky water. And the first question I asked surprised me.

"Was this why you went to London? She wrote to you?"

"Yes."

"Why you?"

"Because I already knew what had been done to her. I was in London in March, when it happened. I called on her, as I usually do, and found her—as you might suppose."

"She must have been glad of you."

"I did what I could."

"Yes. I think . . ."

"What, Olivia?"

"That you should have told me."

"She specifically asked me not to."

I could understand that—or, at least, I ought to have done. But there was something—perhaps not anything important—but just *something* I had not fully grasped. Possibly he had told me and I had not heard. Possibly I had been grappling with my own tangled reactions instead of concentrating on the full horror of hers. This was the worst thing that could possibly have happened to her. I was well aware of it. Maternity to Alys had always seemed to be the ultimate disaster. Madelon had scarcely noticed hers. Whereas I—was I really so hungry for motherhood that I could envy her a child conceived in such bestiality as this? Perhaps I could.

"What can we do for her, Max?"

What would Robin have done?

"Whatever seems best for her, I suppose. There are certain accepted standards of procedure. In the case of a maidservant one turns her off without a reference."

"Max—don't be flippant."

"Oh—it does no harm. It even helps. If she were a mill girl or a shop girl we could give her ten shillings and send her to that old woman in St. Saviour's Passage who is so handy with her knitting needle. One of the Potterton girls—Veronica, the pretty one—was packed off to France rather suddenly once, I remember, to a finishing school, or so they said. And when she came back looking pale and much thinner they married her off to a very dull fellow. I would like to think we could find a better solution than that for Alys."

"Yes."

"What would you do, in her place, Olivia?"

It was a cruel question. I would have *my* child. I shuddered.

"What does Alys want to do—that seems more to the point."

He lit another cigar and flung the match quite viciously into the hearth, his gesture converting it into a dagger.

"Oh—she will do anything she is told to do—anything at all, including suicide, if that should seem convenient."

I got up and stood beside him.

"You are so angry, Max, aren't you?"

"Yes, I believe I am. I don't like to witness defeat. I suppose one admires in others the qualities one lacks oneself, and her courage has always seemed quite miraculous to me."

"I would not say you were lacking in courage, Max."

'But I am. I have audacity, yes—as you have—and tenacity and every intention of having my way. I have suffered a certain amount of physical injury and inflicted some, but only in circumstances that could be turned to my own advantage and which excited me in their way. I could not have endured what she has endured, for an ideal. Women should have the vote. Everybody knows that. No civilized society can expect to enslave half its population forever—only for as long as it is allowed to get away with it. Alys has endured every possible abuse and insult for the cause of women, and what has broken her is her own biology. She is brave no longer. She is terrified of what her mother will say. That saddens me, and because I don't like to be sad, it makes me angry."

She came down to dinner in the kind of white dress with billowing sleeves and a high frilled neck which Aunt Sibylla had always chosen for her and which—her mind on other things—she had continued to buy, a blue sash unevenly fastened around her narrow waist, a cuff-button missing, only a certain hollowness in the cheeks, fine lines of strain around the eyes, deeper ones across her forehead, marring the girlish, almost virginal appearance she had managed, through these grim years, to retain.

She hesitated for a moment at the library door and, hurrying the length of the room, I threw my arms around her, an embrace to which she submitted, I thought, patiently, sweetly, not really liking to be touched but respecting my need to demonstrate—what?—not love, perhaps, but an acknowledgment of those old guilts, a debt which I, who had so disrupted her quiet backwater, must pay over and over again, as often as I could.

"Olivia, I am so sorry to bring you this burden."

"I would have been deeply offended had you taken it to anyone else."

"How kind you are. But other people will be less kind—I think you should know that. They will say . . ."

Her lips trembled and, seeing that she was determined to make her explanation to the end, I quickly made it for her.

"Say what? That you encouraged those men—or enjoyed it? Or that by going out at night as you did you were inviting it? Anyone who says so is either totally naïve or an idiot."

She slid her hand into mine, a narrow, cold little wafer of bone with no flesh on it, and smiled.

402

"Dottie Potterton will say so."

"Not in my hearing, Alys. Not more than once, at any rate."

"And Bessie Greenlaw."

"Alys—do you *care*? You have been to prison."

"Yes. So has Lady Constance Lytton and Mrs. Solomon whose husband was Prime Minister of the Cape, and all those other women doctors and writers and socialites that my mother so enjoys to speak of. But *they* have not gone home in disgrace to bear a bastard child. My mother cannot cope with that."

"Yes she can."

"No. It is beyond the comprehension of her generation and her class. I have hurt her cruelly, I know, but she has been able to conceal it so far. A daughter in prison has been something so unique that she's almost been able to make it sound splendid—particularly when I have been handcuffed with an earl's daughter. But girls who get themselves in the family way are not splendid. She can't raise her eyebrows and talk her way through that and *I* cannot tell her—truly I cannot."

"Olivia will tell her for you," said Max.

"Thank you," she said, turning swiftly towards him, her eyes misty, her mouth tremulously smiling. "Thank you, Max—for everything—always."

For the first few days she was sick, not only in the mornings, as might have been expected, but all day, wretchedly, agonizingly, her body revolting with great violent spasms against the parasite, the alien being which had been grafted so violently within it. She could retain no food but even when her stomach was empty, nausea continued to bend her double, her senses tending to swim away in bouts of dizziness which made her unsteady on her feet and brought her, not a few times, to the ground. But Andrew Rexford was away contesting a by-election and she would see no one else.

She was hoping, I knew, that the constant contraction of her stomach muscles in the act of vomiting might cause her to miscarry. But life does not often arrange its tragedies so neatly. Her sickness eased. The fetus settled more comfortably within her, her body adjusting to its requirements, becoming—despite the total revulsion of her mind—a maternal receptacle, her womb protectively, warmly closing, her breasts preparing their milk. She was carrying the child of brutes and idiots and could not be asked to love it, but her body did not know that and did not care. Her body was female, obedient, fertile, and, separating itself entirely from her shocked and battered mind, began calmly to occupy itself with its allotted task of nurturing the young.

The men who had attacked her had got off not only scot-free but unknowing, uncaring. And they could have had no way of telling, even had they been apprehended and charged, which one had impregnated her. So much for human fatherhood. Odd really, she said, when one thought how often men had tried to break her. Prison had not succeeded. Fractured bones would always heal. Barricades could be torn down, or evaded one way or another. All the punishments and prohibitions which had been devised by the brilliant minds of cabinet ministers had not caused her to deviate a fraction from her purpose. But just one minute seed, planted in her by some lad of poor intelligence, no doubt, and scant prospects, had been all that was needful to stop her in her tracks: to impose upon her, not a term in the Third Division, but a life sentence.

She had considered abortion and had rejected it. The moral issue apart, abortion was often fatal. In the case of a Suffragette it might easily be made public, and her mother could not have borne the disgrace. In any case, Max had said, matters could surely be arranged better than that. Now she was ready to do anything, whatever seemed best—presumably to Max—so long as her mother might be spared.

The weather continued warm and she sat in the garden a great deal, very quietly under the chestnut trees, thin and fine and distant, withdrawing herself—I understood—as she had done in prison, so that she could bear the ordeal, whatever it turned out to be, with outward patience and politeness, a model prisoner.

Open the cage and fly away. The words rang in my head sometimes and, when no one was looking, I wept for her. And for myself, I think, not only for my sterility but because the new cycle of my life with Max, having swung so tantalizingly towards me, had receded, leaving me oddly stranded, feeling myself—as we sat all three together at dinner—to be the outsider in my own home.

Max was up to something. I was well aware of it. I had known him long enough—well enough—to read the signs. They were well in evidence. And, furthermore, there was still that indefinable *something* that was not clear to me, some thread which I could not fit into the pattern of events which had been woven for me—certainly—by Max. He had not lied to me, I was sure of that. Every detail he had given me had been exact. What, then? Why, whenever I saw Alys turn suddenly towards him in the summer heat like a flower to water, did a wordless question leap into my mind and then slip out again, so that a moment later I could not remember it?

I felt the greatest possible compassion for Alys. I not only believed it to be my duty to defend her, but I would have defended her in any case. I did not in any way resent her presence nor her dependence on Max, who probably never allowed her to see the less dependable side of his character. He had always been kind to Alys. She trusted him, which he must find flattering at least, and something of a novelty.

But Alys—despite her experiences of street fighting and the punishment cell in Holloway—was naïve. I did not trust him.

"Max."

"Yes, my pet."

"What are we going to do with her? Time is not on her side you know."

"Quite. I think you will have to go to Bridlington to tell her mother."

"Thank you, Max. That *will* be a pleasure. What will you be doing in the meantime?"

"I have a scheme or two afoot."

She was the color of cold ash the morning I left for Bridlington, her hands shaking, her shoulders unbearably frail as I put my healthy, steady arm around them.

"Tell Sibylla the truth," Max said, "and that we hope to settle matters with the least possible embarrassment to everyone."

"You can't be more specific than that?"

He shook his head, kissed me briefly on the corner of my mouth, put me into the car.

"Straight back from the station, Stevens," he said, "I shall need the car myself later on."

I had been sent away—out of the way, perhaps—and I knew it. I had even accepted it and agreed, without question, to stay three or perhaps four days with Aunt Sibylla who might need my help in coming to terms with the shock.

"Yes, Max," I had said meekly, knowing full well—as he knew—

405

that Sibylla Blackwood would come to terms in her own way with anything, whether I should be there or not.

"You'll send me a telegram, of course, when you're ready to come home—so that I can meet you at the station?"

"Oh yes—of course, Max. I wouldn't dream of coming back suddenly, without letting you know."

"Good. I feel I can rely on that."

We were adversaries again, polished swordsmen, smiling, poised, light-hearted; aware of the folly of trusting one another an inch.

I had not been to Bridlington since the year Robin died and found it unchanged, busier in the summer which made it seem a little smaller but essentially the same; the vicar still observing his seabirds along the cliffs, my aunt bored to distraction without her own maids to bully and the affairs of her village to regulate.

"What a pleasant surprise," she said, sailing majestically into the lounge of my hotel where I had invited her to tea. "And they will have given you the best front bedroom with a balcony overlooking the sea, I suppose, if your husband has had anything to do with it. Well, Olivia—to what do we owe the honor of your presence?"

But, delivered with the tea, came a telegram from Max, saying curtly, as telegrams always do, "Tell Sibylla nothing until you hear from me."

When, I wondered? Exactly when it suited him. And in the meantime I would stay here, well away from Clarrow Fell and whatever he might be planning for Alys.

"Have you news of my daughter?"

"None. Have you?"

I waited five days, strolled by the sea, took stock of my life and of myself, Aunt Sibylla glad of my company although she would not have cared to say so.

"How is dear Madelon? A little closer to becoming Mrs. Potterton, I hope and trust? For I have heard from Esmeralda that Ivor intends to divorce and marry Lois Lasonby—when *she* divorces. My word—how very smart—how terribly convenient."

"And you do not like it at all, Aunt Sibylla. Neither do I."

"Really? I would have thought it altogether your style."

"No, Aunt. My mother's—not mine. Not Victorine's either."

"And Luc? How is he? I should not be at all surprised to see him back here any day with a rich wife—which would be quite *his* style, you will admit. Olivia, are you quite sure you've not seen Alys?"

"Not for ages, Aunt. Are you worried about her?"

"My dear, of course not. What has my daughter ever done to worry me? Had she been Mrs. Clive Potterton by now, or Mrs. de Haan, then I might have had cause to worry. You do know, dear, that your husband sees a great deal of her in London?"

"Yes. Does *that* worry you?"

"I rather thought it might have worried you. I simply wish to make you aware of it because—well, I would not wish my daughter's personal reputation to be in any way tarnished."

"I am sure . . ."

"One can be sure of nothing, Olivia, where men are concerned. Alys, you will agree, is a most attractive woman, no longer in the first bloom of youth to be sure, but with ample time left to make something of herself. Believe me, I do not despair. The Suffragettes are making a great nuisance of themselves at the moment, but their cause will eventually be won, as causes are, and I do believe that those who have been in the forefront, women like Alys who keep on marching in those dreadful processions wearing prison clothes and carrying lighted tapers—you will have seen them?"

"Yes, Aunt."

"Indeed. Who has not. But those women are the very ones who might well emerge as heroines in the end—such is the way of human nature—or "personalities" at the very least. And there are a great many men of mature years, widowers and the like, who would be well suited by a woman of personality. I believe Alys might do better now, with all the experience and the useful friends she has gained, than ten years ago when she had only her youth to recommend her."

"Yes, Aunt."

Opening my handbag to find a handkerchief, I saw Max's telegram, "Tell Sibylla nothing until you hear from me," and I thanked God for it.

I invited my aunt and uncle to dinner and was not greatly surprised when she arrived alone. The vicar had returned late, having spent the afternoon sketching gulls on the cliff top where he had been caught in a heavy shower of rain. He was now fatigued, chilled, unwell. "He is a solitary man," she said stiffly, feeling I was entitled to that much of an apology. Yes indeed, a shadowy man, hardly there at all, who would go out alone with his sketch book and his field-glasses when he learned the truth about Alys, leaving his wife to cope as best she might. Why had she married him? Because she had been approaching thirty, my mother had said, considering that to be reason enough. Why had he married her? Because she had made up her mind that he should. And of course, he had been very handsome—my mother well remembered—and had wanted to give up being a vicar once and become a painter until Sibylla had put a stop to it.

We drank a bottle of champagne between us—totally extravagant, she said, downing her share—I encouraged her to take an after-dinner brandy, and another, and, incautious with wine, she suddenly said to me, "It upsets you, doesn't it, not having children."

"Why yes—as a matter of fact it does."

"I thought so. Well, let me tell you this—Olivia Heron—Mrs. Maxim de Haan—my sister Lavinia's daughter—I had occasion to long for motherhood myself once. Yes, I remember well how very distressing it was, waiting every month in such agony of mind, hoping against hope, and then total desolation—month after month. Oh dear. I was not—well—not seventeen any longer, you see, when I married my husband, and I know there were those who thought it was too late for me. While, to my husband, it made no difference either way, for he was a quiet man even then and did not require much in the way of company. But I—how I longed for a child. How determined I was. I even prayed. And my prayers were answered—not just a child, which would have been wonderful enough, but the daughter I had specifically asked for. Because a son, you see, soon goes off to lead his own life, especially when he marries. But a daughter is always a daughter. One has a companion for life in a daughter, a confidante—or so I imagined. One talks to a daughter, makes plans for her—one has grandchildren. Your mother had all these things without effort, without valuing any one of them—without *deserving them*. Whereas I . . ."

And suddenly quite beside herself she brought her hand, palm down on the table with a sharp slap, setting the brandy glasses dancing. "I will tell you this, Olivia—tonight—because you have filled my head with strong drink—and I will utterly deny it tomorrow. My husband means nothing to me. I expect you know that. He found, years ago, that our way of life did not suit him and so he withdrew from it, removed himself most effectively from his family, his responsibilities, his parish. If Clarrow Fell has a vicar then it is *I*, for my husband does nothing—intends to do nothing—but stand in his pulpit, whenever

408

a curate is unavailable, and smile. I no longer minded that once I had Alys. I could not be ambitious for him but I could be ambitious for her. Why not? She was worthy of the best. We had no money but she had distinction, even as a girl—"something about her" as they say. She could have done well for herself—my daughter—very well. Guy Heron was in love with her. And Robin Esmond. She could have had either one of them if she had said the word. You will admit that."

"Yes, Aunt."

"And your present husband was not indifferent to her, you know. Twice over—if she had stirred herself—she could have been the lady of Clarrow. And since Clive Potterton has turned out to be weak-headed enough to run off with your sister, I am bound to say that, with a little effort, Alys might well have had him too. She was all I ever wanted. She has brought me nothing but heartache and frustration and disappointment. I would annihilate anyone who suggested that. But *I* can say it. My ambitions are at an end. I am getting on in years—I feel it. And if I can just see her married—just that— not to anyone of consequence; to *any* man, in fact, who could be called respectable, that is all I ask."

How could I tell her? I had never shirked a difficult task before. But I had never before been asked to shatter an ageing woman's final, considerably shrunken dream. What could I say?

"Good night, Aunt. Take care."

And the next morning a second telegram was delivered. "Silence is golden, my pet. All resolved. Come home Friday."

It had never been his intention to tell Aunt Sibylla, I realized that. He had used her as a convenient excuse to get me out of the way, knowing that concern for my aunt would keep me in Bridlington whether I suspected him or not. Clever Max. And I had submitted to his scheming as a chess player of experience and skill will submit, nevertheless, to a grand master. Fairly soon now I would be bound to discover the nature of the game he was playing and *then* I would begin to make my moves.

The journey to Bradeswick was tedious and cold, my traveling companions so dull that I closed my eyes to escape them and slept a little, falling into one of those odd sinister dreams when familiar figures turn suddenly to reveal strange faces, when familiar doors open to a landscape that is totally strange.

"Bradeswick!" I awoke with a start, clutched my handbag and

my gloves, the light having faded, while I slept, into evening. Would Max be here to meet me? And if he had sent the chauffeur, what did it signify? Would anyone be here? In my dream I had walked up to the Manor and found it empty; and not recently vacated either, but untenanted for years, cobwebbed and eerie and damp. Just a dream. And if no one came to meet me I would simply take a cab to my mother's and stay there until morning. Whatever happened—no matter what—I would just grit my teeth, as I had been doing all my life, and tackle it. Nevertheless, although the night was not cold, I shivered.

"Olivia?" Max said, from behind me. And for a moment—not long enough I hoped for him to notice the hesitation—I dared not turn to look at him. In my dream he had taken off mask after mask. Had been Max, and then not Max, a hundred characters in one, revealed layer by layer. What now?

"Max!"

"Are you surprised to see me?"

"Of course not. Should I be?"

Clarrow village was very dark as we drove through it, the vicarage closed and silent, the Manor still whole and inhabited, thank God, but no lights shining at the windows of rooms where Alys would have been likely to wait.

So far we had spoken of trains and stations and hotels, the weather at Bridlington, the weather here at Clarrow, the preliminary exchanges, the sounding out of an opponent's strength, the probing of his intentions as a cat delicately paws the ground before risking her weight. But now I concluded that the preliminaries had lasted long enough and said crisply, "Has Alys gone to bed?"

"My dear—I wouldn't care to hazard a guess."

And looking up at him I saw the mask of the card player slide over his face, his wary, keen-eyed Spanish mask, and knew that whatever was about to happen had begun.

"How is she?"

He shrugged, his eyes on the curve of the road as we drew near the house. "I hope she is very well. I haven't seen her today."

"Oh—really. May I know where she is?"

"I hardly know myself."

"Max—this won't do. I realize you have done something and are not expecting me to like it. I knew that when I went to Bridlington. Now then, Max—you said everything was resolved."

He stopped the car, exactly outside the front door, his hands still on the wheel, and gave me a sidelong glance. "Of course. I may have been very clever, Olivia. I may even have brought down several targets with one shot. I hope so."

"What have you done with Alys."

"*With* her—nothing at all. *For* her, a great deal, I hope. The solution to her problem was always quite obvious, you know. After all, it is perfectly right and proper for a woman to have a child. Society could only applaud her for that. What society—and Sibylla Blackwood—cannot tolerate is that she should be unmarried. And there's only one answer to that, my dear. A husband."

"What!"

"A husband, Olivia—a perfectly respectable gentleman, someone she has known all her life and who has always had her liking and her trust. What could be better? She went off yesterday morning to be married by special license—an excellent arrangement for her and for him too, since I know of no man in greater need of a wife than my brother."

He got out of the car, walked around it and opened my door for me.

"Come inside, my pet," he said, "for I really believe we have things to discuss."

TWENTY·FIVE

M rs. Charles had left a cold supper in the library and then, no doubt on the instructions of her master, had retired for the night. I saw a bottle of wine in ice, thin curls of smoked salmon and roast beef, dusty purple grapes, rum truffles in silver dishes, fluted crystal, all elegantly displayed on a tray by the fire.

"Supper. How nice." Was that my voice?

Deftly he filled two glasses, held one out to me, champagne of course. What else?

"Do we have something to celebrate?"

"I'm not sure yet. I hope so."

"Max—what have you done?"

He tasted his wine reflectively, slowly, and then, smiling not at me but rather as if something about me amused him, he said quite pleasantly, "I am afraid, Olivia, that you will have to be generous."

"What do you mean by that?"

"Yes. What do I mean?" He sounded as if he knew his meaning exactly and to the letter. "That he has a wife now as you have a husband. A wife who needs him rather more than you do—and who has not the faintest notion of his entanglement."

For some reason he did not continue, the final word half muffled as he lit a cigar; but I heard it and abandoning all pretenses of cleverness and sophistication, appalled suddenly at the games we had been playing, the time wasted, I said very low, clenching my jaw on every word to stop my teeth—so distressingly—from chattering, "Max—there's never been an entanglement—nothing of the kind—ever."

"Why?"

412

"Max . . . ?"

"Don't distress yourself, Olivia. I feel very certain that you have done nothing to which I could realistically object, for the very good reason that Amyas will have been too decent and too honorable to persuade you. He has been ever thus."

"Yes. I know. But that was not my only reason."

He smiled. "Well—never mind. It's all over now in any case. He married Alys yesterday morning and if you couldn't hurt *me* by running away with him when he was single, I'm quite certain you wouldn't want to hurt Alys now. I knew, of course, all along of his tender feelings for you. I didn't mind—didn't even give it much thought for quite a while. You were something *he* wanted and that *I* had. We were both used to that."

He was speaking bitterly but quite gently. He was not angry with me, did not want to hurt me. I was not sure what he wanted.

"Will you please tell me what you have done." And my voice was a strained, uncertain whisper. For I was not sure what I wanted either.

"Yes. Of course I will."

He refilled his glass and mine and we exchanged smiles, rather politely as strangers do when they are not certain of each other, just curious and perhaps a little hopeful.

"I have done the best I could for her—and for Amyas. Technically there was no skill to it. I merely strolled over to Clarrow Bottom and told him the facts. He saw at once that a husband was needed and as soon as the coast was clear he came riding over here to lay his gallant heart at her feet."

"Max!"

"Flippancy, my pet, has often been my salvation. I cannot be serious in any other way. And so a marriage was arranged."

"What kind of a marriage?"

"Oh—a real one. I believe we may safely assume that much. When she made her vows she intended to keep them. And he will be very good to her. It is not ideal, I grant you. But what is? She will be far better off with him than with her mother. And good God—anything must suit him better than the unhealthy life he has been leading with Maria Long."

"Exactly. Maria Long. Just how do we expect Alys to live comfortably with her?"

"You underestimate me, Olivia. I don't expect it."

"But what can you *do* about it?"

"What I have already done. Money—Olivia. It rarely fails to do the trick."

"She wouldn't leave Amyas for money."

"Wrong, my pet. What it invariably comes down to—and Maria Long was no different—is how much. It has been her ambition to own a small seaside hotel. And ambitions of that kind can only be fulfilled by money. Her brother, who is also my brother, will be led to believe that she has accepted a position as manageress. Not so. But he will be far too relieved at her departure, I imagine, to make close inquiries. And then, there *is* the little matter of her husband. A brute, of course. Maria Long has two secrets, her relationship to Amyas and the whereabouts of her husband, who has been looking for her for years. I know both those secrets. It is a very pretty little hotel."

Yes, of course, if Max had chosen it, then it would be just right, small enough to be managed by Maria herself and a maid or two, big enough to make a profit, conveniently situated to parks and shops and to the sea, its structures sound, its decorative condition excellent. Max would have made no mistakes. I would have made none either.

He had been generous and ruthless at the same time. He had been efficient and calculating as always. Had he also been kind? Had he possibly felt guilt, or remorse? *Max?* I wondered.

"And have you done all this for Amyas or for Alys?"

"Because it had to be done. They will both benefit. And while I don't entirely see her as a farmer's wife, it is a haven from the storm at least, and he will value her for what she is. I am sure of that."

"So—you are quite a magician, Max, aren't you—or a puppeteer."

"I did no more, Olivia, than put the thought into their minds. They are old friends. And you know her views on friendship. When the news gets out no one will be surprised about it."

"Her mother will be much relieved."

"I rather thought she might. And you, Olivia? What do you feel?"

Many things. And then suddenly breaking through them one stark and terrible memory. We had laid him in Clarrow earth where he had not wished to be. Robin. Had we done the same to Alys?

I shuddered and he said quickly, "What is it?"

414

"Oh Lord—all she wanted was to fly away. And all the time there was this dreadful thing lurking in her future, laughing at her—knowing that no matter how hard she struggled she'd end up in the same trap."

I shuddered once again. "How *sad*."

"Yes," he said. "Indeed. But I can't see Amyas trying to cage her. Far from it. He is a man enough—my brother—to appreciate a woman who *is* a woman, not a domestic mouse. He's not so small that he needs a devoted slave to make him feel bigger. And she'll broaden the dimensions of his life quite remarkably, I'd say. They'll be all right."

I sat down on the couch, leaned back and closed my eyes, needing just a moment of quiet to sort through so many shades of reaction and impression, to place in some kind of order the questions I ought to ask, the things I should know: to track down, if I could, that one elusive idea—suspicion—misunderstanding perhaps, which had continued to elude me.

I had never fallen in love with Amyas, I understood that. I had, instead, responded so profoundly to his feeling for me, had valued it—and him—so immensely that, in other circumstances, I could have mirrored it and had been content with it all my days. He had simply wished to offer me the knowledge that I was loved, and that in itself had overwhelmed me.

Yet how ironic—how appropriate perhaps—that the one man who had loved me first and foremost and for so long, the only man in my life who had loved no one else before me or at the same time, should now be married to Alys. Had I paid my debt?

"Olivia," Max said, sitting down beside me, not touching me but the odor of his cigar, the musky fragrance of his cologne a definite physical contact nonetheless. "We could leave it there, my pet—just raise our glasses and wish them well and then go to Monte Carlo or Cannes or anywhere else you fancy in the morning. Perhaps we *should* leave it there."

"No." I had not realized I felt so strongly about it until I heard the decided note in my voice.

"Are you sure? What more can I tell you? What more do you *really* want to hear?"

"I don't know, Max—I don't know—just talk."

There was something to be resolved. I could not name it or

define it but too many times now we had turned away from it, left it hovering uneasily, not altogether out of sight.

"Just talk." And if he went on long enough surely I would pick up, here and there, sufficient words and phrases to remind me of what it was I really *had* to know.

"I'll tell you about Amyas if you like."

"Yes. That will do. Are you nervous, Max—? That is your third cigar."

"I am on uncertain ground, I think. I prefer a cool atmosphere. And when it comes to personal difficulties—with women that is—it suits me far better if they can be resolved by a visit to a good jeweler's shop. My mother taught me that. You may have noticed that although the house she lives in belongs to me, I am not welcome in it unless I appear with a jewel case in my hand."

"Yes. I *had* noticed. And once she has her magnifying glass trained on whatever you have brought her, then she has not the least interest in whether you stay or go."

He smiled. "Quite. Which means, of course, that I grew up believing all women to be like that—rather to your advantage, I would have thought, my pet. Amyas never wanted presents. There was a time when I tried hard to give him—well, the little luxuries I value so much myself, I suppose, and he turned me down."

"He said you always took—and won."

"Oh—he has said the same to me, but in the early days he would have given me the shirt from his back and gone naked himself whereas I, you see, would have managed to lay my hands on two shirts, one way or another—brand-new—best quality—one each. Or perhaps three shirts—two for me and one for him. That is the difference between us."

And now I was the one who smiled.

"Did Amyas look after you when you first came here?"

"He certainly tried. I was an urchin from a foreign gutter. The only English I knew I'd picked up from my father, racing cant and curses mostly, which endeared me to no one. Amyas and I were thrown together because we were nearly the same age. We stayed together because it suited us. When we found out we were brothers I thought it was my turn to start protecting him, since I was the legitimate son of the house with the balance tipped my way. I raised hell when I heard I was going to Hexingham and Amyas to some mediocre place in Bradeswick. Amyas saw the Squire's point of view, and that was the first time we quarreled. I still think I could have worn the Squire down and got him to send us both to Hexingham if Amyas had been ready to co-operate. But he thought we should be grateful to the Squire and not cause him pain."

"Max—you were jealous."

"I often am, my pet. It is the Spaniard in me. I conceal it admirably."

"Yes. You do."

"Amyas never understood it. He went on being reasonable and decent and *grateful*. Not I. He wouldn't believe me when I said the Squire was using him. That upset me and so I made Hexingham suffer for it. But when the Squire finally struck my name from the family Bible and turned me off his land I thought Amyas would come with me. He ought to have come with me. I am still of the same opinion. But your mother was getting up to her high jinks then, your father was going into a decline. The Squire needed Amyas. So did I. The Squire won."

"And since then you've made a point of needing no one."

"I imagine that may have had something to do with it. I could have made his fortune, Olivia. What did the Squire ever give him but hard work and indifference? Even when things were going well in Africa and he had absolutely everything to gain by coming out to join me he wouldn't do it. Your mother had gone. Your father was a sick man. He couldn't desert his post. The Squire needed him. All right— yes—self-interest played a part. In a business like mine I need a man I can trust and Amyas would have been a godsend to me. But if he had trusted me—as he certainly didn't—he'd have been a rich man now. That's what I wanted him to be. I couldn't convince him. I persevered and we quarreled rather badly. When I came back here during the war we quarreled again, because my reappearance was displeasing to the Squire. Amyas was still the Squire's man. My af- fluence meant nothing to him. All he wanted me to do was leave the Squire in peace. Naturally, I did not. I let Amyas know exactly what I intended to do with our ancestral home and lands. He did not like it. I also mentioned—rather crudely I expect—that I'd find it no hardship to include you in the transaction if I could. He liked that even less. He had been looking at you too. I looked again. And whatever my shortcomings, you must admit that I've been looking ever since. The sad thing is, of course, that I would still have been ready to employ him and put a good living his way. I had a dozen profitable little schemes in mind just for him when I came back from Africa and could have thought up a dozen more. He wouldn't listen. In the end all I've been able to do for him is buy his sister a hotel."

"And give him Alys."

"Olivia—surely I have talked enough?"

He got up to pour more wine and, as he gave me my glass, I shook my head, "No—no. You talk so *well* Max. Please go on."

"Do you know what you want me to say?"

"No." But the question was there, hovering on the brink of conscious thought almost—not quite—and then abruptly, "Yes, Max, talk about Alys."

"Yes." And then, taking a long time I thought to light a cigar, fussing needlessly with a match, he said without any expression whatsoever, "Is it wise?"

"I don't know. It seems—relevant."

"What shall I tell you?"

"Max, I don't know. You asked her to marry you once, didn't you?"

He shrugged, looking relieved I thought—oddly so—and smiled. "Ah well, yes I did, but I rather doubt that I expected to be taken seriously."

"And if you had been?"

"Olivia—it was always my intention to marry you."

"For the Manor."

"If we are to begin an investigation of motives, my pet, then what were yours?"

"Money."

"Thank you, Olivia."

"For my honesty, I suppose? I am honest, Max—more often than not. I have been a good wife, too—well haven't I? I have been faithful and agreeable and I have had plenty of opportunities to go astray, believe me, with some of your friends. I have done nothing worse than annoy you sometimes with my relations. And last week when you went to London so mysteriously and I thought you might be bankrupt I spent a whole morning working out how much I could raise on my jewels and my little bits and pieces in the Gatehouse, to help you. So it can't really be for money any longer, can it?"

418

"Darling—I don't quite know what to say to that."

"Something romantic I should have thought. But don't bother. I don't think I'm quite finished yet."

"Olivia—do have some supper, darling. You must have eaten next to nothing today."

"No thank you. It is good to starve a little sometimes. It sharpens the wits."

"You are in a very strange humor."

"Yes. I am."

He turned his face slightly, rather more into the lamplight, and I saw—as one never expected to see in him—an air of tension and fatigue, an impression that his handsome, clever head could ache just like mine; just like anyone's. How old was he? Over forty certainly, and still playing whist until four in the morning far too often and getting up at seven to live up to his reputation as a superb, still lethally accurate gun. I saw now that he was tired. Perhaps he too had not eaten very much today.

"*You* have some supper, Max."

I got up, brisk and purposeful and domestic—good Heavens!—and filled his plate, choosing the very best, looking after him; supplying the bread and salt, the nourishment, obeying the urge to feed, to shelter, to keep warm which is to be found, to some degree, in every woman.

"Would you like coffee?"

"I have sent all the servants to bed, darling. How would we manage coffee?"

"You have not married a king's daughter, Max, you know— just Cinderella. It's been a long time, I admit, but I do believe I can remember what one does about coffee. Shall I?"

"No, darling, because you would have to go into the kitchen, which would take all of fifteen minutes, and I really don't want to spare you for so long."

"How very foolish."

"Yes, isn't it. But exactly what I feel nevertheless."

It was a very tender moment, fragile, built up of intangibles, nuances, as such moments are, no substance to it, nothing that I would be able to define or describe or hold on to when it was gone. I would never forget it.

I leaned forward and kissed him very carefully and gently, just my mouth on his, no other contact until he slid his arms around me and held me just as carefully, a slight tremor in him, a most decided one in me.

And then, still gently and slowly, I released myself and got up, for I had remembered now what it was I had to ask.

I took a few steps, up and down, hoping perhaps that I would forget, that it might suddenly seem unnecessary, unwise. But now, when I would have been glad to lose it, the question remained, so clear, so obvious that I realized I had known it all along. I had not wished to see it. I did not wish to see it now. But there it was, filling my vision, and if I tried to suppress it, then it would surface again, for the rest of my life, at the very moments when it would be least welcome. It would turn sour inside me. It would fester. I must come to terms with it now or try to. For me it was the only way.

"Max—there is something."

"Yes? Won't it keep darling—until morning?"

I shook my head.

"Max—about Alys . . ."

"Oh, Olivia—surely not."

"*Max.* Tell me. You were in London in March when she was attacked. You saw her the next day or even the same night. She was in a terrible state of shock. I understand all that. What happened then?"

I had never thought to see him turn pale but he did so now, only slightly, no more than could have been explained by the lateness of the hour, the fatigue of the day, but I saw it, and understood.

He got up too and standing very close to me, his eyes narrow and keen, his thoughts racing I knew, as mine were, he said tonelessly, "Nothing."

"Max."

"Olivia. Nothing. Absolutely nothing."

"Max, are you lying to me?"

"Possibly I am. Possibly you should accept it."

"Max, I can't do that. You know I can't. I have never left well alone in my whole life—if it *is* well—I'll never give up now until I know the truth. I even wish I could. I *can't.* If you won't tell me, then sooner or later, I'll ask Alys. You wouldn't like me to do that?"

"Not at all."

"I wouldn't like it either. But liking or not liking wouldn't stop me in the end. You must know that."

"Yes," he said, very quietly, "I am afraid I do."

"Max—?"

"Very well."

And he looked very tired.

"You are a woman yourself and so you can imagine the horror of her condition. I went to see her, absolutely by chance, that same night, and I was appalled by it. When I arrived at her flat she could not tolerate me—a man—within a yard of her. And, rather worse than that, she could not tolerate herself. Her disgust with her own body was so profound that it would have been dangerous to leave her alone. By morning she was stable enough not to do away with herself but she was still in great need of distraction. Incredible as it may seem she had never been abroad and so I took her to Amsterdam. I was going there in any case, I admit, so it was easy enough to manage; and her pleasure in a foreign city was a delight to see. I gave her champagne suppers, flowers, all the little frivolities women put out of their minds when they become militant Suffragettes. I even offered her a diamond, which is what one offers in Amsterdam. She refused."

"And you made love to her."

It was not a question but a sorrowful acknowledgment of something already known and understood. All I had to do now was discover whether or not I could bear it.

He leaned forward, staring into the hearth a moment, and I lowered my eyes, preferring not to look at him. "Yes," he said slowly, "of course I did. Olivia—she had to know the difference between what those brutes had done to her and what any normal, decent man would be likely to do. She had been physically raped. She had to be physically loved, and quickly—or it would have been too late. I did not intend it, in that I did not plan it, although I agree that it may have been inevitable. It was an extension of the concern I had for her and the trust which—believe it or not—she had in me. I make no excuses. I know, and she knows, that without it, she would have been ruined for any kind of loving relationship with a man. And therefore—whatever it is going to cost me now—how can I ever say to you that I am sorry?"

I shook my head. There was no need for apology. I understood. But, like Alys, my body could not function so reasonably. My mind accepted the justice, the irony. The intellect, I discovered, could be rational, compassionate, even calm, no matter what the pressure. My body had but one violent and unadulterated reaction. My body was jealous, and leaning back, closing my eyes, I suffered it grimly, held rigid by the shock, tears stinging my eyelids.

"Olivia—for God's sake!"

He sounded startled, considerably alarmed and still keeping my eyes tight shut I began to tell him, "It's all right—it's all right. Just give me a moment. I know I shouldn't behave like this—I know."

"Can you say to me that I was wrong?"

"No. I can't."

"In my place would you not have done the same thing?"

"Very likely I would. In fact—yes *very* likely."

Of course I would. If any man I cared for had been in such dire need of anything my body could give, then I would have given it, without condescension or charity, but freely, frankly, not necessarily with a love that would have bound me to that man for longer than the need lasted, but with love nevertheless. I understood. Regrettably it made no difference to the turmoil I *felt*. That remained an entirely separate matter and jumping to my feet I made a dash for the door, wanting to take my tearful agony away from him until I could subdue it, hammer it if need be into reasonable proportions. But he caught me from behind and held me, my back pressed tight against his chest, until I was calm. And then, turning me in the circle of his arms he held me a while longer.

"Dare I be flattered, Olivia? I hate to see you cry but if you are crying for me then I can only be grateful."

We sat down again and in the great quietness that seemed to be spreading around us—the lull which comes when the subsiding tempest has swept the dead wood away, leaving intact only such things as are steadfast and resolute—I said to him without accusation, "You could be the father of her child."

"No," he said, just as steadily, although he knew what this could mean to me, "I think it unlikely. I took every care."

"But the possibility does exist."

"Yes—remotely—and it haunts me for your sake."

It had haunted Alys too. Perhaps only a particle of doubt remained but because of that she had rejected any idea of abortion or adoption as she may not otherwise have done. Yes, it could be Max's child. And I would have to watch it grow. Very well. I had prided myself all my life on my courage. We would see now what I was really made of. Like Max, I would not have endured prison and degradation

422

as Alys had done. Could I endure this? Could I pass beyond the stage of mere endurance and emerge from it whole and sound and unfettered? I did not know.

"What do you feel for Alys? *Now*, I mean."

He took both my hands in his and leaned towards me, encircling me with his concentration, that intense quiet still building up around us so that our two bodies sitting close together hand in hand, knee pressed against knee, made up an island emerging from deep water; an oasis, perhaps, just appearing in a landscape of dry sand.

"What I have always felt, Olivia. I have admired her purity and her bravery and valued them immensely. Just as I have always valued the same qualities in Amyas. I know my own limitations and I would never have sacrificed my own best interests for the sake of duty as Amyas has done. I was the legitimate son of the house and it was my place to stay here and help the Squire, to accept the responsibilities of my position. He was the by-blow who ought to have been free to go off and make his fortune as I did. I may have cursed him when he refused all those very advantageous offers I made him but by God I admired him too. I would never have had the sheer guts to get myself out of bed every morning, year in and year out, with no time limit to it, no conditions, and waste myself—first for the Squire and then for Maria Long—because I believed it to be right. When I first met Alys I saw a very dainty little bird pecking a way out of its shell, and that aroused my curiosity. Later on I saw Amyas in her. If they succeed in recognizing themselves in each other than I shall not have done too badly for them I think after all. I want her to be happy, Olivia. That is what I feel about Alys. But with me. I would also like him to have some joy in life. It is high time. Olivia—what else?"

"Corfu. You have a child there don't you?"

He shook his head. "A child no longer. A young woman who was married last year—at great expense. She was born in the goldfields in difficult conditions. Her mother died a day later and I had no alternative but to foster her as best I could—a Greek family as it turned out who took her with them, quite soon after, to Corfu. The only part I have ever played in her upbringing has been to pay for it. She has become very much like her foster mother, placid and narrow-minded. We have nothing in common. So—that is what I have in my life, my pet, an avaricious mother, an indifferent daughter—do I have you, Olivia?"

"Yes."

"Once again such instant surrender. I can hardly believe in it."

Time. That was what I most needed. Not much, perhaps, but *time* to adjust not only to the obvious changes that were taking place around me, but to Max himself, time to see him not as the ruthless sophisticate I had first met in the foyer of the Station Hotel but as a man every bit as capable of giving, and suffering, and *needing* as I was myself, a man who had cared about his brother, who had loved a woman in the African goldfields and lost her, who had been disappointed in his child. Time to think of Max as a man who could be trusted. I had been wrong about so many things. I could be wrong again. How could I doubt it? But whatever should happen now, no matter what remnants of the past might remain to worry me, at least, and in full, I had paid my debt to Alys.

TWENTY·SIX

No farmer can remain for long away from his fields, and Amyas soon brought his wife home to Clarrow Bottom.

"My daughter has always been such an impetuous creature," announced Aunt Sibylla, returning post-haste from Bridlington to fill the farmhouse, so recently vacated by Maria Long, with jars of her own prize-winning marmalade, pies made from the fruit of the vicarage garden, hampers of household linen, the trousseau she had started putting aside when Alys had turned fifteen. "Naturally we knew—the vicar and I—how things were between them—have known for years—didn't everyone? My goodness, Lady Potterton, do you really mean to say that you hadn't *noticed*? It was only ever a matter of time—the vicar and I were convinced of that. And naturally one could only approve of dear Amyas. So upright and reliable, and doing so well now—buying more land. Had you not heard that either? Oh yes, naturally, I did implore him to stop her from becoming a Suffragette. But he was quite right, you see, to let her get it out of her system. He said it would make her a more comfortable wife in the end. The dear boy is so wise."

And when it became known that Alys was expecting a child the initial tremor of speculation was soon stifled since no one could be quite certain just when the marriage had taken place.

"I am so glad she has taken my advice and started a family at once," Aunt Sibylla confided to Dottie Potterton, "for when one is no longer seventeen one cannot afford to delay." And that was the end of it.

The house at Clarrow Bottom assumed a different character. Alys took down the net curtains, opened the windows, put branches of greenery and sprays of wild flowers in china pots and then forgot the house entirely, leaving it to the maids while she went out into the fields to talk to Amyas, or sat in the meadow with a book, her hair hanging loose like a girl; forgetting her hat, more often than not, so that by the summer's end her skin was honey gold, her hair almost white. She seemed to be mellowing like the season, ripening rather than putting on weight, her careless appearance and her disregard of all domestic duties annoying her mother, charming Amyas who had had a surfeit of neatness.

"How she will manage to look after that child when it comes I cannot imagine," said her mother.

"Oh—they usually manage to look after themselves mostly, you know," said mine.

"Nonsense," snapped Victorine, "child-rearing is both an art and a science and should not be left to amateurs. I will show her how."

But Alys continued to pursue her own sweet dreamy path, reading her newspapers all morning just as she had done in Cheyne Walk, writing copious letters—her postbag as heavy sometimes as Max's—talking to Amyas, staying up far too late, Aunt Sibylla thought, for a farmer's wife; talking again—talking—talking. How could any woman—my aunt wondered—find so much to say to her husband? While Amyas's attitude to maternal criticism was forthright and simple. He had a dairymaid to churn the butter, a housemaid to sweep the floor, a dear friend who did him the honor of sharing his bed, his table and his name.

"Horses for courses," said Max. "After all one does not harness a thoroughbred to the plow. I'm glad my brother sees that."

"She should get on with her sewing or that poor mite will have nothing to wear," moaned her mother who, since the wedding, had been turning out tiny embroidered garments by the score. But Alys's view of the role she had now undertaken was vastly different. She was a farmer's wife and it was her task not to sit in her parlor doing the fine needlework she hated or to waste her energies fussing about pie-crusts and polishes and invitation cards as her mother did, but to concern herself with farming. Whenever Amyas had to get up in the night to attend a sick cow or deliver a calf she would get up too and help him. One morning when the dairymaid was missing, Alys put on her boots, went into the dairy and, despite her by now fairly advanced condition which made the three-legged stool somewhat hazardous, she milked the herd Amyas had bought from me.

Her aim was not so much to help her husband as to share his labors. She included farming manuals now among her books of poetry and political philosophy and studied them minutely. Did the topic in itself interest her? Not really. But political science—for its own sake—had never greatly fired her enthusiasm either. She simply felt that women should be well informed on every possible issue. The struggle for the vote would eventually be won, she had no doubt of it, and in the meantime women like herself who were forced to be inactive for one reason or another, must use the time to equip themselves: to learn. One should not reap the rewards of any situation without first undertaking the hard labor and although she was now, however surprisingly, a married woman, it was with no thought of being maintained in idleness. If she survived the birth of this child, she told me, then she would immediately conceive another—Amyas was entitled to that, it was little enough to do for him—and then they would work together, not leading the separate lives of man and woman with all the false assumptions and resentments that such a strict division of roles implied, but sharing one life as partners and friends.

"My daughter has always entertained these progressive notions," said Aunt Sibylla, her eyebrows growing supercilious again now that disgrace no longer seemed to threaten, "but time and a little experience will show her that there is no place for progress in marriage. What a man requires is a good dinner on his table, piping hot and not a minute later than *dinner-time*. And no amount of clever talk can hope to compensate him for the lack."

"I do believe," said Max, "that she is about to devote herself to my brother with all the fervor she gave to Suffragism—in which case, happy man. One cannot deny that he has the knack of inspiring devotion."

"He is entitled to yours, Max. If you are fond of him, then why not tell him so?"

"My dear Olivia, he would be considerably startled were I to ride into his farmyard and make him a declaration."

But he rode over to Clarrow Bottom just the same—possibly to see Alys—although Amyas was never far away, reacting with quiet humor and taking no notice whatsoever when Max outlined scheme after grandiose scheme for doubling and trebling his profits.

"He doesn't want to be a rich man, Max."

What had he wanted? Approximately what he now had. Warmth and peace and friendship. And a full acknowledgment at last of kinship. The facts of his birth remained suppressed but, as the husband of my first cousin, he was beyond question a member of the manorial family, coming late and in a left-handed fashion but most truly welcome to the situation for which he had been born. The sight of him, even glimpsed in the distance, gave me pleasure. I wanted him to be happy. That was what I felt about Amyas. But not with me.

Mr. Samuel Greenlaw finally retired to Bournemouth that summer, my mother and Emil Junot and even little Mr. Cross accompanying him. There was to be no marriage. Neither Mr. Greenlaw's heart, it was decided, nor the financial expectations of his daughters-in-law could stand the strain of a wedding. But, in compensation, my mother was to have an allowance—small in her view, princely according to Bessie Greenlaw— for *her* lifetime, not his. And although Bessie and her watchful partner Hattie did not know it, Mr. Greenlaw had already transferred to my mother the ownership of his seaside villa in which, one presumed, she would live very comfortably with Junot when Mr. Greenlaw should be no more.

"I do not wish to discuss it," said Aunt Sibylla, for perhaps the fortieth time. "For the way my sister is exploiting that poor old man sickens me. I cannot imagine what his relations are thinking of to allow it."

But my mother had far more skill with a jar of ointment than one might have supposed, far more patience than Bessie and Hattie combined, was infinitely warmer of heart and much prettier to look at; while no one could choose Mr. Greenlaw an after-dinner cigar or tell him a more amusing after-dinner story than Papa Junot.

"Parasites," said Aunt Sibylla.

"He will die happier with those two around him," said Max, "than those strait-laced bitches who married his sons."

"Shall I sell the house in Aireville Terrace?"

We went together and walked through the familiar rooms still furnished with Miss Jemima Copthorne Heron's heavy Gothic pieces, the garden very much as Victorine had left it years ago.

"We painted this house ourselves from top to bottom, Victorine and I. It nearly killed us."

428

We had been close together then—Victorine, Madelon, Luc—in that distant time before other loyalties or disloyalties or our separate natures had set us on such diverse pathways.

"Keep it," Max said, his arm around my shoulders, "as a souvenir."

"A house? As a keepsake?"

"*What* an idea," snorted Victorine. "I shall come and live here myself and annoy Frances Grey who will certainly not care for my noisy children as neighbors. You will not expect much, I daresay, in the way of rent, for one cannot do wonders on an M.P.'s salary."

She did not see the need, she told me, of moving to London with Andrew when he went to take up his parliamentary duties. Politics—talking about a fatal wound, she called it, instead of stopping the bleeding—did not interest her. If Andrew imagined he could save the world that way then he was welcome to try. But she had the boys to consider, schools, a permanent home, her work behind the tramsheds and at St. Winefrede's Hospital. Much better, she thought, for Andrew to have a flat somewhere in Westminster where he could talk Liberal policies and write his speeches, while she moved into Aireville Terrace, at a nominal rent, where the boys could have a bedroom each, she could re-plant the garden and convert the back kitchen into a still-room for herbal remedies. Andrew would come home during the recess, which amounted, she thought, to six months out of every twelve. And far better for him to interview his constituents in Aireville Terrace than Corporation Square.

"I'm sure he'd like you to go with him, Victorine."

She shrugged. "I daresay he would. But he's a grown man you know. He ought to be able to manage perfectly well without me."

Clearly her boys and the residents of St. Saviour's Passage could not.

I had a letter from Luc announcing his engagement to a Miss Magda Kellermann; a good family said Max, and a reasonably pretty girl from her photograph; thin and dark and very stylish.

"We can go down to the Cape after Christmas," Max offered, "to have a look. Would you like that?"

He wanted to please me. I wanted him to be pleased.

"Darling—I'd love it."

We had started to touch one another a great deal lately, not amorously but the small precious contacts of deep affection, trust, mutual reassurance, his hand suddenly closing over mine, my cheek pressed against his fleeting little caresses too brief for others to notice but which gave warmth to every day.

"That's settled then. We'll call and see my mother on the way back."

"Your mother is an old vulture, Max."

"Yes, but regrettably she's the only one I possess."

"Will you take me to meet your daughter?"

"If you like—although you won't care for her. She's a vulture too, or will be in her day."

"Then how lucky that you have me."

"Yes. I do so absolutely agree with that."

I began to feel not only compelled to touch him, to make certain that he was well and happy and whole, that he was *there*, but with a great desire to give him small presents, little surprises, to produce—like a rabbit from a hat—a certain bottle of wine he believed to be unobtainable, magazine articles he thought he had missed, friends he had not expected to see again for years. I began to talk to him, every remark I made—no matter how great a crowd was present—intended for his consideration, his amusement, his defense should anyone dare, by the slightest hint or the most obscure deed, to criticize. I began to flirt with him, consciously, openly, to my frank delight and his. I began to laugh with him. And it was no surprise to me. The potential had always existed.

"Your husband looks very pleased with himself these days," said Aunt Sibylla, growing tart again since, after all her trouble, she did not seem to be making anything of Alys.

"My husband would not like this to be generally known," I told her confidentially, bubbling over, as I so often seemed to be doing these days, with laughter, "but he is something of an imposter. You may not have realized it but he is an exceptionally kind and responsible man."

Alys, contrary to all expectations, had her child easily and quickly in the autumn, a boy who was referred to by both Alys and Amyas as "our son." I went carefully to see him, testing myself, steeling myself a little, and there he was, healthy, sound, no mark of violence or disease or disgrace anywhere upon him. A brand-new life, unblemished. Neither the child of a stranger's brutality nor of the concern of a true friend. Himself. The clean, unsullied future.

I put my hand into the cradle and touched him lightly, my

fingers enjoying without hunger his warm fragility, his perfect freshness. He was not mine. No child ever would be mine. I regretted it.
But what troubled me most was the thought of Max, waiting at the
Manor tense and anxious about what I could be feeling now. I must
go home at once and set his mind at rest. Children had mothers, and
fathers, if they were lucky. Max had me.

We entertained with enthusiasm all through the Christmas
season, the house full of friends, acquaintances, friends of friends,
complete strangers, champagne for breakfast, Viennese waltzes at noon,
strange, staccato music from America thumped out on our grand piano
until the small hours of the morning by a pale young man who had
simply wandered in, I suspected, to escape the cold. There were letters
and parcels from Luc on Christmas morning; my mother and her whist
table arriving from Bournemouth with the news that Madelon was
finally divorced and had married Clive Potterton just in time for the
birth of their child.

The Clarrow Hunt met at our front door on Boxing Day, drank
their stirrup-cups, rode off and finding no sport, came back for cold
beef and pickles, mulled wine, mince-pies, flirtation. We sent hampers
to every house in the village whether we owned it or not, a case of
champagne to Clarrow Bottom, gave a children's party in the church
hall, sent Christmas presents—chosen by Victorine with an eye to
usefulness rather than artistic merit—to every patient in St. Winefrede's Hospital. I took my nephews to the pantomime in Leeds and
deeply regretted it, realizing that I would have difficulty in facing Miss
Frances Grey when she learned what little monsters I had released
upon her. The weather remained frosty and clear, pale pink mornings
deepening to afternoons of strong, cool sunshine, the air crisp and
delicious on the tongue, dark trees and hedges feathered with snow.
The season had never touched me so deeply. I was aware of every
scent and texture of it, every nuance, woke early every morning eager
to explore every minute of the day.

I was happy.

I was happy with Max.

I was complete.

On New Year's Eve, half an hour or so before midnight, Mrs.
Charles came gliding unobtrusively through the crowded hall with a
message that Mr. de Haan would like to see me—at once, he had
specified—in the garage courtyard. Was something the matter? Mrs.

431

Charles, of course, could not say, could only express an opinion that Mr. de Haan had sounded urgent.

The garage courtyard! It was a place I rarely visited, Stevens invariably bringing the car to the front of the house for me just as the grooms brought the horses. What had happened? What could go wrong now? Please—not now. I shivered and ran, no time to think of finding a coat, the December night by no means ideally suited to a woman in a scanty evening dress of black chiffon held together by a few sequins.

"Max . . ?"

He was standing by the car, my long pale fur over his arm, which he threw quickly around me.

"It's all right, darling. I'm just reliving an adolescent fantasy. Would you care to join me? When I was a young man I thought how very stylish to walk into a room crowded with beautiful women, beckon the very loveliest of them to my side and drive off with her in the most dashing vehicle of the day. It wouldn't have been a Rolls, of course, when I was a young man—a high-perch phaeton probably. And I did send the housekeeper. But then—I knew you'd come."

We drove up the hill—not far—to the top of Clarrow Moor and sat for a while in a most comfortable silence, the village a dim tracery of lights below us, Max smoking a cigar while I, leaning against his shoulder, wrapped like a Christmas parcel in my fur, watched him smoke it, every movement he made a deep and absolute joy.

There was no need to say anything. We sat close together in the dark, enraptured by the simple precious gift of solitude. I was happy—happy with Max. There was just one more thing to wish for.

He finished his cigar and we slid into a familiar embrace, my head against his chest, my furs covering us both.

The year, which had been so good to us, was nearly over. In a little while now a bright New Year would be handed to me, vibrant with possibility and promise, and I knew exactly what I meant to do with it. I wanted—more than that I fully intended—to compensate Max for every bad moment he had ever suffered. I would, one way or another, be sufficient in myself to make up for his greedy, self-centered mother, his impossible father, the harsh discipline of the Squire. I would fill his mind and his senses—and his heart—so that it would no longer matter to him that his daughter was a stranger, Amyas not quite a brother, that so many people regarded him as a man who took

432

and won—when in fact he had given far more than anyone realized. Now I would give to him.

"It's almost midnight," he said.

"Then kiss me, darling. They say that whatever one happens to be doing as the year changes will go on all year long."

I closed my eyes, sighing and smiling at the word which had materialized inside my head. Bliss. A silly word, I'd always thought. But this sensation of dissolving my body into his was—even assisted a little by wine—*blissful*. Magical. I was as enchanted, giddy, bemused as if I had never been kissed before.

"Happy New Year, darling."

Yes. It would be glorious. Down below us in the village church bells began to chime, heralding the first moments of my brief New Year, the best one ever, the year in which I *knew*, from the moment of its commencement, that everything I most desired was safely within my grasp. Lovely, lovely New Year. I could hardly wait to begin this first eager month of it.

It was January, 1914.

TWENTY·SEVEN

I could not understand why we were suddenly at war with Germany. And when Max explained to me the official reasons I could not understand them either.

"Wars happen," he said at last, "because people like them."

No. That could not be true. But Bradeswick was suddenly infected, during that stifling month of August, not with the typhoid which might have been expected at that season, but with the fever for combat and glory, the recruiting officers working overtime to cope with the flood of volunteers; enough to swell the ranks of any army had not so many of them been under-size and under-weight, bandy-legged or crook-shouldered, with too few teeth to eat army rations, or eyesight too defective to see a target, much less hit it.

But these were mainly Victorine's people from behind the tramsheds and, in the slightly better areas of the town where the diet had been sufficient—if sometimes only just—to ward off the more obvious effects of malnutrition, young men from every house in every street enlisted, all pals together, in the same battalion; marching off, conquering heroes in their hearts already, to prove that one English-man was worth a dozen of any other kind, any time.

Had they forgotten the man at the corner of Commercial Street who had lost both legs in Africa and who had squatted at the roadside for as long as I could remember selling matches?

Who gave a thought now to Ladysmith or Mafeking and the young men who had died there, only a dozen years ago? I thought of my brother Guy and shivered.

434

Miss Frances Grey began, very competently, to make a small circle of her acquaintances aware that the likelihood of casualties in the near future would necessitate the forming of committees to organize the provision of bandages, the conversion perhaps of St. Winefrede's into a convalescent home for officers, the knitting of warm scarves and gloves should the war last the winter.

Universities and colleges and the sixth forms of grammar schools emptied. The W.S.P.U. completely abandoned its campaign for the franchise, devoting itself entirely to the war effort, inspired by Mrs. Pankhurst's fervent patriotism and by a measure of common-sense. Someone must run the essential services of the country while the men were away. And if women performed these tasks efficiently, proving themselves perfectly capable of shouldering men's burdens and responsibilities, then any government—Liberal, Tory, Labor or whatever—would find it difficult thereafter to refuse them the same legal and political rights.

My brother-in-law, Andrew Rexford, like every other politician I had ever heard of anywhere in the world, had not wanted a war. "No one," he said, looking harassed, "desires anything but peace."

"Then make it," said Victorine, "and while you're talking about the rights and wrongs of it—you and Frances Grey and Alys— you might like to ask your Lloyd George what's to happen to his soldiers' wives and children while the men are away. War widows might get pensions but these women aren't widows yet, and in the meantime they have to eat. A little soup and bread would see them through the winter a shade more comfortably than ethics. And if that elderly virgin of a Frances Grey lays her hands on St. Winefrede's and tries to turn out my mothers and babies so that she can spend her time administering to officers and gentlemen with her gloves on, I may strangle her."

At least Luc was out of it. I thanked God for that. But then suddenly there was Luc, arriving all bright and breezy, incredibly handsome and tanned, abominably self-assured, using words and expressions that grated on my nerves—what an absolutely first-rate lark it was all going to be, ideal opportunity for a chap to show what he was made of, one had to play the game, of course, and play fair, but there was no doubt that the best team would win. Naturally he would not stay out in South Africa while all the chaps he knew were positively stampeding home to have a crack at the Hun. One could not let the side down.

"Hexingham taught him to think like that," said Max.

And what of Miss Kellermann? Well yes—but she'd wait, of course, for a returning hero. What woman wouldn't? And in any case nothing in the world was going to make him run the risk of a white feather. He could not see it lasting much longer than Christmas in any case.

"I'll be all right, Liv, old girl, you know."

Fervently I hoped, I prayed so.

Ivor Naseby came back from the South of France, not married to Lois, and immediately enlisted. Anyone could have Natasha now, his mother, my mother, anyone at all. He was a soldier, his devotion entirely transferred to the men he commanded, and no one had expected Wellington or Napoleon to stay at home to look after a child.

And then to everyone's surprise there was Madelon, jumping out of her car while it was still moving and running across the grass to me, thin, brittle, quite beautiful, smoking one cigarette after another, laughing, coughing behind a quick jeweled hand, chattering incessantly. Lady Potterton now, although she fell about laughing whenever she thought of it, Clive's father having recently died, making Dottie a widow and Clive a lord. Lady Potterton: mistress of an ancient mansion and a noble estate as she had once been mistress of the Naseby fortune.

And here was her new daughter, Ondine. A pretty name. Yes, she had taken good care of that and had fought off all Clive's suggestions of Dorothea and Theodora and Eustacia. If she could give her children nothing else—and really she rather wondered if she could—then they would have at least these romantic names. Natasha, a Russian princess. Ondine, a water sprite. And how was Clive? Oh well, ready for the fray, of course, and he would look very splendid leading his men into battle, she did not doubt it. Dear Clive. Still wise and wonderful but—well—a little bit bothered sometimes by the difference in their ages. And was she to blame for that? Well, she supposed the war would wake him up a bit, although she had no idea what *she* was going to do about it. Certainly not sit and molder at Dawney Park with Dottie and the baby, as Clive seemed to think. It was all going to be too dreary for words and rather than stay here doing worthy things like rolling bandages, she'd much rather go out to the front with an ambulance, where she'd be likely to find most of her friends.

The next morning I found Max at the gate, watching his horses being ridden away.

"I've given them to Amyas," he said, "before the army comes to commandeer them. If he can prove he needs them for agricultural purposes they may let him keep them—for a while."

"Max—your hunters harnessed to the plow?"

He lit a cigar and then, with a gesture made up of supreme irritation and the most irksome pity and regret, tossed it to the ground.

"Better off at the plow, the poor brutes, than handed over to some damn fool of a cavalry officer who'll ride them straight into the enemy guns shouting "Tally-ho." *They* didn't make this war, whoever else did. Have you ever seen animals in a field of battle? No, how could you. Well, I have. They cower and shiver and they bleed. They don't know what any of it means. They just die. God dammit, Olivia, I'm not staying here to watch the slaughter. Because *men* cower just like the horses, when it gets bad—and cry for their mothers. I've seen it in Africa. Never again. Madeira will be the best place, and soon, while one still can."

"Max, for how long?"

He looked at me strangely, for a long, uncomfortable moment.

"I would anticipate years rather than months. Possibly on a permanent basis."

"And the Manor?"

"Bricks and mortar, my pet, which may have served their purpose—for us at any rate. I think the time has come to face a sorry fact. The good life as we understood it is finished. Win or lose—and I wouldn't like to hazard a guess either way—things will not be the same again. I told you years ago that the pleasures and privileges wouldn't last. Well, we enjoyed them, we *had* them. I don't want to build something second-rate on their ashes. I'd rather move on."

"You want me to sell the Manor, don't you?"

It was the sacrifice I would never have made for Robin. Max knew that. He made no reply. After a moment, facing him fairly and squarely I said, "The Manor means as much to me now as it always did. Possibly more. My roots are here. Everything of real importance that has happened to me in my life has happened here. And apart from that I love it. My family are here too. Victorine may need my support one day because if Andrew finds some pretty little girl to keep him company she may take it harder than she imagines. God knows what will happen to Madelon and Luc. I daren't think. All I can really do is offer them a home when they need it. A base. The Manor represents all that. But yes, Max. I'll sell it. I'll come with you. We can go today and make the arrangements."

"Olivia," he said, rather gruffly for him "I do love you. I suppose you did know that?"

He could be in no doubt any longer of my love for him.

We went to London the following day to tie up the loose ends of the many schemes he had afoot, the train full of recruits, every platform gay with bunting and flags, Union Jacks draped everywhere.

"They're trusting Kitchener again," Max said, closing his eyes. "Dear God—and the same old fools they had in the Transvaal. Olivia—if you *knew* . . ."

"Yes, darling."

London was even more frenzied, more hysterically, tragically gay, the streets full of laughing, cheering, weeping women, watching, blowing kisses, making promises, throwing flowers as, to the music of military bands, tall sergeants in the prime of middle life, their broad chests ablaze with medals, marched their thin, young recruits away.

"Ten years from now," said Max bitterly, "the only ones who'll remember it are those who lost their eyesight or their limbs, and those who have to live with them. They're being taken to die. Do you know that?"

Yes, I knew.

"And it won't be just rifle fire and shells and dysentery that does the trick. They don't know yet what it feels like to stand facing the enemy with an empty gun in your hand and an empty belly because some idiot has lost the supply wagons or another idiot in Whitehall has forgotten to order the supplies. They'll find out, just like they did in Africa."

I gave no opinions. I allowed his bitterness to run its course and prepared myself to meet whatever it should lead to. I loved him. However wrong this war, or any war, might be, I would never have chosen to walk away from it when so many of my family and friends could not. I did not choose to sell the Manor. But I had chosen Max. I would keep my word.

We dined at the Carlton as we usually did, surrounded by young crusaders, pledging themselves in vintage champagne to what had come to seem a holy cause, this war to end all wars, their handsome, healthy faces alight with sincerity.

438

"God dammit," snarled Max, "they think it's all white horses and armor and Sir Galahad. It's hunger and filth and lying in the mud when you're wounded because they forgot to pack the medical supplies. By Christ, whoever called it a contest in blunders was absolutely right."

"Napoleon," I said.

"Olivia?"

"Yes, darling."

"I'm not running away you know."

"Max—you're not military age, thank God. You have no reason to run."

"Olivia—if they got desperate enough, they'd take Sam Greenlaw."

We slept late. He left me alone to shop, although there was nothing I cared to buy, and when he came back to the hotel later in the day, his humor was entirely different.

"All right, Olivia—all right."

"All right what, darling?"

"I have given in. I have enlisted."

"You—have—done—*what!*"

I reached him in one movement and with such force that we fell over together into an armchair.

"Max—oh God—oh no."

And then, seeing the quite wicked glee in his eyes, I clutched hard at his shoulders, trying to shake him, and cried out, "No you haven't. You're too old. They wouldn't take you."

"They've taken Clive Potterton. He's about the same age as me."

"He's a professional soldier so don't lie to me." And I punctuated every word with a blow to his chest.

He caught my hands, kissed them, and eased me into a sitting position on his knee.

"And I, my darling, am a professional—what?—provider of luxuries for those who can afford them, and luxuries, in wartime, can consist of bread and bullets. Olivia, would you care to move into a rather graceful little house in Belgravia?"

"Max—what have you done?"

"Well, I have bought a graceful little house in Belgravia, for one thing—or rather taken an option, which I'll confirm if it suits you. I don't know about domestic staff because all the girls here seem to be running off to the nearest armaments factory. I expect you can bring a couple of maids down from Clarrow."

"Max!"

"Olivia." And getting up he crossed over to the fireplace and lit a cigar.

"I told you I'm not brave. I'm not. And I don't believe in any of this. Their "war to end all wars" is more likely to start another than anything else. And I don't give a damn what happens to governments and generals—anybody's generals. They'll come out of it all right in any case. I tried not to care about those poor young devils, with their pasty faces and their best Sunday suits on, marching off to the slaughter, or those extremely fine young gentlemen—and I am speaking very sincerely—at the Carlton last night. They *were* Sir Galahad in their hearts, every one of them, and it touched mine. It troubled me, quite a lot, thinking of them with their empty guns, cheering on their men just the same, giving "the chaps" the last of their rations and going hungry themselves because a gentleman takes responsibility, puts others before himself and plays the game. I really tried not to care, and if there'd been nothing I could do to help it wouldn't have mattered a damn whether I cared or not. I tried to convince myself there was nothing I could do, or that plenty of others could do it just as well. It didn't work. So I went to Whitehall to see several friends of mine in high places who expressed themselves delighted to use my services and my expertise, as a civilian without rank, and without pay of course, but apparently appreciated. Because they know I never let my customers down. Which leads me to the matter of a small house in Belgravia."

"Max de Haan," I said, walking towards him, "Hexingham gentleman, after all. I am so proud of you."

"Don't be. I don't want to do any of this. I shall be in a foul humor for the duration of the war, I warn you."

"I shall be proud of you if I please," and then, suddenly, as a cold wind slices through the warmth of a room when a door opens a thought struck me. "They wouldn't send you to the front, would they? *Max*—they wouldn't."

"Good gracious me, darling, how could they do that. I'm far too old. You said so yourself."

He was being flippant. It was always a bad sign. Fear flickered into my mind like a nervous thread of electricity—great fear. He was fit and alert and a crack shot.

"Oh yes they would if it suited them—not to fight perhaps but to get information—have a look—Max."

He pulled me towards him and held me very close, muffling my voice against his chest.

"Hush, darling, do hush. I think you can rely on me to avoid it."

"Avoid it! You'll just tell them that you're not going—you're a civilian, they can't make you. They can't, can they?"

Suddenly I was no longer sure. If they could take our horses and St. Winefrede's and the Manor too if it could be of any use to them, then where was the end of it? Fear again.

"Promise me, Max." Pity was one thing, and responsiblity, and I entirely approved of them. Heroics were quite another.

"All right, darling. If you promise me not to fill this little house in Belgravia I keep telling you about, or at least not too often, with Madelon and her assorted infants and husbands. Or with Luc and whatever bright young thing happens to take his fancy when he's on leave."

"I promise."

We walked down to Belgravia to inspect what I had already decided, without looking at it, was to be our new home. An elegant little house as it turned out with long Regency windows and gracious empty rooms unburdened by the past.

"Shall we buy it?"

"Yes, Max—if you haven't bought it already. Shall I sell the Manor?"

He smiled. "That, my darling, is entirely up to you. Sell it or let it or convert it, or keep it, just as you please. It is yours absolutely and always has been so far as I've been concerned. Is it really such a vital issue—now?"

I shook my head. No. The need for possession was over. It had been resolved.

"There is only one thing I would really like you to do for me, darling."

"Yes, Max. I hope it is difficult and complicated and will take a great deal of my time."

"Oh, absolutely."

"What then?"

"If you could just—be with me, then I would be exceedingly content with that."